The Mukden Disciple

by
W.E.D. Wilson

Table of Contents

For Colt and Cody.
No father is prouder of his sons
than I am of you.

War is an ugly thing, but not the ugliest of things. The decayed and degraded state of moral patriotism that believes that nothing is worth war is much worse. A man who has nothing for which he is willing to fight, nothing he cares about more than his own personal safety, is a miserable creature who has no chance of being free unless made and kept so by the exertions' of better men than himself.

John Stuart Mill

Chapter 1 - A New Beginning

Poulsbo, Washington was enjoying a beautiful sunny Saturday, a rarity for the month of April. The residents were taking advantage of the sunny day by milling about in the old downtown area. A more telling testament to the good weather was all of the convertible tops lowered while the car's owners drove through the town.

Twenty miles due west of Seattle and across the Puget Sound, Poulsbo had been a staple in the area since the 1880's. First settled by Norwegian fishermen, the town so tightly clung to its roots that Norwegian was the primary language until World War II. The locals had a saying, "Welcome to Poulsbo, turn your clock back fifty years."

Resting atop a small hill overlooking the town stood a large Craftsman home, built in the 1920's by the great grandfather of its current resident, Kirk Hanson. The house stood majestically overlooking Poulsbo harbor and Liberty Bay. Painted in earth tones of green, tan, and brown, the three thousand square foot home was one of Poulsbo's most elegant residences.

Other than two remodeling endeavors in 1965 and 2007, the structure had retained its original configuration, with one exception; the addition of a six-car garage and shop in the back of the house.

The inside of the home was equally as elegant. Retaining its beautiful wood cabinets, hardwood floors, and tile kitchen counters, the only changes that had been made were to upgrade the wiring and plumbing. Kirk's great grandfather, the founder of Poulsbo construction, had taken great care to build a home that would stand the test of time.

Normally, Kirk and his wife Maria would be out on the porch enjoying a cup of coffee on such a beautiful Saturday, but the house was abuzz with activity in preparation for the evening's festivities at the state capital in Olympia.

Maria was standing in the kitchen, fastening the clasp on her necklace as she waited for her husband to finish dressing in the second story bedroom. The five-foot-ten black haired beauty was adorned in a full length black satin evening gown. Her high heels placed her just one inch below the height of her husband. At fifty-seven-years-old, her once jet black shoulder length hair had been slightly streaked with gray, accenting the dark features of her face.

The statuesque Italian-American was the first non-Norwegian to marry into the family in its entire time in the United States, something her mother-in-law had said was "the best thing to happen to the family since they settled in Poulsbo." Maria's parents had emigrated from Naples, Italy in 1954 and settled in Seattle. Their only daughter was born the following year.

Maria had wanted to be a lawyer as far back as she could remember. Since her parents were unable to afford to put their daughter through law school, Maria paid her University of Washington tuition largely through modeling jobs. Even after graduation, she had received numerous offers for a modeling career, but gave it all up for a law practice. The strong willed woman had refused all offers that took her away from her career path, with the exception of one, the offer of marriage from a blond haired, blue eyed man named Kirk Hanson.

Kirk and Maria had met when they reluctantly agreed to a blind date, set up by their mutual friends. Their fate was sealed when they saw each other for the first time over dinner. The two all but ignored the other couple at the table that night. Six months later, they were married. The bond between the two was forged almost immediately, something they both marveled at.

Maria looked into the mirror and checked her hair. She rolled her

2

left wrist over and looked at her watch. Concerned about the time, she walked to the handrail of the staircase. Balancing on her right foot, she leaned forward and looked up toward the second floor, speaking loudly, "Come on, Honey, its one o'clock, we need to get going."

Kirk's voice bellowed from the bedroom, "Almost ready, just trying to get the bowtie for this monkey suit tied."

Maria walked back into the kitchen and opened her purse. Pulling the perfume bottle out, she dabbed some of the liquid on her wrist. As she gently rubbed her wrists together, the phone rang. Flipping her hair to one side, she placed the receiver on her ear. "Hello?"

The deep gravelly voice of her father-in-law responded from the other end. "Hey, Sweetie, it's Dad."

"Hi, Dad! You guys are cutting it a little short, aren't you? You were supposed to be here by now," Maria joked.

Jerry Hanson's voice cracked slightly as he responded. "We've had a little difficulty getting there, honey."

Maria frowned as she heard his normally rock-solid voice waver. "What's the matter, Dad? Are you and Mom okay?"

Jerry struggled to control his breathing as he responded. "We got into an accident on Interstate Five. I'm calling you from the police car right now."

Maria felt her heart start to race as she tried to control her emotions. "Oh no, oh no-"

Jerry Hanson spoke quickly, interrupting his daughter-in-law. "Maria, it's okay. Your mother and I are fine. They're taking us to Tacoma General for a check-up just as a precaution. I promise you, we're fine."

Maria tried unsuccessfully to place her emotions in check. "Hold on, Dad, I need to get Kirk on the line." She placed her hand over the receiver and called out to Kirk, "Honey! It's your Dad on the phone."

Kirk Hanson exited the Master bedroom, tugging at his tuxedo, and rolling his head around his neck in protest. As he descended the stairs he spoke loudly. "Man I hate these things. Whoever invented these monkey suits should be drawn and quartered." The two hundred and twenty pound father and husband always looked chiseled, and fit.

As he stopped in front of Maria he smirked. "What?" he said in a deep and loud voice.

Maria had a look of concern on her face as she covered the receiver with her left hand. "It's your father. He and Inger have been in an accident!"

Kirk quickly grabbed the phone from his wife. "Dad, are you guys okay?"

Trying to maintain a calming tone to his voice, Jerry responded to Kirk. "Son, your mother and I are okay. She just got a little shaken up, but she's fine. My left arm is a little sore from the impact, but I'll be fine. The ambulance is going to transport us to Tacoma General to be checked out. The car, on the other hand, didn't make out so well. I think it may be a total."

Responding quickly, Kirk fired back, "Dad, we'll be there in driving time."

With authority, Jerry spoke louder. "Oh no you won't. You guys are not going to miss out on the award ceremony tonight. Don't you dare!"

Maria had been selected, along with eleven other people in the State of Washington, to receive the Governors "Humanitarian Award" for the year. Her lifetime of legal pro-bono work on behalf of the poor had been recognized throughout the state. The entire family was beaming with pride over the award, especially her father-in-law.

"Dad, you need us. That ceremony does *not* take priority over your health. Besides, there's no one to watch Bobby, so we won't be able to go anyway."

With an even more commanding voice Jerry replied, "Look, Son, I only called to tell you that I already called someone to watch Bobby. He'll be there in about ten minutes."

"Dad, the court said Bobby has to be in the care of a family member until his probation is over. I can't leave him in the care of a stranger."

"He won't be in the care of a stranger. I called Walter and he said he'd be happy to watch him until they release your mother and me."

Taking a big breath, and trying not to get upset, Jerry responded to his father, "Dad, your friend Walter is an eighty four year old man with a heart condition. Bobby would have him for lunch."

"Kirk, Walter can handle himself. He's known Bobby since his birth. It'll be fine. Besides, he's already on his way there from Bremerton."

"I don't know Dad, I just don't feel comfortable with this."

"Look, Son, as soon as the hospital releases us, I'll get a cab back to the house, get the truck, and drive right there. Your coming here is going to be a waste of time. At least wait until Walter gets there before you make a decision. Promise me you'll at least talk to Walter."

"Okay, Dad. But *you promise me* you'll keep us posted as to how you're doing."

In a decidedly calmer voice, Jerry agreed. "We will, Son. I'll call you when we're leaving the hospital."

"Alright, Dad, I'll talk to you then. Give Mom our best." Kirk held the phone out in front of him and whipped it to the side in frustration as he depressed the off button. He slammed the phone on the counter and turned toward his wife. "Well, he insists they're both fine," Kirk announced in an irritated voice with both hands raised in the air. "Says they'll be here as soon as they're released from the hospital. Says they'll be okay," he stated with a smirk.

Maria tilted her head to the side and looked at Kirk in a questioning manner. "And did I get that right, he's sending Walter to watch Bobby?"

"Yup, be here in a few minutes," Kirk responded with a half smile.

"Honey, you were right when you told your dad that no one outside the family can watch Bobby. I don't want to try and explain this to the judge."

Karl Robert "Bobby" Hanson was the youngest child of Kirk and Maria. After having three boys early in the marriage, they were surprised when Maria became pregnant twelve years after their third son was born. Bobby had been the ideal son; a straight "A" student and an exceptional athlete, until the death of his oldest brother Eric. He'd always been the closest to Eric and took his untimely death hard. Eric had been attending law school and was coming home to Poulsbo for Thanksgiving when he was killed by a careless motorist in Seattle. Bobby changed almost overnight. The court found the other driver guiltless in the accident, something Bobby could not, and would not, accept.

After watching the man's house for a month and determining its occupant's habits, Bobby broke in and took an axe to its interior. The damage was extensive and cost Kirk and Maria almost a hundred thousand dollars.

The judge wasn't as forgiving as the house's owner, however. He ordered the damages be paid and sentenced Bobby to six months of community service and custodial probation, until Bobby's eighteenth birthday. Incarceration had been avoided only because of the judges understanding of the exigent circumstances of the death of Bobby's older brother.

The Hanson family had endured fourteen months of the sentence so far and was on the final sixty days, something Kirk and Maria didn't want to jeopardize. The incident could have been resolved and the entire family could have attended the award ceremony had Bobby not refused to attend. Both Maria and Kirk had never allowed themselves to give up on helping Bobby through the ordeal but Bobby, however, had given up on himself.

Kirk placed both his hands on the kitchen countertop and lowered his head. "I know, Honey, but Dad was right, We can't miss this night; it's too important for you. I kind of agree with him, let's at least listen to Walter when he gets here."

Maria was clearly worried about the decision, but left it in Kirk's hands. "Okay, Honey, we'll do what you think is best, but I'm still worried about this. I would have preferred for him to go tonight, but obviously that's not an option. Not with the way he's been behaving."

Kirk placed his hand on Maria's shoulder. "Let me go up to his room and tell him Walter will be staying here with him while we're gone." Kirk turned and walked toward the stairs leading to the second floor. He turned and smiled at Maria. "Can't imagine this is going to go over too well."

Maria took a deep breath and responded with raised eyebrows. "Bet you're right."

Maria had taken Eric's death particularly hard, but Bobby clearly had suffered the most. Kirk and Maria had dedicated everything to ensuring their careers never took them away from the task of raising their boys in a happy and productive family. Their commitment had paid off. Each of the boys had turned out to be studious, hardworking and respectful. But that all came crashing down that Friday evening Eric was killed in the car crash. The family was hit hard, but Bobby set out on a personal path of destruction.

Having an adult member of the family with him constantly had become an incredible burden to both Kirk and Maria, and a hindrance to their careers, but it was something they dedicated themselves to, no matter the circumstances or consequences. There would be no more pain for the family if Kirk had anything to do with it.

Kirk knocked on Bobby's bedroom door. The response was anything but cordial. "Yeah. Come in." Kirk opened the door and stepped inside. The seventeen-year-old was lying on the bed in his high school sweat pants and shirt with his X-Box controller in his hands furiously playing "Call of Duty." At six foot one inches tall and one hundred and eighty-five pounds, the handsome and athletic Bobby was a force to be reckoned with on the football field.

Kirk stood erect looking at Bobby, waiting for the young man to do the proper thing and acknowledge him. Bobby slowly turned his head toward his father and with a blank expression responded, "What?"

Kirk fought the urge to grab Bobby by the shirt and remind him of the manners he used to have. He took in a slow deep breath to suppress his anger and responded, "Your mother and I are almost ready to leave. Your grandparents were in a car accident and won't be able to get here for a while."

With a total lack of emotion on his face, Bobby responded, "They okay?"

"They'll be fine, but they won't be able to get here in time to be with you before we leave," Kirk replied.

"I'll be fine. I'll just wait for Granddad and Grandma to get here."

Kirk stepped closer to Bobby and spoke with greater purpose. "Bobby, you know you can't be alone; the judge's orders were specific. Besides, your grandfather called Walter Brown, and he's coming to stay with you until they can get here."

Bobby jerked up on the bed and furiously replied, "Dad, I'm seventeen years old, I don't need a baby sitter!"

"Non-negotiable, Bobby, Mr. Brown will be here shortly. I want you to come down and greet him when he gets here."

"Fine!" Bobby replied defiantly as he swung around and returned his focus to the video game.

Kirk exited the room, pulling the door closed behind him. He stopped and dropped his head, taking in a long, slow, breath and exhaling before walking down the hall. He looked up at the ceiling as he spoke softly. "Please get us through this. Please." He turned and walk down the stairs.

In spite of endless attempts to reach his youngest son, Kirk realized on some level that he was losing the battle. He'd tried every tactic except anger to try and reach Bobby, and refused to resort to any form of antagonism. Bobby certainly wouldn't respond to that. Both he and Maria were at a loss as to what to do. They had decided to let time heal the wounds.

As Kirk reached the bottom of the stairs he heard the front doorbell ring. He opened the door to see his father's friend, Walter Brown, standing in front of him. "Please come in, Walter," he said with a big smile.

The eighty-four-year-old Walter was dressed in bib overalls with a long sleeved work shirt underneath. At five foot ten, the white-haired man was hardly an imposing figure. His white moustache adorned a tanned and wrinkled face that always seemed to have a smile on it. A life of hard work in a greasy environment had permanently soiled the old man's wrinkled hands. In spite of his age, the one hundred seventy-five pound man walked as erect as he did at twenty. The retired machinist held out his right hand toward Kirk.

The two men shook hands firmly. "Good to see you, Walt!" Kirk said with a smile. Kirk was always amazed at the strength in the old man's hands.

The soft and gentle voice responded, "Good to see you, too, Kirk." Walter gestured at himself with open hands as he spoke. "Sorry about the clothes; I didn't have much time to get ready after your father called."

"That's okay, Walt, we appreciate you coming by," Kirk responded as Maria entered the room.

Maria smiled her usual beaming smile as she approached Walter. She reached out to give him a hug, but Walter stepped back and joked.

"Oh no, Maria! You don't want to touch these overalls. They're clean, but by machinists' standards."

Maria stepped forward and hugged Walter tightly. "You're forgetting that I married into a blue collar family." She laughed as she kissed Walter on the cheek.

Walter raised his eyebrows and whistled. "Wow, look at you two. How grand you both look. You're gonna be the best lookin' couple at the event."

"Not me, but Maria will turn heads, as usual," Kirk responded as he tilted his head toward his wife.

"Thank you," she said with a shy smile. Never comfortable with praise, Maria quickly changed the subject. "Walter, we really appreciate this, but are you sure it'll be okay?"

Walter swung the open palm of his right hand away from his body. "Easy peasy. Bobby's a good kid. We'll be fine."

With concern, Kirk responded, "It's not *you* we're worried about, Walter; it's Bobby. He's become a bit difficult since the accident. Not to mention we're worried about Mom and Dad. We were thinking it might be better to just call it off tonight."

Walter's expression turned serious as he looked at Kirk and Maria. "Look, your mother and father are okay. I've known Jerry a lot longer than you have, and he's always told it straight. If he says they're fine, then that's good enough for me. As to Bobby, we'll do some peck pounding and talk about motorcycles. Don't worry, everything will be fine."

Maria and Kirk looked at each other. She nodded approvingly. "Okay, but please call us if you need anything. Inger was going to cook for everyone tonight, so I'm afraid there's nothing prepared," she responded.

"Not to worry, I'll whip something up, or we'll order pizza. We'll be fine, you guys."

Kirk nodded. "Thanks, Walt. Let me get Bobby down here." Kirk turned toward the stairs and called to his son. "Bobby, could you come down here please?"

Maria stood arms folded as she waited for Bobby to come down the stairs. Still not comfortable with the arrangement, she cautiously

9

decided to trust that Walter could handle her son. However, she knew her thoughts wouldn't be totally focused on tonight's ceremony and all that it entailed.

Bobby slowly walked down the stairs in response to his father's request. He stopped at the bottom with his hands shoved deep into his pockets.

Kirk looked at his son. "Bobby, Mr. Brown has been nice enough to spend the evening with you while we're in Olympia. We'll get back as soon as we possibly can, it shouldn't take long."

Walter put his hand out toward Bobby. "Hi, Bobby, it's good to see you."

Bobby pulled his right hand out of his pocket to shake hands. He looked down at the floor as he spoke. "Hi."

Trying not to telegraph her concern, Maria smiled and uncrossed her arms as she spoke nervously, "Okay, you guys, have fun. You have our cell phone numbers if you need us."

Walter smiled and clapped his hands together, rubbing them as if washing. "Okay, you better get going. Bobby and I are gonna be just fine."

Bobby turned and walked back up the stairs without saying anything. Maria looked at Walter and said apologetically, "I'm so sorry, Walter; he's going through a tough time right now."

Walter nodded as he responded. "I know, Maria, no apology necessary. He'll get through it, time heals all wounds."

Maria didn't respond; she only smiled as she looked back at him. Kirk looked at his watch and sprung into action. "Good grief, we better get going. It's a good two hours down to the capitol."

Walter followed as Kirk stepped forward and opened the door for his wife. Maria felt the need to offer help once more before they left. "Remember, if you need us, please call," she pleaded as she stepped out onto the porch.

"Stop worrying! I will. Have fun and make us all proud." Walter grinned as he closed the door behind them.

Maria held onto Kirk's right bicep tightly with both her arms as they walked to the car. "I hope everything will be okay," she stated with concern.

Kirk opened the passenger's side door and held it for Maria as she climbed in. "It's gonna be fine, Honey, quit worrying," Kirk assured his wife as he closed the door.

Maria stared out the window saying a silent prayer as Kirk strapped himself in and started the car.

Chapter 2 - Old Knowledge

Walter stood at the bottom of the stairs looking up toward the second floor. He took in a deep breath and slowly exhaled. "Okay, Brown, you've had tougher jobs than this," he muttered, as he climbed the stairs and walked to Bobby's room. With his large, calloused right hand, Walter tapped against the door. "Bobby?"

"Yeah?" the voice on the other side responded.

Walter opened the door slightly and stuck his head inside the room. "Just thought I'd see what you wanted for dinner, Bobby."

"Nothing," he replied curtly.

Walter looked to see a full back pack sitting on the floor next to Bobby's bed. "Okay, Bobby, if there's anything you need, just let me know."

Bobby nodded as he continued to play his video game.

Walter closed the door and walked back downstairs. Bobby's grandfather, Jerry Hanson, had spoken to his old friend Walter about the arrest. Jerry had grieved over Eric's death for months, but was visibly more upset by how Bobby had reacted. It's tough enough to lose a family member, but to watch an existing member of the family deteriorate was much worse. The family seemed to be paralyzed as to how to help Bobby. Offers to take his grandson to a Mariners game had been declined several times. Even his favorite sport of motorcycle racing had been ignored since the accident. No one had a clue how to help this young man, who seemed to be spiraling downward with each day.

As soon as Walter left, Bobby dropped the controller for the video game onto the bed and reached for the telephone. He looked cautiously toward the door as he punched in the numbers to his girlfriend's house. A young female voice on the other end answered, "Hello?"

Bobby spoke in a low voice, "Hey, Baby, it's me."

Annie Richards responded, clearly excited. "Are you still coming?"

"Yeah, I'll be there in about a half hour. I have to lose this lame old dude my parents stuck me with. I'll get there as quickly as I can," Bobby replied as he hung up the phone.

The one thing Bobby refused to give up on was seeing his girlfriend. Annie had been over to the Hansons' for dinner and homework sessions on several occasions during the probation, but it was nothing compared to spending time alone ... something Bobby and Annie both found unacceptable.

In the kitchen, Walter opened the refrigerator and started loading up his arms with produce. He opened the freezer and looked for some meat to prepare beef stew. "Ah, this'll do," he said to himself as he pulled a pack of diced beef from the freezer. He placed the package of beef into the microwave and punched in the numbers for the "defrost" cycle. He placed the vegetables on the counter and pulled out the cutting board from the rack in the cabinet.

Upstairs, Bobby slid off his workout pants and pulled on a pair of jeans, glancing unconsciously at the bedroom door as he laced up his boots. He grabbed his cell phone from the nightstand and stuck it into his pants pocket. Trying to be quiet, Bobby lifted the backpack off the floor and slid it over his right shoulder. He slowly turned the doorknob and cracked the door open slightly to look out into the hallway. He heard the water running downstairs in the kitchen and decided it was clear. Stepping out of the room, he gently eased the door shut. Walking slowly toward the stairs, he stepped as quietly as he could. Once he reached the stairs, he moved all the way to the left side of the staircase as he descended, a trick he'd learned to prevent the ninety-year-old stairs from creaking.

Walter stood at the kitchen sink cutting up vegetables for the stew with the water running. He was whistling softly and enjoying the afternoon sun as it shone through the window.

Once Bobby reached the bottom of the stairs, he could hear Walter in the kitchen. He looked behind him one more time before he walked to the back door at the east end of the house. He turned the knob and slowly opened it. Once outside, he quietly closed the door behind him, taking in a deep breath. He'd been unconsciously taking shallow breaths to avoid making too much noise. He glanced behind him as he crept toward the door to the garage. Opening the door, he quickly stepped inside and pulled it closed.

The twenty-five hundred square foot garage housed his father's woodworking tools and equipment, a fifteen foot long workbench, and enough room for six vehicles. The enclosure had the unique aroma of sawdust, gasoline, and motor oil. It was the perfect place for a family of men to drip testosterone. Parked in front of his father's black 2005 Ford work truck was Bobby's true passion, his 2000 Ducati 996R sport motorcycle. The red 150 mile per hour rocket ship had been a gift from his grandfather after Bobby received his driver's license.

Bobby secured his backpack to the rear fender and lifted the helmet from the right hand grip. He walked to the work bench, picked up the garage door opener and clipped it to the handlebars. He carefully put the key into the ignition and sat on the bike. Lifting the bike off the kickstand, he pulled his full face helmet on and closed the visor. While straddling the bike, he rolled it to the garage door. He knew he would have to start the bike, raise the door, and speed down the driveway all in unison to avoid being stopped by Walter Brown.

He turned the ignition key while his other hand rested on the garage door opener. His right thumb depressed the black button and the starter cranked. Bobby lifted off the starter button when the engine failed to fire. He checked the fuel valve and found it to be open. He sat back up and depressed the starter button one more time. The starter engaged, but failed to start the engine for the second time.

Bobby put the kickstand down and got off the bike. He removed his helmet and knelt next to the engine to see what the problem was. As he looked intently at the bike, the voice behind him announced, "It ain't gonna start, kid."

Startled, Bobby shot to his feet. He stood silently, staring at Walter Brown, who was standing next to the entrance door of the garage. Walter raised his right hand to reveal the bike's coil wire. Embarrassed and angry, Bobby responded in the only manner he could after being caught attempting to violate the conditions of his probation. "Gimee that right now!" he ordered.

Walter put the coil wire into his pocket and shook his head in the negative. Bobby took a step toward Walter and raised his right fist. "Look, old man, I don't wanna hurt you. You'd better hand it over to me or I'll take it from you."

Walter stared at Bobby with a small grin. "That ain't gonna happen either, kid."

"What does it matter to you if I leave? You don't have any control over me, you old bastard," Bobby spat with clenched fists.

Calm and purposeful, Walter attempted to negotiate a safe conclusion to the dilemma. "Look, Bobby, your parents asked me to watch over you. I take that responsibility seriously. Once your parents get home you can do what you like. But while I'm here, nothing's going to happen to you while you're under my watch, so let's just go back inside, have some dinner, and talk about this. And don't swear kid, it's low rent."

The diplomacy approach didn't work. Bobby's temper was rapidly elevating. "I'm warning you, old man, GIVE THAT TO ME NOW!"

Walter, with a more serious expression, again shook his head no. Deciding to make his escape on foot, Bobby depressed the button on the garage door opener. Nothing happened. Walter pointed the index finger of his right hand toward the door controller next to him. The switch was in the off position.

Bobby threw the controller to the floor and pulled his jacket off, letting it fall on the concrete. "Okay, old man. Just remember, I warned you." Bobby pulled his motorcycle gloves off and tossed them aside. He widened his stance and drew his right fist back to his waist. "I'm trained in Tae Kwan Do, and I'm gonna kick your ass!"

Walter slowly slid his right foot to the rear, balancing his stance. "Don't even think about it, kid. You're outclassed."

Bobby moved forward quickly and threw a straight on punch at Walter's face. The old man moved his head to the side and grabbed Bobby's right arm, pulling him forward and down to the ground. Walter stepped back and regained his stance, facing the young man. An enraged Bobby quickly stood and got into a lower profile with his fists drawn to his side. He grunted loudly as his right foot kicked out straight toward Walter's groin. "KEAAA!"

Walters left fist remained at chest level as his right fist drove down hard on Bobby's right shin. The intense pain shot through Bobby's leg as he hopped backward. "You son-of-a-bitch! I'll kill you!" Bobby lunged toward Walter with his right fist cocked and roared loudly, "AAAH!"

Walter moved forward and to the right of the punch. As he grabbed Bobby's right fist with his left hand, his right fist drove a punch into Bobby's upper chest, just below his neck. Walter immediately pulled Bobby's right hand back toward him, again forcing the young man to the ground. His left hand twisted Bobby's now powerless hand into a lock. Lying on his back and writhing in pain, Bobby's body went limp in submission.

Walter lifted Bobby to his feet with the wrist lock still on his hand. "You done, or am I gonna have to thump on you some more?"

Bobby nodded in surrender as he struggled to get his breath; the pain in his chest was forcing his shoulders forward. Walter let go of the young man's hand and set him on the stool next to the work bench. "You gonna be okay, kid?" Walter asked, with concern in his voice.

Trying to get his breath, and twisting in pain, Bobby responded, "My chest hurts."

Walter put his left hand on Bobby's upper back while he placed his right palm on the young man's upper chest. His fingers slowly worked on the area he'd punched. With a quick move, Walter twisted his right hand and pushed in hard. "Sit up straight and take in a deep breath, kid. You'll be okay now."

Bobby slowly took in a deep breath and stretched his chest out. With surprise in his voice, he looked up at Walter. "I've never been hit so hard."

"I didn't hit you hard, Bobby, I checked my punch. If I'd have hit you full on, we'd be planning your funeral tonight."

16

"Son-of-a-bitch that hurt!" Bobby announced.

Scowling, Walter responded, "I told you before kid, don't swear."

"Why not?" Bobby asked, sarcastically.

Walter sat on the stool next to Bobby. "Because profanity is the linguistical crutch of a verbally vacuous and inarticulate asshole, that's why!"

Bobby tried to smile, but couldn't. He continued to rub his chest with his right hand. "How'd you stop the pain in my chest so quickly?"

"Something I learned a long time ago."

Bobby looked at Walter with a newly found respect. He couldn't contain his curiosity. "What did you do to me? You were so fast, and you hardly moved! I mean, I've never seen someone so fast, and you're, well, I mean you're -"

"You mean I'm so old, right?" Walter asked with a smirk.

"Well, yeah, I mean, I'm sorry, but yeah, you're so old," Bobby said almost apologetically.

"It's not about strength, size, power, or even age, Bobby. It's skill level and basic geometry." Walter answered.

"What art did you use on me?" Bobby asked.

"Kung Fu."

"Where did you learn Kung Fu?"

With his hands on his knees, Walter lowered his head. "About a million years ago in China."

Bobby couldn't contain his excitement. "You were in China? That's so cool. My Tae Kwan Do instructor has been to China. He's good, but not even close to as good as you."

"Tae Kwan Do?" Walter smirked. "You better get your money back, kid."

"What, don't you think Tae Kwan Do is a good art?" Bobby asked.

"It's a *very* good art, Bobby, but it's not the art; it's the instructor and the heart of the student. You got no heart, kid." Walter said as he

17

stood. "Come on Bobby; let's get you into the house." Walter reached under Bobby's right arm and helped him up from the side. He walked a weak Bobby to the door and exited the garage. Pulling the door closed behind them, Walter slowly walked Bobby toward the house.

"Man, I sure thought I could kick your ass," Bobby said as they walked.

"You got some mouth on you, kid," Walter replied with disgust in his voice.

A more reserved Bobby responded, "I'm sorry. I mean, I just thought I wouldn't have any trouble taking you."

Walter chuckled as they approached the house. "Come on, tough guy; let's get you something to eat."

Chapter 3 - An Old Friend

A completely humbled Bobby walked into the kitchen aided by Walter. The old man helped Bobby sit at the kitchen counter, then walked to the refrigerator and pulled out a can of iced tea. He pulled the tab, opening the can, and placed it in front of Bobby. "Thank you," the young man replied.

Walter turned back toward the counter and started loading the vegetables into the pot. He turned the water on and covered the ingredients. Walking to the microwave, he pulled out the stew meat and opened the package. Bobby looked across the counter toward Walter. "Dude, would you like teach me some moves?"

In a quiet voice, Walter responded without looking up. "My name is Walter Brown. Most people call me Walter, some call me sir." He turned his head toward Bobby, "But you can call me Mr. Brown, not dude."

Bobby responded apologetically. "I'm sorry, Mr. Brown. Would you please teach me some moves?"

After placing the meat in the pot, Walter opened the spice cabinet. He responded while looking for the spices he needed. "Now why would I do that?"

"Please, Mr. Brown. I mean, you're like the best I've ever seen. I could totally learn a lot from you," Bobby said pleadingly.

Walter dumped the spices into the pot and placed the lid on top. He turned the stove top on and turned to face Bobby. "Look, kid, it's like I said; you got no heart. I'm not gonna give an angry kid like you the tools to seriously hurt someone. Maybe if you had ten more years and a boat load more gray matter in your skull I'd consider it, but not while you got this giant chip on your shoulder. My answer is no."

Bobby remained persistent. "Come on, man, I mean Mr. Brown, I'll do what you say. Please."

Walter walked to the counter across from Bobby. He placed his hands on the countertop and looked into Bobby's eyes. "Look, son, you've got a lot of issues you're dealing with. I know it was tough to suffer through the death of your brother, but you're taking your anger out on your whole family. They're hurting for you, especially your grandfather."

"My grandfather? What's he so worried about?" Bobby responded with surprise.

"He loves you. Isn't that reason enough? He's my friend, and it hurts me to see him so worried about a member of his family." Walter leaned in closer to Bobby and spoke with purpose. "When your brother died, I watched your grandfather cry like a baby. He used to spend hours at my house talking about how much it hurt. And then he had to go through a whole different kind of hurt when you went nuts and trashed that mans house. He's hurting, and he doesn't know how to deal with it."

Bobby scowled as he responded, "Yeah, well, that dirt bag deserved it for killing Eric."

Walter's voice rose as he responded. "You don't think he's hurting, too?"

Bobby rolled his eyes. "Why is he hurting? He's the one who killed someone."

Walter reached across the counter and tapped Bobby's chest as he spoke. "See what I mean, kid? You got no heart."

Bobby had a curious look. "I don't understand."

"Why do you think you were spared from some serious jail

time?" Bobby shrugged in response. "Because that man pleaded with the judge not to give you jail time. He killed someone, and he just wanted the pain to go away." Bobby's brow furrowed inquisitively as Walter continued. "When you take a life, it weighs on your shoulders like a thousand-pound rock, *if* you have any conscience. It tears at your insides like a cancer. It's something that remains with you until the day you die. It's something you would never wish on another human being. Believe me when I tell you, Bobby, it's something you never want to experience."

"How do you know? Did you kill someone?" Bobby asked.

Walter lowered his head and responded in a quiet voice. "Yes, many times, and there's not a day goes by but what I don't ask God for forgiveness."

"When did you kill someone?"

"In Korea," Walter responded solemnly.

"Wow, you were in Korea … like what, in the Army?" Bobby asked.

"ARMY! Bite your tongue, kid. I was a Marine," Walter responded proudly.

Bobby took a sip from his iced tea. "None of *my* family was in the military," he replied, almost apologetically.

Walter pulled a stool around the counter and sat across from Bobby. "Yeah, well, some people serve in different capacities."

"How did they serve?" Bobby replied with a smirk.

"Your family was in the construction business for a hundred years Bobby. They're almost single handedly responsible for the construction of the Bremerton Naval Shipyard. Your great grandfather during World War Two, your grandfather during the Korean War, and your father during the Viet Nam War. But the single most important service they ever performed was to raise a healthy, happy, and productive family. My service in the military can't even begin to compare to theirs."

Bobby was learning information about his family that he never thought he could. A new light had been shed on his family heritage by someone not even in the family. It was giving him a lot to digest. Wanting to know more about this man's involvement in his family,

21

Bobby inquired further, "Where'd you meet my grandfather?"

"I first met Jerry at a motorcycle race in the fifties," Walter responded.

Surprised by the statement, Bobby replied, "I didn't know granddad used to watch motorcycle races."

"Watch?" Walter replied with a laugh. "He used to race."

"You guys raced motorcycles! I know he used to ride them, I just didn't know he used to race, too," Bobby said with excitement.

"Yeah, he was good, too. He cleaned my clock the first race we were in."

Bobby was opening up for the first time in over a year. He found himself excited to talk with someone about something other than his legal problems. He was truly beginning to enjoy a meaningful conversation for the first time in months.

"Like most young guys, we were consumed by motorcycles. We rode 'em, fixed 'em, raced 'em, and then talked about 'em. Once we got older, we got busy raising a family and making a living, and they faded into the background. Never lost the love for it, though."

Bobby smiled as he responded, "Yeah, granddad seemed pretty proud when he gave me my bike."

Bobby had been riding a motorcycle since he was ten years old. First the small less powerful scooters, then the low end dirt bikes, then finally street bikes. His natural talents on a motorcycle hadn't gone unnoticed by his parents and grandparents. After consultation with Bobby's parents, his grandparents purchased him the motorcycle.

"Do you know the story behind that bike?" Walter asked.

"Granddad said it'd been wrecked and that he had someone put it back together."

"Nope," Walter replied. "He bought it from a guy who had dumped it on the freeway. We loaded it into the back of my truck and took it over to my garage. It was pretty messed up. We spent almost a year putting it back together. Jerry tore the bike down and spent months rebuilding the frame. Your grandfather is one heck of a welder. He spent even more time on the fiberglass body panels. He must have spent a hundred hours in the Ducati dealership, and even more time looking through books to get the frame and paintjob just right."

"Who did the engine?" Bobby asked.

"I did," Walter said proudly as he tapped his chest. Walter Brown had been a machinist at the Bremerton Naval Shipyard for forty years. After retiring, he'd continued to hire himself out for side work to augment his income until the death of his wife in 1998. He rarely worked in his garage after that, but jumped at the chance to help his old friend restore a bike for his grandson.

Bobby smiled widely as he responded, "No shit, I'm sorry, Mr. Brown." Bobby immediately responded after violating Walters's request. "Granddad said it's the fastest Ducati anywhere in the Pacific Northwest."

"And it is," Walter stated emphatically.

"How come my dad or granddad never talked about this stuff? I don't get it; they never said anything to me about it," Bobby mused.

"Ah, don't worry about it, Bobby. It's a guy thing. Maybe when you get married and have your own kids you'll understand." Walter laughed as he continued. "Besides, it also has a lot to do with that whole Norwegian thing. That tough as nails Viking heritage you were born into. More 'Do than Say.'"

Bobby lowered his head, staring at his iced tea. "Yeah, sometimes I don't think Dad cared about Eric dying. He never wanted to talk about it. Mom either."

Walter's head moved from side to side as he responded, "Bobby, you just don't get it. Why do you demand others mourn in the same way you do?

"Look, when my wife got sick in 1998, she went into the hospital for exploratory surgery. They went in and found two arteries totally blocked. Before they could finish, she had a bad reaction and died. Now, my daughter won't go into a hospital to see anyone, ever! The only experience she has with hospitals is that when someone goes in, they don't come out. That's how she deals with it.

"I could have drowned my sorrows in alcohol. I could have driven my car off a bridge, or I just could have given up. I chose to get on with life and wait till I die to see her again. Your mother and father took solace in the church. It's how they're dealing with it. Cut 'em some slack, kid; they're hurting too. The best way they know how to deal with it is to turn it over to God."

Bobby sat silent as he contemplated what Walter had said. Youth and inexperience was the only thing he could draw upon when Eric died. Bobby had watched his parents mourn silently for over a year. Whenever he approached them about Eric's death, they would hug him and walk away. Mistakenly feeling that no one cared, he acted out the only way he knew how; violently.

Bobby's back straightened as he responded, "Yeah, well, I don't believe in God anymore. If He's so great, then how come He let Eric die?"

"Why do you want to put this on God? It isn't His fault. He just wants to be there to comfort people when they're hurting. To you, this is only about Bobby Hanson." Walter got up to check on the stew. He went on after stirring the pot with the wooden spoon. "You have a job to do, Bobby, and the sooner you get on with life and fulfill what God has for you, the better off you'll be," Walter said as he sat back down at the counter.

"Don't tell me you're gonna give me that whole 'God speech' my parents are always laying on me," Bobby said with disgust in his voice.

"What speech is that, Bobby?" Walter shot back.

"That whole thing about it being God's will. I've heard enough of that since Eric died," Bobby said defiantly. "I've had about enough of the whole 'God thing,' he said as his head dropped down.

Walter took in a deep breath as he looked at the young man seated in front of him. It pained him to see Bobby suffering so much, and he didn't know how to deal with it. His mouth slowly turned into a small grin as he pondered Bobby's condition. "I'm not gonna give you the 'God speech,' as you call it, just thought I'd tell you how others deal with it, Bobby. Just call it useful information for you to file away for future use.

"But just because you don't want to acknowledge God, don't put others down who do rely on Him. Your choice, Bobby, just don't deny others their choice."

Bobby lifted his head and looked toward Walter. I'm sorry, Mr. Brown, I didn't mean it that way. It's just that everyone wants to tell me what to do. All I want is to be left alone," he said apologetically.

Walter's lips pursed as he mused over Bobby's comments. "Bobby, they aren't trying to tell you what to do, or even what to feel, they've just been down the road a lot farther than you, and want to save you the hurt of bad experiences they think you could avoid."

"Mr. Brown, I'm seventeen, I can make my own decisions," Bobby said stubbornly. "I don't need anybody's help."

"But you still need us old geezers to help you down the road, Bobby. Don't you?" Walter said with his head tilted to the side.

"No, I can do it on my own," he said with a furrowed brow.

Walter took in a deep breath and exhaled slowly in frustration. "Well, you're asking this 'God Freak' old man to teach you Kung Fu, aren't you? Seems like you are asking for the wisdom of someone older than you right now, huh?"

Bobby remained silent as he looked at Walter with a blank stare. "I'm Sorry, Mr. Brown. You're right. I apologize, but I'd still like you to teach me."

Walter leaned back in his seat and looked at Bobby, analyzing the young man. "Tell you what, kid. If you can comply with my conditions, maybe I'll consider it."

Bobby sat up excitedly. "Anything you say, Mr. Brown. I promise I'll do what you say."

Walter held his right palm out toward Bobby. "Don't jump in till you know how deep it is, Bobby. You may not like the conditions," Walter warned.

"I'll do what you say, Mr. Brown, I promise," Bobby responded.

Walter stood and looked Bobby in the eyes. "Okay, here are my conditions. No more fights at school. You've been bullying some of the other kids."

"How do you know that?" Bobby said as he leaned back in his seat.

"I'm old, Bobby, not stupid. The word gets around."

"Okay," Bobby responded sheepishly.

"Next, you be at my house to train when I say so, no excuses."

25

"I can do that," he responded with a smile.

"Next, I want you to apologize to that man for destroying his house," Walter demanded.

"What!" Bobby exclaimed.

"That's right, Bobby, and I want you to tell him you forgive him for Eric's death," Walter said with authority.

Bobby leaned back in his chair and rolled his eyes. "Oh, man, that's not fair. Why do I have to do that?"

"Because I want you to help ease the pain that man is suffering. This is one condition that's nonnegotiable. You don't have to see him in person. You can write him a letter, but I want to read it before we send it," Walter stated emphatically.

Bobby lowered his head and spoke softly. "Okay, I will."

Walter closed out his conditions. "And last, you sit through a story I want to tell you. After I finish, I'll decide whether or not to teach you." Walter extended his right hand toward Bobby. "Agreed?"

Bobby shook Walter's hand. "Agreed. But could you just teach me one thing before you tell me that story?" he asked.

"What's that?" Walter curiously asked.

"That thing you did to my wrist out in the garage," Bobby responded.

Walter chuckled. "Okay, I suppose I could do that. Move your fist toward my head."

Bobby moved his right fist toward Walter's head. Slowly, Walter raised the back of his open left hand to meet Bobby's lower arm. His palm turned outward and slid down to Bobby's hand. He grasped Bobby's hand and rolled it counterclockwise away from Bobby. Walter continued rolling Bobby's wrist until his whole body submitted to the move by falling to his right. Walter let go and spoke softly. "There you go."

Bobby rubbed his wrist and responded, "I don't get it."

Walter stood and walked to the end of the counter by the phone. He tore off a sheet of the notepad and sat back down. Holding the sheet between his thumb and fingers horizontally, he rotated the paper one-hundred-eighty degrees, then rotated it back. "That's the secret, kid."

"I don't understand."

"Don't worry, Bobby, you will." Wanting Bobby to discover the process for himself, he responded with a smile. Walter stood and walked to the stove. Stirring the pot for another time, he looked back to see Bobby rotating the piece of paper back and forth in his hand. Walter put the lid back onto the pot and sat back down. "Bobby, do you know what it means to have a Heart of Service?"

Bobby put the paper down and looked at Walter. "No, what's that?"

"To serve others, no matter the cost. To do for others with no expectation of reward. To give of yourself without regard for your safety or well being, and to serve without bringing attention to yourself."

Bobby had a confused look as Walter continued. "Your father, mother, grandmother, and grandfather have that heart. Your mother gives her time and legal skills with no hope or expectation of being repaid. Since he retired, your father fixes up old homes for a living, but also fixes houses of the poor and needy. Your grandparents have given of themselves to help the underprivileged for decades, not to mention your grandfather rebuilding that bike of yours, then giving the credit to someone else. That's the heart of service, Bobby," Walter said, while pointing toward the young man.

Bobby was confused. "So that's the key to Kung Fu?"

"No, Bobby, Walter said while nodding his head in the negative, "It's the key to life. And as much as you whine about God, it's also a part of His commandments. We're here to serve, and the martial arts and every other thing in life can benefit from a heart of service."

"Where did you learn about it?" Bobby asked.

"I had a friend a long time ago who taught me the meaning of service, honor, duty, and loyalty. I owe everything I am today to that man," Walter responded.

"Who was he?" Bobby asked inquisitively.

Walter spoke reverently of the man. "He was a Sergeant in the Marine Corps. We were both stationed at the US Consulate in Mukden, China together."

"Wow, and that's where you learned Kung Fu?" Bobby said excitedly.

"Yup," Walter responded. "I enlisted in the Marine Corps in late 1945 when the war was winding down. By the time I was trained, it was early 1946. I was too late for the war, so the Marine Corp sent me to China instead. Normally, the Marine Detachments are only at the Embassies, but we were sent to Mukden, or Shenyang as it's called now, because of the conflicts between the Nationalists and the Communists. When I got to the consulate, Rusty was already there."

"His name was Rusty?" Bobby asked.

"Yeah, Rusty Harrigan. He was a big guy from Philadelphia. Good lookin' kid with that perfect Marine Corps recruiting poster look. I was brand new and full of energy. Rusty took me under his wing and helped me fit in, and also kept my foot out of my mouth," Walter said with a smile.

"He was a pretty tough guy, huh?" Bobby asked.

"Yeah, he was, but also fair. He was one of those 'God Freaks' you talk about," Walter said with a smile.

Bobby was feeling sorry for making the statement earlier about God, something Walter was reminding him of repeatedly.

Walter continued with his story. "We all thought it was going to be a cushy assignment, but what we didn't know is that we were about to be in the middle of the most evil acts of the twentieth century."

"What do you mean, evil?" Bobby asked.

"Do you know who the most blood-thirsty tyrant of the twentieth century was Bobby?" Walter asked.

"Yeah, Hitler."

"Nope, he was a piker. He only killed somewhere between six and nine million people," Walter responded.

"Was it that dude from Russia?" Bobby asked.

"By dude, I assume you mean Joseph Stalin?"

"Yeah, that's the guy."

"Nope, bush league. He wasn't even close. He only killed around twelve million." Walter said as he looked at Bobby.

"Then I don't know," Bobby replied.

"It was Mao Tse-tung," Walter announced.

"Who?" Bobby asked.

"Mao Tse-tung, Mao Zedeong, The great Helmsman, Chairman Mao, good grief, Bobby, don't they teach you anything in school?" Walter said with disgust in his voice.

"Oh yeah, yeah, Chairman Mao. My history teacher told us about him. She said he did a lot of great things for the Chinese people," Bobby said after remembering the name.

"Great things?" Walter said angrily. "Your teacher's all wet. She wasn't there to see it; I was. That blood-thirsty animal killed over forty-five-million of his own countrymen in what was called 'The great leap forward.' He starved his own people to death for his great experiment, Bobby. By the end of his reign, he'd killed over eighty million people. He was a whole different level of evil. And, at one point, he was killing fifteen thousand Christians a day in China. Great things, my butt!"

Bobby's brow was furrowed. "Why would he kill Christians? I mean, like what did they do?"

"It's the tenants of Communism, Bobby. Every tyrant or despot has to separate the population from God if they want total control. They have to establish that there is no higher authority than the state."

"Wow," Bobby said reverently. "How did someone like that get into power?"

Walter took in a deep breath. "Well, we all have to take some responsibility. The United States initially sided with Chiang Kai-shek over Mao, the leader of the Communist Party. Chiang-Kai-shek and his followers were incompetent and corrupt, but we stuck by him instead of the Communist rebels. Chiang didn't like the Americans very much, and he certainly didn't like the Communists either, but he would have been a whole lot better than that thug Mao.

"There were a group of American diplomats called the China Hands who reported favorably on the Chinese Communists, and the United States began negotiations with Mao. After it all ended, Mao threw us out of China.

29

"The history of our relations with China has been grim at best. The Chinese were snubbed at the Treaty of Versailles after the First World War. Britain had crapped on them for decades, along with the Germans, Russians, French, and Japanese. Even the Dutch had a hand in the chaos. All of the western empires had a policy of Gunboat Diplomacy in China going back to the eighteen hundreds to protect their shipping interests there. I guess China finally got tired of western influence and meddling. The whole thing fell apart in 1949.

"Chiang led the Nationalists, while Mao led the Communists. Mao finally won out, and Chiang fled to Taiwan. After gaining total control, Mao went on a killing spree that made the crusades look like child's play. Rusty and I were there at the peak of the trouble."

"I didn't know he did all that," Bobby said with surprise.

Walter pointed his finger at Bobby. "You might mention that to your teacher next time you see her." Walter checked the stew and announced its completion. "Come on, Bobby, set the table. We're ready to eat." Walter smiled as he watched Bobby hurry to set the table. Might be hope for this kid after all, he said to himself. There just might be some hope.

Chapter 4 - The China Hands

Despite his initial reluctance, Bobby was finding the afternoon with Walter to be an enjoyment, rather than an impediment to his plans. His youthful inexperience and misplaced hubris were in direct conflict with his desire to be with this elderly man. He ate the stew voraciously in the hope that Walter would continue the story of his friend if he finished.

With purposeful cunning, Walter looked up at Bobby. "The stew okay?"

"Yes, Sir," Bobby replied. "Mr. Brown, could you continue your story about you and Rusty?"

Walter tore another piece from the loaf of French bread. "You still ready to comply with my conditions?"

"Yes, Sir."

"Okay. Then, if you still agree, I'll tell you the story." Walter put his elbows on the table and clasped his hands together, resting his chin on his hands. "The US Consulate we were at was in Mukden, China. The city was first founded around 300 BC. It remained relatively unimportant until the 1920's. Since then it's been a major industrial center in China.

"It's located in the northeast section of the country, about a hundred miles from the North Korean border. Soviet forces occupied Shenyang in early August 1945 after Japan surrendered. The Soviets were replaced by the Chinese Nationalists, who were flown in on U.S. transport planes.

"During the Chinese Civil War, Mukden remained a Nationalist stronghold from 1946 to 1948, although the Chinese communists controlled the surrounding countryside. It was captured by the communists on 30 October 1948. It was during that time from 1946 to 1949 that Rusty and I were assigned there.

"There were ten Marines at the Consulate, and we were under strict orders to represent the United States in a professional manner. The building had been the Russian Consulate before we occupied it in the 1920's, so it was a natural fit for security. The US opened the consulate back up in 1945 and staffed it, along with a detachment of Marines. Mukden had been a trouble spot throughout the thirties and forties with all kinds of violence and civil unrest.

"The Nationalist occupation brought stability. We were allowed to go into the city on a regular basis, but always in civilian clothing. All the Marines assigned there walked on eggshells while they were off the Consulate grounds, not wanting to bring shame on the United States.

"Rusty had been reading about the Chinese culture since before I got there and was fascinated about the Chinese martial arts. He was completely taken by the power of the art of Kung Fu, yet how smooth and effortless it appeared to be in its application. We both wanted to learn, but didn't know how to go about it. We set out to find a teacher. We had asked a bunch of the locals where to find an instructor, but were always told no. We finally found someone one day, in an unlikely place. Little did we know it would change our lives forever."

1946

Walter Brown stood from the kitchen table and walked to the counter to give his dishes to the Chinese worker standing next to the sink. The man smiled and bowed toward Walter as he took the dish and utensils. The seventeen-year-old Marine Corps Private was clad in his khaki fatigues that were bloused to show his highly polished combat boots. His five-foot-ten inch one hundred and seventy-five-pound frame was topped by a freshly trimmed crew-cut hair style. The New Hampshire native smiled at the worker and thanked him as he turned to leave. He glanced at his wristwatch and hurried his pace to get to the barracks to change his clothes. Walter opened the door to the bay and stepped inside.

As he closed the door behind him, he heard his friend Rusty Harrigan call out to him. "Hurry up Walt, we're gonna be late."

Rusty, a blond-haired, blue eyed Philadelphia native was folding his fatigues to place them into his foot locker. The six-foot-three-inch, two-hundred-pound Marine was built like a brick. The tough and chiseled eighteen-year-old man had a command presence about him that most people could only hope for. Rusty's Commanding Officer (CO), Capt Jose Rivera, had already taken steps to recommend Rusty for Officers Candidate School (OCS) due to his talents and his leadership abilities. Everyone liked and respected the young Marine.

Walter began stripping his clothes off to get dressed in his "civvies," a term members of the military gave to their civilian clothing. Walter pulled on his slacks and shirt and sat on the edge of his bunk to put on his shoes. He turned his head toward Rusty with excitement in his voice. "Do you think this place will know who to contact?"

Rusty was kneeling in front of his foot locker closing the lock. "Hope so, Walt. We've about run out of options."

Rusty and Walter had been looking for a Kung Fu teacher for three months now and were on the verge of giving up. They only had two more places to check. The locals were *not* open to helping the Americans, and in some cases were outright hostile. The owner of the local watering hole the Marines at the Consulate frequented had told Rusty and Walter about two places that might help. The two Marines were excited to follow-up on the leads.

Walter closed and locked his foot locker and grabbed his wool coat. "Ready," Walter announced as they walked from the squad bay. Turning down the hall to walk to the exit door, the two men were stopped by Capt. Rivera.

"Corporal Harrigan," Rivera said firmly as he approached the men.

The thirty-one-year-old Mexican-American officer looked small standing in front of Rusty, but still cut a commanding figure. The Iwo Jima survivor had the complete loyalty and respect of all the Marines at the Consulate and the complete confidence of the Consul General. When he spoke, everyone at the consulate listened.

Rusty stopped and stood at attention. "Yes, Sir."

Rivera's eyes looked up at Rusty. "Is the inspection of all the weapons complete, Corporal?"

Rusty remained at attention while responding. "Yes Sir, the report is on your desk, Sir." Rusty responded sharply.

Rivera looked toward Walter. "You guys headed downtown?"

"Yes Sir." Walter responded.

Rivera pointed toward Walter while looking at Rusty. "Okay, but be careful. We don't want this wet-nose killed in a Chinese bar."

"No, Sir," Rusty said with a smile. He pulled a pack of Beeman's gum from his pocket, holding it out toward Rivera. "Stick of gum, Sir?"

"Negative, Corporal, got my own." He looked toward the two Marines and smiled. "Dismissed," Rivera said while turning and walking away.

Walter looked back to ensure Capt Rivera was out of ear shot. "Wet-nose?" he said, disgusted.

Rusty looked at Walter as they were walking and smiled. "Don't take it personally, Walt. He doesn't mean anything by it. If he's not giving you jazz, that's when you should start to worry." Rusty and Walter exited the building into the courtyard of the Consulate. The walled compound and buildings had been meticulously maintained since the United States had taken control of the facility. The Consulate sat in the center of the city, strategically located for the diplomatic purpose it was meant to fill.

As the capital of the Liaoning Province, Mukden is an important industrial center. Since the 1920's the city has exploded industrially, and everyone, including the Japanese, Russians, British, and the United States wanted influence in the city.

Fall was clearly underway as evidenced by an absence of leaves on the surrounding trees. The cold air bit at Walter and Rusty's nostrils as they approached the entrance gate. Private David Butcher stood watch at the gate and readied himself to check Rusty and Walter's identification. The two men produced their ID and "Liberty Cards," authorizing them to leave the compound. They opened the gate and stepped out into the city.

The gray clouds covering the city prevented the strong odor of smoke from the factories, livestock, and aromas from the local eateries from escaping. It made for an unusual and unwelcome smell. Walter had been told that "You'll get used to it." He would find that the memory of the aroma would be with him for the rest of his life.

Walter and Rusty ran to the main street next to the Consulate just in time to catch the trolley. The men jumped on board as the trolley operator slowed the car down. With a smile to the operator, Rusty showed him the piece of paper that displayed the name and address of the place they were going. The operator smiled back and responded in broken English, "Okay, I take."

A never-ending sea of people dominated the landscape as the trolley car made its way through the city. Absent from their faces, however, was any emotion. Anger, joy, sadness; nothing appeared to be on their minds other than the task at hand. Rusty found himself missing the hustle and bustle of Philadelphia. At least back home people had passion on their faces. But for all its pitfalls, Mukden had an eerie politeness about it. He found himself fascinated with the Chinese people.

At the edge of the old city, the driver waved at the two men as the trolley came to a halt. Rusty and Walter stood and walked to the front of the car. The driver pointed toward the alley next to the trolley and smiled. "You go there."

Rusty bowed and thanked the driver with a smile. He and Walter stepped off the trolley and walked to the entrance of the alley. Rusty pulled the paper from his pocket and studied the characters written on it. They slowly walked down the alley as he scanned the signs on the shop fronts. At the end of the alley, Rusty looked up to see the sign on the store that looked like the writing on the paper. "Hope this is it," he said as the two men opened the door and stepped into the store.

The brass bell at the top of the door clanged as the door was opened then closed. They looked at the inside with puzzlement on their faces. The aroma of spices and herbs filled their nostrils as they stood silent, taking in the view.

A countertop ran all the way down the left side of the shop with shelves behind it. On the shelves were large glass jars with metal lids. Inside the jars were what they surmised to be the spices and herbs. The remaining floor space was taken up with tables containing more of the glass jars. Every bit of usable space was occupied with inventory.

They looked to see an elderly couple behind the counter, both with becoming smiles. One lone customer stood at the counter, an elderly gentleman in humble Chinese clothing. As the three people looked at the two Americans, Rusty raised the piece of paper to show the shop keeper and accidently dropped it onto the ground. After reaching down to pick up the paper, Rusty stepped forward to the counter and put on his best public relations smile. He leaned forward and spoke as slowly as he thought necessary.

"Could you please help us? We are looking for a martial arts school, someone to teach us Kung Fu."

Rusty stepped back as the old man's smile turned to a scowl. At a volume just below shouting the old man waved his arms wildly at Rusty. "You go now! You get out."

Both men immediately stepped backwards toward the door as Rusty apologized. "I'm sorry. Please, I'm *very* sorry."

Walter closed the door behind him as they stepped into the alley. Not unfamiliar with the response, they were both surprised, however, at how adamant the old man had been. "That was pretty brutal," Walter said as they stopped midway down the alley.

Rusty lifted the paper and looked at it closely. "Well, that makes seventeen down and only one to go. Maybe eighteen is the charm, huh?"

"I'm beginning to think this is a dead end, Rusty," Walter said with disappointment in his voice.

Rusty and Walter turned as they heard the door to the shop open and close behind them. The elderly customer who had been at the counter was walking toward them. The old man had his arms crossed with each arm enclosed inside the sleeve of the opposing arm. He smiled broadly as he approached. He was looking directly at the two men and slowed as he approached them.

Bowing as he stopped in front of them, the old man looked toward Rusty and spoke softly. "You want learn Kung Fu?"

Rusty smiled with excitement as he responded, "Yes, we do."

The old man pulled his right hand from the sleeve and placed it on his chest. "I am Tao Chung."

Rusty placed his right hand on his chest as he responded. "I am Rusty Harrigan and this is Walter Brown."

Tao placed his hands back inside his sleeves and looked at Rusty. "You come with me."

"Do you know someone who can teach us?" Rusty asked.

"Yes, know someone. Please, you come with me."

The tall and thin seventy-year-old man was dressed in traditional Chinese clothing that was obviously old and tattered. His long gray hair was woven into a pony tail that fell halfway down his back. His equally long gray beard outlined a wrinkled and weathered face that had the air of decades of both wisdom and conflict.

Rusty and Walter walked next to the old man as they travelled farther and farther from the edge of the city. Both buildings and people were becoming scarce as they continued to walk. The old Chinese man was suspiciously quiet as they walked away from the city, something that left Rusty and Walter apprehensive about continuing to follow him. Beginning to become concerned, Rusty asked Tao, "How much farther are we going?"

Tao pointed down the dirt road approximately a quarter of a mile away and responded, "There."

As they looked to where Tao was taking them, they could see a walled compound with several old buildings inside. Large trees surrounded the enclosure that had the appearance of offering a tremendous amount of shade in the spring and summer months. The old stone wall was ten feet in height and was showing signs of its hundred year existence. The wooden entrance gate sat under a stone arch of Chinese design and had carvings in the wood of two dragons, one on each gate. The dried out wood had signs of cracking throughout the gates, displaying the lack of care they had received over decades of use.

As they reached the gates, Walter looked to the left to see two wooden fish hanging by a string attached to the wall. "What are these?" he asked.

Without responding, Tao opened the gate. "Please, come in," he said, motioning with his right hand and a broad smile.

Rusty and Walter hesitated, neither wanting to enter an unknown place where danger could greet them. Tao repeated the request. "Please, is safe, come in."

The two men entered the compound and stood silent as Tao closed the gate behind them. They stared in wonder at what once appeared to be a nice compound years before, but had fallen into disrepair. The wall surrounded a three-acre complex, with five buildings strategically placed against the three rear walls. In the center of the rear wall was the largest of the buildings. A large porch accented the building, with steps ascending down each side.

To the left, there was a long narrow building with a dozen doors to it, implying there were twelve individual rooms. In the dirt courtyard, was evidence of a recent harvest of crops, based on the even rows of tended earth. Chickens and ducks wandered about as a handful of people attended to chores.

This certainly didn't look like a Kung Fu school to Rusty, and he was beginning to think they had been duped. A middle-aged man emerged from the center building and ran toward Tao. Without acknowledging the two Americans, the man greeted Tao, speaking in Chinese. Tao reached into the pocket of his coat and produced a paper bag. The man took the package and bowed. He turned and ran back toward the main building.

Becoming annoyed, Rusty addressed Tao, "Is this your Kung Fu studio?"

Tao bent down to the ground and rested on his knees, then sat back on his heels. He took his right index finger and made an arc in the dirt approximately ten-inches long. He placed his hands in his lap and looked up to Rusty and Walter. Rusty bent down to the ground and rested on his knees. He placed his right index finger at the start of Tao's arc, then drew an arc under the first one, crossing Tao's arc three inches from the finish. The final drawing resembled a fish with an open tail. Tao bowed his head toward Rusty.

The two men stood and faced each other. Rusty smiled at Tao. "How did you know?"

Tao reached out and touched the silver crucifix hanging around Rusty's neck. Normally hidden beneath his shirt, the one inch long pendant had fallen outside his shirt when he'd bent over to pick up the paper in the shop where Tao had first seen them.

With a confused look, Walter questioned Rusty. "I don't get it. What just happened?"

Rusty spoke while still facing Tao. "In the first century of Christianity, believers were being persecuted. When they would meet someone they suspected of being a Christian, they would draw one side of a fish, usually with the toe of their sandal. If the other person was a Christian, they would complete the drawing, creating a fish. If they weren't Christian, it just looked like a meaningless line in the dirt. And since Christians are being persecuted here in China, he just wanted to be sure before he identified himself. These people are Christians, Walter."

Even more puzzled than before, Walter pressed for an answer. "But a fish? What does a fish have to do with Christianity?"

"It's the universal symbol for Christ, Walt." Rusty smiled at Tao. "That's why you have the two wooden fish hanging from the wall."

Tao bowed toward Rusty in agreement.

"A fish, I don't get it, Rusty," Walter protested.

Rusty turned to Walter. "Jesus was always using a fish, or fishing, to identify with him or his cause. The two fish are representative of the two fish and five loaves of bread he used to feed the people at the Sermon on the Mount. He told his disciples to be a fisher of men, and so on. There are countless references to fish or fishing in the Bible." Rusty turned toward Tao. "But I don't understand; why did you say you knew a Kung Fu teacher?"

Tao bowed toward the men. "I am teacher."

"You know Kung Fu?" a surprised Rusty asked.

"Yes, am master of Shaolin Kung Fu," Tao responded. Tao placed his hand on Rusty's shoulder. "Please, come inside for tea. We talk there."

Walter walked beside Rusty as they followed Tao toward the main building and looked toward Rusty as he spoke. "Where the hell did you learn that stuff about the fish?"

"Sunday school, Walt. Every Christian kid knows that story."

"Yeah, well I don't," Walter responded defiantly.

Without looking toward Walter, Rusty replied with a smile. "Don't worry, Walt, you will."

Chapter 5 - New Friends, Old Skills

Bobby Hanson had been leaning forward in his seat since Walter had started telling the story of him and Rusty. The eager seventeen-year-old was filled with questions and pressed Walter. "What did Tao mean by Shaolin Kung Fu? Is that like what was in the TV show Kung Fu?"

"No, Bobby, nothing like that. Shaolin Kung Fu was an art created by the Shaolin monks sometime around 400 AD. The holy Shaolin temple was established on the mountain of Sung in the Honan Province and remained the symbol of Buddhism's power in China for centuries. It also represented the ultimate dominion of Buddhism over all other religions for the next one-thousand years. The temple was built during China's Feudal Age, when warlords ruled over separate regions in China. It was a time when bandits, thieves, and murderers were commonplace. The high priests of the temple researched and devised unique and powerful techniques and trained all of the monks in those arts to combat the violence and maintain Buddhism's dominance.

"According to legend, the monks devised extremely powerful techniques that allowed them to punch through concrete walls, regenerate, and heal at a faster rate, and to be able to walk on the surface of the water. All of those arts came together to form what's

41

known as Shaolin Kung Fu. No one really believes those powers existed, and even if they did, they were lost over the last six-hundred or so years. In spite of that, Shaolin Kung Fu remains the most effective and powerful martial art today. And bet you didn't know this, virtually all other arts such as Karate, Judo, and Tai Kwan Do were variants of the techniques that originated from Shaolin Kung Fu. So while your art of Tai Kwan Do is extremely effective, it has its roots in Kung Fu."

Bobby's mouth was agape in amazement as he listened to Walter. He was consumed by curiosity over the knowledge he was receiving. "So then you were like a Buddhist."

Walter smiled as he responded. "No, Bobby, I'm a Christian. I just learned from someone who had been a Buddhist and converted to Christianity."

"Yeah, but you weren't a Christian when you were learning, were you?"

"No, I didn't become a Christian until years after I was in China," Walter explained.

"Was that because of Rusty?"

Walter slowly nodded. "Yes, it was, Bobby. Rusty was a good man, and he became a role model and mentor. He was a dear friend."

"So like what happened to him?"

Walter stood from the table. "You're gonna let me finish this story, aren't you?"

"Yeah, I'm sorry," Bobby said apologetically.

Walter picked up his bowl and utensils and started walking toward the kitchen. "Come on, Bobby, I'll tell you while we do the dishes. I'll wash, you dry."

★ ★ ★

Rusty and Walter followed Tao inside the main building. In spite of the state of disrepair, the old structure still showed signs of its once grand beauty. Everywhere they looked, hand carved wooden beams and arches could be seen.

On the back wall of the room was a large stone fireplace with a brightly burning fire inside. Rusty and Walter welcomed the warmth on such a cold fall afternoon.

A large table that looked to seat in excess of twenty people was the centerpiece of the four-thousand-square-foot main room. The dining table sat close to the fireplace and offered a warm and comfortable meeting place for the twenty-two occupants of the facility. Around the walls of the room were small, simple beds used for the congregation.

Tao led Rusty and Walter toward the only bed that was occupied. The young girl lying in the bed was covered by numerous blankets and shook uncontrollably from fever. The elderly man who had met Tao at the front gate was standing over her and was holding a cup with liquid in it. The contents of the bag that Tao had brought were being administered to the child. Tao placed his left palm on the girl's forehead and smiled at her.

Tao turned toward Rusty and Walter. "Please, we have tea now."

Rusty and Walter followed Tao to the dining table. Directly in front of the fireplace was a metal table with pots and cooking utensils on it. Tao placed three old tin cups on the table and lifted a pot from the metal table. He poured the steaming, pale liquid into the cups and gestured with his left hand for the two men to sit.

Rusty and Walter took off their coats and sat at the table close to the fire. Rusty lifted the cup and took a sip of the tea. It was hot and delicious, but had a distinct metallic taste from the pot. He immediately thought of the difficulties this group of people must be experiencing. The humble and Spartan accommodations these people were living in could only be because they chose this life. They were living in seclusion from their fellow countrymen, and Rusty was humbled by the thought that they preferred this life to the better conditions in the city.

He was intensely curious and wanted to know the reasons for their choice. "Tao, are all the people here Christian?"

Tao smiled and waved his hand around the room. "Yes, all Christian."

"Why do you live here together?" Walter asked.

"All Christians in China are, parsec, uh presec-"

"Persecuted?" Rusty stated politely.

43

"Yes, persecuted," Tao responded. "Sorry, English not good."

"Why does the government persecute you?" Walter asked.

Tao took a sip from his tea before responding. "Buddhism is religion of China. Long ago, warlords ruled over China, and many people killed. Buddhism brought peace to land. When western countries come to China, they bring Christianity. Many Chinese change to new religion. Chinese fear losing traditions, and blame west. Christians then persecuted." Tao smiled at his correct pronunciation.

"You speak well. Where did you learn how to speak English?" Rusty asked.

"Daughter teach. This was orphanage for many years. Daughter work for missionaries from America and learn English."

"Is she a Christian?" Walter asked

"Yes, daughter was Christian."

"Was?" Rusty asked.

"Daughter was killed by Nationalist soldiers because she was Christian. She was speaking against Nationalists, and was taken. She died in prison," Tao said with a soft voice.

Rusty's brow furrowed as he responded, "I'm *very* sorry, Tao. Did she have a husband or children?"

"No, she dedicate life to orphanage. Never marry."

"How did you become a Christian?" Walter asked.

"Visited daughter in prison. She said she forgave people who put her in prison, ask me to forgive them, too. She achieved total peace from Christianity. I wanted total peace like daughter, so became Christian. Daughter also ask I watch over and protect other Christians at orphanage."

"But didn't the Nationalists round up all the Christians here at the orphanage?" Rusty asked.

"Yes, take many Christians away. Some hide in town. For two year we wait, then come back to orphanage to be together."

"Don't the Nationalists know you're here?" Rusty asked.

"Yes, but they not know we Christian."

44

Rusty had a perplexed look. "But then why did you bring us here? I don't understand why you need us."

Tao smiled as he responded. "To teach … we need Christian teacher."

"Don't you have bibles here at the orphanage?" Rusty asked

"No, all bibles taken by Nationalists. We need teacher. You have bible?"

"Yes, I have a bible at the Consulate, but I don't know how good of a teacher I can be," Rusty replied apologetically. "Besides, I don't speak Chinese. No one will know what I'm saying."

"Only three people here not speak English. We help them." Tao smiled broadly. "You teach Bible, I teach Kung Fu."

"But, Tao, I only have one bible. There won't be enough to go around."

Tao reached across the table and grasped Rusty's hand. "We copy bible. Jesus will help, Rusty. You help us please. He will find way. You will see, please, you teach us." Tao pleaded.

Rusty gave Walter an incredulous look, then took in a deep breath and slowly let it out. "Of course I'll help. I'll bring the bible the next time we come."

Walter was overcome with curiosity about Tao's background. "Tao, how did you become a Kung Fu teacher?"

"Now I am Christian and teach new Christians Kung Fu."

"But then where did you learn Kung Fu from?" Walter asked.

"My family come from Shaolin Monks, many, many generations ago. Our fathers teach Kung Fu to sons. No sons, no students."

Rusty gave Tao a warm smile as he reinforced his commitment. "I'd be pleased to teach you, Tao."

Tao bowed in acknowledgement. "Good, now you stay for food."

"Oh no, Tao, we're not hungry. We ate before we left the Consulate. Besides, we need to get back for duty. When do you want us here?"

"You come when can," Tao responded.

"We can come most evenings, and during almost every weekend if that's okay," Rusty replied.

"That be fine," Tao said with a smile.

Rusty and Walter stood and put their coats on as Tao came around the table and stood in front of them. Walter bowed as he looked at Tao. "Thank you, Tao."

"No, thank you. You have made old man very happy," He said with a smile.

Rusty and Walter turned and walked to the door as Tao watched them leave. After entering the courtyard, and out of earshot of the people, Walter addressed Rusty. "Rusty, we should have stayed for dinner. I wanted to start learning."

Rusty turned his head toward Walter as they walked. "Walt, these people barely have enough food for themselves. They certainly don't have enough to feed two hungry Marines. We'll bring some food next time we come so we can contribute."

Walter felt ashamed for not seeing what Rusty had clearly understood about the people in the compound. As they closed the gate behind them, Walter addressed Rusty again. "Rusty, this might be a bad idea, getting involved in the local's problems. I don't think Rivera would like it."

"Walt, I can't deny a request to teach them. We were placed in front of these people for a reason, and I'm not going to ignore them." Rusty explained.

"I don't understand; what do you mean 'placed in front of them for a reason'?" Walter protested.

"Don't worry, Walt, you will," Rusty said with a smile.

"You're always saying that," Walter replied.

Rusty laughed as the two men continued to walk.

Bobby interrupted Walter as he was hanging up the dish towel. "Wait a minute, Mr. Brown, I saw the *The Bruce Lee Story*;" he got into trouble in China Town in San Francisco because he was teaching Americans Kung Fu. You're not supposed to teach non-Chinese the art. How come Tao could do it?"

"Bobby, Tao left his old life when he became a Christian. He was no longer loyal to the old ways. He was becoming a whole new person," Walter explained.

"I don't understand, Mr. Brown" Bobby protested.

"Don't worry, Bobby, you will."

"Oh, I see, you're gonna pull that same thing on me that Rusty pulled on you," Bobby said with contempt in his voice.

Without responding to Bobby, Walter smiled and continued. "We were both excited to get started and went back to the orphanage two days later."

The early morning sun shone brightly as Rusty and Walter entered the compound. Walter closed the gate behind them as they walked in. The two men labored under the cover of their coats and the large linen sacks they carried. They both perspired as they struggled under the weight. As they crossed the courtyard, the occupants all looked up from their tasks and bowed toward the two men with smiles. They smiled back at the people and bowed slightly as they walked.

"Wow, big change from the first time we saw them, huh?" Walter stated.

"My guess is that Tao spoke to them," Rusty responded.

The two men walked up the steps and knocked on the front door. The door slowly opened and revealed the old man whom they had seen caring for the young girl greeting them. He smiled widely and bowed repeatedly toward the two men. "Please come in" the old man said softly.

Once inside, the old man placed his right hand on his chest and addressed them. "I am Ho Shen."

Rusty smiled back and responded. "I am Rusty Harrigan."

Walter smiled at Ho and responded, "I am Walter Brown."

Ho shook each man's hand. "Am honored meet you both." He turned to his right and pointed to the center of the meeting room. "Master Tao be happy see you. Please, come in."

Walter and Rusty saw Tao instructing five young men in the center of the room. The men were in a line in front of Tao, approximately ten feet from each other. Each was holding six-foot-long wooden staffs and turning them around their bodies in unison. The ballet was mesmerizing to watch. Each moved in harmony perfectly as they spun the staffs around their bodies. Walter and Rusty watched the movements with amazement. Each movement was smooth yet powerful in its application. Rusty was excited to finally be able to learn the art and imagined performing these moves himself.

The five young men spun the staffs around their bodies one last time and finished by placing the staffs vertically next to their right side. The young men bowed toward Tao as they finished. Tao spoke in Chinese to the men, then bowed toward them. The five men walked to the east wall and placed the staffs in the rack on the wall. The men smiled and bowed as they walked past Rusty and Walter, then exited the building.

Tao walked toward Rusty and Walter, smiling as he addressed them. "Thank you for coming."

"Were those your students?" Walter asked.

"Yes, all students."

"Are they Christians?" Rusty asked.

"Yes, Christians from village."

"Why don't they live here with you?" Rusty wanted to know.

"They all new Christians. They live in village and come here to train and worship. One day maybe have to stay here all time," Tao responded.

Rusty reached behind his back and pulled a book from his waistband. "Here's the bible you asked for, Tao."

Tao took the bible and held it reverently in his open palms, bent over, and kissed the book. "Thank you," he replied.

Tao turned and motioned to Ho. The old man hurried toward them. As he stopped in front of Tao, his eyes opened wide. Tao held out the bible and Ho slowly took the book in the same reverent manner in which Tao had received it.

Ho looked at Rusty as he spoke. "It is my honor copy this bible. God bless you."

Rusty had never in his life seen such excitement or reverence regarding the Bible or Christianity. He felt ashamed at his own countrymen that they took such matters routinely. If only Christians back home in the United States could see these people and their sacrifices just to be able to worship God, he thought. Rusty knew this was a moment he would remember for his entire life.

Tao turned back toward the two men. "Now we train."

Rusty remembered the contents of their sacks. "Oh, we brought something for you," he said as they opened the bags. Walter and Rusty walked to the table and began pulling food from the sacks. Potatoes, butter, crackers, rice, and cans of spices now filled the end of the table. Tao's eyes opened wide as he saw the food in front of him.

Tao looked pleadingly toward Rusty. "You not take this from work, do you?"

Rusty immediately knew what Tao was saying. "Oh no, Tao, we didn't get this from the Consulate. We got this at the market."

Tao smiled at Rusty and clasped his right forearm with his hands. "Thank you, thank you both," he said, smiling at Rusty and Walter.

"I did get something from the store at the Consulate, though." Rusty reached into his shirt pocket and removed the last item, a bar of chocolate. "This is for the little girl who's sick," Rusty said as he looked toward the bed. "Where is she?" he asked as he saw the empty bed.

"Mee Ling in kitchen helping cook," Tao replied. "I give her chocolate."

"Wow, fast recovery," Walter said in a low voice as he leaned in toward Rusty.

"I'll say," Rusty responded.

"Now, we train," Tao stated, not responding to Walter's statement. "I give you three things to practice. Work hard, train each day, learn these three things, then I give you more to learn."

Rusty and Walter took their coats off and hung them on the backs of the chairs. They both turned toward Tao with excitement on their faces. Tao led them to the west end of the room, where he pointed toward the floor. They looked to see four red lines painted on the floor. The lines intersected to form what looked like an asterisk. Each line was four-feet in length and four inches wide. Tao stood in the center of the lines with his left heel against the instep of his right foot. "Do as I do," he said.

Rusty and Walter stood on each side of Tao and placed their feet in the same positions. Tao moved his left foot up to the end of the line in front of him and immediately brought his right foot in behind. He quickly moved his right foot back to the center, immediately bringing his left foot back next to his right foot. He quickly duplicated the entire move on each of the lines of the asterisk. His eyes and hands remained forward as he completed each of the moves. When he finished, he looked to Rusty and Walter.

The two men clumsily stepped up and down as they attempted to duplicate Tao's moves. "No, not lift foot high. Move quickly, keep balance." Tao watched as they stumbled through the exercise. Tao stopped them. "You watch again." Tao moved quickly through the exercise again. "See? Keep feet low." The second time the men were smoother, but still needed a lot of practice.

Tao faced Walter and held up his left hand. "You hold up left hand." Walter complied and held up an open hand, palm toward Tao. Tao placed his open palm against Walters and began to push against it. Instinctively, Walter increased pressure until he was pressing hard against Tao's hand. Suddenly, Tao pulled his hand back and Walter fell forward. Tao stepped to the rear with his right foot, sliding his left foot behind, and grasped Walter's wrist, pulling him to the ground.

Walter stood back up and raised his palm. "Can we do that again?" he asked.

Tao nodded as he raised his hand. Again they applied pressure to each other's hands. When Tao tried the same thing, Walter was ready and released the pressure rather than fall forward. Tao immediately stepped forward and pushed Walter to the floor, landing on his back. Tao bent forward and looked Walter in the face. "Keep balance, understand?" Tao asked.

"Yes," Walter responded.

Tao helped Walter stand, then turned toward Rusty and reached inside his pocket. He pulled out a thin piece of wood that was five-inches by three-inches. He held the piece of wood between his thumb and fingers with his palm down. He rotated his wrist clockwise until his thumb was on top and the wood was horizontal. Tao passed the wood to Rusty. "You do," he said.

50

Rusty held the wood the way Tao had, and rotated it one-hundred-eighty degrees clockwise until his thumb was on top. Tao looked at him. "Now rotate more in same direction."

Rusty tried to rotate the wood farther, but found his whole arm was moving. "I can't," he protested.

"Put back with thumb on bottom," Tao requested. Tao watched as he complied. "Now turn other way."

With his fingers on top, he tried to rotate his wrist counterclockwise. Rusty found he couldn't comply.

"Now hold hand out without wood," Tao said.

Rusty held out his right hand palm-down as instructed. Tao reached out with his left hand and quickly rotated Rusty's hand counterclockwise. Rusty immediately fell forward and down to the floor. When he got back up, Tao instructed him to put out his hand again in the same manner. This time, Tao rotated Rusty's hand clockwise. The difference was dramatic; Rusty flew off his feet and fell to the ground on his back.

Tao looked down at Rusty. "You understand?" he asked.

"Yes, Sir," Rusty responded while lying on his back.

Once Rusty and Walter were again facing Tao, their instructor addressed them. "You practice these three. Keep doing until learn. Then we go next lesson."

Rusty was rubbing his wrist as he turned and faced Walter. "Did you see that? He didn't even breathe hard!" Rusty said with amazement in his voice.

"Yeah, makes you not want to shake his hand, huh?"

The two men laughed as they began practicing the moves.

Chapter 6 - Trouble Begins

Rusty and Walter were in the barracks practicing the moves they learned from Tao. It was duty day for both of them, and going to Tao's compound wasn't possible, as they had to remain at the Consulate during the entire twenty-four-hour period. They were in their fatigues and practicing hard before Rusty had to assume guard duty in the next hour.

Their movements were becoming smoother as they practiced on the makeshift asterisk made from tape on the floor. Trying not to look too interested, the other Marines in the barracks glanced toward the two men with curiosity. Corporal Brian Manning walked toward the two men and crossed his arms.

"You two are spending way too much time with the Slope Heads. You're even starting to look like them," Manning said, smiling at the other Marines in the barracks.

Rusty immediately halted his exercises and turned toward Manning. "I don't like that word very much, Manning. I'd appreciate it if you wouldn't use it around me."

The nineteen-year-old six-foot-three, two-hundred-pound Marine puffed his chest out and continued. "I don't care what you think,

Harrigan. The whole lot of them should be bombed like we did in Hiroshima and Nagasaki."

Rusty's brow furrowed. "If it's a fight you're looking for Brian, I'd be happy to comply. If not, leave us alone," Rusty ordered.

Manning smiled back at Rusty. "Oh, what you gonna do, kick my ass with that Chinese ballet shit you're doing?" Manning scoffed, while he waved his hands back and forth in front of Rusty.

Walter stepped next to Rusty as he addressed Manning. "Come on, Rusty, forget about this guy. He's just mad because he found out his parents weren't married when he was born."

Manning's teeth clenched as he cocked his fist back. He threw a straight-on punch toward Walter with his right fist. Walter slid his foot to the right of his body, avoiding the blow. He placed the back of his left hand against the oncoming fist and rotated his hand, gripping Brian's wrist tightly.

While holding onto his now open hand, Walter pulled hard, bringing Brian's body toward him. He then rolled Brian's hand clockwise as he reversed the movement, lifting Manning's body off the floor. Manning came crashing down to Walter's right side in a heap.

With the wrist lock still on him, Walter bent over with a smirk and addressed the Marine. "Wow, what do you know? That Chinese ballet crap really works. And don't cuss anymore in front of Rusty; as he said, he doesn't like it very much." Manning's face was racked with pain as Walter held on tightly to his wrist.

Walter's eyes opened wide as he continued. "And before you think about taking on Rusty here, you'd be wise to know that he's a whole lot better at this Chinese crap than I am. Now say you're sorry, Brian, before I rip your arm off."

With his right arm bent unnaturally, Brian Manning squeaked out the words, "I'm sorry, Rusty."

Walter let the Marine up from the ground. As Brian stood, Walter spoke quietly, "Now run off and play with your friends."

With surprise on his face, Rusty looked toward Walter. "Wow, what do you know, that Chinese stuff really does work, huh?" The two men laughed as they bowed while facing each other.

At that moment, Captain Rivera entered the barracks and let loose his booming voice. "Alright ladies, all hands report immediately to the conference room for a meeting with the Consul General!" The men stood silent, looking at Rivera. "Don't make me repeat myself!" he emphasized with a louder voice.

The Marines knew better than to test their Captain. They quickly straightened themselves and hurried toward the conference room. Rusty and Walter were the last out of the barracks and checked each other to ensure their uniforms were in order as they walked.

"What do you think this is all about, Rusty?" Walter asked with a concerned voice.

Rusty shook his head as he replied, "Don't know, Walt. The Consul Generals never have an 'all hands' meeting except for when they're being replaced, and he's not due to rotate out anytime soon. We'll just have to see."

The conference room was small, but adequate for all ten of the Consulate staff. The accompanying Marine detachment however would have to stand against the wall for the meeting.

The large wooden table in the center of the room seated twelve people. At the far end of the table stood a small podium, with the seal of the United States of America hanging on the front. The American and Marine Corps flags stood tall behind the podium.

The dark, windowless room was artificially lit with ceiling lights and three table lamps on stands sitting next to overstuffed chairs. Dark wood paneled walls lined the conference room and housed bookshelves on two sides.

On the back wall were three large photographs, the President of the United States, Harry S. Truman, the Secretary of State, James F. Byrnes, and Brendan Allen Smith, the Consul General, Mukden China.

The entire staff of the consulate was seated at the conference table when Walter and Rusty entered the room. Rivera followed them into the room and stood next to Walter. He elbowed Walter and leaned in toward him, whispering softly, "Nice moves there, Private. You sure put Manning in his place."

Walter nervously smiled back. "Thank you, Sir."

The Consul General entered the room with a folder under his arm

54

and stepped to the podium. The forty-five-year-old was slight in build and sported a small moustache that gave him a professorial appearance. Placing the folder on top of the podium and opening it, he took in a deep breath before addressing the Consulate staff. General Smith looked around the room. "Are we all here?"

Captain Rivera spoke first. "We're all present with the exception of Private Wade, Sir. He's on guard duty."

Smith looked toward his assistant Gary Parker. "I see the staff is all here. Very well, Captain Rivera, will you see to it private Wade is briefed after the meeting?"

"Yes Sir, as soon as we're done, Sir."

Smith waved toward the occupants of the room with open hands. "I'm sorry for interrupting your afternoon, but we have very important information to pass on.

"The entire content of this briefing is to be considered classified and not to be discussed outside of the Consulate. Intelligence sources indicate that the Communist forces in China will be moving against the Nationalist Forces in the near future. The Nationalists here in Mukden are, for the most part, surrounded by the Communists. Should they move against the Nationalists, we feel the city could be overrun in a matter of days.

"We're unsure as to the outcome this presents for the Consulate, but feel that if the Communists are victorious, Mao Tse-tung will allow us to remain here in Mukden. Should hostilities break out, under no circumstances will we become involved. If you're outside the Consulate when that happens, you're to return immediately. Captain Rivera, do we have enough pistols to arm the staff?"

Rivera stood erect. "Yes, Sir, we have more than enough, and I can provide training if needed."

"Very well, I don't think it necessary at this point, but Embassy and Consulate staffs have had to be armed here in China before. Let's hope it doesn't come to that. That being said, I think we should have the Marine detachment go to the airfield for any mail or diplomatic pouches until further notice. Is that possible, Captain?"

"Yes, Sir, I'll see to it immediately after the meeting." Rivera responded.

Smith took another deep breath and let it out slowly before

speaking. "If we're ordered to leave Mukden, the Army has assured me that they can have transport planes here from Japan within hours. Before leaving, all Consulate documents are to be destroyed, so we need to follow State Department guidelines for destruction of sensitive material. If we have to leave quickly, you'll only be allowed to take a small bag of personal items; so I suggest you prioritize your personal items accordingly and be ready for that scenario should it unfold. If we're ordered out, then you're all to follow Capt Rivera's orders to the letter; he's in charge of security. This is, of course, all precautionary. We only want to be prepared for the worst-case scenario."

Rivera raised his hand. "Sir, are the Communists reinforcing their positions outside the city?"

"The Army tells us that they're not. They feel that an attack on the city will only occur if they gain strength and have victories in other areas of the country. There are four key cities in China where the Nationalists have a stronghold: Xuzhou, Taiyuan, Nanjing, and here in Mukden. If they're successful in the other areas, then they will, in all probability begin building their forces up around Mukden. So far, the only thing that has stopped them is the superior numbers of Nationalists here in the city."

"The policy of only going into the city in civilian clothing is still in force, with the exception of the weekly trips to the airfield," Smith said, while addressing Rivera.

"Yes, Sir," Rivera acknowledged.

"Well, ladies and gentlemen, that about sums it up. We'll have weekly meetings for all personnel until further notice. If there are no further questions-" Smith looked the crowd over quickly, "Then we can adjourn." Smith collected his notebook from the podium and walked from the room.

As the other staff members followed, Rivera spoke to the Marines. "Okay, gentlemen, listen up. I want the guard doubled until further notice. I want the weapons checked and all the magazines loaded."

Private Manning spoke up first. "Captain, can we still go into the city?"

"Yes, but if hostilities begin, I want you all back in the compound most Ricky-Tik. Understood?"

56

The Marines all responded loudly. "Yes, Sir."

Rivera turned toward Rusty. "Harrigan, make up a new schedule for doubling the guard, and also for the weekly trips to the airfield."

"Yes, Sir," Rusty responded.

"Alright, gentlemen, we have work to do. Let's get after it."

Rusty and Walter were the last to leave the room. Walter looked toward Rusty as he spoke. "I hope we can still go to Tao's."

Rusty responded as they walked. "I don't see a problem with it, Walt, but it may come down to us not being able to go there sometime in the future."

"I hope the people at the mission will be okay, Rusty."

"Me, too, Walt--me too."

Bobby was completely enthralled with Walter's story and was leaning forward with his chin resting in his hands. He interrupted Walter. "Mr. Brown, if it was getting so dangerous, why didn't the Consulate staff just leave China?"

"It was our job, Bobby. Just because it gets a little dicey out there doesn't mean you can pack up and come home. We had a job to do, and we had to stay if there was any hope of establishing relations with China after the conflict. You sign up for the job, you finish it," Walter responded.

Bobby lifted his head out of his hands. "Did the Communists take over the city after that?"

"Not right away. It took another two years. It wasn't until October of 1948 that the Communists finally entered the city."

"Were there a lot of battles there?" Bobby asked.

"Not really. The Communists just basically walked in and occupied it. They began it with a bombardment, but for the most part they just walked in and the Nationalists abandoned their positions. There was a lot of chaos, though. I've never seen so many people trying to get out of a city before. The train station was a madhouse, and people were leaving by any means possible. By the time the Communists entered, it looked like a ghost town."

"Did the Communists make it hard on you after they took over?"

"It was clear they didn't want us there. Threats and intimidation were always there any time we interacted with their military. The whole lot of 'em were nothing but a bunch of thugs dressed in uniforms. The worst of them was a Chinese Communist Colonel named Sheng Li. You could have written volumes about his brutality."

"Did you ever meet him?"

"Yeah, we had a couple of run-ins with him. He was educated here in the United States, spoke perfect English. We trained and educated him, then he turned on us. I'd have given real money to get the chance to drop that cockroach," Walter said with a scowl on his face. "The only solace I have in life is that I outlived that maggot."

"Gee, Mr. Brown, was he really that bad?" Bobby asked.

"I'm pretty certain he killed two of the people at the orphanage, or had them killed. Sure would have been nice to put him in the crosshairs of my M-1." Walter smiled at the idea.

"So were you able to keep going to Tao's during that time?" Bobby asked.

"Yes, we were. We went there regularly until late 1948."

"What happened then?"

"The beloved Chairman Mao, along with Colonel Li, had us held in the Consulate for almost a year."

"So, you were like prisoners?"

"Yeah, we were there for almost a year stuck behind the walls of that Consulate. Wasn't my most favorite time. After that, we were all taken to Tientsin China, just south of Beijing. We were all taken by boat out into the China Sea and transferred to the SS Lakeland Victory, then back home to San Francisco."

"Did you go to Korea after that?"

"No, I mustered out of the Marine Corp and went back home. I was there for almost a year, then I was recalled to go to Korea after the war started."

Bobby had a curious look. "So then you only learned Kung Fu for a little over two years?"

"Yes, just over two years, Bobby. We trained almost daily, though. Rusty and I would train at Tao's for two or three hours, then Rusty would have Bible studies. His teaching was as intense as Tao's instruction. It made for some late evenings, but he finally got through the whole Bible."

"So how did you get so good at it if you only trained for two years?"

"I applied the principles I had learned, then practiced every day. I was taught the basics in about two years, but it's taken my whole life to try to achieve perfection, and I'll probably die before I can have that perfection."

Bobby had a dejected look as he listened to Walter. "You mean it's gonna take me my whole life to learn Kung Fu?"

"Nothing worth having in life is easy, Bobby. If it was easy, they'd get a monkey to do it. That applies to everything you do. Besides, you're young; you've got your whole life ahead of you."

Bobby was shaking his head as he thought about the concept of spending his whole life trying to master something. He had a curious look as he spoke. "Why did Corporal Manning have such an attitude?"

Walter sat at the counter across from Bobby. "Most bullies have low self-esteem, Bobby. Sometimes we need to be reminded that we're acting inappropriately. Brian turned out to be a good man; it just took a while for him to realize what was proper and what wasn't."

Bobby sat back in his chair. "So I guess you're, like, trying to tell me I have low self-esteem because of fights at school, huh?"

Walter leaned in toward Bobby. "Not sayin that at all, Bobby, I said most bullies. Your problems came about as a result of you trying to deal with your brother's death. Whole different ball of wax."

Bobby seemed satisfied with Walter's explanation of his difficulties at school. Nonetheless, he was feeling bad regarding his conduct, especially by being confronted about it from someone he was beginning to respect. He felt the need to change the subject. "Mr. Brown, what does 'Most Ricky-Tik' mean?"

Walter laughed as he responded. The phrase Ricky-Tic is derived from *Rikki-Tikki-Tavi*, a short story in *The Jungle Book* by Rudyard Kipling; it's about the adventures of a mongoose that kills a cobra. It's commonly used in the US Military as a slang term for 'quickly'.

"Rudyard Kipling? Who's that?" Bobby asked.

Walter was shaking his head side-to-side as he responded. "Rudyard Kipling was an author from the late eighteen-hundreds. You seriously need to change schools or start watching more old Disney movies. You spend way too much time on the football field. I'm going to alter my agreement with you to also include the reading of some classic books."

Bobby smiled. "Okay, Mr. Brown."

Walter stood and walked toward the refrigerator. "Okay, let me get us something to drink and I'll continue with the story."

Chapter 7 - David's Faith

The threat of the Communist takeover in Mukden was elevating, and had become the daily discussion at the Consulate for the security briefings. The Marines were being kept at an elevated level of security based on the Consul Generals briefings, and it was beginning to take a toll on morale.

Captain Rivera knew instinctively that trouble was in their future, he just didn't know how bad it would get. Based on how the Chinese Communists were being influenced by the "Godless Russians," as he referred to them, it wouldn't be long before the Communists flexed their muscles.

Rivera's Marines didn't have any combat experience, but he still had every confidence in their abilities. He had been accelerating their training and performing drills since the first day. It was his job to keep them on alert and ready for the day when confrontation from the Communists became a reality. Hopefully that day would come later than sooner.

Almost a year had passed since Rusty and Walter had entered the compound of the orphanage and met the occupants living there. Their martial arts skills were growing rapidly, and the thirst they had for more knowledge was unquenchable. Walter and Rusty were also quickly becoming like family members. Each time they entered the compound; the residents would stop what they were doing and greet them with smiles. Their young lives were being forever changed.

Walter and Rusty entered the compound with their usual bundles of food to see some of the believers working in the yard. It was late summer in the Liaoning Province, and the crops were almost ready to be harvested at the orphanage. The majority of the workers were in the rice fields two miles west of the compound, harvesting the meager crop that would hopefully get them through the winter months. The two young marines continued to bring as much food as they could during each visit they made to the orphanage.

As they walked toward the main building, each of the believers looked up and smiled at them and waved while calling out their names. As they were busy responding to each of the believers, the front door of the main building burst open to reveal Mee Ling with a huge smile on her face as she ran toward the two men.

Rusty and Walter dropped their bundles and prepared to receive the usual hugs from the young girl. Before she had even reached them, she was shouting loudly, "Uncle Rusty, Uncle Walter." The young girl leapt into Rusty's awaiting arms. He lifted her up to his chest and hugged her tightly. When he set her back down, she jumped into Walt's arms and hugged him equally as tight.

She looked into Rusty's eyes with anticipation as she stood in front of the two men. Rusty pointed toward Walter as he spoke. "He has it today honey," he said with a smile.

Mee Ling turned toward Walt and smiled with wide eyes. He reached into his shirt pocket and pulled out the large bar of Hershey's chocolate. He spoke as he handed it to the excited young girl, "Make sure you share it with the others."

"I will," the young girl responded. "Thank you, Uncle Walter."

Walt placed his hand on her head as he responded, "You're welcome, honey."

The two men smiled as they watched Mee Ling run back into the building clutching her prize tightly. They picked up their bundles and continued toward the main building. "She's growing up fast," Walt announced.

"Yeah, she's getting bigger by the day," Rusty said with a smile.

The two men entered the main building to see Tao demonstrating the techniques of the six foot long staff called a Bo. He was displaying his skills to the five Chinese students sitting on the floor in front of him.

Ho Shen approached Rusty and Walter and bowed as he stopped in front of them. The two men bowed in return.

Rusty set his bundle on the floor as he spoke. "I'm sorry, Ho, are we late?" he stated with concern.

Ho responded quickly to his friend. "No, Rusty, Master Tao teaching new moves to older students. Will begin training for you after he done. Please watch, he stated as he picked up the bundles, "Please, watch Master Tao."

Rusty and Walter sat on the floor with their legs crossed along with the other students, as they watched Tao demonstrate the techniques of the Bo. Rusty was mesmerized as he watched the ballet being performed in front of him. This was why he had wanted to find a Kung Fu teacher, what had drawn him to the art; the perfection fascinated him.

He was watching the result of a lifetime of dedication to a skill that Tao so perfectly displayed. Tao spun the Bo around his body as if it were part of him. Each move was gracefully performed, yet powerfully executed. Rusty marveled at how a man in his seventies could be so agile and powerful. Tao performed as if he were a teenager. This was the beginning of Tao's instruction for the Bo and was primarily directed toward his two American students.

Rusty had not only a newfound respect for the Chinese people, but he also marveled at their humility and honor. He never saw them complain. They never asked for luxuries or splendor, only to exist in peace. He'd watched them scratch out a meager existence in the dirt of their compound, laboring to grow enough food for the winter, yet they always smiled at him when he would come to be with them. Rusty had grown to love the Chinese people.

Tao completed his demonstration by spinning the Bo above his head and bringing it down next to his right side. The students all stood and bowed toward him. Tao motioned for the students to come forward with their Bo's.

Rusty and Walter stepped toward him, holding their Bo's clumsily in both their hands. Tao held his Bo in his right hand, with even amounts of the staff on each side of his hand. He held it out in front of him horizontally, looking at his students. He began moving it in a figure eight manner in front of his body, slowly increasing the speed until the staff became a blur to the onlookers. He finished by bringing one end of the Bo around behind him, resting on the back of his shoulder as his feet were wide apart. The other end was pointing down to the ground at his right side. Rusty smiled as he watched the smooth operation.

Tao pointed toward his students and nodded. The six people in front of him began spinning their Bo's in front of them in a figure eight. Walter was having difficulty with the coordination and moved his hand wide as he struggled with the move. Rusty's attempts were better, but not by much.

Tao moved in front of Rusty and Walter. Looking at the two men, he spoke softly. "Must make hand smooth. Hold Bo in left hand."

The two men put the Bo's in their left hands and looked back at Tao. "Now hold fist out." They complied. "Now make move without Bo."

They held their right fists out in front of them and moved in a figure eight. The movements were smooth and tight. "Need to do same with Bo."

Rusty stopped the movement and looked at his Mentor. "Master, what does the movement do?"

"When do right, can stop attack from front," Tao responded.

"It can stop any attack?" Walter asked.

"Not all." Tao motioned for Chow Yun to come in front of him and waited for him to implement the move. As Chow was spinning the Bo in front of him, Tao held his Bo with both hands. He slid his right foot to the rear, pointing one end of the Bo in front of him. He spoke as he concentrated on Chow's Bo. "Must see move, find opening."

With lightning speed, Tao moved forward and stuck the Bo into the spinning circle. In one continuous move, he flipped the Bo from Chow's hand and rotated his staff, striking Chow in the stomach, checking his blow before hurting his student.

Walter's eyes popped open as he watched the move. "Wow, that was incredible."

Tao held his hand out toward Rusty and Walter. "Must practice."

The two men put the staffs in their right hand and continued to practice with the other students. Each continued to spin the staffs, making the circle smaller and smaller as they focused on the movement.

After practicing for an hour, Tao interrupted them and asked Ho Shen to come forward with his Bo. Ho stopped in front of Tao and bowed toward him. The two men slowly began to move their staffs toward each other in attacking moves. They were purposely moving the staffs slowly so the students could see the moves, and counter moves. After ten minutes of demonstration, Tao and Ho stopped and turned toward the students.

Tao motioned toward the group with his open palm. "Choose partner and practice." He looked toward Walter and pointed to the floor in front of him. "Please, Walter, come." Walter stepped toward Tao with his Bo.

Ho smiled at Rusty and nodded. Rusty smiled back and stepped toward him holding his Bo. The group of men began attacking each other slowly with moves and counter moves.

Rusty moved his Bo aggressively toward Ho. Each move was countered, and reversed on him. He gradually began to increase his speed as he became more confident. The clicking noise of the Bo's contacting each other became louder as the two men moved faster and faster. Rusty was relaxing his stance as he focused more and more on his technique. Seeing the weakness, Ho quickly lowered himself to the ground and swung the Bo counter-clockwise, striking Rusty behind his knees. Rusty's legs collapsed and he fell to the floor with a thud.

Ho looked at Rusty as he stood back up. "Must keep feet firm Rusty," Ho said with purpose.

Rusty stood back up and gained a solid stance as he faced Ho again. The two men returned to their drills, moving with more purpose. Rusty was in complete focus as he watched the moves coming from Ho. He was getting faster, and more aggressive as he attacked his partner. Each time Ho moved in with a blow, Rusty stopped it, and immediately went on the offensive.

When Ho lowered his body to repeat the move toward Rusty's knees, Rusty jammed the end of the Bo on the floor, stopping the blow. Ho immediately reversed the move and swung the Bo in the opposite direction as he stood. Rusty quickly swung the Bo to the other side of his body to stop the blow coming toward the left side of his head, but lost the grip in his right hand. The end of Ho's Bo struck Rusty's right temple hard. The loud crack of the Bo against Rusty's head echoed through the room as he collapsed onto the floor.

After several minutes, Rusty regained consciousness and slowly opened his eyes from being knocked out. He looked up to see Ho, Tao, and Walter looking back down at him. The figures of the men slowly came into focus as he regained consciousness.

Ho looked compassionately at Rusty as he spoke. "Sorry Rusty. Hit you too hard, very sorry."

Rusty gently touched the knot on the side of his head as he responded. "It's okay Ho, my fault. I lost my grip on the Bo."

Tao looked down at his friend as he spoke. "You be okay, Rusty?"

The big man smiled back. "I'm fine, Master."

Tao and Walter returned to their drills as Rusty stayed seated on the floor. Ho sat down in front of Rusty as he placed his hand on the side of Rusty's head.

"Be fine Rusty, all be fine," he stated.

"I know, I'm just angry I lost my grip."

Ho smiled at his friend. "Still learning Rusty. I hit many times when learning," he said while slapping Rusty on the arm. Ho changed the tone of his voice as he looked at his friend. "Rusty, what you want from life?"

Rusty chuckled as he looked at Ho. "What kind of a question is that, Ho?"

"Want to know what my friend want from life. Care about friend."

Rusty raised his eyebrows as he grinned. "Don't know, maybe to get married and have some children."

"What do for work?" Ho asked.

'Don't know, maybe stay in the Marine Corps. I haven't thought

66

about it very much," he responded.

"You like Marine Corps?"

"Yeah, it lets me see the world. I didn't see anything outside of Philadelphia until I joined," he responded.

"You go back home when done in China?" Ho asked.

"Nah, I want to live somewhere that has some mountains and trees. Kinda tired of the city. What about you, what do you want from life, Ho?"

Ho grinned as he responded. Want be like King David, want be blameless before God. King David say he blameless before God. All sins forgiven." Ho stuck his chest out as he continued. "Yes, want be blameless before God."

Rusty grinned as he looked at his friend. He felt ashamed about his own selfish desires after listening to the simple request of this humble man sitting in front of him. He smiled at his friend as he stood. "We all want that, Ho."

As the two men stood, Tao announced the completion of the training. "Done for today. Good practice, we eat now."

Rusty and Ho placed their Bo's in the holders and walked to the table. The humble meal was being brought to the table by the children. The four large bowls of rice laced with vegetables and spices were placed on the tables with a plate of bread next to each bowl. Mee Ling smiled at Rusty as he approached the table. He grinned back at her as he sat down. The young orphan girl had attached herself to the two Marines, and was viewing them as her surrogate family. As Rusty sat down, he gently touched the side of his head with his fingers, trying to stop the throbbing in his head. Tao looked at his friend and smiled as he sat down across from him.

Chapter 8 - The New Occupiers

October 1948

Rusty and Walter entered Tao's compound laden with their weekly supply of food for the occupants. The packages were smaller now, but continued nonetheless.

Commerce in the city had been reduced to a minimum. Communist troops had occupied Mukden for three months. Under the direction of General Lin Piao, they had walked into Mukden virtually unopposed and now had complete control over the city. The factories were empty, and most of the stores were abandoned. Those who hadn't fled before the occupation now lived in both fear and poverty. Many had been taken to the factories to gear up for needed production to feed the engine of Communism that dominated the once proud city.

As fall came to the Liaoning province, Mukden was besieged by trash and fallen leaves in the streets. A cold wind howled through the once bustling city, and an eerie feeling of dread for the coming totalitarian rule consumed everything.

The American Consulate had been allowed to remain open for the time being, although Mao Tse-tung and the Russian troops in the area would have preferred otherwise. A new Consul General had been posted in Mukden, Robert Allen Marsh, a tough as nails administrator dedicated to salvaging what he could of the deteriorated relationship the United States now had with the Chinese Communists. Marsh had been accompanied by his wife for his assignment. Both he and Vera were excited for the posting, but worried about the stability of China.

The entire Consulate walked on pins and needles, waiting for the time they would be thrown out of the country. Marsh had told the staff "that the day was coming, it was just a matter of when." Although the Consulate staff was allowed to leave the compound for short trips into town, most were now carrying sidearms for their self protection. Times in Mukden had drastically changed, and not for the better.

It had been two years and ten months since Rusty and Walter had first met Tao. The bonds that had been created between them and the group at the orphanage since that day would last a lifetime. Rusty's Bible studies had become a treasured gift to the people occupying the compound. Even Walter found himself asking questions during some of the sessions, something that surprised even him.

Rusty and Walter opened the door to the main building and stepped inside. The fireplace was glowing hot in the large room and was welcome to the two men after such a cold walk from the Consulate. Before they could set the bags down, Mee Ling ran toward them. "Uncle Rusty," the young girl shouted as she hugged the big man tightly. Mee Ling let go of Rusty and immediately hugged Walter. "Hello, Uncle Walter," she said as she stood between the men. Now ten-years-old, the girl was growing into a beautiful young lady.

Rusty reached into his pocket and produced three Hershey bars. He held them out toward Mee Ling. "Here you go. Share them with the others." The excited young girl ran off with her treats. It amazed both Walter and Rusty how something as simple as chocolate could create such a bond.

They looked to see Tao approaching from the back of the room, armed with his usual smile. Rusty and Walter walked to the table to place their weekly delivery on top. Tao bowed as he stopped in front of them. Rusty and Walter bowed in return. Tao reached out toward the two men, grasping their arms tightly. "Come, sit. We talk."

Rusty and Walter hadn't seen Tao so reserved before. Concern fell over them as they sat at the table. Tao placed three cups on the table and filled them with tea. Placing the pot back on the iron table next to the fireplace, he sat across from his friends. Tao looked pleadingly

69

toward them as he spoke. "Ask favor, you not come here anymore."

Rusty's brow furrowed as he responded "Why, Master" Have we done something wrong?"

The old man reached across the table, patted the men's hands, and smiled. "No, do nothing wrong. You both good friends. Has become dangerous here. Worry you both are in danger by coming here."

Walter looked at his friend, deeply concerned. "Has something happened, Master?"

"Communists come here two time. Afraid they looking for Christians. If you found here, they take you away to prison."

"Have they taken any of you away?" Rusty asked.

Tao lowered his head as he spoke. "Not take from here, but have taken two students from village, Zhu Dong and Chen Yang. They taken to prison. If speak, they tell about us here. Very dangerous for you come here anymore."

"But, Master, we have to continue our training. There's so much more we need to learn," Walter said pleadingly.

Tao smiled at him. "Already know what you need. Have taught you all I can; just need practice. Have been good students."

Rusty looked at his master and friend. "But Master, Tao, we haven't finished our Bible studies. You need to learn so much more."

Tao placed his hand on his chest. "Already know what we need. All we must do is practice," he said with a smile, repeating his explanation.

Tao stood, walked to the end of the room, and motioned to Ho Shen. The elderly man picked up a package wrapped in rice paper and walked back to the table with Tao. He held out the package toward Rusty and smiled. Rusty tore open the package to see his bible, now covered in a heavy silk binder. The front of the binder was adorned with a beautiful hand-stitched pheasant on the upper portion, with Chinese writing sewn on the bottom. He looked at Ho. "What does it say?" he asked.

"It say 'To our friend and teacher, Rusty Harrigan.'"

Rusty could feel his emotions overpowering him. He fought to hold back tears welling up inside. He took a deep breath before speaking. "This is the most wonderful gift I've ever received. I'll treasure it for as long as I live." He bowed toward Ho with a huge smile.

The old man smiled back at Rusty and bowed in return.

"Did you get enough bibles copied for everyone?" he asked Ho.

"Yes, all copied. Thank you, Rusty. God bless you."

Rusty looked pleadingly toward Tao as he started to speak. Wise beyond his years, Tao knew it was best to have the two men leave without further conversation. He reached out, touched Rusty on the shoulder, and nodded with a smile. Understanding what Tao was doing, Rusty bowed toward his master. "Say goodbye to Mee Ling for us."

Tao nodded and smiled back as Walter and Rusty turned to leave. As the two men walked to the door, they saw all of the occupants of the room look toward them and bow as they walked past. When they reached the door, Rusty looked back and smiled at Tao and Ho. Tao placed his palms together and lowered his head, smiling back. The two men closed the door behind them.

The walk back to the Consulate was both long and painfully silent. Neither Rusty nor Walter felt the need for talking; they merely reflected on a chapter to their life that was coming to a close. When they were only eight blocks from the Consulate, they heard the sound of a vehicle behind them. Both men turned around to see a troop transport truck approaching.

Rusty slowly slid his bible into the large left pocket of his coat. The truck came to an abrupt halt ten yards from the men. Ten Chinese Communist soldiers exited the rear of the truck and ran toward the men with their rifles at the ready. The men stopped in front of Rusty and Walter in a line and pointed their weapons at them. Rusty and Walter slowly slid their hands into their pockets. Each man put a firm grip on the Colt .45 that lay in their right pockets.

Colonel Sheng Li exited the right side of the truck and casually walked toward them with his hands clasped behind his back. The forty-one-year-old Colonel was thin and towered over his men at six-feet-three-inches-tall. His uniform was impeccable, right down to the highly polished calf high brown leather boots. His long trench coat accented his height and gave him a sinister look. Colonel Li stepped around his men and walked to where Rusty and Walter were standing.

As he stopped in front of them there was an arrogant smile on his face. "Corporal Harrigan, Private Brown, what are you doing walking around in my city?"

Both men were surprised to hear a member of the Chinese military speak such fluent English. Rusty responded with surprise in his voice. "Sir, we were just going back to the Consulate. How do you know our names, Colonel?"

His hands still clasped behind his back, Colonel Li calmly responded, "We know each of the members of the Consulate and everything about them, Corporal. For instance, you can each hand over the Colt .45's in your pockets, and don't bother denying it. We know each of you carry sidearms when you leave the Consulate." Colonel Li held out his right hand toward Rusty. "Yours first, Corporal."

Keeping his eyes locked on the Colonel, Rusty slowly pulled the .45 out of his right pocket. He turned the weapon around and held it out toward Colonel Li, grip first. Li took the weapon and dropped the magazine out into his left hand. He began ejecting the .45 rounds from the magazine with his left thumb. When the magazine was empty, he ejected the last round from the chamber. He slid the magazine back into the weapon and handed it back to Rusty. "Now yours, Private," he said while looking at Walter.

Walter glared at Li and stood still. "Walt, give him your weapon, now!" Rusty ordered.

Walter slowly pulled the weapon out of his pocket and surrendered it. Col. Li emptied the weapon in the same manner as he had Rusty's and handed it back to Walter. The sixteen live rounds from the pistols now lay on the ground in front of him. Returning his hands to the small of his back, Li addressed the now disarmed Marines. "Gentlemen, what were you doing at the orphanage?"

Rusty felt his stomach tie into a knot as he heard Colonel Li ask the question. How much did he know about Tao and the others at the orphanage? he thought. Rusty drew on the only thing he could think of. "I want to be a doctor after I get out of the Marine Corp, and Tao Chung has been teaching me about herbal remedies."

"And how did you know he was a healer?" Li asked.

"I was in an herb shop not far from here two years ago and met him. He's been teaching me since then," Rusty responded.

"And what about you? Do you want to be a doctor?" Li asked Walter.

Walter smirked at the Colonel. "No, I want to be a fireman. I just go where my friend goes."

Colonel Li bristled at Walter's response. "Well, gentlemen, I'm afraid your days of going to the orphanage are over. From this point on, the only movement outside of the Consulate will be for your weekly diplomatic runs to the airfield."

"Does the Consul General know about this, Colonel?" Rusty demanded.

"He was told an hour ago. He said there were only two people outside the Consulate; Private Brown and Corporal Harrigan. We informed him we would return you. So to put it in your parlance, gentlemen, you need to 'hightail it back there'," Li said while leaning toward the men.

"Are we under arrest, Colonel?" Rusty asked.

"Not at the moment, Corporal, but if you don't comply, you will be."

"You speak awfully good English for a tyrannical Communist thug, Colonel," Walter said defiantly.

Colonel Li turned to face Walter. His face was emotionless as he responded "You persist on trying to provoke me, Private Brown. It would do well for you to keep your mouth shut at this point, or I'll have you shot where you stand. And if it's any of your business, I have a Masters Degree in Philosophy from Columbia, which by the way, your government paid for. And after living in your country for six years, I can say without reservation that I can hardly wait for the day when your country falls to a third-world Communist nation." Li leaned in closer toward Walter. "Did this tyrannical communist thug explain it to you clearly enough?"

Walter snapped to attention. "Yes, Sir!" he replied defiantly.

"Now, I want the two of you to get in the back of the truck before I lose my temper and shoot you both." Li stepped aside and motioned with his left hand for them to walk to the truck.

Walter and Rusty stepped inside the truck and sat on the jump seats with the ten soldiers surrounding them. The driver started the

73

engine and drove the eight remaining blocks to the Consulate. When the truck stopped, Colonel Li exited the passenger side and walked to the rear of the truck. He motioned for the two men to exit the rear. Rusty and Walter stepped down out of the bed of the truck and walked to the gate of the Consulate.

After opening the gate, Walter turned defiantly toward the Colonel and spoke. "Thanks for the ride, Colonel. I hope we meet again someday."

Colonel Li smiled at Walter. "Oh, you can count on it, Private," he replied before getting back into the truck. The vehicle drove off as Rusty and Walter stopped inside the compound next to the guard shack. With his weapon at port arms, Corporal Manning addressed the two men. "The Captain said to send you two to the duty hut to see him as soon as you got back."

"Okay, Manning," Rusty responded as they turned to walk toward the main building. Rusty was shaking his head while they walked. "Someday, Walt, that attitude of yours will get you into big trouble."

Still fuming, Walter spoke with purpose. "I wasn't going to let that asshole get the better of us, Rusty."

Rusty stopped in his tracks and faced Walter. "Walt, what were you thinking? All he had to do was search us and he would have found the bible I have in my pocket. With the Chinese writing on it, I'm sure a tyrannical communist college graduate can figure out that Tao and his people are Christians. You could have placed them all in harm's way, and I've told you before, don't cuss around me!"

Walter felt ashamed after realizing that his pride could have endangered Tao and the people at the orphanage. He lowered his head as he responded, "I'm sorry, Rusty, I didn't think of that. It won't happen again," he said apologetically.

"Walt, the best soldier uses his head before his heart. You've got to start thinking before you jump," Rusty said, clearly disappointed.

Walter responded the only way he could after being dressed down. "I'm sorry, Rusty."

The men walked to the duty hut and knocked on the door. "Enter!" came from the other side.

Walter and Rusty entered the room and snapped to attention. "Sir, you told us to report," Rusty bellowed.

74

"At ease," Captain Rivera replied. "Have a seat, gentlemen."

The two men took seats across from the Captain and sat erect in their chairs. "Good to see you made it back unharmed, gentlemen. Did Colonel Li find you, or did you make it back here by yourselves?"

"No, Sir, he found us about eight blocks from the Consulate and drove us back," Rusty responded.

Rivera lit a cigarette before going further. He took a long drag from the smoke and exhaled slowly. "Then there's no need telling you that we're all confined to the Consulate until further notice."

"No, Sir," the two men responded.

"Were you treated properly?"

Rusty sat forward in his seat. "He took our ammunition from us, Sir, but we still have our pistols. Other than that, we were treated okay."

Rivera leaned back in his seat. "The Consul General believes that we'll be thrown out of the country sometime in the very near future. We're allowed to make weekly trips to the airfield for provisions and diplomatic pouches. Other than that, we're confined here. I'm sorry, gentlemen, this means you won't be able to go to that place you guys are always frequenting."

Rusty and Walter decided not to tell the Captain about Tao's conversation with them. Like good soldiers, they accepted their orders. "We understand, Sir," Rusty responded.

"General Marsh briefed us an hour ago about the situation. Colonel Li told the General about the confinement only about two hours ago, so there are a lot of unanswered questions that remain. We've set food rationing in place until further notice, as we don't know when we'll receive provisions. It's going to get tight around here, so I need you to stay frosty. General Marsh remains in negotiations with the Chinese Communists and will brief us of any changes." Rivera extinguished his cigarette in the ashtray and leaned back in his chair. "That's about all we know so far. I need you men to get into uniform and comply with the daily routine posted outside the squad bay." Rivera looked toward Walter. "Private, please leave us. I'd like to have a few words with Corporal Harrigan now."

Walter stood and snapped to attention. "Yes, Sir." Walter did an about-face and left the room.

Rivera opened the top drawer to his desk, pulled out a bundle of Sergeants stripes, and threw them across the desk toward Rusty. "Get these sewn onto your uniforms immediately, Sergeant Harrigan."

Rusty took the bundle and looked at Rivera with surprise. "Sir, I-"

"Harrigan, you're the perfect choice. You're a natural born leader, Son, and since Sergeant Weston left us six-months ago, we've needed a replacement. And before you start getting humble on me, you're gonna earn every bit of pay those things come with." Rivera said while pointing to the bundle of stripes. He reached back into the desk and retrieved another bundle. He handed them to Rusty. "Here are Brown's corporal stripes; we need a replacement for you. Thought it best if you presented them to him."

Rusty remained awestruck and sat speechless in his chair.

"I also received paperwork for your acceptance to Officers Candidate School. Unfortunately, we won't be able to comply with that until we get outta here."

"Thank you, Sir. I won't let you down," Rusty responded with confidence.

"I'm counting on that, Sergeant," Rivera said with a smile.

Rivera's tone changed as he went on. "Rusty, we've got a helluva problem here. The Communists have got us boxed in. At anytime we could all find ourselves in a Chinese prison. We already have reports that there are US servicemen in the factories here in forced labor, some of them Marines. I can't stress how difficult this is. I need you to keep the men both calm and occupied. I don't need these guys losing their head and discharging a round into one of the Chinese soldiers, much as some of those bastards deserve it," Rivera said with a smile.

"And since the cancellation of leave, transfers, and discharges here, the men are on edge. I need you to keep them in order." Due to the impending hostilities in China, the Marine Corp had cancelled all orders for the Marines stationed in Mukden.

"I will, Sir," Rusty responded.

Rivera stood and held his hand out toward Rusty. He stood and took Rivera's hand. "I want to be the first to congratulate you,

Sergeant Harrigan," Rivera said, firmly shaking Rusty's hand. "And give my congratulations to Brown as well."

"Thank you, Sir," Rusty replied.

"Now get into uniform and get some chow," Rivera ordered.

Rusty saluted smartly and did an about-face. Stepping into the hall, he closed the door behind him. He stood quietly and stared at the bundles of stripes in his hand. He smiled as he spoke quietly to himself. "Baptism by fire, Harrigan."

Chapter 9 - Evils Hand

Mukden, China's prison system, had a history like no other in the world, save the horrors of the holocaust camps under Hitler's regime. First used by occupying Japanese forces during the thirties and forties, the prison systems in Manchuria began gearing up after the surrender of British, Australian, and American forces in the Far East in 1942.

The vast amount of prisoners of war from Bataan in the Philippines came through Mukden. They were forced to work supporting the Japanese war effort in the Manchurian Machine Tool Factory, while some others worked at a leather tannery, a textile mill, and a steel and lumber mill. Along with British and Australian forces from Singapore, thirty-five-percent of these servicemen housed at Mukden died horrible deaths from the treatment they received.

If they didn't die from the beatings, they passed away from malnutrition, dysentery, or pneumonia. Those prisoners who escaped and were recaptured were returned to the complex and tied to wooden poles while their fellow prisoners watched the Japanese guards shoot them. Even these deaths were mild compared to the countless prisoners subjected to horrific medical experiments.

After the Russian Army liberated the POW's in September 1945, it was widely thought that the brutality of the Japanese Army could never be replicated. Little did anyone realize that the Communist leadership in China would not only meet, but exceed the Japanese horrors under the leadership of Chairman Mao.

The vast majority of the structures comprising the Mukden prison were constructed of brick. The wooden barracks, however, were hastily built to house the tremendous amount of excess prisoners of war who came through Mukden. In the center of the complex stood the red brick main building. The long and narrow brick structure housed the original cells and became the center for the new Chinese Communist campaign for reeducation.

Early morning sunlight illuminated the front of the main building and brought welcome warmth to the frigid morning air. A lone flat brown staff car entered the complex and drove to the entrance of the main building. The vehicle stopped in front of the building's entrance door. Steam rose in tendrils from the exhaust of the vehicle as it sat idling, waiting for its passenger to exit.

Colonel Li stepped from the rear of the vehicle and put on his trench coat. He reached inside the back of the car and retrieved his valise from the rear seat. He motioned to the driver to leave as he walked to the door. Once inside, the Colonel was greeted by the guard. Even in the Chinese language, it was clear the guard feared his superior.

"Good morning, Sir!" The guard said loudly as he snapped to attention.

Without acknowledging the man, Li stepped away and walked down the long hall toward the interrogation room. The dank interior possessed an odor that could have only come from its unclean occupants and a substandard sewage system.

Colonel Li entered the interrogation room and briskly closed the door behind him. Eight men occupied the room, all of whom snapped to attention upon Li's entrance. The inside of the room was warm from the two stoves burning intensely at each end. Lighting for the room came from four ceiling lamps, the shrouds of which focused the light down into large circular areas surrounding the center of the room. Four wooden tables eight feet in length were strategically placed in the middle and stood four feet tall. Colonel Li stepped to the first table and placed his valise on it. After removing his coat, Li turned to the senior officer and spoke. "Are the two prisoners ready?"

"Yes, Sir," Major Hung responded.

"Very well, bring them in."

While Major Hung left the room accompanied by four of the other men, Colonel Li opened his valise and removed two of the folders inside. He placed the folders onto the table and walked to the side of the room, picking up two wooden chairs. He placed the chairs directly under one of the ceiling lamps. Li went back to the table and began reviewing the contents of the folders.

The door to the room flung open, and two prisoners were brought in. The two men had their hands tied behind them and were gagged. The guards shoved the two in the chairs and began tying them with ropes securely to their seats. Once their feet and chests were secured, the men stepped back from the prisoners.

Li strolled over to the prisoners while rolling up the sleeves of his shirt and looked deep into the faces of the two men.

Colonel Li returned to the table and removed two bibles from his valise. Each book was covered in linen, with a hand-stitched pheasant on the top and its owner's name below. Li spoke with purpose as he looked at the men. "Mr. Dong, Mr. Yang, before this day is out, you will tell me where these bibles came from, and you'll also tell me where your church and followers are."

The two trembling men sweated profusely as they looked back at Col Li. Li motioned toward Zhu, barking out his command. "Remove this one's gag."

One of the men stepped forward and removed the gag from Zhu's mouth. "Where did you get this bible?" Li demanded.

Zhu's trembling voice replied. "We got them in the city."

"From where in the city?"

"From a man who was selling them on the street."

"You're lying to me. I'll ask you again, where did you get this bible?" Li again demanded.

Zhu's entire body was shaking violently. "From a man selling them on the street," he repeated.

"Where is your church?" Li snapped.

"We don't have a church. Chen and I read the Bible by ourselves."

Li stepped back and snapped his fingers at the guards. Two of the guards untied the ropes holding Zhu to the chair, while another tied Zhu's feet together and stood him up. With his hands still tied behind him, the guards tied ropes around his arms just above Zhu's elbows and fed the loose end of the rope through a pulley attached to the ceiling. Chen watched as his friend was lifted off the floor by his elbows. Zhu screamed in pain as his legs twisted below him.

Li snapped his fingers again and the guards lowered Zhu back to the ground. Li stepped back in front of Zhu and repeated his question. "Where are your church members?" he demanded.

Forcing the words out of his mouth, Zhu responded with pain in his voice. "We have no church. We worship alone."

Li snapped his fingers again, and the guards lifted Zhu back off the ground. Zhu's screams echoed through the prison. After five minutes of writhing, and almost to the point of passing out, Li snapped his fingers again and Zhu was lowered back down.

"I tell you what I'll do. If you deny Jesus Christ here and now, I'll untie you, and you can go home. Will you deny Jesus Christ?"

Colonel Li knew he could watch Zhu after he was let out of prison and ultimately find the other followers. He looked deeply into Zhu's eyes and repeated his question. "Will you deny Jesus? Deny him, and all of this will stop."

Unable to stand, Zhu's body was being held up by the ropes. He spoke between gasps for air. "I will not deny my Lord, I will not deny Jesus!"

Colonel Li looked toward the guards. "Put him back in the chair and gag him." Li turned toward Chen and looked into his eyes. "Either you or your friend will answer my questions, or you *will* die today. The choice for you is to decide how painful your death will be." Li turned back toward Zhu and drew his revolver. Li emptied the cylinder and kept one live round in his hand while Zhu and Chen were watching. Li put the live round in one of the empty chambers and spun the cylinder, snapping it closed. He stepped to the side and placed the revolver to Zhu's head. Cocking the weapon, he looked to the guards standing next to Chen. "Take the gag out of his mouth."

Once the gag was removed, Li addressed Chen. "Where is your church?" he demanded.

A trembling Chen responded, "We have no church!"

Li pulled the trigger and the hammer fell on an empty chamber with a hollow click. Immediately cocking the weapon again, Li continued his questioning. "Where are the rest of your followers?" he said, louder.

Chen's voice grew louder in answer. "We have no other members! We worship alone!"

Li pulled the trigger and a second click was heard. Immediately cocking the weapon again, he repeated his question to Chen. "Where are your other members?"

A crying and desperate Chen shouted at the top of his voice, "WE HAVE NO OTHER FOLLOWERS!"

The hammer of the weapon found its mark and the round discharged with a loud explosion. Zhu's lifeless body fell to the side and onto the floor.

Chen screamed in horror as he cried uncontrollably, "Zhuuuu!"

Wiping the blood from his hands with a towel, Li stepped in front of Chen. "You'll tell me what I want to know, or die today. But your death won't come as swift as your friend's. You'll die a long and painful death."

Li stepped toward the table and unrolled the sleeves of his shirt. After putting his coat back on, he turned toward Major Hung. "Soften him up. I'll be back this afternoon to finish."

Major Hung's lips were pursed as he looked on at what was unfolding. He'd lived through the horrors of the Japanese occupation and had lost many of his friends and countrymen. After the Japanese had left, there were still Chinese walking the streets with visible scars from torture at the hands of the Japanese. He had thought those horrors were in China's past; he was finding that not to be true. Hung responded in a lower than normal voice as Li was walking toward the door. "Yes, Sir."

★ ★ ★

Rusty and Walter were in the Squad Bay practicing their Kung Fu techniques with six of the other Marines. Rusty had decided to occupy the other Marines' free time by teaching them martial arts. The idea had worked. He had kept them occupied with something they were eager to learn, keeping their minds off what was happening to them. Captain Rivera had immediately understood Rusty's actions, which reinforced his choice in recommending Rusty for Officers Candidate School.

Rusty and Walter were showing the men the earliest moves they had learned from Tao. Rusty moved to the side of a blow Walter directed toward him and placed the lock on Walter's hand, twisting it into submission and sending Walter sprawling.

After letting Walter back up from the ground, he turned toward the men. "Okay, pair up and try it on each other," He ordered.

The six men paired off and began practicing the moves on each other. Walter observed Brian Manning's technique and stepped toward him. "No, Brian, you have to maintain the proper stance while you're doing it or your opponent can turn it against you." Walter stepped in front of Brian. "Stand the way you were with your feet close together and I'll throw a punch at you."

Brian placed his feet together and readied himself for Walter's punch. Walter threw the punch at Brian, and while Brian was deflecting the blow, Walter moved toward Brian, pushing against him. Because of Brian's weak stance, Walter was able to easily push him to the ground.

"What happened?" Brian asked as Walter was helping him up.

Walter held his open hand out toward Brian, palm out. "Place your open hand against mine."

Brian complied, and the two men were facing each other, touching their right palms together. As Walter increased pressure, Brian applied equal opposing pressure. Suddenly, Walter moved his hand to the rear, pulling an unbalanced Brian toward him and down to the ground.

When Brian got up, he looked at Walter and said, "I don't get it, Walt."

Walter smiled and replied, "Don't worry, bud. You will," while slapping Brian's shoulder with his open right hand.

Captain Rivera entered the squad bay and let go his booming voice. "Alright, ladies, 'all hands' meeting in the conference room.

Let's go."

The men immediately dropped what they were doing and filed out of the room. Rusty remained behind and was the last to leave, ensuring everyone was out of the room. As Rusty started to leave, Rivera stepped close to him. "Good job, Sergeant; that was a brilliant idea to keep the men focused on martial arts. They've taken to it like a duck to water."

"Thank you, Sir," Rusty responded.

The two men walked to the conference room and stepped inside. Rivera closed the door behind him. Consular General Marsh was dressed in casual clothes and had a five-o-clock shadow. He looked tired from all the responsibilities that had been heaped upon his shoulders. He took in a deep breath before he addressed the staff.

"Ladies and gentlemen, I had a conference with General Lin Piao this morning, the Commanding Officer for the Communist forces in the Liaoning Province, and it appears we're here for quite some time.

"The good news is that thanks to our rationing program set up by Capt. Rivera, we can remain here for quite some time, although that wouldn't be our best choice." He smiled as he looked over the group. "Hopefully we'll be able to leave soon, although General Piao has indicated otherwise. We've become political pawns for the Communists to use against our government.

"I'm proud of each and every one of you. You've managed to make the best of a difficult situation. The new Communist regime has been brutal against its own people, and we have unconfirmed reports of genocide being committed against their own citizens. Under Chairman Mao's direction, Christians are being persecuted around the country. We can't confirm if that's going on here in Mukden, but believe even if it's not, it most assuredly will in the future.

"We have reports that the Chinese Communists are using many of its citizens for forced labor in the factories around the city. Sadly, we've also heard reports that there are even some Americans who have been pressed into service at the factories, although this can't be confirmed, either.

"The United States is protesting the persecutions through the United Nations, and we remain hopeful there will be results. The Chinese government is in bed with the Russians, so negotiating has become difficult at best. When I asked General Piao about the allegations, he denied them, and if my Chinese is up to speed, I was told it's none of my business. From all indications, I'm afraid that any hope of relations with China has been lost. All we can hope for at this time is to be able to leave China and continue negotiations once we're back home.

"I'm sorry I don't have any better news for you, but I'll continue to keep you posted as we get any new information. Again, I want to thank you all for the sacrifices you've made." Marsh lowered his head and uttered his final words. "Dismissed."

"Okay, gentlemen, let's get back to it," Rivera ordered.

Rusty and Walter slowly walked back to the Squad Bay. Before entering, Walter stopped Rusty. "Rusty, did you hear that? Tao and the people at the orphanage are in danger."

Rusty took in a deep breath. "You don't know that, Walter. Besides, didn't you hear the General? Those reports are unconfirmed. Forget about it, Walt. Everything will be okay," Rusty said firmly.

Walter walked into the Squad Bay grumbling to himself. Rusty was clearly concerned, but didn't want Walter worrying about Tao. He needed his friend to be focused on his duties at the Consulate. He whispered a prayer before entering the Squad Bay. "Lord, watch out for them, please."

Colonel Li entered the interrogation room to see Chen Yang sitting in a chair in front of him. Chen was covered in blood and had multiple bruises, cuts, and lesions all over his body. His head was drooped down, his chin resting on his chest. His hands were now tied in front of him and hung limp in his lap. Both of his arms had been broken above the elbows from blows received from steel rods at the hands of the guards. Li took his coat off and placed it on the table next to Chen. Li then stepped in front of Chen and lifted his head by the hair and spoke to him.

"Where's your church?" Li calmly asked.

Blood covered almost all of Chen's face. His right cheek was swollen, and his lips were puffed out from the blows he'd received. He was exhausted and weak from the beatings. Chen looked at the Colonel, his face devoid of emotion.

"Where are your followers?" Li asked.

85

Chen forced a smile through his blood stained lips and refused to respond.

Li let go of his hair and turned toward Major Hung. "Bind him with his arms next to his body. Cover his head, but leave his eyes and nose uncovered."

Major Hung and three of the guards lifted Chen from the chair and laid him on the table. Chen screamed from the pain as the men moved him. The guards began wrapping his entire body with linen wraps.

"Take him to the other end of the building." Li ordered.

Major Hung turned to the guards. "Carry him to the construction site at the end of the building."

Colonel Li exited the room and walked the one hundred yards to the other end of the prison. He entered the doorway and into the unfinished utility room and ordered the construction workers to halt their work. Each of the workers dropped their tools and stood back against the wall.

As Major Hung and the guards brought Chen into the room, Li calmly made his intentions clear. "Place him in the wall."

The workers looked at each other in horror as they realized what was about to unfold. The guards stood Chen up and placed him inside the unfinished brick wall. There was just enough room for Chen to stand in the unfinished fireplace chimney enclosure. Chen's shoulders touched each side of the opening, and his head butted against a steel plate at the top.

Li pointed to the two guards. "Hold him in and don't let him fall forward." Li turned to the two workers standing against the wall. "Brick him in the wall."

The workers nervously looked at each other, then toward Colonel Li. "Sir, we can't-" one began.

Li pulled his pistol out of the holster and pointed it toward the men. "Do it or I'll shoot you both!" he commanded.

The two workers began applying mortar to the bricks and putting them in place. Col Li and the guards watched as the men placed bricks up the wall, closing Chen into the compartment. The workers breathed heavily and trembled as they completed their task.

Major Hung stood in the background with his head down, looking at the floor. He could not look on as Chen was bricked into the wall.

When the bricks were two rows from completion, Li ordered the workers to step back. He stepped forward and looked into Chen's eyes.

"If you deny your Jesus, I'll tell them to open the wall and you can go home. If you want to deny him, blink twice and I'll let you out."

A terrified Chen was breathing heavily through his nose, and his body was trembling violently. He groaned loudly through the wraps over his mouth.

"Deny him, and you'll be set free," Li repeated.

Chen groaned loudly, but fought to keep his eyes wide open.

A defeated Colonel Li turned to the workers. "Brick it up."

As the last brick was being placed in the wall, the men saw Chen's eyes open wide, staring back at them in horror.

The two workers were trembling with terror as they turned toward Colonel Li. Li looked toward Major Hung and spoke. "I want guards posted outside the door for five days. No one gets in here. Understood?"

Major Hung stood silent with his mouth open as he stared at the wall. He couldn't wipe the image of Chen's terrified eyes from his mind.

Li leaned in toward Hung. "Major, did you hear my orders?"

Major Hung snapped his head toward Colonel Li. "Yes, Sir!" he responded.

Li reached into his valise and removed the two bibles from inside. "Burn these," he said as he handed them to the Major. Li closed his valise and walked from the room. Hung's head was down as he held the bibles. He turned toward the wall one last time and took in a deep breath, slowly letting it out. He turned and walked from the room in silence.

Chapter 10 - Communism Unleashed

Bobby sat silent with his mouth unconsciously open wide as he listened to Walter. His youth and inexperience was finding it difficult to process the information he was hearing. "Wow, Mr. Brown, that couldn't have happened. I mean like that's totally messed up," Bobby stated with a furrowed brow.

Walter took a sip from his cup of coffee before responding. "It did happen, Bobby, and many other things far worse. The Nationalists were pretty brutal as well, but nothing could prepare the Chinese people for the Communists and their brutality."

"Why didn't the government step in and stop it?" Bobby asked.

Walter leaned forward in his chair. "Bobby, the government authorized it. It came down right from the top. Mao Tse-tung needed to purge any remnant of Christianity from his country if he had any hope of controlling the people. He saw western religious influence as a major threat to China."

Bobby had a confused look. "It doesn't make any sense, Mr. Brown. You said that Buddhism was the religion of China. If he feared religion, then why didn't he get rid of the Buddhists?"

"It was the *state-sanctioned* religion, Bobby. Totalitarian rulers have always feared Christianity because it offers freedom. Buddhism bows to the power of the state; Christianity only bows to Christ. Most all of the despots since communism took hold in the beginning of the 1900's have been atheists. Hitler was an atheist, Benito Mussolini was an atheist, Stalin, Pol pot, Mao, Castro, pick your favorite lunatic leader and you'll almost always find they were atheists."

"Why did the Chinese people allow someone like that to get power? I mean, like, couldn't they stop Mao from getting control?" Bobby asked.

"Bobby, you're looking at other parts of the world through American eyeglasses. The rest of the world doesn't operate like we do. They don't have a system like ours to control maniacs from getting into power. Even if someone gets into office here who runs afoul of the best interest of the United States, we can vote them out, they can't. The 'bully system' is the only way they gain power. One of Mao's famous quotes was 'Power comes largely from the barrel of a gun.' He didn't care what the people wanted; he only wanted to maintain *his* power."

Bobby wasn't going to let this go without further explanation. "But the people could have replaced him."

"Who would they have replaced him with, Bobby?"

"I don't know. Anybody would have been better."

"No, under their system, the next guy would, or could, have been worse. That's where Mao's statement about power coming from the barrel of a gun is so troubling. The next leader would have been equally as brutal. Power corrupts; absolute power corrupts absolutely."

"Where did you hear that?" Bobby asked.

"It's a quote from Lord Acton," Walter responded.

"Who?"

"Look, Bobby, you're not going to learn, much less retain it if I keep telling you this stuff. Write it down and research it along with all the other questions you've had," Walter said with a smile.

Bobby leaned over to the end of the counter and picked up the pen and notepad. He quickly wrote down the name <u>Lord Acton</u> and set the pen down. He looked back toward Walter and continued his questions. "But, like, they could have fought back."

"With what? The people weren't armed. What would they oppose them with? Every dictator takes the weapons from the citizens as soon as they come into power," Walter explained.

Bobby's face lit up with realization. "Wow, that's why the Martial Arts first trained with tools like chains, ropes, staffs and stuff like that, huh? 'Cause they didn't have weapons."

Walter put his index finger to Bobby's forehead. "Now you're using this, Bobby," he responded with a smile.

"But, Mr. Brown, there's one thing I still don't understand. If Mao killed the Christians, how come there are still Christians in China today?"

"It's the one immutable fact of Christianity, Bobby. If you kill one Christian, ten take their place. Totalitarian régimes throughout history never understood that. Christianity empowers the weak, the powerless, the infirmed, and the poor."

Bobby sat silently as he heard Walter's words. His new mentor was giving him an unfiltered version of data he'd never heard in school. Excitement welled up inside him as he realized he was spending a special day with someone he never dreamed he could learn so much from.

Walter stood and walked toward the refrigerator. "I think we need ice cream before we go on, don't you?"

"Yeah, that sounds good," Bobby said with a smile.

★ ★ ★

The full moon shone brightly over Mukden through a cloudless sky. An eerie silence covered the once busy city that could now best be described as a ghost town. Not even the animals were heard. The entire city appeared as if it had been painted with a pallet of black, brown, and gray. An unseasonably warm front had moved in and had given some relief from the normal frigid conditions of fall.

At the center of the city, the US Consulate was no exception to the still night. The only movements in the compound were the two Marine guards walking the grounds, standing guard over the complex. In the barracks, the rest of the Marines were fast asleep in their bunks, with the exception of Sgt. Rusty Harrigan. Rusty lay on his back under the cover of the bedding, with his hands clasped together on his chest. He looked up at the ceiling, almost in a trance, as he thought of nothing but the occupants of the orphanage.

Rusty had been unable to sleep through the night, since hearing about the dangers for Christians in China since the communist takeover. He feared the worst for Tao and the people at the orphanage, but felt powerless to do anything. Rusty rolled over his left wrist and looked at his watch. The face displayed 3:15 a.m. He knew any further attempts to sleep were futile.

Rusty rolled out of bed and placed his feet on the floor. He winced as the cold stone floor bit at his bare feet. He stepped to his locker and started getting dressed. As he was lacing up his boots, Private David Butcher entered the barracks and approached Rusty.

"Is everything okay, Sarge?" Butcher asked in a low whisper.

Rusty looked toward Butcher and responded quietly. "Yeah, I'm okay, just can't sleep. Why are you in here?"

Butcher pointed to the end of the barracks. "I need to wake up Manning; he's got the duty after me."

"Is everything on the grounds okay?" Rusty asked.

"Yeah, everything's Jake, Sarge."

Rusty smiled at the New York native. Butcher was part of the post war jet set that was defining the American youth. Butcher couldn't respond with fine or okay; he felt the need to say 'everything's Jake.' Rusty tolerated his slips in front of the enlisted men, but told Butcher in no uncertain terms not to use that language around the Captain or the Consulate staff. He liked the New York native and found him to be an asset, but his tolerance stopped at being called 'Daddy-o'. "Is there any coffee made?" Rusty asked.

"Yeah, fresh pot, Sarge."

"Okay, get some rest." Rusty responded.

"Okay, Sarge."

Butcher turned and walked toward Manning's bunk as Rusty lifted his coat from the rack. He exited the room, quietly closed the door behind him, and walked to the kitchen. The small light over the stove was on, allowing just enough light to see the coffee maker.

Rusty poured himself a large cup of coffee and walked back out of the kitchen. He turned and walked up the stairs to the roof access door. Rusty set his coffee cup on the flag cabinet by the door and buttoned his coat. He put his cover on his head, picked up his coffee, and opened the door to the roof of the Consulate. Before closing the door, he unlocked the door knob and stepped out onto the flat rooftop. Rusty closed his eyes and took in a deep breath of fresh morning air before walking to the rail that bordered the roof.

Rusty leaned out and rested his forearms on the barrier, holding his coffee cup in both hands. He looked down into the courtyard to see Private Sheridan walking the grounds. Sheridan looked up to see Rusty, and waved at him. Rusty responded with the open palm of his right hand. He looked back out over the city and went into deep thought about the orphanage.

He tried in vain to rid himself from the feeling of dread that had overwhelmed him. The people at the orphanage had touched him deeply and now held a special place in his heart. Tao had become his surrogate father, and the remainder of the group had become his extended family.

Since the news of the persecution of Christians throughout China, he could think of nothing else. He wanted desperately to help them, but didn't know how it could be accomplished. The conflict within him was growing as he thought about the near certainty of them being killed by the Communists. Without his help they would die; with his help, they could also die.

One thing was certain, his career, and possibly his life, would be over if he helped them. He closed his eyes trying to block out the thoughts.

Rusty heard the roof access door open behind him. He turned to see Captain Rivera stepping out onto the roof. Rusty snapped to attention and saluted. "Good morning, Sir."

Rivera returned the salute. "As you were, Sergeant," Rivera responded. Rivera set his coffee cup down on the roof and pulled a cigarette from the pack in his coat pocket. He turned toward the roof cupola and opened the Zippo lighter. With both hands cupping the lighter and hiding the flame, he lit his cigarette. Rivera picked up his coffee cup and walked to the roof rail next to Rusty, leaning onto the edge. "Didn't expect to see you here, Sergeant," Rivera stated.

"Just needed a quiet place to think, Sir."

"I know what you mean; I come up here every morning. I like to look out over the city before the sun comes up."

"If you would like, Sir, I'll leave so you can have the time to yourself," Rusty offered.

"No, that's okay. Don't need to be alone; I just like having the high ground," Rivera responded with a smile.

Rusty looked at Rivera curiously. "High ground, Sir?"

"Since Iwo, I hate having someone with higher ground than me," Rivera responded with a half smile.

"When were you on Iwo Jima, Sir?"

"March of '45."

"And they had the high ground, Sir?" Rusty asked.

"Yeah, the Japs were up on Mount Suribachi and had the high ground. Since then I like to be higher than anyone else." Rivera turned his head toward Rusty. "Pretty weird, huh?"

"No, Sir, it doesn't sound weird to me. Was it pretty tough there, Sir?"

From 19 February to 26 March 1945, the Marines fought one of the bloodiest battles of World War II. During the thirty-five day battle, 6,800 Marines had been killed. Of the 22,060 Japanese defenders, only two-hundred-and-sixteen had been taken prisoner. The rest had either been killed or were missing and presumed dead. For Rivera, the engagement resulted in his being awarded the Navy Cross, Purple Heart, and scars to his body, both internally and externally.

Rivera grunted comically. "Wasn't good, but we got through it. What brings you up here?" Rivera asked.

Rusty picked up on the fact that Rivera obviously wanted to change the subject. "Couldn't sleep, Sir. Just wanted to get some fresh air."

Rivera looked straight ahead as he responded. "Yeah, it's peaceful up here. Gets my mind off the job for a while."

"How long have you been in the Corps, Sir?" Rusty asked.

Rivera took a long drag from his cigarette before answering. "Signed up on December 8th; the day after Pearl Harbor."

93

"Wow, Sir, so you were there for the whole war."

"Yeah, from the beginning. So what about you? What got you into the Corps?"

Rusty looked out over the city as he spoke. "I tried to join when I was seventeen, but my grandfather wouldn't sign the waver for me. I had to wait until I was eighteen. He said he wanted me to be the 'first Harrigan' to get a high school diploma," Rusty said with a smile.

"Well, he was right. How come your father or mother wouldn't sign for you?"

Rusty turned to look at Rivera. "They were killed in a car crash when I was five. My grandparents raised me."

"I'm sorry, Rusty. No brothers or sisters?"

"No, Sir. One uncle, my father's brother is still alive, but we don't get along very well. He wasn't too happy when I joined the Corps. Said it was a 'fool's errand'," Rusty said with a chuckle.

"Was he in the military?" Rivera asked.

"No, Sir, he had a disability. Said it was his back, but my grandfather said it was really his eyes. Granddad said Uncle Gary told him he just couldn't see that crap." Rusty avoided using the more descriptive word.

Rivera laughed at the statement. "Not a patriot, huh?"

"No, we got into a huge fight over me going into the Corps. I told him that someone who is lucky enough to live in the United States should be willing to serve his country. I guess that cut too close to the bone for him, so he took a poke at me. That was the last time I saw him."

Rivera took a long drag from his cigarette and spoke while exhaling. "That very thing was best said by Thomas Paine. 'Those who expect to reap the blessings of freedom must undergo the fatigue of supporting it.'"

"What did he mean by that, Sir?"

"Rusty, most often it's the things we don't want to do that need to be done the most."

Rusty tilted his head to the side in reflection. "Yes, Sir, I suppose that's true." His lips pursed as he mused over Rivera's statement.

94

Rivera moistened his left forefinger and thumb and crushed his smoke out between them. "Well, it's about time to get to work," he said as he placed the dead smoke into his pocket.

Rusty straightened up and turned toward the door. "Yes, Sir, I've got to get going as well. I have to make out the duty roster for the rest of the week."

Rivera smiled at Rusty as he turned to enter the door. "Nice conversation, Sergeant. Glad you were up here."

"Thank you, Sir."

Rusty walked down the stairs toward the duty hut. He opened the door and walked over to the desk. Once seated, he removed a sheet of paper from the desk and inserted it into the typewriter. After typing the hours of guard duty on the paper, he pulled the paper from the typewriter. He wrote the names of the six marines onto the corresponding time slots. The last name he entered for the 10:00 pm to 2:00 am position was Corporal Walter Brown.

Rusty picked the paper up from the desk and stepped outside the duty hut to the cork board hanging on the wall. After removing an unused pushpin from the bottom, Rusty held the paper against the board. After taking in a deep breath and letting it out slowly, Rusty stabbed the pin into the top of the paper forcefully and stared at the roster with a furrowed brow. "What needs to be done the most?" he whispered to himself before turning to walk to the barracks.

The Spartan conditions of the newly established Army headquarters in Mukden were tolerated by most of the occupants, with the exception of the officers. As bad as the conditions were, however, it was palatial compared to their accommodations outside the city before the occupation. Raiding the empty businesses and homes had provided them with some creature comforts, but they still worked in less than ideal conditions.

Colonel Li was sitting at his desk going over paperwork with Major Hung. His desk was bare, with the exception of a blotter left over from the previous Nationalist Colonel. Colonel Li was sipping tea as he read the reports from the previous evening. His subordinate, Major Hung sat across from him, preparing to answer the barrage of questions that always followed a briefing with his superior.

Li looked up from the papers, addressing Major Hung. "From this report, it would appear that there are still Nationalist soldiers within the city, Major."

A nervous Major Hung responded, "We're having difficulty locating them, Colonel. The citizens are hiding them."

"Major, we're here to comply with the orders from the Chairman. He wants them rounded up, and we *will* comply. I don't care what you have to do, I want them found."

"Yes, Sir," Hung responded.

"The General says that the factories are almost ready to begin production, but we'll need more workers. Starting tomorrow, I want everyone who can work taken to the factories, even the children. You're to leave the farmers to their fields for food production, but the remainder will be pressed into service for production."

"Yes, Sir," Hung responded. "What is to happen to the Americans at the Consulate, Sir?"

"When the Chairman has decided that they're no longer serving a political purpose, they will be released to return to America. Until then, they're to remain in the Consulate."

"Do you still want my men to remain posted around the Consulate?" Hung asked.

"Yes, and I want them highly visible. I want the Americans to see them whenever they look outside the compound." Li took a long sip from his cup of tea. "Now, these Christians, have we made any progress in finding anymore of them?"

Hung leaned forward in his chair. "No, Sir, we believe we've found all of them."

Colonel Li sat back in his chair and looked directly into Major Hung's eyes. "Major, if there's one thing I learned while living in America, it's that Christians are like rodents. You can never get rid of them all. They multiply just like cockroaches. Starting tomorrow I want you to take the men and make a house-by-house search to find them."

"It's difficult to identify them, Colonel. They obviously don't have any identifying features, and their dress is normal," Hung responded.

"Tear every house apart and look for bibles. Christians are never far from their bibles," Li stated.

"Very well, Sir. Is there anything else for this morning?"

Li looked back to his desk as he responded, "No, that will be all for now."

Major Hung gathered his papers and stepped to the door. As he was opening the door he heard Colonel Li behind him. "Send in my aid, Major."

"Yes, Sir."

Li leaned forward in his seat. "And Major-"

"Yes, Sir."

"Find those Christians!"

"Yes, Sir," Hung replied before closing the door.

Chapter 11 - Rusty's Revelation

Walter was sitting in the kitchen eating his morning meal and readying himself for the day's work. Unlike Rusty, Walter described himself as a night person. He had a difficult time enjoying the morning, but welcomed the busy schedule Rusty had assigned to the Marines since the confinement at the Consulate. He hated not being tasked with a meaningful job and detested the military phrase "look busy." Normally, his above average work ethic would often push him well into the night accomplishing a task, but he then preferred to sleep in, rather than "wake up with the chickens," as he often stated. All of that, of course, changed with his enlistment in the Marine Corps. Walter was enjoying the last of his coffee before getting ready to leave the kitchen, when Rusty sat at the table across from him.

"Good morning, Sergeant," Walter said with a sarcastic smile.

Rusty placed his folder on the table before speaking. "I see your usual morning face is on. Will we be enjoying your attitude throughout the day, or will you at least smile once in a while for us?" Rusty said with a grin.

"Okay, just for you, I'll smile today." Walter chuckled.

Rusty's tone changed suddenly as he addressed his friend. "Walt,

I have something important to ask of you."

The look of concern on Rusty's face told Walter that he needed to be serious. "Of course, Rusty. What do you need?"

Rusty looked around the kitchen to ensure no one was there or in earshot. He leaned in close toward Walter. "Walt, I put you on the ten-to-two watch tonight."

"I know, no problem. I don't mind," Walter interjected.

Rusty forced a small grin. "I know you don't, but there's something I need you to do for me. No matter what happens, I need you to be on the west wall of the compound at midnight."

Walter's brow furrowed with a curious look toward his friend. "Okay, I suppose I could do that," he said, lifting his open palms from the table in an inquisitive manner.

Rusty leaned in toward Walter. "And no matter what you see, you won't say anything. I need you to be completely silent."

Walter started to chuckle when he realized what Rusty was asking of him. "Wait just one damned minute, Rusty; you're not going to do this." Walter looked around the room and lowered his voice to a whisper. "Have you lost your mind? They'll hang you for this. How in the hell are you going to help Tao by getting yourself thrown out of the Marine Corps, or worse yet, killed by Colonel Li? This is madness, Rusty."

"Walt, if not me, who? Every one of those people will be killed if I don't help."

"Rusty, you can't take on the problems of the whole world. This is none of our business. This isn't even our country! If I've learned anything from you, it's that we need to respect the laws of the country we're in. I'm telling you, you can't do this!"

"My mind is made up, Walt. I need you to cover for me for as long as you can. That's all I'm asking."

"Okay, then. Good grief I can't believe I'm saying this. I need to go with you. If you're going to do this, you'll need my help."

"Absolutely not! We can't leave Captain Rivera totally naked. Since you got promoted to Corporal, Rivera will be relying on you. He'll need you here. I'm just one guy. You can make it without me, but they can't do it with both of us gone."

Walter leaned back in his chair with disgust on his face. "You're throwing away a commission, Rusty. They were going to make you an officer."

"I know, Walt," Rusty replied with sadness in his eyes. "I've been thinking a lot about this since we were briefed about the Communists killing the Christians. There are more important things in life than thinking about ourselves. I couldn't live with myself knowing I could've helped, but didn't."

Walter could see he wasn't going to talk Rusty out of doing this. He took in a deep breath and exhaled slowly. "Okay, Rusty, I'll keep my mouth shut. I hope you're prepared for this. You better have a plan."

"I do. I just hope God helps me with it." Rusty put his right hand across the table toward Walt.

Walter shook his friend's hand with a tight grip. "So do I." Walter further tightened his grip on Rusty's hand and looked deep into his eyes. "So do I."

Tao Chung and Ho Chen sat at the table in the orphanage drinking tea. A feeling of dread had fallen over the congregation since the Communists had taken over the city. The group had focused their attention on the one thing that seemed to give them comfort, their study of the bible. Since the Communist invasion, the group had hidden their bibles in the grain sacks in the storage room. Tao had even taken down the two wooden fish from the gates of the compound. They knew that at any time the Communist soldiers could enter the complex and remove them all for use in the factories. Fear had gripped the entire group of believers.

Ho looked up from the table and addressed his friend. "Master, you know the soldiers will come here soon. We should prepare for that time?"

"Nothing can be done, my old friend. There's no place to go, nothing we can do, and nowhere to hide. We have over twenty people here, many who are old. An is expecting her first child. If we go out into the cold we could lose her and the baby. No my friend, we should stay here, Jesus will protect us; we must be obedient."

"Master, the Communists killed Zhu and Chen because they were Christians; they'll kill us too. We must do something."

Tao leaned toward his old friend and looked deep into his eyes. "We will do something, we shall trust in the Lord Jesus."

Ho stood and walked toward the fireplace on Tao's side of the table. He placed his hand on Tao's shoulder as he walked by. "I hope you're right, my friend."

Walter walked the grounds of the Consulate with his M-1 Garand slung over his right shoulder. He unconsciously checked his wristwatch every five minutes, hoping that midnight wouldn't arrive.

This night would prove to be the longest watch he'd ever stood. He tried in vain to stop the shakes that had taken over his body. Walter cursed himself for agreeing to be a part of Rusty's plan. His old friend was destroying his life, and Walter was powerless to stop him.

He moved closer to the west wall, looking back across the courtyard toward Private Butcher. He'd wanted to talk to Rusty throughout the day, but each time he would look at Rusty, Rusty would just smile and walk away. He looked at his watch again, fifteen minutes to midnight. Boy, I can hardly wait for this night to be over, he thought.

Rusty was lying on his back in his bunk with the blanket pulled up to his neck. As he stared up at the ceiling, he thought of countless reasons why he should stop what he was about to do, but he couldn't find one reason why he shouldn't do it. He tilted his head to the left, looking throughout the barracks to see if any of the men were awake. Satisfied that all was quiet, he slowly slipped out from under the blanket. Fully dressed in his civilian clothes, Rusty stood and pulled the blanket back up over the bunk. He pulled on his coat and quietly walked toward the door, closing it behind him.

Rusty walked to the roof access stairwell and quietly placed his feet on each step, slowly climbing to the top. Once he reached the top of the stairwell, he opened the flag cabinet, and pulled out his rucksack and the large bundle next to it. He placed his arms in the loops of the rucksack and pulled it up his back, securing it tightly with the buckle in the front. He reached back into the locker and removed the rolled up one-hundred-foot length of rope. With all of his gear, he opened the bolt to the roof door and stepped outside.

Rusty looped the end of the rope through the handrail and leaned over the edge, looking down to the alley below. Moving back, he tied the bundle to the end of the rope and looked back down to the alley. He saw a Chinese soldier walking his post below. He patiently waited for the soldier to reach the end of the compound and turn the corner before lowering the rope and the bundle to the ground. He stepped out over the handrail and grasped the rope tightly in his hands. Leaning out, he glanced back into the compound and saw Walter looking back up at him. Walter raised his right hand, palm open, toward his friend. Rusty nodded toward Walter and slowly rappelled down the rope.

Walter sighed as he looked at his friend for one final time, wondering if he would ever see Rusty again. His mind was abuzz with the thoughts of what he was going to say to Captain Rivera. This isn't going to be pretty, he thought. Walter walked away from the west wall and toward the main gate.

At the bottom, Rusty pulled on one end of the rope, allowing it to release from the handrail and fall to the ground in front of him. He quickly gathered the rope and moved into the dark between two buildings across from the west wall of the Consulate.

As he looked out from the dark, he saw another Chinese soldier walking down the alley toward him. He froze, trying not to move, his heart racing as the man approached him. Rusty was sure that the man could hear his heart pounding in his chest. He slowly moved his hand inside his coat, placing a firm grip on the Colt 45 on his hip. Rusty watched as the soldier walked calmly past him. He then rolled the rope up as quietly as he possibly could and tied the loose ends off. Rusty slid his left arm through the rope and placed it over his head and under his left arm. He picked up the bundle from the ground and moved out slowly between the buildings.

Walter stepped inside the Consulate and walked down the hall to the roof access stairwell. He climbed the steps and opened the roof access door. Stepping out onto the roof, he looked out over the area around the Consulate, trying to see Rusty. The only movement he could see was the two Chinese soldiers slowly walking their posts around the Consulate. He took in a deep breath and sighed as he spoke softly, "Good luck, Bud, I'm gonna miss you." Walter stepped back into the building and locked the door behind him.

★ ★ ★

Rusty was slowly working his way through the city using the

back streets. Although virtually empty, the occasional military patrols would pass by each of his positions making their way through the city. He was frustrated at the slower pace he was making as a result of hiding from the patrols.

Finally reaching the southwest edge of the city, Rusty stopped at the end of a group of buildings. He surveyed the open ground between him and the outer wall of the city. Built in 1680, the ten mile long outer city wall was constructed to protect the urban area of Mukden, which wasn't protected by the smaller inner city wall built in 1625. He looked a hundred yards to his right to see an open portion of the wall, collapsed by shelling from the Communists. To his left, approximately three hundred yards away, was the gate that led to the bridge over the Shen River, leading to the orphanage. Light from the three-quarter moon wasn't helping his plan of concealment, and the open ground posed a threat to his ability to move unnoticed.

After several minutes of looking and listening for activity, Rusty moved quickly toward the collapsed portion of the wall, looking left and right as he moved over the open ground. He slowed his pace as he approached the breached portion of the wall, stopping at the opening. As he stepped in, two young Chinese men stepped from behind the wall, blocking his exit. Rusty stepped back to gain distance between him and the men, but heard a third man behind him.

Rusty slowly turned around in a circle accessing the movements of the three. He let go of the bundle in his right hand and slowly lifted his hand to his waist, releasing the buckle of his rucksack. He prepared for what he knew to be the inevitable. Knowing the rubble from the collapsed wall underneath his feet would make it difficult to move quickly, he glanced down for a smoother surface. Rusty moved to his left as the largest of the young men spoke in Chinese. Rusty shrugged with a smile and pointed to his ears, indicating he didn't understand. The man pointed to Rusty's bags and smiled.

Rusty slid his right foot behind him and shook his head no. The young man's smile turned to a scowl as he brought the six-inch knife around in front of him.

As the man stepped toward him, Rusty lowered his head and shoulders, dropping the rope and the rucksack to his left and swiftly struck out with a high kick to the man's chest. The young man fell backwards hard, knocking the wind out of him. In a continuous move, Rusty lowered himself down, pivoting to the right on the ball of his left foot, spinning around and hitting the second man with his leg at the knees, cleaning the man's legs out from under him.

He quickly stood and readied himself for the third man who was now lunging toward him. Rusty stepped to the side of the oncoming man and swung his left forearm toward the man's throat. The one-hundred-twenty-pound assailant had no chance against Rusty's mass; he collapsed in a heap.

Before Rusty could turn around to face the second man again, he felt the sting of a knife slashing through his coat and into his left shoulder. Gritting his teeth and groaning in pain, Rusty stepped into the man, denying him the use of his knife hand. Rusty cocked his right hand back and struck out with a powerful punch to the man's throat. He could feel the bones and cartilage of the man's throat collapsing beneath the blow. As he released his grip, the man's lifeless body fell over on its back.

Rusty quickly turned around as he heard movement behind him. He looked to see the first man running away, carrying his two bags. He quickly bent over, picked up one of the stones from the rubble, and hurled it toward the thief. The heavy stone struck the man square in the back, knocking him to the ground. Rusty started running toward him, in an attempt to stop him from getting back up. As he closed the gap between him and the thief, he heard the noise of a vehicle approaching. He saw the lights from a truck coming from behind the buildings eighty yards away. Rusty dove the last ten feet onto the top of the thief's back.

Rusty quickly placed his left hand over the man's mouth as he began to call out. The muffled screams from the man threatened to bring attention to their location as the truck stopped. Rusty pulled the 45 from his belt holster and struck the man's neck hard. All motion from the thief ceased, and Rusty focused his attention on the truck.

In the distance, he could see a Chinese soldier stand up through the roof access hatch of the cab and turn on the flood light. Rusty slowly cocked the hammer of his .45 as the beam from the light moved through the rubble-strewn area. The lumps of stone and debris from the wall provided a minimum amount of cover for the four bodies that lay on them. Rusty remained motionless as the beam of light slowly swept back and forth over them. The idling engine was the only sound that could be heard as the light continued searching the area. After several minutes, the soldier turned off the light and lowered himself back down into the cab. The truck slowly moved out, continuing its southerly direction.

Rusty slowly stood and retrieved the bundles from in front of the now unconscious man lying at his feet. With the bundles in his left hand, he grabbed the man at the collar and dragged him back to the opening in the wall.

Dropping the bundles next to the rope, he pulled each of the men behind the wall and out of sight. After moving his items behind the wall, Rusty slowly removed his coat to inspect the wound. The slash was shallower than he'd thought, and finding the blood only oozing rather than gushing, Rusty breathed a sigh of relief.

He pulled his K-Bar knife out of its sheath, bent over the unconscious man, and cut away a large portion of his shirt. Rusty wrapped the linen around his upper arm over the wound and tied it using his teeth to hold one end of the wrap as he tied it off. He carefully put his coat on, then put the gear on his back and shoulder.

As he was straightening his rucksack, one of the men groaned as he came back into consciousness. Rusty rotated the Ka-Bar in his hand and struck the man hard on the forehead with the handle end of the knife. The man's body went limp again. Rusty put the knife back into the sheath and looked down at the man. "Just isn't your day, is it?"

He looked in both directions along the south side of the wall for any activity. Finding it quiet, he crept out slowly toward the Shen River. He hadn't calculated how he was going to get across the river, but knew walking across the bridge while the Chinese Army was posted there wouldn't be an option. He began mentally preparing himself for what was bound to be a cold swim.

Chapter 12 - The Trek Begins

Walking in a southwesterly direction on the north side of the Shen River, Rusty was trying to put some distance between him and the bridge. As the river turned south, he looked behind him to see the bridge no longer in sight. He knelt down and untied the bundle, pulling out the folded tarpaulin. He unfolded the dark green tarp and placed his coat, rucksack, and rope inside, along with the other items. Pulling the corners together, he tied the large bundle tightly at the top, leaving enough rope to tie a loop for him to pull over his shoulder.

The fall weather had slowed both the river's volume and current, but did little to stem the bone-chilling cold the water presented. The river was still moving fast, and he knew crossing it would be difficult, especially with the wound on his left shoulder.

Rusty looked around for signs of danger as he slowly stepped into the water, making his way around the rocks along the shore. He groaned as he waded in deeper, feeling the cold close around his legs.

With the rope around his neck and shoulder, he lowered himself into the deep water. Pushing himself off, he began taking powerful strokes against the current. The fast moving water, aided by the heavy bundle around his shoulder, pulled him quickly down the river.

Rusty fought to get to the other side with all of his strength. The wound on his left arm was burning as he placed one hand in front of the other, pulling at the water. The opposite shore was only twenty-yards away, but the bitter cold was taking its toll. As he closed on the shoreline, he could feel his muscles tightening from the frigid water.

He pulled himself onto the shore and rolled onto his right side, giving some relief to the wound on his left shoulder. Now out of the water, his body began to tremble from the cold.

He pulled the bundle out of the water and untied the top. He hurried to get the coat on over his water-soaked clothing. Once he'd put the coat back on, he wrapped himself in the tarpaulin and pulled on the rucksack. Closing the bundle, he picked up his other gear and walked up the embankment to get his bearings.

The river had carried him three hundred yards downstream and two miles from the road leading to the orphanage. With his hands still shaking, he opened his compass to get his bearings. He knew he'd been pulled way downstream, but was unsure just how far he'd been taken. He closed the compass and stepped off on an eastern heading to intersect the road.

The big man felt uncomfortable traveling with so few trees for cover. He was out in the open, and didn't like it. The rolling hills offered him little opportunity to hide from view, should someone come along. He knew he was being overly cautious in such a remote area, but to be discovered so soon after leaving the Consulate would prove dangerous at best, deadly at worst.

As he crested the hill, he looked down to see the road below him. His eyes followed the road to the north, and he could see a dark outline of the orphanage dimly illuminated by the moonlight. Way off in the distance to the north, he could see the moonlit outline of the city of Mukden.

His body still trembled from the cold as he made his way down the hill toward the orphanage. Almost at the bottom of the hill, Rusty froze in his tracks as the headlights of a truck pierced the darkness. He dropped to the ground, lying on his stomach as the vehicle approached.

As he lay on the ground, he was certain his position would be given away because he was shivering so uncontrollably. As the headlights of the vehicle grew closer, Rusty could see that it appeared to be the same truck searching for him back at the wall of the city.

The truck sped by without incident.

Letting out a deep shuddering breath, he stood and continued toward the orphanage. His paranoia was kicking in, and he fought the urge to move slowly. He needed to get to the orphanage to get warm and to get the people to safety. The thought of the truck that had passed couldn't be wiped from his mind. Could they still be looking for him? Did they have a layover at the bridge or changing of the guard? "Stop it, Harrigan!" he said out loud as he continued toward the orphanage.

He could now see the walls of the orphanage ahead as he quickened his pace. The compound was dark and eerily quiet, even for this late at night. Rusty reached the front gate and tugged at the doors, only to find them locked from the other side by the beam spreading across both gate doors. Rusty looked around to make sure no one was approaching. He threw his bundles over the top and jumped up to grab the top of the eight foot gate. He pulled hard and lifted his left leg over the top, then slid his body over onto the other side and dropped to the ground.

Picking up his bundles, he walked toward the front door of the complex. He was beginning to become concerned as the compound looked vacant. He reached the steps and began to walk up when a sudden flash of pain shot through his legs. He was catapulted into the air as his legs were cleaned out from under him. Rusty looked up to see Tao standing over him, pointing the end of a six foot staff at his head.

Tao had a surprised look as he stared down at Rusty. He quickly stowed his staff and extended his hand. "Rusty, why you here?"

Rusty reached out to grab Tao's outstretched hand. He spoke as Tao helped him up from the ground. "I came to warn you," Rusty responded.

Tao reached out and touched Rusty's shoulder. "You are wet, Rusty. Come in, get warm."

The two men walked inside the main building to see a low burning fire in the fireplace. As they approached the table, Ho came out from the shadows with his staff. Tao looked at his friend. "Ho, get tea; Rusty cold."

As Ho hurried to get some tea, Rusty eased close to the fire. As he started taking off his wet clothes, Ho handed him a cup of hot tea.

Rusty's trembling hands brought the cup to his lips and sipped slowly.

Tao looked at Rusty's shoulder and opened his eyes wide. "Rusty, you hurt!"

Rusty's voice shook as he responded, "I got into a fight with some thieves at the city wall."

Tao leaned in and looked at Rusty's shoulder and spoke to Ho in Chinese. Ho immediately turned and ran from the room. Tao pulled a chair next to the fire as he spoke to Rusty. "Sit, please."

Rusty sat in the chair and continued to sip the hot liquid. Tao inspected Rusty's wound as he spoke. "Rusty, why you here? Is dangerous for you be here."

"Tao, we got information that they're going throughout China killing all the Christians they find. You need to get out of here."

Tao's voice was unshaken, almost reverent as he responded. "We know, Rusty; Zhu Dong and Chen Yang were killed by Communists."

Rusty lowered his head as he heard the words. The two men he'd known for the past two and a half years, two men who had become his friends and extended family, had had their lives snuffed out by the godless thugs who now occupied the city. His mission now took on an even greater sense of urgency. He had to get these people out of China.

Walter Brown stood in front of Private Cody Bledsoe in the courtyard as they exchanged gear for the changing of the guard. Cody took the M-1 Garand from Walter, checked the chamber, and slung it over his shoulder. Walter stood tall as he faced Cody. "I stand relieved," He said firmly.

Cody placed his right thumb between his chest and the rifle sling and relaxed his stance. "Anything happening, Walt?"

"Nah, it's like a graveyard out here." Walter turned his head looking toward the main gate where a Chinese Army soldier was walking by. "Even the goons are bored."

Cody looked toward the Chinese soldier. "How long do you think this'll last, Walt?"

Walter took a deep breath and slowly let it out. "Don't know. One thing's for sure, though. We're probably gonna get thrown out of China before it's all over."

"I sure as hell hope so; I wanna get home."

"Me, too, Cody." Walter could see the look of concern on Cody's face, but avoided a lengthy explanation as to the reason for his distance.

"Is everything okay Walt?" Cody asked.

He looked out over the city as he responded, "It's nothing, just getting cabin fever. These walls are starting to close in on me."

"Yeah, me, too," Cody responded with a frown. "If it wasn't for Sergeant Harrigan keeping us busy, I think I'd go nuts around here. He sure is a good man."

Walter lowered his head as he responded, "Yup, he sure is." Walter's lips pursed into a faint smile as he turned to walk away. "See ya later, Cody."

Private Bledsoe stared at Walter as he walked away. He'd never seen Walter so detached. Oh well, he thought, he's probably just as tired of this as the rest of us are. Cody turned away and began walking the grounds.

Walter looked out over the skyline of the city as he walked to the entry door of the main building. He couldn't get Rusty out of his mind. He was sure that at any time the Chinese would bring Rusty back to the Consulate either in chains or stretched out on a slab. Walter opened the door and walked down the hall to the kitchen. He looked at his watch. The dial displayed 2:10 am. Walt had been constantly looking at his watch for four hours now, worrying about his friend. He pulled a cup down from the cabinet, filled it with coffee, and sat at the table. He'd been trying to come up with some kind of explanation when Captain Rivera would confront him in just a few short hours. He knew Rivera would be screaming at him once he found out Rusty was gone. He decided the best approach to take with Rivera was to play dumb. Walter smiled as the thought crossed his mind. You should be able to pull that off, Brown.

★ ★ ★

Rusty sat in front of the fireplace in his underwear, wrapped in a blanket for warmth as Tao stitched up his wound. His clothes were hung by the fire drying out. Ho sat in a chair next to Tao and kept bringing Rusty cups of tea.

"Rusty, you need to go back to Consulate. Not safe for you here," Tao said, while applying the herb-lined dressing to Rusty's shoulder.

Rusty turned his head toward Tao and spoke. "Master, I came to take you out of here. It's no longer safe for you to stay here."

Tao finished tying the bandage to Rusty's arm and leaned in toward his friend. "Rusty, what you ask is not possible, we must not leave. You must go back before you caught."

Rusty pulled the blanket up over his shoulder. "Master, I can't go back. It's too late for that. They'll come here for you and the others, and all that you've worked for will be lost. You must realize they'll kill you and everyone here."

Tao smiled at his friend and placed his hand on Rusty's arm. "Rusty, you not worry. The Lord will protect us. Jesus will find way to care for us."

"Tao, they're killing Christians all over China. Sooner or later they'll come here," Rusty pleaded.

"Rusty, if I am to die, then it my honor to die for Jesus. He die for me."

Rusty's voice was louder as he pleaded with Tao. "Except that if you die, they'll kill the others here, too. Men, women, children; they'll all die. They will rape the women and torture the men. Even the children will be killed. Tao, you can't want that on your head. You must leave with me now."

Tao's brow furrowed as he spoke. "Rusty, Jesus will find way. He will care for us some way."

A smirk came across Rusty's face as he responded. "Tao, maybe He sent me to find a way to care for you. Maybe I was supposed to come here for you." Rusty leaned in close to his friend. "Look, Tao, I'd never tell you anything about Kung Fu because you're my teacher and my friend. You should listen to me now, because I've been your teacher of the bible. Please trust me as I've trusted you. We must leave."

Tao was silent as he pondered Rusty's words. "Rusty, where we go? If we leave, they find us."

Rusty turned in his chair and pulled his rucksack on the table top toward him. Rusty spoke as he opened the sack. "Tao, I have maps and charts from the Consulate." Rusty opened the map and placed it on the table in front of Tao. "We can follow the river from here down to Yingkou. Once we're there, we can get transportation by boat to Japan."

Tao grimaced as he responded. "Rusty, Japanese hate us. We go Japan, we die."

Rusty reached into the rucksack for a second time and pulled out a stack of documents. "Tao, I have signed Visas here; enough for all of you. They've been signed by the Consular General and can't be rescinded. Once we get to Japan, you can go to the US Embassy and get transportation to the United States."

Tao's eyes opened wide. "We can go America?"

"Yes, Tao, all of you. You can all go to America."

Ho smiled broadly as he grasped Rusty's left hand. "Rusty, we can live in America? This true?"

Rusty patted Ho's hand with his right palm. "Yes Ho, you can live anywhere in America you want."

Ho turned toward Tao with a beaming smile. "Master Tao, I can be with my family in San Francisco."

Tao turned toward Rusty. "Rusty, how we get to Yingkou? Is very cold now. We have children and old people. How we get there?"

"We can follow the river down to Yingkou; it'll take us four days, five at the most. We can travel at night to avoid detection. We'll need to take five days of food and plenty of warm clothes, but the point is, we can do this, Tao. We can make it out of here."

"It be faster we go Dandong, Rusty," Ho responded.

"The mountains between here and there are too much of a problem Besides, it's right on the border with North Korea, and they're too unstable right now."

Tao nodded in acknowledgement. "You think we can do, Rusty?"

"Yes, Master, we can, but we must hurry. We need to get as far from here as we can tonight. We need to leave now!"

Tao sat up erect in his seat and set his jaw. "Then we leave now."

112

Ho immediately set into action with a beaming smile. He ran quickly from the room to wake the others and get them ready to leave. Rusty stood from the chair and began putting his clothes on as Tao went to the kitchen to gather his things.

Rusty knew that the going would be difficult, but if the people of the orphanage were to have a chance at life, they would have to leave China. The only part of his plan he hadn't worked out yet was how they were going to find a boat in Yingkou. Everything hinged on finding a boat, but he decided not to focus on that problem until he had to. He leaned his head back and opened his eyes wide. "Okay, Lord, gonna need you on this one."

As Rusty was loading his rucksack and tying off the items in his bundle, Mee Ling approached him with a huge smile. "Uncle Rusty, we go America?"

Rusty smiled as he looked down at the little girl. "Yes, sweetie, it's true; we're going to America."

Mee Ling vaulted herself toward Rusty and hugged him tightly around his waist. "Thank you, Uncle Rusty. Thank you very much!"

A tear fell down Rusty's cheek as he held the little girl tightly. Mee Ling was the sole survivor from her family, after her parents and her two brothers had been murdered by the Nationalists. Tao had found her hungry and alone on the edge of the city. Until Rusty's arrival, she had stayed away from everyone but Tao. That all changed when Rusty showed up at the orphanage doors. His bible studies and English lessons had cemented the little girl to him tighter than he could have imagined; that plus the occasional Hershey's chocolate bar.

Rusty knelt in front of the little girl and reached into his shirt pocket as he addressed her. "I don't have any chocolate, but would you like a stick of gum?" Rusty said as he held out a piece of Beeman's gum. "Sorry, it's still a little wet from the river."

She took the gum and smiled. "Thank you, Uncle Rusty."

Rusty stood and placed his right palm on the girls head as he smiled broadly. He turned to see Ho approaching.

"We have food and blankets for everyone. We also have some pots to cook in," Ho stated.

"Okay, but we have to pack light. Leave the pots, Ho; we can't have a fire for cooking. Just grab what food you can. We need to make twenty miles a day to pull this off, Ho." Rusty turned toward the center of the room to see the remainder of the twenty-one people from the orphanage gathered. His lips pursed as the reality of the situation hit him. He scanned the group to see elderly men and women, young children, and an expectant mother in front of him. Every one of them was beaming with broad smiles at the news of going to America. In spite of the worry that plagued him, he placed a broad smile on his face as he walked toward them.

His attention focused on the three young students of Tao's. They were the remaining three from Tao's original group of five Christian students after the deaths of Zhu Dong and Chen Yang. He knew he'd be relying on their strength and energy to get these people to Yingkou.

Tao walked to Rusty, carrying a large bundle on his back. He smiled at Rusty and bowed toward him. "We all ready," Tao said as his right hand gestured to the crowd.

"Okay, let's get going."

The believers moved toward the rear of the compound where the back gate stood. Rusty brought up the rear with Mee Ling close at his side. They stepped from the building and into the back courtyard where a moonlit night welcomed them.

Tao waited next to the gate holding onto his staff as the people filed through and into the countryside. He looked back toward the compound one last time. Ten years of his life had been spent in the orphanage, and it was gone in as many minutes. The group disappeared into the tree-covered hill next to the compound.

Chapter 13 - A New Exodus

Captain Rivera stepped out onto the roof and into the early morning light. He turned toward the building and ignited his Zippo lighter, setting fire to his cigarette. He took a long drag and exhaled slowly as he looked out over the city in the soft light just before sunrise.

His instincts told him that the time for conflict with the Chinese Communists was getting close, and he had to ensure that his men were prepared to protect the Consulate staff. That "Godless fat man," as he referred to Chairman Mao, couldn't keep his ego in check much longer. He was hoping that the end would be a quiet escort to the airfield for the men and women of the Consulate, but needed to prepare for a "worst-case scenario." The burden of command was weighing heavily on him.

Rivera wetted his right thumb and forefinger with saliva and crushed the smoke out between them. He held the extinguished cigarette in his right palm and opened the access door to the stairwell. After reaching the bottom of the stairs, he turned down the hall and toward the kitchen. He opened the door and looked inside to see four of his Marines sitting at the table having breakfast. He leaned into the room and addressed them. "Has anyone seen Sergeant Harrigan?"

"No, Sir," the Marines responded.

As he walked toward the conference room, Rivera passed Walter. "Corporal, have you seen Harrigan?"

Walter stopped in front of Rivera. "No Sir, I just got up. Haven't seen him."

"Is he out on guard duty?"

"No, Sir," Walter replied.

"Okay. If you see him, tell him to meet me in the duty hut."

"I will, Sir." Walter turned and walked away from Rivera toward the kitchen. He raised his eyebrows and opened his eyes wide as he walked to the kitchen. "First salvo avoided," he said softly, under his breath.

Rivera walked out the main entrance of the building and into the courtyard. He looked to see the two Marines on guard duty, Private Gary Wade and Private Nick Sheridan, standing in the center of the courtyard talking to each other. The two snapped to attention and saluted as he stopped in front of them.

Rivera returned the salute. "Either of you two seen Sergeant Harrigan?"

"No, Sir," the two Marines responded in unison.

Rivera looked confused as he spoke. "Okay, if you see him, tell him to meet me in the Duty Hut."

"Yes, Sir," they replied.

As Rivera turned to walk back into the building, he spoke loudly while turned away from them. "And break it up, Marines; keep your attention on the perimeter walls."

"Yes, Sir!" they responded loudly.

Sheridan and Wade watched Rivera as he walked away. "The old man seems to be on edge lately," Wade stated.

"Yeah, it must be driving him nuts to have to sit inside this compound without being able to confront the enemy."

"Yeah, I'd hate to have the old man mad at me," Wade responded as they walked away from each other.

116

Rivera walked inside and turned again down the hall toward the kitchen. All of the Marines were out of the kitchen and had begun the daily routine. Rivera poured himself a cup of coffee and walked back out. He stepped into the duty hut and sat behind the desk, taking a sip from his cup. He opened the folder, placing it on the blotter, and began reading the evening report from Sergeant Rusty Harrigan.

As he was reviewing the pages of the report, his telephone rang. He picked up the receiver and addressed the caller. "Captain Rivera."

The voice on the other end was Judy Francis, the Administrative Assistant. "Captain Rivera, could you please come to my office? There's something I need to talk to you about."

"Of course, I'll be right there." Rivera stood and walked from the room and down the long hall to the administrative office. He knocked on the door and waited for the response. "Come in," Judy Francis announced.

He opened the door and stepped inside. "How can I help you?"

Judy was standing next to the filing cabinet with folders in both her hands. The top of her desk was piled with documents from the cabinet. She had a look of panic on her face as she addressed Rivera. "Captain, I don't know how this has happened, but I'm missing twenty-five Visas."

Rivera's brow furrowed as he stepped toward Judy. "Are you sure?"

"Yes, I'm positive. I keep them all in the top drawer for easy access."

"But we haven't used any for months now. Are you sure?" Rivera repeated his query.

"Captain Rivera, I'm positive. The General requires I do a weekly check of the forms, and I started the first thing this morning with my audit. I'm positive."

"Who has access to the cabinet?" Rivera asked.

"The General, Mr. Parker, you, and me. I thought I'd ask you before I brought it to Mr. Marsh's attention."

Rivera was perplexed. "I keep my set of keys in the duty hut, but I can guarantee that none of my guys would use them. Let me check with the men, but I'm certain they wouldn't access your office without permission from you, me, or the General, not if they wanted to live to see their grandchildren."

"Okay, but I have to tell Mr. Marsh about this."

"Of course, tell him immediately, and I'll get back to you within the hour," Rivera responded as he walked from the office.

Rivera could feel his anxiety level rise as he walked back to the duty hut. He rolled his wrist over and glanced at his watch. 0630 hours, where the hell is Harrigan? I need some answers, he thought. As he passed by the squad bay he was approached by Corporal Manning.

"Sir, have you seen Sergeant Harrigan?" Manning asked.

"No, I'm trying to find him myself."

"Sir, I have a problem in the armory."

Rivera froze in his tracks. "What do you mean, 'a problem?'?"

"I'm missing a .45 and eight clips, Sir."

Rivera's blood ran cold as the realization of what was happening hit him. "Son-of-a-bitch!" he shouted.

Manning took two steps back as Rivera's voice bellowed through the hall. "Corporal, get your ass back in the armory and give me a complete inventory, and I want it ten minutes ago!"

"Yes, Sir," Manning replied as he hurried off to the armory.

Rivera began pacing the hall, fuming, as he realized what was happening. He turned left, then right, then left again, as his blood pressure climbed. "Brown!" He said out loud. "Where the hell is Brown?"

He stormed down the hall and turned into the squad bay. Walter was sweeping the floor of the bay as Rivera's voice boomed through the enclosure. "Private Brown, get your ass in the duty hut, now!" Rivera shouted, then walked out and back to his office.

Walter dropped the broom on the floor and hurried off to the duty hut. He knocked on the door with his fist. "ENTER!" he heard Rivera bark back.

Walter stepped inside and closed the door behind him. He snapped to attention and responded, "Yes, Sir."

118

Rivera was pacing in front of his desk. He stopped in front of Walter as he spoke. "Private, I'm gonna ask this question just once, and I'd better get the answer I want! Where the hell is Sergeant Harrigan?"

Still at attention, Walter put the best confused look on his face he could muster up. "I don't know, Sir, I haven't seen him."

Rivera's jaw was pulsing as he spoke to Brown. "Private, I have a missing Sergeant, a missing .45 with eight clips of ammunition, and twenty-five missing visas. Now it doesn't take a PhD to figure out what happened. Harrigan has gone to help those people at the orphanage, and he wouldn't have left without telling you. You two are as thick as thieves. If one of you eats, the other one takes a dump, so don't tell me you don't know what happened to him."

Walter relaxed his stance and looked at Rivera pleadingly. "But Sir, *I don't* know what happened to him." Walter pleaded.

Rivera's fists clenched as he moved within inches of Walter's face. "I didn't tell you to stand at ease!"

Walter snapped back to attention and thrust his chest out. He saw Rivera's fists clench as he glanced down.

"If you're lying to me, I'll field strip your blood-soaked body with a butter knife! Do you understand me, Marine?"

Walter's shoulders snapped back as he responded, "Yes, Sir!"

"You better hope you're not lying to me." Rivera could see he wasn't going to get anything out of Walter. He turned his back toward the young Marine. "Dismissed!" Rivera said with disgust in his voice.

Walter saluted, did an about face, and walked from the room. He closed the door behind him and walked back to the squad bay. When he entered, he was greeted by Cody Bledsoe and David Butcher. Bledsoe moved in close toward Walter and spoke softly to avoid detection, "What the hell happened in there? We could hear the old man screaming from here."

Walter was still shaking from the dressing down he'd received. "It looks like Rusty took off last night," he said while looking down.

"What the hell do you mean, Brown?" Cody replied.

"I mean it looks like he went over the wall, went AWOL, skipped out. What the hell do you think I mean?" Walt was venting some of his own rage for not only lying, but having to endure Rivera's wrath.

David Butcher leaned back on his heels. "I don't believe it. Sergeant Harrigan wouldn't bug out, not on his own men, he wouldn't."

"Well, it looks like that's exactly what he did Dave, so leave me the hell alone about it," Walter replied as he picked up the broom and continued his chores.

The two Marines stood staring at each other in amazement at what they had heard. The thought that the Marine they all respected so much could abandon them was unthinkable. They all walked away in silence.

Captain Rivera stood, furious and confused, in the middle of the duty hut. He was trying to digest the morning's events when a knock on the door interrupted him. "WHAT?" he responded.

The door slowly and cautiously opened to reveal Consular General Robert Allen Marsh standing in the doorway. "Is it safe to enter, Captain?"

Rivera's professionalism immediately kicked in. "I'm sorry, Sir. How can I help you?"

General Marsh looked tired from the heavy weight he was carrying on his shoulders. Whatever difficulties Rivera was experiencing, Marsh was receiving it tenfold. The usually energetic man was now fatigued and beaten down by the responsibilities of his office. He was looking forward to leaving China with his staff. "Judy suggested I come and see you. Something about some missing visas."

Rivera pressed the palms of his hands on his forehead and slowly ran them down his face. "I'm sorry, General, please have a seat," he said while gesturing to an empty chair with his right hand.

"Am I gonna be angry at what you have to tell me, Captain?" Marsh said while sitting in the chair.

"I was, Sir," Rivera responded as he fell into his chair. "It appears that Sergeant Harrigan has gone AWOL."

Marsh fell back into the seat of his chair upon hearing Rivera's words. He closed his eyes and lowered his head. "Oh no, not Harrigan, not him, why?"

"Well, I don't have all the facts, but I'm guessing it has a lot to do with the Chinese people at that old orphanage he and Brown were going to. After your briefing about the Chinese Communists killing all the Christians, he became distraught. My guess is he's trying to get them out of the country."

Marsh spoke as his head tipped back, looking at the ceiling. "Well, that would explain the missing visas."

"And the missing .45 and eight clips I was told about," Rivera added.

Before Marsh could respond, a knock came on the door. "Enter!" Rivera said loudly.

Brian Manning opened the door and looked at Capt. Rivera. "I'm sorry to interrupt, Sir, but I inventoried everything. Besides the .45 and clips, there's a rucksack, a length of rope, two K-bars, six K-rats, and a tarp missing."

Rivera's jaw set as he heard the report. "Very well, Manning; that'll be all."

"Yes, Sir," Manning said as he turned around and closed the door behind him.

Marsh looked at Rivera. Well, that confirms it. He's trying to get them out of the country."

"Yes Sir." Rivera let out a huge breath before responding. "I'm sorry, General; I'm afraid the Corp let you down."

"They'll kill him if they find him, you know."

"Not if I kill him first," Rivera responded, striking the top of his desk with his right fist.

General Marsh's tone changed as he became less formal with his subordinate. "I wouldn't take it so personal, Joe; at least Rusty's doing something about all of this."

Rivera leaned back in his chair. "What in the world do you mean, Sir?"

"Look, Joe, I've spent the last year lodging protest after protest about the murders and the treatment of the Chinese people. At least Rusty did something about it, even if it was wrong."

"That doesn't excuse it, Sir. We're talking about desertion here.

Forget the Chinese Communists; our government will hang him for this if they catch him."

"I know Joe, but the kid did more in one day than I've been able to do in an entire year. Who knows, he may be judged better than me at diplomacy after this is all over with."

Rivera's head fell forward looking at the floor. "Damn it ... I had high hopes for that kid and he just throws it away." Rivera said with disgust in his voice.

"I know, Joe; I thought the kid had great potential too. One thing's for sure, though; we can't take this to the Chinese. They'll bring him back in a box."

"I know, Sir, that's the damnable thing about it. I can't go get him. And sooner or later they'll find out he's missing."

Marsh took in a deep breath and exhaled slowly. "Well, we'll deal with that when the time comes. If and when we get out of here, I'll brief Central Command about the whole thing."

"You don't want to send them a message now, Sir?" Rivera asked.

"Good Lord, no! The Chinese may be loose cannons, but they're not stupid. If they intercept a message about him leaving, they'll hunt him down and kill him on the spot. We can deal with this once we get to Japan, which is where Rusty is probably headed." Marsh's head leaned back as he spoke. "What do you think his chances of getting there are, Joe?"

Rivera pulled a smoke out of the pack of cigarettes on his desk and placed it between his lips. "Slim to none. He has no combat experience, limited resources, no Intel, and a bunch of civilians to move over a hundred miles." He opened his Zippo lighter and lit the cigarette, letting out a large cloud of smoke. "One in a thousand, tops."

"How does this hurt us? I mean, can we do the job without him?"

"It'll be tough, but we'll manage, Sir."

Marsh stood and looked toward Rivera. "Well then it doesn't do us any good to worry about it now. Let's just get on with business until we have to address it. We'll take this one step at a time."

Rivera looked up at Marsh. "Yeah, like a mine field."

Marsh's lips pursed as he responded, "I suppose so." He turned and walked from the room, closing the door behind him.

Rivera stood and looked out his office window. The incredible anger over the incident was slowly leaving him as he stared out the window and into the courtyard. "Good luck, kid." He took a long drag from his smoke and crushed it out in the ashtray. "You're gonna need it."

★ ★ ★

Bobby leaned back in his seat with a disappointed look on his face. The story he was being told had taken a decidedly different direction, and his furrowed brow told Walter he didn't like it.

"What's the matter, Bobby, you don't like what happened?" Walter asked.

"Well, no, I mean, like you didn't like it either, did you? Rusty taking off like that really sucked. I mean, he left you guys all alone," Bobby said with both hands in the air, palms up.

Walter's lips pursed as he responded. "No, Bobby, I didn't much like it, but eventually I understood it had to be done."

"But he had a duty to be with you guys, I mean… he took an oath and all, didn't he?"

"Yes, he did, Bobby, and it tore him up inside to do it, but he knew he had to get them out, and that took priority."

Bobby looked confused. "But his duty was to obey orders, and he didn't. He was supposed to stay at the Consulate, and he went AWILL."

Walter chuckled. "It's AWOL Bobby. It means, <u>Absent</u> <u>Without</u> <u>Leave</u>."

Still angry at the thought of Rusty's actions, Bobby was responding in his usual manner when he got confused. "Whatever, it still sucks that he left you guys."

"But he had higher orders, Bobby," Walter replied.

"Oh don't tell me this is another one of those God Things you're always talking about."

"Yup, sure is. Rusty didn't have any options to ignore either order, whether it came from Rivera or God. That's why he was so

123

conflicted. The thought of leaving the Consulate ate at his gut like an acid. He was tormented by it; and in the end, he knew he had to do what the Lord wanted him to do."

"So what, like, God came down and told him to do it?" Bobby asked, still confused.

"No, Bobby; He doesn't speak to you in the literal sense."

"Then what the hell *does* he do?" Bobby caught himself before Walter could respond. "I'm sorry, Mr. Brown. I apologize, it's just that I don't get why he would run away from his duty."

"Bobby, if you're a Christian, you don't have a choice. You do what you're told, when you're told to do it. He doesn't part the heavens and send lightning bolts down to hit you; that stuff's for Hollywood. He places it on your heart; He burdens you with it until you respond. He makes it impossible to ignore Him."

"But you were mad at Him, too, weren't you?"

"I sure was. I didn't understand any better than you do now. It wasn't until I became a Christian, years later, that I finally understood he didn't have any choice in the matter. The Lord wanted those people saved, and He chose Rusty to do it."

"So what, God destroys his life and that's okay?" Bobby asked angrily.

Walter shook his head as he responded, "Bobby, it's not about this life. It's about the next one. If you're defiant here, then you'll be defiant there. God can't allow even a miniscule amount of rebellion in heaven. A life of service to God isn't for wimps, Bobby. A choice to follow him means compliance to His will, even to the point of death, should it be required."

"Man, that doesn't sound cool," Bobby said defiantly.

"Again, Bobby, you're putting too much emphasis on this life, and not on eternity. God doesn't give you a huge bank account, a Mercedes, and a mansion in the hills if you accept him. If He did that, he'd have a bunch of materialistic drones who would leave the minute the money petered out and the car broke down.

The best soldiers in the military snap to attention and say 'Yes, Sir,' and do what they're told without questioning orders. Why is it so easy to understand the military structure, but so easy to dismiss

124

God's? Rusty loved the Marine Corps very much; and loved his country even more. But there's one thing you need to understand, Bobby. God doesn't sit in heaven wrapped in an American flag. So what we think is important, God most often views as irrelevant."

Bobby leaned forward as he reflected on Walter's words. It was appearing to him that there was no end to how little he knew about what life was all about.

Chapter 14 - The Huge Responsibility

The morning sun was now just below the horizon as the line of Christians from the orphanage walked slowly southwest, away from their home. Rusty and Tao were in the front, along with the older people and the children. The rear was being brought up by the younger people, along with Tao's students. Rusty wanted the pace of the group to be set by those who were the slowest, to better determine when rest was needed. His task for the first night had been to put as much distance between them and the orphanage as possible. According to his mental calculations, they had travelled about ten miles. The going had been relatively easy so far, but the mountains lying ahead were going to make the travel significantly slower, and of greater concern, more hazardous.

The weather had been cooperating and remaining in the high sixties during the day, but dipping into the forties at night. Rusty had hoped for the weather to remain warm during their trek, but knew that eventually a cold front would be moving into their area.

The road to Yingkou was west of them, approximately two miles away. Rusty knew they would eventually have to cross the road to avoid the large cities that ahead to the south. Moving farther east was also not an option, due to the difficult terrain. The heavy traffic of the road, however, was going to be difficult to get across undetected. His task was becoming more and more difficult.

As Rusty turned his head and looked behind him, he saw only smiling faces looking back. These people had placed all their faith in his promises and his abilities. The consequence of his decision to take them away from their home was being brought to light.

Tao placed his right hand on Rusty's shoulder as they walked. "Rusty, time we rest for the night. Everyone tired, need rest."

Rusty looked at his watch and stopped in his tracks. The line of people stopped behind him as Rusty turned to face them. "You're right, Tao; we've been moving for a long time now. Let's move into that clump of trees over there and set up camp," Rusty said while pointing about a hundred yards to their left.

The group moved out and began walking toward the tree line as the sun slowly rose above the horizon. Rusty continued into the trees about thirty yards and stopped in a small clearing. He watched as a *very* pregnant An Zhao slowly sat on the ground against a tree, with the help of her husband, Wu. Rusty felt badly for driving the group so hard, especially after seeing the exhausted look on An's face.

Rusty waited until the entire group was in the clearing before he relaxed. Everyone gathered closely together in the center. Each person carried packs hastily made from sheets of linen, holding a small amount of food and what possessions they could gather. Rusty watched as they pulled pieces of dried fruit and cooked rice in rolled up paper from their packs. Each person took a few bites, and then placed the remainder back in their packs. Even without being told, everyone in the group was rationing their food. None were complaining, none were groaning from hunger. Not even fatigue seemed to bother them. His respect and love for the Chinese continued to grow at every step in his involvement with them.

Rusty stepped toward Tao and asked for his help in assigning tasks. "Tao, can you please ask one of the men to stand guard over the perimeter while we rest? If he can watch for two hours until sunset that would be a big help."

Tao smiled back at him. "Rusty, you ask. You lead us now; they listen to you."

Rusty smiled back at Tao. "Okay," he responded. He stepped toward the four youngest men in the group and addressed them. "We need to post guards on the perimeter; I need to have each of you take a two-hour shift. Wake me up for one of the shifts as well."

Each of the men bowed toward Rusty and spoke to each other in Chinese. Two of the men walked away from the group, one going north, the other going south. Rusty bowed to the remaining two men. He walked back to the center of the group and sat next to Tao. He reached into his rucksack and pulled one of the rations from his pack.

After opening the pack, he set the cans and packets on the ground in front of him. He opened the small paper wrapper that contained the can opener and began opening the cans of food. A curious Tao watched in wonder at what Rusty was doing.

"What is this, Rusty?"

Rusty looked at Tao and responded, "They're K-rations, Tao. A 'ready to eat meal' used by the military."

First introduced in 1943, the K-rations had taken the place of the heavier C-rations. Breakfast had veal, dinner was spam, and supper was sausage. Each meal had condiments of cheese, crackers, candy, and gum, drink mixes including coffee, toilet paper, and cigarettes. The wax box that contained the meal could be burned to heat the meals, although it barely completed the job. Neither the K or C rations were very appealing to the GI's.

Tao continued to look on in amazement as Rusty opened the cans. "What kind of food, Rusty?"

Rusty smiled as he responded. "Mystery meat, Tao." Rusty handed Tao his spoon and held out the can toward him. Tao dipped the spoon into the can and withdrew some of the meat. He slowly put the spoon into his mouth and rolled the food around inside for a moment. "Not very good, Rusty," he said after swallowing the meat.

Rusty laughed out loud as he responded "No, it's not, Tao."

Rusty passed the cheese and crackers around the group, then placed the gum and toilet paper into his pocket. He looked about twenty feet away and smiled at Mee Ling, motioning for her to come to him. She smiled and stepped toward Rusty. He held out the chocolate bar toward her. "Here you go; share it with the others."

Mee Ling smiled as she took the chocolate. "Thank you, Rusty." She hurried off to share her treasure with the other children.

Rusty ate from the can as he leaned back against the tree, speaking to Tao between bites. "We're going to have difficulty getting over the hills tonight, Tao. I saw a draw between the mountains that might be passable, but it's still going to be tough."

"It be okay, Rusty. Everything be okay," Tao said with a smile.

"I sure wish I had your optimism, Tao," Rusty replied.

"You right Rusty; I was wrong. This God's will for you take us away. All things His will," Tao said, waving his right hand in the air.

"You're right about that, Tao, but it's still going to be tough."

Tao looked at Rusty with intensity while he spoke. "If God help Moses, He help us. Hard for Moses, but God help. Same for you. Very hard, but God help."

Rusty looked back at Tao. "Well, I'm certainly no Moses, Tao, and that ain't Mount Sinai," he said while pointing toward the mountains to the south.

"Not matter; His will. Remember, you teach us. God provide."

Rusty smiled as he looked at Tao. "You're right; His will."

Rusty was awe struck at the faith of these new Christians. They had been jerked out of their homes, told to walk over a hundred miles, and with only a promise of a better life. He was in awe of their optimism.

Rusty held out another can of K-rats toward Tao. "Do you want more, Tao?"

Tao's nose turned up as he responded, "No, Rusty, not need food. What is hometown like, Rusty?"

"Philadelphia, it's like any other town, I suppose. Tough town, but still my home."

"Is town where all brothers love each other, right?" Tao asked.

Rusty chuckled. "It's kind of grown away from the whole 'Brotherly love' thing. It's not like it used to be when the country was founded. But I guess it's like that all over America. Times change," he said.

"You not like Philadelphia anymore?"

"No, I like it fine, Tao. It's where I grew up, it's where my family is from. It's just changed a lot."

"Yes, Mukden same way. Not same since I was boy. First British, then Japanese, then Communists. Not same anymore. Understand what you say, not same." Tao looked inquisitively toward Rusty. "Rusty, can live in America anywhere we want?"

"Yes, Tao, anywhere you want."

"Not need permission to go anywhere?"

Rusty smiled. "No, you can go anywhere you want, at any time. You don't need permission from anyone. Is there a place you want to go when you get there?"

Tao smiled broadly. "Want to see Texas. Want to see Old West."

Rusty smiled as he responded. "Why in the world would you want to see Texas, Tao? It's nothing like China."

"American missionary who at orphanage from Texas. He say everyone free in Texas. All free, do what I want, no one bother."

"Well, he's right; Texas leaves everyone alone, and there's a lot of space there. It's the biggest state, and no one will bother you, that's for sure."

Tao thrust his chest out and stated with certainty, "Yes, Texas place I want to be."

Rusty stood and placed his hand on Tao's shoulder. "Well, we'll make sure you get to Texas then." Rusty walked the ground around the group checking on them one last time before he settled in. The others in the group were lying down for some rest, covering themselves with what they could to keep warm. He walked to the edge of the tree line and looked out toward the north one last time. He stood still and listened for any noise in the distance, but heard nothing. He turned around and walked back into the camp. Rusty walked to his bags and retrieved the tarp from his belongings. He stepped over to where Mee Ling and the other children were lying and spread the cover over the sleeping children. He smiled as he looked down to see Mee Ling holding the chocolate he'd given her close to her chest while she slept.

As Rusty walked past An Zhao and her husband, Wu stood and smiled at him. He spoke in Chinese, none of which Rusty could understand. Rusty glanced down at An with a puzzled look. An smiled and translated for her husband. "Wu say thank you for helping us. He say God send you to care for us. He also say our baby will be raised in America because of you. He very happy, Rusty, I very happy. God bless you, Rusty."

Rusty turned back toward Wu and smiled. As he was about to respond with you're welcome, Wu reached out and gave the big man a huge hug. Rusty bowed and smiled at the husband and wife, then turned away from them with tears welling up in his eyes. He walked back to his spot and laid his head down on the rucksack. He'd been up now for almost thirty hours, and his body groaned with fatigue. Rusty reached up with his right hand and wiped tears from his eyes. He rolled over off his injured shoulder to relieve the pain as he settled in for some rest. He closed his eyes and fell off to sleep immediately.

Tao, watching, rolled his head back skyward after looking at Rusty. He smiled as he closed his eyes.

The column of three trucks slowed as they approached the orphanage. Major Hung rode in the passenger side of the lead truck. He was about to follow an order that was eating at him, something that had started to give him sleepless nights, the rounding up of Christians in the Liaoning Province. He shut his eyes tightly in an effort to blot out the image of Chen Yang as he was bricked into the wall of the prison.

The driver looked toward Major Hung. "Sir, do you want us to stop in front of the compound?"

Hung remained silent, staring at the approaching orphanage.

The driver repeated his request. "Sir?"

Snapping back into consciousness, Hung turned toward the driver. "Yes?"

"Sir, do you want us to stop at the gates in front of the compound?" the driver repeated.

"Yes, that would be fine," Hung responded as he brought his focus back to the business at hand.

As the three trucks came to a halt at the main gate of the compound, the men in the rear of the trucks immediately jumped out with their rifles in hand and ran to the gate. Major Hung exited the lead truck and barked out his orders. "Split up and surround the complex. I want ten men here with me." The men scrambled in compliance with his orders.

He pointed toward one of the soldiers. "Knock on the gate." The soldier turned his rifle around and banged on the gate with the butt of the weapon. After there was no response, Hung pointed toward the gate. The soldier hit the gate again with his rifle butt three times.

After waiting almost a minute, Hung ordered the man over the wall. Two of the soldiers held a rifle between them, and the soldier stepped onto it. The two men lifted him to the top and over the wall. After removing the wooden beam that held the doors closed, the soldier opened the gates, allowing entry for the others.

Major Hung and the nine men entered the vacant compound to see the remaining soldiers coming from the rear of the complex. "Check all of the out buildings," he shouted to the approaching men. He waved his arms towards the ten men. "Okay, check the main building."

Hung walked up the steps toward the main entrance. He followed the men with his hands clasped behind him. The soldiers scurried around the building looking for occupants as the Major stood in the center of the main room.

Hung was struck by the humble conditions of the orphanage. At one end of the great room, towels and rags hung on a line to dry. At the other end of the room were makeshift beds lining the wall.

He walked to the fireplace behind the dining table to see the tea pot and tin cups placed on the metal stand. He placed his hand on the pot to check the temperature and found it to be cold. He took the metal poker and disturbed the ashes in the fireplace, and found glowing embers under the ashes. He mentally calculated that the fire had gone out about six hours ago.

He noticed small linen patches on the hearth and bent down to retrieve them. His brow furrowed as he found them to be covered in blood. While he was bent over, he noticed two small pieces of paper under the table. He reached out to retrieve them and stood back up. As he unraveled the crumpled pieces he saw a white wrapper with a horizontal red stripe across the front. The writing read Beeman's gum. "The Americans were here", he said in a low voice. As his sergeant approached, Hung put the gum wrapper into his jacket pocket.

"Major, we've checked the entire compound, and there is no one here. There's no clothing or personal items anywhere, and it looks like they took almost all of the food. The kitchen is pretty much empty, Sir," the sergeant reported.

"Very well, Sergeant. It appears they've left for good. Let's get back to headquarters and report to Colonel Li. There's nothing more we can do here."

The task of rounding up the Christians was becoming a burden he no longer wanted to shoulder. He wanted this over as quickly as possible so he could get back to what he knew; being an Infantry Commander. He found himself longing for the days before the occupation. Major Hung looked around the room one last time before he left to rejoin his men.

Chapter 15 - A Troubled Mind

A heavy snowfall had moved into the area and was covering the group of believers with six inches of new snow. With no one to warn them of the drastic drop in temperature, the members were quickly slipping into unconsciousness. The black, cloud-covered sky offered little light, with the exception of the one quarter moon that fought to shine through the clouds. The fifteen degree temperature was slowly claiming the younger members and rapidly rendering the older ones immobile. The entire group of Christian followers was slowly dying.

Beyond the clearing, a lone Chinese soldier moved slowly through the darkness, his steps silenced by the fresh snow. His slow and even breathing was clearly visible in the cold air of the evening and was controlled in an attempt to quiet his approach. His uniform hat was placed low on his forehead, and the collar of his coat was turned up, concealing his face. His glove-covered hands were held out low in front of him, with his back arched forward, giving him a cat-like stance, ready to react to any threat. Leading his advance was the revolver held in his right hand, telegraphing his intentions.

As the soldier reached the tree line, he stopped to survey the surrounding area. Satisfied he'd not been discovered, he slowly stepped into the trees. Each step was soft and carefully placed to avoid stepping on fallen branches hidden beneath the snow.

As he approached the clearing, he lowered his stance even further. Stopping behind a tree at the edge of the clearing, he looked out over the group and found no signs of life. He inched out into the group and carefully looked at each person lying on the ground.

The children appeared to be dead as he looked down to see the gray tone to their faces. His eyes slowly scanned the area, searching for his target. He stopped as his eyes fell on Rusty Harrigan. He slowly crept toward Rusty, his revolver targeting the big man.

Barely conscious, Rusty's eyes slowly opened to see the sinister figure moving toward him just ten yards away. As the soldier slowly raised his head, the hat brim revealed to him that it was Colonel Li.

Rusty tried to move, but felt like his body was in quicksand. The cold had taken its toll; he was helpless to move. He concentrated with all his effort to rise, but he couldn't; he was frozen to the ground.

Li moved closer toward him and smiled as he pointed the revolver directly at him. The Colonel slowly cocked the hammer of the revolver back and took aim at Rusty's head. Every muscle of Rusty's body cried out as he tried to react. Li laughed loudly as he pulled the trigger. The earsplitting explosion and fire from the revolver echoed through the valley.

Rusty sat up from a dead sleep, sweat pouring from his face and neck. His eyes frantically scanned the clearing, looking for any threat. His heavy breathing had awakened Tao, lying just three feet away.

"Rusty, you okay?" Tao said with concern in his voice.

Still coming into consciousness, Rusty wiped his face with his open hands. "Bad dream," He said through his hands as they tightly griped his face.

Tao sat up and looked at his friend. "When mind in trouble, body cry out. Must clear mind Rusty."

Rusty was sitting up with his head hung down. He smiled as he responded, "Easier said than done, Tao."

Tao's brow furrowed as he looked at Rusty. "Why you so troubled?"

Rusty looked over at his friend. "It's nothing, Tao, just worried about getting us through all this."

"Will be fine, Rusty, all things be fine." Tao turned his body to face his friend. "Rusty, remember what you teach that Moses say to God?"

With his head still down, Rusty smiled. "No, but I have a feeling you're gonna remind me."

"Moses say he has seen and done many things, he has been many places, but one thing he know for sure is 'You are Lord.' Just need to know He is Lord. He take care of everything."

Rusty stood and responded to Tao with a chuckle. "You know, Tao, I don't know why you needed me; you know the bible better than I do."

Tao stood and faced his friend, placing his right hand on Rusty's arm. "Had good teacher."

Rusty chuckled again, placing his hand on Tao's shoulder. "Tell me that if we get outta here." Rusty looked at his watch. The dial read 5:00 pm. He realized that he hadn't been awakened for his turn at guard duty. He placed the .45 in his holster and bent down to gather his things. He looked up to see the young student Chow Yun approaching him. Chow stopped and addressed him.

"Rusty, almost time we go." The seventeen year old Chow had his bow and quiver of arrows slung over his shoulder and a tired look on his face.

"Chow, you were supposed to wake me up for my turn at post," Rusty said while placing his belongings in his rucksack.

"You very tired, need sleep. We okey-dokey." Chow had learned the slang term for okay from Walter Brown's repeated use at the orphanage.

"Okay, Chow, but from now on, you wake me up for watch. Okay?"

"Okey-dokey, Rusty."

"Tao, could you get the rest of the people up and fed? I'll take the last watch before we leave," Rusty asked.

Tao smiled and bowed toward Rusty as he was walking away. As

136

Rusty passed by the children still huddled under the tarp, he smiled at a now awake Mee Ling. Her beaming smile reminded him of why he was doing this. He stepped toward the edge of the tree line and stood behind one of the trees, looking out toward the north.

Rusty reached into his pocket and retrieved the packet of crackers from his K-rats. The crackers were hardly making a dent in the void of his stomach, but would hold off the hunger pangs for at least this evening. He took a sip from his canteen as he looked out over the landscape. The full weight of his responsibility was hanging over him. He closed his eyes tightly as the vision from his earlier dream entered his mind.

The setting sun was now moving behind the mountains to the west of the Mukden Prison. All throughout the complex, fireplaces and stoves were being stoked in an effort to combat the falling temperature. Colonel Li sat at his desk in the room at the end of the complex, reading the day's reports from garrisons all around the Liaoning Province. The fire from his standing stove burned brightly as he looked over his papers. The lone desk lamp illuminated his work space in the windowless office.

Li looked up from the desk as he heard the knock on the door. "Come in" he responded.

Major Hung opened the door and entered the office. Clearly tired from the day's work, Hung exhaled loudly as he closed the door behind him. "The last load of the day is being processed, Colonel."

Li looked to his subordinate. "What's the total for the day, Major?"

Hung placed his file onto the Colonel's desk as he spoke. "Three hundred and fifty-eight, Sir."

"Excellent," Li replied as he dropped his pen on the desk and leaned back in his chair. "That makes it just under three-thousand for the entire province. The Chairman will be pleased. You may have the guards begin the executions first thing in the morning. Make sure the graves are dug before you start, Major."

Hung leaned in toward the Colonel as he spoke. "But, Sir, we need time to determine which are Christians and which are Nationalist sympathizers. There are also elderly and children in with them."

Li scowled as he stood from his desk. "The old men and women are of no concern to me. The children are the only ones I want screened. They can work in the factories, so long as they're not Christians."

"But, Sir, we acted only on the word of informants. There's nothing certain to confirm whether they're Christians or not. Besides, we need people for the planting in the spring; shouldn't we hold out enough for the fields?" Hung reasoned.

Li folded his arms and looked at Hung. "Major, there won't be enough food for all the people as it is. I'm not going to have useless eaters sitting around for six-months emptying food warehouses that are already too low in inventory. If we need workers for the fields, we can truck them in here in the spring. The one thing for sure in this country is that there are always more people. Besides, the Chairman will be announcing his new plan for the country soon."

"A new plan? What new plan, Colonel?" Hung asked.

"It's called The Great Leap Forward. It should end all of our problems for food production. So don't worry about the prisoners; they can be replaced, if needed."

Major Hung found himself searching for a way to reason with his Colonel to prevent the total slaughter of the people he'd brought to the prison. His role in the genocide was wearing heavily on him. "But, Sir, at least give me one more day to be sure about the status of those who were brought in."

Li's brow furrowed as he looked at the Major. "I'm not certain that you're in compliance with our orders, Major. If you can't comply, then I can have you removed and replace you with someone who is. I'm beginning to think that you are not with me on this, Major."

Major Hung knew what "being replaced" meant. He'd be thrown in with the rest of the prisoners and scheduled for termination. He decided to back away from his argument for now. "I'm absolutely with you, Colonel; I'm committed to compliance with our orders. I'm sorry; I won't say anything further."

"Very good, Major, see that you don't." Li returned to his seat and looked up at Major Hung. "Did you bring in the suspects from the old orphanage with the group today?"

Hung pointed to the seat in front of Li's desk. "May I, Sir?"

Li nodded in the affirmative.

Hung spoke as he was sitting in the chair. "We went there this morning; it was our first stop. The compound had been abandoned sometime before we arrived."

"Abandoned!" Li shouted. "Where have they gone?"

"We don't know, Sir. We checked the surrounding countryside and found no signs of them."

"And none of them were brought in with the others?"

"No, Sir," Hung responded.

Li sat back in his chair and pulled at his chin with his right hand. "They couldn't have gone south; the Koreans would pick them up. Going west only gets them closer to their demise. The mountains to the east are too difficult for them." He looked toward Hung. "Have you finished checking the city?"

"Yes, Sir, the city has been checked completely."

"Very well. Take your men to the north first thing in the morning. You'll probably find them working their way up to the border. They couldn't have made it far." Li leaned across his desk toward Major Hung. "Find them, Major! You're dismissed," Li said waving his hand in the air.

Major Hung responded sharply, "Yes, Sir."

Hung stepped from the room and closed the door behind him. It was becoming obvious to him that his days were numbered. He didn't want anymore of this, and he was certain that Colonel Li would have him transferred if he didn't comply with the orders. He shook his head as he walked down the hall of the prison.

Rusty turned around to see Chow Yun approaching him from the rear. As he stopped, Chow spoke to his friend. "Rusty, we ready to leave."

"Has everyone eaten?"

"Yes, all eaten, ready to leave."

Rusty looked up to the sky and determined that it was dark enough to move out without being seen. He turned and walked back into the clearing. He found all the members standing waiting for him to give the order to move out to the south. He placed his hand on Mee Ling's head as he walked past her and smiled. He looked down to see that someone had tied up his bundle using the tarp. He put his rucksack on and slung the rope and bundle over his shoulder. He looked over the group as he spoke. "Is all the paper and trash picked up?"

Tao responded for the group. "Yes, nothing left, all ready."

Rusty led off, with the children and elders following. The younger men brought up the rear.

Conversation for the group had dropped to a minimum, and any words spoken were at just above a whisper. Even the children had curtailed their usual chatter. The clouds had moved out, and the night sky was illuminated by an unobstructed moon. Although the temperature had dropped by three degrees from the prior night, it was still somewhat warm. Rusty continually pulled the compass out from his pocket to check his bearings. He made minor corrections in his directions each time, continuing in a southwesterly direction.

The four miles to the base of the mountain had been travelled quickly. The grade was becoming steeper now, and the older people were breathing harder as the incline increased. Rusty looked ahead to see the pass and tried to make an easier path for them in the limited light.

Just one hundred yards ahead, Rusty made out what appeared to be an animal trail at the base of the mountain. He pointed to the trail and spoke to Tao as he walked toward it. "Up there, that's where we have to go." He was certainly relieved there was a path; he didn't want to walk around the base of the mountain. There were too many settlements the closer they got to the main road, and it would put them miles outside of their route.

Tao looked at the imposing incline with unease. "Rusty, this be too hard for people. Have old people and children. An is with child, need more help than husband Wu can give. Why can't go around mountain?"

Rusty stopped at the beginning of the trail and removed the map and flashlight from his rucksack. "This is the only mountain we have to go over, Tao. Once we get over this mountain, we can walk the base of the next mountain range down to Anshan."

Rusty bent down on his knees and covered the lens of the flashlight. The red lens offered little light, but denied any light to be seen beyond their position. He opened the map on the ground, tracing their proposed path with his index finger. "If we go around this mountain, we'll get too close to Dengta, and the risk of being discovered is greater." His finger continued in a southerly direction on the map. "Once we get to Anshan, we can cross over and enter the valley. It'll be a straight shot to Yingkou."

Bent over on one knee, Tao studied the map. "But will be hard going through valley, much open area to travel."

"Yes, but fewer people, Tao. The only problem that we'll have is if the weather gets colder. The lower temperatures would be hard for the people to take if we're out in the open. But from what I can see, this is our best path." Rusty folded the map and stowed the flashlight in his pack. "We'll have to keep a close watch on An, the elders, and the children. We can put the children between us and have the younger men help An." Rusty was as worried about the trek over the mountain as Tao was, but he didn't want to telegraph his fear.

Tao stood as he spoke, "Okay Rusty. You lead."

Rusty began forming the group into single file, with the children behind him, and in front of Tao. He placed the four youngest men around An and her husband Wu, with Chow Yun at the rear of the column. Once the line was formed, he stepped out and began the walk up the mountainside. He turned around to check on the group and saw Mee Ling smiling her usual smile at him. He gently touched her on the head and continued his drive.

The trail, though well formed, was narrow and getting steeper and less manageable. The trail wound through trees at the lower level, but was now turning into more of a loose rock and gravel configuration, with fewer trees. Rusty looked back down the mountain and, in the limited moonlight, determined that they had climbed about three-quarters of the way up. The decision to make the climb at night was proving to be a mistake, but one that was too late to reverse.

Rusty's footing was getting looser at every step. He stopped the group and pulled the rope from around his neck. He tied the end off around his waist and passed the coil of rope behind him, instructing everyone to hold on tightly to the rope. Once the rope had made it to the last person, he slowly stepped out again.

Rusty continued to fight the increased grade of the trail, slipping

141

and falling to his knees time and again. The going had become extremely slow due to the grade and the pace that An and the older members were setting. They had taken at least a dozen breaks during the climb. Rusty looked at the luminous dial of his watch to find that they had been walking for five hours. It was now ten-thirty, and he began worrying about getting back down the mountain and across the valley before the sun came up the next morning.

Rusty looked ahead and saw the top of the pass, just fifty-yards away. He knew they had to stop for rest, because the muscles of his legs were burning. How much worse would it be for the others? As he took the last steps to the plateau he breathed a sigh of relief. The others finished the walk to the top and gathered around him in the three-hundred-square-foot area at the top of the pass.

He untied the rope from around his waist and stepped to the other side of the pass. The three-thousand-five-hundred-foot elevation provided a stunning view of the landscape below. He looked to the south to see the lights of Liaoyang on the other side of the valley below them and off to the west. Farther to the south, he saw what he surmised was Anshan, the place where they would cross over the road and river. He turned around to look north and was pleased to no longer see the lights of Mukden in the distance. The farther away from Mukden, the better, he said to himself.

As he turned back to look at the path down the mountain, his blood ran cold. The southern side of the mountain was steeper. The path followed the side of the mountain in an easterly direction. There would be no protection for them on their right side. He couldn't see the path farther than about two-hundred-yards, but assumed the remainder of the journey would be as perilous as the beginning. He walked back to the group to rest before the descent.

Chapter 16 - A Friend's Sacrifice

Rusty moved through the group of people hoping to encourage them with his smiles. He was satisfied to see that it was working so far, especially for the children. He stepped toward Tao and motioned with his head to follow him to the other side of the pass. Tao stopped next to Rusty and asked with a look of concern "What you need, Rusty?"

Rusty spoke softly to his friend. "Tao, look at the path below us."

Tao looked down the mountain to see the perilous path that lay before them. He slowly turned toward Rusty. "How we do this? Is dangerous Rusty."

"I know. It's too late to turn back now; we have to go down, but it's gonna be slow." Rusty placed his hand on his friend's shoulder. "We need to put an older person with each child, a stronger one next to a weaker one, and keep close to each other."

"Okay, Rusty, we go down slowly."

The two men walked back to the group and began placing them in the order they had discussed. Once they had the group staged, Tao began speaking to them in Chinese, telling them how dangerous the trip down the mountain was going to be. Looks of concern covered their faces as they heard the warning. Each of them began looking toward Rusty as Tao finished his instructions. Rusty smiled at them as he stepped through the group. He secured the rope around the waists of the strongest men throughout the line, ensuring an anchor should someone slip.

As he walked back to the head of the column of people, he stopped in front of An Zhao and her husband Wu. He looked caringly at the couple. "An, we need you to set the pace for us. Whatever you do, don't go too fast. We don't need the baby coming while we're on the trail. Please take it slow," he said with a smile.

An placed her hand on Rusty's arm. "Be fine, Rusty; we all be fine. You get us down mountain, all be okay."

Rusty smiled one last time at the couple and stepped to the front of the line. He loaded himself with his packs and pulled on his leather gloves. He slowly stepped out with each of the followers moving behind him in order, clinging tightly to the rope. The drop-off was to their right, and Rusty had placed the rope between them and the cliff's edge. Rusty knew his plan wasn't perfect, but it was what he would live with. The path was three-feet wide and appeared to be broad enough to negotiate, but consisted of loose rock. Rusty was finding it difficult to keep his footing. He found it easier to place his feet flat on the path, rather than a heel-to-toe approach. No matter what the method, it was still slow going for them.

Thirty minutes into the descent, Rusty held his hand up, signaling the members to stop. He looked at his watch and found the time to be ten to midnight. He looked out over the valley below to assess their progress. In the limited light, he determined they still had another three-thousand feet of elevation to negotiate.

He couldn't make out the condition of the path ahead for more than two hundred yards, but didn't see the condition improving. As Rusty turned to look behind him, he found the usual smiles to be gone. Everyone was holding tightly to the rope and looking to the path ahead of them, with the exception of Mee Ling. At a position of four people behind him, the young girl still had a look of confidence as she smiled back. Tao was in the middle of the line, with his unwavering calm face on display.

Rusty held his hand up and made his announcement. "Okay, move out slowly."

The group stepped out slowly as they began to move down the

mountain again. They had walked about three hundred yards when Rusty saw the path bending to the left to follow the line of a ravine in the mountain. The path was getting narrower the farther they ventured toward the depression and darker as it moved away from the moonlight. As he entered the limited light, Rusty found himself wishing they had taken the longer route around the mountain, even if it had exposed them.

They were barely moving now, as each step was cautiously made in the dark. Rusty looked across the depression, and sighed with relief to see a wider, less steep path in the moonlight. He smiled and turned around to check on the group. Just as his eyes fell on the group behind him, he saw Mee Ling stepping onto a pile of loose gravel beneath her feet. Every muscle in Rusty's body cried out as he saw her slip over the edge and fall away below into the night, screaming.

Rusty frantically freed himself from the rope, but before he could get free, Lao Pan was climbing down over the edge. Fear gripped Rusty by the throat. In a low voice he kept repeating his plea. "Oh, Lord, please, not Mee Ling! Lord, please, not this little girl." As Rusty was on his knees by the edge he heard Mee Ling cry out from below, "Help me, Uncle Rusty!"

Rusty reached into his pocket and scrambled to retrieve his flashlight, frantically removing the red lens from the bulb cover. As he turned the light on, he could see Mee Ling hanging from a ledge, forty-feet below. She was clinging to an outcropped rock, looking up toward him.

Lao Pan was quickly climbing down toward her. The forty-two-year-old man was moving as quickly as he could, understanding that Mee Ling couldn't hold on for long. Rusty passed the light to Tao, who had worked his way to the front to help, and quickly tied a loop in the end of the rope, preparing to lower it to Lao. "Hold tight, Mee Ling; we'll get you! Hold on tight, honey!"

"Hurry, Uncle Rusty!" the frightened voice called out from below.

Rusty looked down to see Lao Pan within five feet of her. The light illuminated the two, but disappeared beyond them into the darkness. When Lao Pan was within reach of her, he held tightly to a rock with his left hand and reached down to her with his right hand. His feet pressed against a ledge to his right. He frantically called out to Rusty, "Rusty, I see ledge below, shine light!"

Rusty moved the light to the left and saw a five-by-five-foot ledge below to the right of Mee Ling. She screamed as her left hand slipped free from the rock. Barely clinging to the rock with her right hand, Lao reached out and grabbed her right arm.

Rusty and Tao watched, neither breathing, as Lao swung her back and forth, trying to get enough momentum to drop her to the safety of the ledge. With all of his strength, he pulled her back to the right for a final swing. As Mee Ling swung toward the ledge, the rock gave way under Lao Pan's left hand. Everyone cried out in horror as Lao Pan disappeared into the darkness below. They could hear his terrified screams slowly fade as he plummeted to the valley floor below. Rusty shined the light to his left to see Mee Ling lying in a heap on the ledge. He cried out to her below, "Mee Ling, are you okay?"

The meek, groaning voice of the little girl drifted up from the ledge. "Uncle Rusty, come get me please. Hurry please!"

Rusty tore the bundles from his back and pulled the rope over his head and down around his back, with the knot in front of him. He looked to Tao as he spoke. "Get more men to hold onto the rope. I'll need you to pull me up when I get her." Without waiting for a response, he stepped over the ledge and began his climb down. Tao barked orders to the men in Chinese, while slowly feeding rope down for Rusty's descent.

Rusty tried to blot out Lao's horrific death as he climbed down toward Mee Ling. There would be time for mourning later; the task at hand was what he focused on for now. His steps were careful and calculated. He checked the integrity of each edge he placed his feet and hands on. Aided by the light from above, his descent was going quickly.

After a nail-biting fifteen minutes, Rusty reached the ledge and gathered Mee Ling into his arms. The sobbing girl held on tightly to him as she shivered uncontrollably. Rusty looked down at her as he swept the tears gently away from her face with his big hands. "It's okay, sweetie, you're safe now."

Rusty lifted her against his chest, placing her arms around his neck and over the rope. He looked back up and called out to Tao, "Okay, bring us up."

The ascent was rapid, aided by his foot placements, and Rusty quickly found himself back on the ledge with Mee Ling. Tao lifted her from the rope and hugged her tightly. Rusty sat on the ledge, catching his breath. Mee Ling got on her knees and hugged Rusty tightly around his neck. "I knew you would save me, Uncle Rusty. I love you."

Tears filled his eyes as the big man whispered. "I love you, too, honey."

This evening had been difficult for the followers. They had saved a treasured young life, but lost a valued friend. Rusty looked in vain at the darkness below him and closed his eyes.

Major Hung stood on the side of the road at the head of a ten truck caravan. The engines of the trucks hummed at idle awaiting the arrival of his men. The midnight cold was clearly visible from his breath. The ear warmers of his military hat were lowered, protecting him from the frigid night air as he slapped his arms around his chest trying to keep the blood flowing.

Hung had utilized a time-tested strategy for finding the believers. He'd determined their travel from the orphanage to be no more than twenty-five miles since their departure. He'd placed a hundred soldiers on the edge of Mukden, spread out over a ten mile area moving north. He then placed the same amount of soldiers in the City of Tieling, twenty-five miles north of Mukden, moving south. Major Hung was stopping every five miles, waiting to get reports from his men as they pushed from both the south and the north.

Major Hung disagreed with Colonel Li about the direction the people at the orphanage had taken. He was convinced they had moved south, but refused to disagree with his superior officer. Li believed the group would try to remain in the countryside and avoid capture. Hung knew the only way to escape the impending persecutions was to leave the country, and the quickest way out was by boat, probably via Yingkou or Dandong. In any event, he knew he would ultimately be going south for them once the search of the north didn't pan out. Colonel Li would insist.

A sergeant emerged from the tree line south of the road with two of his troops a hundred yards away. Major Hung threw down his cigarette and crushed out the smoke under his boot, waiting for the report from his subordinate. The remainder of his men would continue the march south until the army met in the middle, where they would be picked up by the trucks.

The sergeant stopped in front of Major Hung and saluted.

"Nothing to report, Major; there's no sign of them."

The Major returned the salute. "Very well, Sergeant; continue your push south."

The sergeant saluted and returned to his drive southward. Hung grumbled under his breath as he walked to the other side of the truck. "Only a fool would waste such time on this." There was only one saving grace for him in this fruitless effort; it delayed the capture of the believers he was starting to identify with. Killing his own countrymen for political purposes was weighing heavily on his conscience. "What evil has fallen on this country?" he said to himself.

As he stepped into the passenger's side of the lead truck he barked at the driver, "Move south to the next check point!" The driver acknowledged the order and started the truck moving.

The believers' journey to the bottom of the mountain was almost at an end. They were only five-hundred feet above the valley floor, and the path had widened considerably. Even the grade had lessened to a comfortable three percent. None of the believers had uttered a word since Lao Pan's death; the only sounds that could be heard were their feet in the gravel on the path. The death of their friend had struck them all silent. Lao Pan had been a trusted friend in the compound for many years. He'd never complained and had always been available for duties assigned by his trusted master, Tao Chung.

Rusty looked ahead to the valley beyond and guessed they had another seven to eight miles before they could set up camp for the day. As they reached the bottom, Rusty turned his head back to look at the mountain pass they had just negotiated and breathed a sigh of relief. He looked at his watch to see it was 3:30 am. He pulled out his canteen and took a long swig of water from the container. Now in the trees, Rusty pulled the compass from his pocket and checked his bearings. He adjusted his direction and continued his march.

The rope had been rolled back up when the path had widened and placed around his shoulder. The weight of his packs and the rope was beginning to take its toll on him, but he focused his attention on the task at hand. Nothing was going to deter him from this mission. He was going to get this group of people out of China if it was the last thing he did. Rusty's eyes shut tightly as the image of Lao Pan's fall kept replaying in his head. The senseless death of his friend had only strengthened his resolve.

Rusty was so focused on the direction they were headed that he nearly jumped when Tao placed a hand on his shoulder. "Rusty, need to rest. People tired."

Without looking to Tao, Rusty responded while continuing to walk, "We have to get to the other side of the valley before dawn."

Tao repeated his request. "Rusty, people tired, need to stop for rest."

Rusty stopped and spun around with a scowl on his face. At an elevated volume he protested Tao's request. "We have to get to the other side of this valley before dawn! I'm not going to be caught out in the open!"

"Rusty, please, need rest."

Rusty brought both his fists to chest level as he responded, "I will not fail these people!"

Tao looked concerned as he gently responded by placing his right palm on Rusty's chest. "Rusty, Lao's death not your fault." Rusty took in a quick breath, but before he could launch back, Tao applied more pressure to his chest and leaned in closer. He spoke softly, but with purpose. "Rusty, Lao was friend, we all sad he gone. But he save Mee Ling. Don't dishonor his death. Give him honor by remembering him. Be proud of his sacrifice." Tao patted his friend's chest as he turned and told the people to rest.

Rusty stood alone as he stared back at the group. He wanted to be angry, but couldn't; he knew Tao was right. He sat down and placed his arms on his knees as he watched the people sitting down to rest. Tao was right, but his ego wouldn't let him acknowledge it. He was learning a valuable lesson about life, from someone who had lived it far longer than he had.

The lead truck stopped at the side of the road, fifteen miles north of Mukden. As Major Hung exited the right side of the truck, he looked to see the soldiers emerging from the tree lines on both sides of the road. The push from both Mukden and Tieling had taken less than five hours for the soldiers, moving from both directions at a three-mile-per-hour march. Major Hung moved into the open field next to the road to meet with his sergeants.

The men began walking to the trucks to get warm inside the

covered beds as the sergeants walked to where Hung stood. Hung lit a cigarette and looked to the men. "Well, anything to report?"

Sergeant Chang spoke up first. "No, Sir, we saw nothing. We were spread out from the base of the mountain all the way to the other side of the valley across the river, and there was no sign that anyone had been travelling through the area."

Hung looked to Sergeant Hin. "And you?"

"Nothing, Sir. My men found a few small villages and checked them thoroughly, but no signs that anyone had travelled through them. If they came through here, they would have had to walk the top of the mountain or swim the river. Neither option is possible in the cold. Is it possible they could have gone west, Sir?"

Major Hung took a long drag from his cigarette and responded, "No, only a fool would go closer to the center of power. No, it's either north or south."

"We could check the area again, Sir, if you want," Sergeant Yuen offered.

"No, that won't be necessary." Hung rubbed the back of his neck with his open hand and looked to the north. "We'll check inside the city of Tieling, then report back to the Colonel."

The two sergeants responded in unison, "Yes, Sir," and turned to walk to the trucks.

Hung walked to the side of his truck and took one last drag from his cigarette before entering the cab. He spoke through the smoke exiting his lungs, "Insanity; absolute insanity."

Chapter 17 - The Noose Tightens

The group of believers stepped into a clearing at the base of the mountain ten miles east of Liaoyang. The five-hundred-square-foot opening sat against the mountain in a natural cove, protected on three sides. It was just after five a.m., and the sun was creeping over the mountains to the east. With fatigue biting at all his muscles, Rusty dropped the packs at his feet. Tao set his bundle next to Rusty and sat on the ground with his legs folded.

Rusty motioned for Chow Yun to come to him as he was untying his bundle. The young man stopped in front of Rusty and smiled. "Yun, we have the mountain on three sides of us here, so we'll only need one guard this time. Can you take the first watch?"

"Yes, Rusty, can take first time."

"Okay, stand watch for two hours, then I'll take over so you can get something to eat."

"Okey-dokey," Chow Yun replied as he turned and walked away.

Rusty sat with his back to his rucksack, picked up his second box of K-rations, and started to open it. He closed his eyes tightly as the image of Lao Pan falling into the darkness haunted him. He dropped the box between his legs and covered his face with his hands. Losing a member of the group weighed heavily on him, in spite of Tao's encouraging words.

Tao was sitting next to him, eating some of the rice from his pack and trying to give Rusty some space in his grief. Rusty took in a deep breath and went back to opening the box of food. With his head down, looking into the box of K-rats, he addressed his friend. "Did Lao have any family?"

"No, wife and sons dead," Tao responded.

Rusty wanted something, anything to ease the pain he was feeling; just one shred of humanity to understand this violent land. "How do you people do it? How do you live around so much pain, suffering, and loss?" Rusty asked.

"God's help," he replied.

Rusty turned toward his friend. "I'm not talking about Christians, Tao; I'm talking about the Chinese people. How can you tolerate the injustices heaped on you? Your own countrymen kill you by the bushel baskets full, and no one speaks out."

"Has always been that way, Rusty. Biggest stick has biggest voice. People have no voice."

"I've never seen such evil leveled toward such good and decent people. The Chinese people are treated like barnyard livestock; used for some leader's purpose, then thrown away."

Tao placed his hand on Rusty's shoulder. "Rusty, you come from free country, hard for you to see how Chinese live. You not able to take on pains of world. God only give you what you can do, no more. I know you sad about Lao Pan, but can't take all problems of world on shoulders. Can only do what are given. Lao Pan die with hope of freedom, you give that to him. Was God's plan he die. Accept God's plan Rusty, not take on all pain, too much for you."

Rusty pondered Tao's words as he finished opening the cans of food from his pack. He placed the crackers and condiments in his pocket and gathered the cans of food in his arms and stood up. As he was stepping away, he turned toward Tao and spoke. "None of that helps, Tao. Lao Pan died, and I was responsible for his safety." He turned back around and walked away to pass out the food from his box.

★ ★ ★

The streets surrounding the Consulate were quiet and appeared to be abandoned as Colonel Li's staff car approached the main gate. The truck that followed was filled with twenty of his troops, all armed with rifles. Colonel Li exited the passenger's side of the car as it stopped. He stood tall next to the car as the men exited the truck and formed up behind him.

Private Nick Sheridan was already on the phone to Captain Rivera. The voice on the other end bellowed out, "Rivera!"

"Captain, this is Private Sheridan. Colonel Li is here with twenty of his men. You better get out here, Sir!"

Rivera hung up the phone and called Judy Francis. "Hello?" Judy answered.

"Judy, this is Capt Rivera; we need the General out at the front gate immediately." Rivera didn't wait for a response. He was hanging the phone up and running out of his office. As he headed for the courtyard, he stopped in front of Walter Brown in the hall. "Brown, get all hands out at the front gate with their weapons. I want you on the roof checking the perimeter."

"Yes, Sir!" Brown shouted as he turned and ran for the squad bay.

Rivera burst through the courtyard door to find Sheridan standing in front of the main gate with his M-1 Garand at port arms. He slowed his pace as he approached, taking an assessment of the situation. As he stopped in front of the gate, he could hear the Marines filing out of the door behind him. They lined up behind him with their rifles at port arms.

Colonel Li smiled at Rivera as he looked around the courtyard. "I'm impressed Captain, but you're outclassed."

Rivera bit back his irritation, remaining professional as he responded. "Colonel, how may I help you?"

"I'm here with business for General Marsh."

"He's on his way out here, Colonel."

Li craned his neck looking around the courtyard. "I don't see Sergeant Harrigan, Captain; where is he?"

"He's inside guarding the building, Colonel," Rivera quickly responded.

"Too bad. I enjoy seeing him keep Corporal Brown's foot out of his mouth," Li stated with a smile.

"So do I, Colonel," Rivera responded with a frown.

General Marsh stopped in front of the gate and addressed Colonel Li. "Colonel, how may we help you?" Marsh said with his arms folded.

"General, you're being charged with espionage. We're here to confiscate your radio and all related equipment. You will accompany me to the office of General Lin Piao, where you'll be prepared for trial."

Anger flooded over General Marsh as he responded, "You're insane, Colonel. I won't respond to your trumped up charges, and I will *not* give up our radio, under any circumstances."

"General, your facility is involved in the crime of espionage, and you *will* turn over your radio immediately, or we'll take it."

The General was becoming angrier by the minute. "You've had us confined to this compound for months now. We haven't had the opportunity for espionage, even if we wanted to. Lastly, this is sovereign United States territory. You will not enter these grounds under any circumstances. Do I make myself clear, Colonel?"

"As you wish, General." Li turned and waved his hand toward his men. As he did, the Chinese soldiers brought their weapons to the ready.

Rivera shouted to his men as he kept his focus forward. "At the ready!" The thump was heard all around the compound as every Marine put their left foot forward, pointing their weapons out in front of them with the barrels elevated. Rivera pulled his .45 from its holster, chambered a round, and held it to his side, pointed at the ground. "Colonel Li, no matter what happens next, I can guarantee you that the first round fired will enter your skull," Rivera stated emphatically.

Colonel Li looked to the top of the building to see Corporal Brown aiming a rifle at him.

Marsh stepped toward the gate and spoke to Li. "Colonel, you may have us confined to these grounds against our will; there's nothing we can do about that. But I can also guarantee you something - if any U S citizen dies as a result of your actions, the United States will level this city. You can either leave here or seal your fate, the choice is yours."

Li scowled at the men on the other side of the fence. He'd gambled on bluffing the Americans into giving up their radio. His superiors believed the Americans would give in when confronted. Li had known better because of his many years in the United States. He knew they would never cave, but he hadn't planned on being dressed down. He straightened his spine and responded, "Have it your way, General Marsh. Just remember, you brought this on yourself." Li waved his hand in the air and stepped to his car. His men entered the truck and the two vehicles drove from the front of the Consulate.

General Marsh turned to face Captain Rivera. "Well, it looks like things are going to get tough around here. Can we increase the guard around the Consulate?"

"No problem, Sir, consider it done," Rivera responded.

"Thank you, Joe," Marsh replied as he turned and walked back to the inside of the building.

Rivera looked toward the Marines. "I need you all to be in the courtyard until we're sure they won't try to come inside. I'll get a duty roster posted shortly and get you all relieved as soon as I can. Until then, keep your eyes peeled."

"Yes, Sir," the men responded in unison.

He stood around his Marines, looking at them with a smile. "I'm proud of every one of you. You did well." Rivera stepped away from the men and waved toward Walt, indicating he wanted him down from the roof. Walter waved back and started down the stairs. Walter met Rivera at the bottom of the stairs with his weapon at port arms. "Yes, Sir."

"Brown, I need you to make up a duty roster. I want three men on guard at all times, two in the yard and one on the roof. Put someone on the roof until you get a schedule made up. No one enters this compound without the expressed permission of the Consular General, understood?"

"Yes, Sir," Walter responded.

Before walking away, he slapped Walter on the shoulder. "You did well, Brown." Rivera turned and walked toward General Marsh's office. Walter stood in the hallway with a confused look. He'd never seen the "Old Man" so friendly. "I'll be damned," He said as he turned to walk to the duty hut.

Captain Rivera walked to the radio room and stepped inside. The General had just finished his radio transmission to the staff in Japan. Marsh looked at Rivera and raised his eyebrows. "Well, we're on our own for awhile. They're going to contact Washington and let us know."

"What can they do?" Rivera asked.

"Not much without putting teeth into it." Marsh rubbed the back of his neck with his right hand. "They'll lodge a protest, and Mao will tell them to 'sit on it.' I think we'll ultimately get out of here once Mao has sucked all the political energy he can out of the situation. Until then, we'll have to hunker down and tighten our belts. Looks like the rationing program you put in place a while back is going to pay off, Joe," Marsh said, while patting Rivera on the back. "How long can we hold out?"

Rivera shot back with his usual efficiency. "Three months tops, Sir, without the Chinese allowing us to resupply."

Marsh took a deep breath and exhaled before responding. "Joe, you know that Li will be back, right? His ego won't let him get past the hurt you just put on him."

"We'll be ready for him, Sir," Rivera responded.

"I know, Joe; I just hope we can hold him off until Washington makes a decision."

Rivera tilted his head with a skeptical look. "Washington make a decision, Sir? My eighty-year-old grandmother has a better chance of getting pregnant than those clowns do making a decision."

Marsh smiled as he responded, "You're right about that. So what do we do until then?"

"Play the waiting game, General."

"Well then." Marsh slapped his hands together and rubbed them vigorously with a huge smile. "Let's warm up the cribbage board." Both men laughed as they walked from the radio room.

★ ★ ★

156

"Mr. Brown, how bad did it get at the Consulate?"

Walter rubbed the back of his neck as he responded, "It got pretty bad, Bobby; we went on a tighter schedule of rationing and geared up for a conflict. The Chinese cut off our electricity and water, so things got a little dicey for a while. The Consular General was worried about the situation, but felt they would just saber rattle, then let us go. Rivera, on the other hand, just knew the Chinese were going to come over the wall at any moment.

"The American government ordered the consulate closed and called for the withdrawal of the people stationed there. Marsh was unable to do this because of the charges of espionage. With the crisis worsening, President Harry S. Truman called upon American allies to withhold recognition of Mao Zedong's People's Liberation Army (PLA).

"In November 1949, Marsh was ultimately brought to trial, and the American public's anger was on the verge of explosive. President Truman was under severe attack for losing China to the Communists, so he couldn't afford to show weakness in the face of the Chinese Communists.

"We learned later that President Truman had met with his military advisors to discuss the feasibility of a rescue operation. Washington showed great restraint because it was still looking for opportunities for reaching an accommodation with the People's Republic of China (PRC).

"Secretary of State, Dean Acheson, conveyed the message to Beijing that the US wouldn't recognize the new Chinese government until all the Americans at Mukden was released. On November 24, 1949, Marsh, along with the rest of us, was charged with inciting-to-riot and ordered to be deported. We finally left China in December 1949.

"The whole thing lasted almost a year, by which time the already fragile US relations with the Chinese Communists had been damaged virtually beyond repair. Any possibilities that might have existed for US recognition of the PRC became remote. In retrospect, the whole incident was the beginning of the confrontation between the United States and the People's Republic of China that lasted until President Nixon finally normalized relations in 1972."

"Wow! That must have been pretty intense. So, then, you all got out of China, huh?"

Walter smirked as he responded. "No, Bobby, we all stayed in China until we died."

Bobby smiled as he realized what he'd said. He turned serious as he asked his next question. "Mr. Brown, would you have shot Colonel Li that day at the Consulate?"

Walter's lips pursed. "In a New York second, Bobby."

Bobby raised his arms in the air. "You should have. He killed your friends."

Walter leaned in toward Bobby as he responded. "Did you not learn anything from our discussion about the man who hit your brother?"

"That's different!" Bobby shot back. "Colonel Li was a bloodthirsty killer; the man who hit Eric did it by accident!"

Walter smiled at Bobby as he stared into his eyes. Realization dawned on Bobby's face. He sat back in his chair contemplating his words, silent. His blank stare said all that Walter needed to know. "Tough thing to realize that you've been wrong, isn't it?"

Bobby's head dipped down as he responded, "Yes, Sir," he replied. "But Colonel Li would have killed you all, right?"

"Different set of circumstances, Bobby. If he would have had his men fire, then we would have responded."

"But you'd still be dead."

Walter put a smile on his lips. "But he'd have been the first one down. That being said, I would have been defending the lives of my fellow Marines and the Consulate staff, not committing murder. Whole different set of circumstances, Bobby."

Bobby leaned back in his chair, processing what his newfound mentor had just told him.

Colonel Li burst through the door to his office and slammed his valise down on his desk. The morning at the Consulate had proven less than productive and had turned into a complete embarrassment for him. As he removed his coat, he heard a knock on the door.

"Enter!"

Major Hung stepped inside the office and closed the door behind him. He stood at attention, waiting for the Colonel to acknowledge him.

"Ah, Major Hung; I hope you have good news for me about the Christians."

Major Hung took his hat off and responded to his superior. "I'm afraid not, Colonel. We covered every square foot of ground between here and Tieling. The Christians were nowhere to be found, Sir."

Li sat behind his desk and lit a cigarette. He took a long draw from the smoke and exhaled as he spoke. "Even in the valley west of the road?"

"Yes, Sir, we were spread out over a ten-mile-wide area and saw nothing. Not even a shoe print was found."

Li rolled the end of his cigarette in the ashtray. "And you still think they could have gone south?"

"Yes, Sir, the southern route is still the easiest to negotiate, and there are only two possible destinations, Yingkou or Dandong."

Li motioned for Major Hung to sit. "But they would run up against the sea at either place, and they're not likely to get on a boat at either."

Major Hung sat in the chair as he responded. "I don't think they've thought that through enough, Colonel. They would know that if they go north, they'll wind up in the Soviet Union or Mongolia. Stalin would turn them back over to us if they went there, and the journey to Mongolia is both too far and too dangerous. And as you mentioned before, the terrain to the east is virtually impossible to traverse, and going west toward Beijing just gets them closer to being captured. No, Sir, I still think they went south."

Li stood from his desk and walked to the window looking out over the street. He stood, pulling at his chin as he thought about his dilemma. He took a drag from his cigarette and turned back to Major Hung. "Okay, Major, get some men moving down toward Yingkou and Dandong. Start them moving through the countryside toward both destinations. When you're done making your push, leave a detachment in both places."

"Yes, Sir."

Li sat back down at his desk. "Make sure it's done by tomorrow morning before you return; we have a job to do at the American Consulate."

Hung's brow furrowed. "Is there something wrong, Colonel?"

Li took a long drag from the cigarette before crushing it out in the ashtray. "We have to arrest the American Consular General."

"I don't understand, Sir; why do we need to arrest him?" Hung asked.

"Beijing wants him tried for espionage."

"But, Sir, Espionage? That doesn't make any sense; they've been confined to the Consulate," Hung questioned.

"I suspect the Chairman wants to embarrass the United States. Either way, we need to pick him up tomorrow. I went there this morning to retrieve him, but the Marines were prepared to defend him. Tomorrow morning we'll put a hundred men around the compound and take him by force if necessary. I'll need you here at five a.m., Major."

"I'll be here, Sir."

Chapter 18 - The Enemy Closes

Rusty looked up to the sky to see the sun falling behind the mountain. He rolled his wrist over to look at the dial on his watch, ten minutes to six. He glanced around the camp and saw everyone putting their belongings into their sacks. He stood tall and arched his back, trying to get rid of the nagging pain in his back that came from sleeping on the ground. He found himself missing his bed at the Consulate, uncomfortable as it was.

Rusty removed his coat and pulled his shirt down over his left arm, looking at his wound. Lowering the bandage away from the wound, he was surprised to see that it was almost healed. Tao appeared next to him and wrapped his hands around Rusty's left bicep. "Look good, Rusty. Be okay soon," Tao said, placing the bandage back over the wound.

Rusty smiled at his friend. "I'll say. You continue to amaze me, Master. Where did you learn how to dress wounds?"

"From family. Old family secret, Rusty," Tao said with a smile.

"I know a couple of Corpsmen who would like to meet you," Rusty said with a laugh.

161

As he was putting his coat on, Ho Chen ran into the camp and hurried toward Rusty. Clearly excited, he spoke in as low a voice as possible. "Rusty, men coming!"

"How many?"

Out of breath, Ho replied "Ten, maybe twelve, coming from north."

Rusty turned to Tao. "Get everyone to the back of the clearing against the mountain, and keep them quiet!" he ordered. He motioned for Ho to come with him.

Rusty and Ho crouched down and moved quietly toward the edge of the clearing. They lowered themselves to the ground as they saw the men moving toward them. Rusty could see they were soldiers, and counted ten of them as they approached the believers' position. They were spread out, with about a hundred yards between them.

Although the sun was down over the horizon, there was still enough light to make an escape impossible if they were discovered. He calculated the soldiers were about half a mile away.

Rusty's worst fear had been confirmed; the Chinese Army had been to the orphanage and discovered they were missing. This surely wasn't a routine patrol. The soldiers appeared to be moving to the right of their position, probably to hug the side of the mountain with their left flank. Rusty motioned to Ho to move back to the camp.

The two men stepped slowly backwards into the cover of the trees. Once they were back in the camp, Rusty found the entire group huddled against the mountain in the back of the cove. He and Ho moved back next to the group and dropped to their knees, waiting for the soldiers to approach.

He looked to the children and held a finger to his lips, motioning for them to stay silent. They nodded, acknowledging his request. Rusty pulled his .45 from its holster and brought it out in front of him. Tao placed his hand on Rusty's arm and shook his head in the negative. Tao whispered in Chinese to the men surrounding him. They all pulled their bows out in front of them and knocked an arrow in the string, waiting for the impending threat.

Rusty couldn't see through the trees to tell how close the men were, but strained his ears to hear any sounds coming from beyond the tree line. He knew there had to be more than the ten men; they wouldn't send so few soldiers to look for them. There were certainly more soldiers than a man with a pistol and four men with bows could handle. His mind was racing, trying to formulate a plan.

He could hear men talking in the distance and guessed they were about fifty yards away. As he listened to the conversation, it appeared as though they were turning toward the west. He needed to get a look to confirm his suspicions.

Rusty slowly inched forward on his hands and knees toward the tree line. As he approached the clearing, he could see that the men had turned right toward Liaoyang. He slowly stood and breathed a sigh of relief.

Just as he started to turn around to walk back into the camp, he heard the sound of footsteps to his right. He slowly moved his head around the tree to see a Chinese soldier approaching him from twenty yards away.

Ho Chen rubbed his left thigh, trying to relieve the cramp that had set in. The pain was increasing as he pressed on the muscle hard. With little relief, Ho tried to move quietly and stretch his leg out. As he extended his leg, his foot slipped and scraped across the ground, rustling the leaves loudly.

The Chinese soldier stopped, turned, and listened carefully to locate where the sound had come from. He began to slowly move toward Rusty's position with his rifle at the ready, inching his way closer. Rusty holstered his weapon and pulled his K-bar from its sheath, holding it tightly in his right hand against his chest.

Hidden behind the tree, Rusty listened for the man's footsteps, gripping his knife tighter. Slowly, the soldier moved closer and closer to Rusty's position. When the man was ten yards from Rusty, a brown-eared pheasant was flushed from its resting place and fluttered away. The startled soldier let out a quick breath and laughed, relaxing. He turned and walked away, moving west to rejoin his group.

Rusty peered around the tree and saw the man retreating. When the soldier was far enough away, Rusty let out a deep breath; he'd been unconsciously holding it the entire time. He relaxed and put the knife back into its sheath. Rusty waited until the man was out of sight, then walked back into the camp. As he approached the group, Ho bowed in front of him. "Very sorry, Rusty."

Rusty patted his friend on the shoulder as he walked past him.

"That's okay, Ho, he's gone now." He stepped toward Tao and picked his coat up from the ground. "They're walking toward Liaoyang," Rusty spoke quickly as he put his coat on. "I'll take Ho with me and follow them. I need you to follow us, far enough behind with the group so you're not heard. I'll send Ho back to warn you if they stop." Rusty put the rest of his packs on as he continued. "Give us a twenty minute head start, then follow, staying close to the tree line. Tell everyone to be as quiet as possible, okay?"

Tao didn't say a word; he merely nodded in agreement as Rusty stepped away. Rusty turned toward Ho. "Come with me, Ho; we need to get in close to the soldiers and see if we can determine where they're going."

"Yes, Rusty," Ho responded.

The two men quickly moved out from the camp to follow the soldiers before they got too far ahead.

Walter Brown was sitting at a table in the kitchen of the consulate drinking a cup of coffee. He had both his hands wrapped around the cup as he stared into it. His emotions were getting the better of him as he thought about his friend and mentor.

Rusty had taken the same oath as he had when joining the Marine Corps. He couldn't understand why his friend had left the Consulate, especially during such difficult times. In his heart he knew that Rusty had done the noble thing, but he couldn't understand why he hadn't done the right thing.

His agnostic upbringing couldn't contemplate such a selfless act, performed solely for religious reasons, especially for people who weren't even his countrymen. His mood had changed since Rusty left, and not for the better. Even though he was struggling with his friend's absence, he found himself wishing he'd gone with him to help. Rusty's departure was eating at him like a cancer.

Captain Rivera walked into the kitchen and over to the cupboard. He removed a cup and placed a spoon of instant coffee into it, then filled it with hot water from the kettle. Rivera turned and stepped to the table, taking a seat across from Walter.

He took a sip of the coffee and groaned as the liquid hit his tongue. "Yuck!" he said loudly with his nose turned up. "Powdered eggs, powdered milk, and instant coffee, don't know if I'll be able to survive this."

Walter knew that Rivera was making small talk and probably had larger issues on his mind. Still stinging from his 'dressing down,' Walter mumbled in a low voice, "It's not so bad, Sir. Could be worse."

Rivera looked at Walter, who had his head down looking into his coffee cup. "Yeah, we could be in the Navy, huh?"

Walter smiled in spite of himself, while still looking down. Rivera reached into his pocket and pulled out a folded piece of paper. He unfolded the document and placed it on the table. Sliding the paper across to Walter he tapped it with his index finger.

Walter looked at the paper, then up at Rivera. "What's this, Sir?"

"It's the order making you a sergeant, Corporal."

"I don't understand, Sir. Why me?"

"It's a field promotion, Brown. I need a sergeant, and you're the obvious choice. We'll make the order official once we get to Japan. You've done an exceptional job keeping the men on their toes, and you have the confidence of everyone here. The men respect you, and I trust you."

"You trust me, Sir? I mean, I thought you, well-"

"Look, Brown, there's no getting around it, I was pissed when Harrigan left and I took it out on you." Rivera held his hand out toward Walter, palm out. "This isn't an apology; just an explanation. I respect what you did. You didn't rat out a shipmate; you stuck by your guns. I know he told you where he was going, and it's no secret he's trying to get those people out of the country, but you stood firm by your friend." Walter looked at his commanding officer with a blank stare. "You don't need to respond, Brown. I'm just letting you know its okay."

With a curious look, Walter responded to Rivera, "Thank you, Sir."

Rivera held his hand out toward Walter. "Congratulations, Sergeant." Walter shook his hand firmly and folded the paper back up, placing it into his pocket. "You're gonna have to take the stripes off Harrigan's uniforms. I'm fresh out," Rivera said with a smile.

"Thank you, Sir." Walter looked back down at his coffee before

speaking. "If he *was* trying to get those people out of the country-"
He looked back up at Rivera with a smile, "what would his chances
be?"

Rivera pulled a cigarette from his pocket and set fire to it with his
Zippo. "Not very good," he said while blowing a cloud of smoke out.
"The Chinese won't stop until they get him. That would be a major
political victory for them. They'll put him in a Chinese prison for
very, very long time." Rivera could tell from the look on Walter's face
that he had poured cold water on any hope of him seeing his friend
again. He sat up erect. "But, hey, Harrigan's a resourceful guy, right?
He may just pull it off."

Walter smiled back at him. "Yeah, he is. And if he did run into the
Chinese Army, I'd bet he'd come out on the best end of it. I'd hate to
have him mad at me," Walter said with a smile.

Rivera stood from the table and took the last swig from his coffee
cup. "You're right about that, Brown."

As Rivera walked from the kitchen, Walter smiled and murmured
to himself, "Well, I'll be damned. He's human after all."

Tao mentally calculated that Rusty and Ho had been gone about
twenty minutes. He gathered the believers around him and told them
to be quiet during their journey, as the Army was moving in the same
direction they were and wasn't far. He placed the children in the rear
of the column of people with the older members and brought the
young men, armed with their bows, to the front. They all set out,
moving slowly along the base of the mountain toward Liaoyang.

Rusty and Ho walked as softly as they could, staying as close to
the tree line as possible. Neither man spoke as they made their way.
The Chinese soldiers weren't visible in the distance, even with the
moonlight, but Rusty calculated that they were, at maximum, a mile
ahead.

The evenings were getting colder, and Rusty worried that snow
was on the way, not to mention his concern over a pregnant An Zhao.
If An had her baby during the journey, it would set them back days.
There was no end to the worry that consumed Rusty. He stopped in
his tracks and closed his eyes tightly trying to rid his mind of the
thoughts that washed over him.

Ho stopped and looked at his friend, worried. "You okay, Rusty?"

he whispered softly.

Rusty opened his eyes and whispered back to Ho with a smile, "I'm fine, just tired."

Ho knew that his friend was troubled about the journey, especially since the death of Lao Pan. Ho worried about the big man, but felt powerless to help him.

The lights from the city of Liaoyang were less than five miles away and illuminated the skyline. Even the mountain that had been the sentinel on their left was fading as it slowly came down to the valley floor, the closer it got to the city. The main road had to be close to them, Rusty thought, but none of that mattered as long as their path was blocked by the soldiers ahead.

As they heard voices in the distance ahead, the two men froze in their tracks. They moved to their left quickly to the cover of the trees. Not sure how far away they were from the voices, they made their way slowly ahead, toward them. Rusty thought they were close, but couldn't see anything. He inched forward as Ho followed behind.

The voices were becoming louder as the two men moved forward, so he knew the soldiers were stationary. He and Ho dropped to the ground and crawled toward the voices. Still in the cover of the tree line, they stopped as they saw the headlights of several trucks stopped on the side of the main road. Lying on their bellies, the two men listened to the conversation twenty yards in front of them. Rusty whispered to Ho, "What are they saying?"

"Officer asking men if they found anything. Men say they not see anyone and no signs of people traveling." Ho paused as he listened further. "The officer say the men to go to Yingkou and wait for Christians from orphanage. Rusty, they know we gone."

Rusty looked at the group of soldiers and counted at least fifty men. "How could they know where we were going?" His mind was racing with possibilities. Did they know he'd snuck out of the Consulate? Did they know he was the one who took the people from the orphanage? How did they know Yingkou was their destination? His mind was swimming in speculation. He leaned in toward Ho to listen for more information.

"Officer say he going back to Mukden, and men should take trucks to Yingkou," Ho whispered.

167

Major Hung suddenly stopped speaking and slowly turned his head toward where Rusty and Ho were hiding. It appeared as though he was looking directly at them. His eyes bore a hole into the trees as he listened. Rusty and Ho didn't move as they looked back toward him, certain he'd heard them. After several minutes, Major Hung slowly turned his head back toward his men and finished his conversation.

Ho nervously whispered, "He know we here, Rusty."

Rusty tried to reassure his friend. "No, Ho, he didn't see us; maybe he thought he heard something. We're okay." Rusty thought Hung had seen them as well, but didn't want to alarm Ho. His focus returned to the conversation. "What did he just say?"

"He say people from orphanage not to be killed. Men are to tell him when they get Christians and wait for him."

They watched as Major Hung got into the nearest truck, which looked to be headed back toward Mukden. The rest of the men got into the remaining three trucks and drove to the south. Rusty stood and watched them until they were out of sight. He breathed a sigh of relief. "Go back and get the rest and bring them here. I'll wait to see if there are anymore soldiers."

Still nervous from the encounter, Ho quickly moved out toward the believers. Rusty stood guard at the base of the hill, using the time to compose himself. He lifted his canteen to his lips and took a drink from the container as his eyes panned the horizon.

Riding in the passenger's side of the truck, Major Hung had that burning in his stomach every soldier gets when they know someone has been watching them. His military instincts were kicking in, and he couldn't get rid of the feeling. Had someone been looking at him, or was it just his senses on overdrive? Shaking his head in protest, he decided to file the incident away in the back of his mind. He took in a deep breath and slowly let it out as he settled in for the ride back to headquarters.

Chapter 19 - When Leadership Counts

Rusty pulled the compass from his pocket and checked his bearings, surveying the ground before him. They were on the outskirts of Liaoyang, about twenty miles north of Anshan. He pulled the map and flashlight from his pack and knelt to the ground to study them.

After placing the red lens on the flashlight, he got as close to the ground as possible and removed his coat, placing it over his head to avoid anyone seeing the light. The map showed low hills to the east of Anshan and a clear path to Haicheng. Since hearing Major Hung's conversation, he preferred to stay close to the hills where more ample tree cover would be available for their encampments during the day. He didn't want to take any unnecessary chances.

He pulled a pencil from his shirt pocket and traced a new path for them. After turning the light off, he stood, placing the light and map back into his pack.

Rusty's mind was abuzz with different strategies as to how to deal with their ultimate arrival into Yingkou. The new path he'd laid out would keep them farther from the larger cities, but time was running out for them. He had An Zhao to worry about.

169

His ultimate worry, however, had always been how to get through the large city of Yingkou without being detected. He knew his nationality, size, and the way he was dressed would make him stick out like a sore thumb. "Worry about that when the time comes, Harrigan," He whispered to himself.

Rusty turned to see the group of followers approaching him from the rear. Tao and Ho were in the front of the group and were moving slower than usual due to the earlier encounter. Tao smiled as he saw Rusty. He quickly moved toward him to be away from the others. He put his arm around Rusty's shoulder and moved him away from the group. "Rusty, Ho say army know we gone. They looking for us!"

"I know, Master; we knew at some point they would find out that we were gone. This doesn't change anything; we still have a solid plan." He wasn't going to let Tao know he was deeply concerned about their safety. He needed to display as much strength as he could muster up to keep the group calm.

"Rusty, Ho say they wait for us in Yingkou. How we get through?" Tao replied.

Placing his hand on Tao's shoulder, he responded, "It'll be fine, Tao, we'll make it through this, you have my word. Now let's get them moving. We have to get past Anshan before morning."

"Okay, Rusty," Tao responded with a worried look.

The group of followers set out headed south toward the City of Anshan. As Rusty turned to look back, he saw the beaming smile of Mee Ling looking back at him. It was one of the few things that kept him going.

 ★ ★ ★

The early morning hours at the Consulate had taken a different tone since the confinement. The staff moved slower and with less purpose than before. The hope of leaving their imprisonment was slowly evaporating as the days ground on. General Marsh knew their situation was dire and tried every day to rally the people at the Consulate, but his efforts were waning the longer the confinement went on. The daily cribbage and bridge games were about the only thing keeping the staff sane.

The Consulate had been without electricity and water for a long time. While they had plenty of food for now, they had been reduced to using candles for light. Taking a bath had been one of the earliest

170

casualties of the confinement, and the bitter cold had forced them to layer more and more clothing on their bodies as the Chinese did, to combat the cold.

The United States was in no mood to enter another conflict so soon after World War II and appeared on the surface to be powerless in the face of the Chinese Communists. Mao Tse-tung was riding high on his newly found power.

Sergeant Walter Brown knocked on Captain Rivera's door. A more subdued response than normal came from the other side. "Enter." Walter opened the door to see his superior officer sitting back in the chair with his feet on the desk reading his morning briefs. He looked up to see Walter. "Oh, Brown. Come on in" he said while putting his feet back on the floor. "What can I do for you?"

Walter stood at attention as he responded, "Sir, I reworked the-"

"Brown, sit down, please," Rivera said while gesturing to the chair in front of his desk.

Walter sat in the chair and continued. "I reworked the figures on the food and water rations, and I think we can squeeze another ten days out of the rations, Sir."

"Really? How did you do that?" Rivera said with skepticism.

"I was talking with Private Wade, and he said we could combine some ingredients from the K-rats with some of our stores and stretch them out."

"How would he know that?" Rivera asked.

"His father owns a restaurant in St. Louis, Sir."

Rivera put a smile on his face. "Well, I'll be damned." He sat up. "You just learned the third rule of leadership, Brown. 'Listen to the men under you.'"

"What's the first and second rule, Sir?" Walter asked.

"Rule number one, 'The Old Man is always right.' Rule number two, 'In the event of the impossible hypothesis that the Old Man could be wrong, refer back to rule number one.'"

Walter smiled as he looked back at Rivera. "Yes, Sir," he responded.

"I'm pleased with the work you've done, Brown. The men are

responding to you because they respect you. Good work, and tell Wade I said job well done."

"I will, Sir. One other thing, Captain, if we-" Brown stopped as the telephone rang.

Rivera picked up the receiver. "Rivera."

The voice on the other end was Private Butcher. "Sir, three trucks are pulling up in front of the Consulate, Sir. It looks like Colonel Li."

"Understood!" Rivera responded as he slammed the receiver down and stood. "Get on the roof with a weapon, Brown. The Chinese are back."

"Yes, Sir!" Walter replied as he turned and ran out of the office.

Rivera grabbed the belt with his .45 and ran from the office. As he passed Gary Parker, the Consular General's assistant, he barked out his command. "Tell the General that Col Li is back." Without waiting for a response, Rivera hurried toward the exterior door. He was buckling the belt around his waist as he exited the building into the courtyard. Once outside, he looked up to the roof to see Sergeant Brown holding his weapon at port arms. The remainder of the Marines formed up behind Private Butcher. As he approached them, he could see Colonel Li walking to the gate.

Colonel Li had his hands in the pockets of his coat, with his collar turned up around his neck. He smiled broadly as Rivera stopped in front of the gate. "Captain, I'm impressed to see the response time."

Rivera stood at parade rest, with his hands behind his back. "Colonel, what do you want this time? You're beginning to become a bother."

"Captain, we're here to arrest General Marsh. I trust you won't resist again."

Rivera looked beyond to see five trucks parked in front of the gate. He estimated that the Chinese had approximately one hundred soldiers surrounding the Consulate. It was clear that Colonel Li meant to take the General this time.

"You tried that once before, Colonel. As I recall, you weren't that successful." Rivera looked to see Major Hung walk up.

"As you can see, this time I came prepared," Li replied, nodding to the right toward Major Hung.

General Marsh stopped next to Captain Rivera and looked directly at Col Li. "Colonel, why must you persist on bothering us? We remain behind these walls virtually prisoners on our own property, yet you continue to harass us for your own amusement. Why don't you just leave us alone, Colonel?"

Colonel Li stepped up next to the gate as he responded. "General Marsh, we have over a hundred soldiers surrounding the Consulate. If you look on the roofs surrounding us, you'll see rifles aimed at all of you, to include the Marine on the roof. We're here to arrest you for the charge of espionage and inciting a riot. You will come with us now."

General Marsh stepped in front of Captain Rivera and stopped at the gate, just inches from Colonel Li. "Colonel, you know these charges are bogus. No one would be happier to leave this country than me, but we remain here because of your actions. The only reason you continue to harass us is for political gain."

"You remain because of the crimes you have committed. That *is* the issue, nothing else. Now, you will come with us, or we will take you by force."

General Marsh shot back at Li. "You can't do that, Colonel; this is sovereign United States territory."

Colonel Li leaned in closer toward Marsh. "This is China, General, not the United States. You *will* come with us, or the blood of your subordinates will be on your head. I quote one of your past presidents, 'Walk softly and carry a big stick.' We have the bigger stick, General, and this is your last chance to comply." Li snapped his fingers, and the soldiers aimed their rifles toward the General and the Marines behind the gate. "Choose your next words carefully, General. They may just be your last."

Captain Rivera quickly brought the Marines to the ready in response. General Marsh whipped around holding the palm of his right hand up toward Rivera, shaking his head in the negative. He turned back around toward Colonel Li. "Colonel, you wouldn't dare attack this facility!"

Colonel Li raised his right hand, readying his men. "Yes, I would. The decision is yours. Last warning, General."

General Marsh set his jaw, his eyes boring a hole in Li's head as he made his decision. He knew that an exchange of gunfire in the courtyard of the Consulate would solve nothing and only exacerbate the position the United States was in with the Chinese government. He opted for the diplomatic position. "Captain Rivera, please step forward."

Rivera stepped next to the General and responded, "Yes, Sir."

"Captain, I'm going with Colonel Li."

"Sir, you can't-"

Marsh's head snapped toward Rivera. "The decision has been made, Captain. I'm going with them. Please tell Mr. Parker that he is in charge now, and watch out for my wife, please. I'll be back as soon as this nonsense is resolved." Marsh placed his hand on Rivera's shoulder and smiled at him. "Besides, one less mouth to feed, right? It'll be fine, Joe. Take care of everyone while I'm gone."

"I will, Sir." Rivera replied.

Marsh opened the gate and stepped toward Colonel Li. Rivera, and the other Marines watched as Marsh was placed in the staff car with the Colonel. Rivera turned around and faced his men as the car drove away. He took in a deep breath and exhaled slowly. "Dismissed," he ordered as he walked away from the men. He was furious, but complied with the orders of the General. He fought the urge to slam the door as he entered the building.

As he passed the stairwell, he saw Walter standing at the bottom waiting for him. Holding his weapon at port arms, Walter looked at his superior with a questioning face. "Why did he leave, Sir?"

"He didn't have a choice, Brown. He knew eventually that he'd have to go."

Walt looked at Rivera with pleading eyes. "But, Sir, we could have stopped them."

"We have civilians here, Sergeant; he didn't want them to suffer," Rivera replied.

"But without the General here, they'll just come in and take the rest of us."

"General Marsh knew they ultimately wanted *him*. His hope was that they would leave the rest of us alone. He's the 'big fish' they always wanted. They'll leave us alone now, Brown," Rivera concluded.

"I sure hope so, Sir."

Rivera pulled the pack of cigarettes out of his breast pocket and reached inside for a smoke. After finding it empty, he crushed it in his hand. "Well, that's the end of that. Sure could use a stick of Beeman's gum from Harrigan right now." He smiled at Walter. "Oh, by the way, Brown, what was the other thing you wanted to talk to me about before?"

Walter put a smirk on his face. "I was going to talk to you about what would happen if the Chinese came back, Sir."

Rivera turned and walked away as he replied, "Guess that's not an issue now."

As the sun crept up over the horizon, the group of believers settled in a grove of trees two miles north of Anshan. They had made good time during the night, in spite of the reduced pace they were now traveling, caused by the Chinese Army.

Rusty pulled one of the three remaining K-rats from his pack and began opening it. As usual, he pulled the bags of condiments from the pack and placed them into his pockets. He stepped toward An and Wu, handing them one of the opened cans of meat. Wu stood and bowed toward him with his usual smile. Rusty looked down at An to see her weaving strands of hair together as she sat against a tree. The pieces of hair were ten inches in length and jet black in color. She was focused intently on weaving the hair into tight rows, tugging at them after every loop she made. He assumed that whatever she was making, it was something for the impending birth of her child.

He knelt next to her. "Very pretty, An, for your baby?"

An looked up and smiled. "Yes, for baby."

"Are you feeling okay to continue?"

An reached out with her free hand and patted Rusty's right arm. "All fine, Rusty, everything fine," she replied assuring.

Rusty stood and responded, "Please, tell us if we need to go slower, okay?"

"All fine, be okay." She replied as she went back to work on her project.

Rusty finished passing the food out to the group and sat back down next to Tao. He pulled the crackers from his pocket and began to eat. "Sure hope An can wait to have the baby until we get to Japan," he mused.

"All will be fine, Rusty, everything be fine," Tao said as he ate from his packet of rice.

His looked at Tao. "You sound like An. I can't believe the optimism you people have."

"What 'optumusm'?" Tao responded.

Rusty smiled as he spoke. "Positive attitude. I can't believe how positive you all are."

Tao waved his hand around the group. "We know we doing what Jesus want. All have op, tum, ism." He smiled back.

Rusty returned the smile as he turned to lay his head on the pack. With every day, and every encounter, he loved the Chinese people more.

The four Chinese soldiers led General Marsh into the Shenyang prison with his hands tied behind him. Following the group, Colonel Li watched with glee as he was taken to his cell. Marsh stood silent as the guard opened the cell door while another untied his hands. Marsh rubbed his wrists as he stepped inside. He turned around to see Colonel Li closing the door with a smile on his lips.

"I hope you find the accommodations acceptable, General. Best we could do on such short notice."

Marsh smiled back at his captor. "I'm sure it will be fine, Colonel; it's bigger than my room at the Consulate," Marsh countered, smiling broadly at Li.

Colonel Li scowled as he turned and walked away. Marsh stood in the center of the cell and stretched his arms out wide, touching each side of the dark room. He took in a deep breath and slowly let it out. This was the first time in his life he'd been incarcerated. The experience was new to him. He backed against the stone wall and slid to the ground, settling on the dirt floor. He placed his head in his hands as his thoughts went to his wife and children, wondering if he'd ever see them again.

Chapter 20 - A Mother's Task

The full moon shone brightly over the followers as they approached the eastern side of Anshan. The temperature had dropped to thirty-five-degrees during the night, and with a cloudless sky, there was no hope of it getting any warmer. The smells from the city assaulted Rusty's senses as they drew closer to Anshan. He imagined that living in nineteenth century America would have been much the same, beautiful open spaces and crowded dank cities.

The countryside he'd seen since arriving was spectacular. The spring and summer foliage, and majestic mountains, were some of the most beautiful he'd ever seen. Even the winter in China possessed a beauty he'd never experienced. Prior to joining the Marine Corp, he'd never been outside of Pennsylvania. The train ride he took from Philadelphia to San Francisco after boot camp had taken him through some of the most incredible countryside he'd ever seen. He promised himself to return to the west once he was out of the Corp. The small towns and open spaces of California, Nevada, Utah, and Wyoming appealed to him after spending a lifetime of living in a crowded city.

Rusty was jerked back into consciousness by Tao's hand on his shoulder. "Rusty, time for rest."

Rusty looked at his watch. "Twelve-thirty. I'm sorry, Tao, I kinda lost track of time. Let's gather everyone in close together and take thirty minutes for rest."

Tao bowed to Rusty and began gathering the group around into a tight circle. Rusty used the opportunity to check their location. He pulled the map, compass and flashlight from his pack. After visually surveying the surrounding landscape, he crouched to the ground and covered himself with his coat. He turned the flashlight on, illuminating the map. He could see that they were about fifty miles from Yingkou and, barring any unforeseen circumstances, he figured they would get there in two to three days. Satisfied, he turned the light off and pulled his coat back on. After putting the gear back into the pack, he sat next to Tao.

"Well, with a little luck, we'll be in Yingkou in no more than three days," he said while pulling the packet of crackers from his coat pocket.

Tao sat with his legs crossed as he responded, "Is good; all be fine, Rusty. Soon be on way to America."

"Don't get the cart before the horse, Master; we still have to get through Yingkou. And you're not thinking about the long boat ride through the Bohai Sea, then around South Korea to Japan. We still have a long ways to go."

Without looking at Rusty, Tao patted Rusty on the forearm. "Be okay, Rusty, all be fine," he said while looking out over the countryside.

Rusty shook his head. Did Tao never worry about anything? he thought. Either Tao had the best 'poker face' on the planet, or he simply refused to worry.

Rusty looked over the group of followers seated in the camp. Old people, and young people, not a lot in the middle, he thought. Four energetic young men, along with Tao and Ho for protection. Two Bo's, one pistol, and four bows and a few handfuls of arrows. It wasn't the security force he would have preferred, but it was what he had to work with.

Rusty looked toward An, who was once again working on her project. She was intensely focused as she weaved the hair tight, pulling it hard each time she would add another strand, tightly wrapping it around small pieces of wood. She looked up at him and

178

smiled as she paused. Rusty returned the smile as he looked at her and her husband Wu. The hope in all of these people's faces was amazing to him. Oppression and persecution were things he'd never experienced until his time in China. Were it him, he'd be torn about leaving his country, but these people found peace in their departure.

He looked at his watch to see they had been sitting for the prescribed thirty minutes. Rusty stood, putting the bags on his shoulders. "Time to go," he said to the group.

The believers all stood without saying a word and looked toward Rusty. He stepped out with Tao and Ho behind him. "Four hours to Haicheng," he said softly.

Walter stood on the roof of the Consulate looking out over the city. The bright moonlight gave him a clear view of everything around him. It was getting colder during the evenings, which forced all the Marines to wear bulkier clothing than normal.

He rubbed his gloved hands together to get warm as he stamped his feet to keep circulation in his legs. Privates Wade and Butcher walked the grounds of the Consulate, keeping a close watch on the entrance gate, while the Chinese soldiers patrolled the perimeter of the Consulate walls.

While tensions remained high, everyone wanted this over, including the Chinese. Wade wanted to return to his native Arizona to get warm again, and Butcher had committed to moving there himself after his time in China. The cold and the confinement were taking its toll on everyone.

Walter watched the two dozen Chinese soldiers surrounding the Consulate, with their rifles slung over their shoulders. He had little respect for them as a military force, but did respect their dedication. He often quipped that "There are so many of them that if we ever had to do battle with the Chinese, we'd run out of ammo before we could kill 'em all."

Walter looked up to the midnight sky as he stretched up on the balls of his feet. He found himself daydreaming about what he was going to do when he got back home. A steak, he thought, The biggest T-bone I can find with a baked potato, that's gonna be my first meal. Two blocks away, the shouting of Chinese soldiers brought him back to reality. He strained his eyes to see two soldiers running toward a lone woman walking on the street, their rifles pointed at her. The woman stopped and raised her hands high in the air as they approached. To his horror, the two soldiers leveled their rifles and shot her. Walter jumped back in surprise as he watched the woman fall to the ground in a heap.

Walter pulled the M-1 off his shoulder and knelt on the roof, waiting with the butt of the weapon resting on the roof in his right hand.

Behind him, the roof access door flung open to reveal Captain Rivera with a .45 in his hand. "What the hell is going on?" he said as he knelt next to Walter.

In low a voice, Walter responded. "They shot an old woman. They just shot her, for no reason!" he said while pointing toward the soldiers two blocks away.

From the street, the two soldiers looked up to the roof of the Consulate to see the two men kneeling. They began screaming at Walter and Rivera in Chinese. Rivera looked down in the courtyard to see all the Marines taking up positions around the compound, ready to respond to the threat. Brown and Rivera crouched in the prone position as they looked on.

The two soldiers raised their rifles and began shooting toward Brown and Rivera. The rounds impacted the cupola above their heads as the soldiers continued to fire toward them. Walter took aim with his Garrand and shouted to Rivera, "I can take 'em, Sir!"

Rivera shouted back at Walter, "Negative, Brown! Get back inside!" The two men quickly slid backwards toward the door as rounds continued to buzz over their heads, impacting the building. Once Walter moved into the building, Rivera slid his body over the threshold, pulling the door closed from the bottom. Once inside, the two men descended the staircase and ran into the courtyard to check on the other men.

With their weapons at the ready, Brown and Rivera stood by the door and surveyed the grounds. They could see the other Marines behind cover around the courtyard, waiting for any threat. Rivera turned toward Walter and barked, "Get back inside and keep guard over the civilians. Gather them into the squad bay and wait for my orders!"

"Yes, Sir!" Walter responded as he turned to go back into the building.

Rivera moved quickly to the right, staying close to the building with his pistol in front of him. He stopped next to Manning, who was at the inside corner of the building, scanning the tops of the buildings outside the Consulate compound.

Without looking at Rivera, Manning whispered to his superior. "What the hell is going on, Sir?"

"Two Chinese soldiers killed a woman on the street outside, then fired at Brown and me."

"They shot an innocent woman?" Manning said as his head snapped toward Rivera. "What kind of an animal would do that?"

"The worst kind, Manning. Keep alert, and under no circumstances fire on anyone unless they come through there," Rivera said, pointing toward the main gate.

"Yes, Sir," Manning responded.

Rivera continued to move around the compound, making contact with the remaining Marines to make sure the situation didn't elevate.

Walter had gathered the Consulate staff together in the squad bay and stoked the fire in the stove for them to keep warm. He walked from window to window checking the exterior for threats with his rifle in hand.

Assistant Consular General Gary Parker stood and approached Walter. "Sergeant, what's happening out there?"

Not wanting to alarm the others, Walter responded in as generic a tone as he could. "Sir, when Captain Rivera gets in here he can brief you. I think you need to wait for him, Sir."

"Then I need to get out there and talk to him," Parker responded.

"Sir, that would be a *very* bad idea. I'm afraid I can't let you go out there. It's not safe. You need to wait for the Captain, Sir."

Parker didn't like being in the dark, but knew Walter was correct, so he stepped back toward the group. As he was about to sit down, Captain Rivera entered the squad bay. "Captain, what's happening out there?" Parker demanded.

Rivera motioned for Parker to follow him into the hall. Once Parker closed the door behind him, Rivera spoke softly. "Sir, the

181

Chinese soldiers killed a woman two blocks from the Consulate. When they looked up and saw Brown and me on the roof, they fired several rounds at us."

"Good Lord, are they coming into the Consulate?" Parker asked nervously.

"I don't think so, Sir; they would have done so already. They were probably surprised to see that there were witnesses and just panicked. Sooner or later, though, they'll probably come here for us, since we saw the woman die."

Parker was shaking his head as he spoke. "I don't think so. General Marsh and I spoke a couple of days before he left. I agree with his assessment that, once they got him, the rest of us would be left alone. He was the real prize they were looking for."

"I hope you're right, Sir, but I'm not only worried about you and the other staff members; I'm also worried about the potential danger for my men. The Chinese will take them to the labor camps and use them in the factories," Rivera responded.

"Not if you're disarmed. If we turn over the weapons, they'll have no reason to see us as a threat."

Rivera's head jerked in disbelief. "You're joking, right?"

"No, I'm not joking, Captain. If the Chinese come here again, I'm ordering you to surrender your weapons."

"Sir, that didn't work for the Germans, the Poles, or even the Chinese when the Japanese came here. How in the hell is it going to work for us?"

"The only chance we have is that the Chinese view us as a non-threat. So long as we're armed, the potential exists for them to enter the compound with gunfire, then maybe some of the civilians *will* get killed."

Rivera's back straightened as he spoke. "With all due respect, Sir, if you're wrong, they'll hang you higher than Hayman. I want you to note that I'm complying with this order under protest."

Parker's jaw set firmly as he responded, "Duly noted, Captain."

Parker turned and entered the squad bay, slamming the door behind him. Rivera stood in the hall with a disgusted look. He spoke out loud as he turned to walk to the duty hut. "Bureaucrats, I'll sure be glad when I'm retired!"

★ ★ ★

Rusty looked ahead about five-hundred-yards and saw buildings scattered over the countryside. Small homes with outbuildings were blocking their path around the southeastern end of Anshan. He looked farther to the east and found more buildings still. He stopped, looked at his watch, and discovered they didn't have the time to walk around the populated area before the sun came up. The closer they got to Yingkou, the more populated it was becoming. He now had an additional worry, remaining unnoticed during their daytime encampments. They had to get to the other side of the main road.

He gathered everyone around him and spoke softly. "We have to walk through the settlement ahead of us; I need everyone to be absolutely silent."

Tao and Ho translated Rusty's words to the three in the group who didn't speak English. Each nodded in agreement after hearing the warning with somber looks. Rusty smiled back at them, nodding.

The closer the believers came to the houses, the closer they gathered to each other. Mostly out of fear of being detected, they were unconsciously huddling together. Such a tightly gathered group ran completely afoul of everything Rusty had been taught in the Marine Corp. Despite his attempts to spread them out, they continued to group closer together.

As they approached a small shed twenty yards from its main house, Rusty stopped and whispered for Tao and Ho to have the group spread out. He watched as the two men whispered softly to the others, then turned around to lead them out. As he turned around, he found himself face-to-face with a young teenage boy at the edge of the shed holding a wooden bucket. Startled, the young man screamed and turned to run.

Before Rusty could react to get the group out of sight, an old man came running from the house waving a large knife in his hand. The young boy ran to the man and held on tightly to him. Rusty instinctively pulled his pistol from its holster and held it low next to him.

As the old man stared back at them, Tao stepped toward him. "Master, don't!" Rusty warned.

Tao turned toward Rusty as he walked toward the old man. "Be

183

fine, Rusty, all be fine."

While his eyes were locked on the old man, Rusty muttered under his breath, "I sure wish he'd quit saying that."

Tao stopped in front of the old man and bowed. The man bowed in return and listened as Tao spoke to him in Chinese. The old man's look changed from a scowl to a smile as Tao continued. None of the believers could hear what was being said, but relaxed as they saw the man's change of expression.

Tao turned toward the group and motioned for Rusty to join him. Rusty placed the .45 in his pocket and stepped toward the men. Tao continued to speak to the man as Rusty stopped in front of them. Tao finished his sentence with the words "Rusty Harrigan," as he gestured with his left hand toward Rusty. The old man bowed toward Rusty. "Rusty, this is Qiang Hwang and his grandson, Gan."

Rusty bowed toward the old man and his grandson with a small smile. "Rusty, he say we can stay and rest." Rusty looked toward Qiang who was smiling and nodding. "He have warm food for us. All be fine, Rusty."

Rusty turned toward Tao with a look of concern. "Master, what did you tell him about us?"

"I say we going to Yingkou, then going to America."

Rusty's eyebrows shot up when he heard the words. "Master, we can't be telling people where we're going. You don't know him; he might tell someone, and then where will we be? Not a good idea, Master!"

"Rusty, Jesus watch over us. Will not let anything happen. He take care of us."

"I hope you're right, Master."

Qiang Hwang smiled and motioned for everyone to enter his house. Despite his trepidation, Rusty had to admit that the temporary departure from the cold, coupled with a hot meal, would do wonders for the group. The believers all hurried toward the house, smiling, as Rusty stood by the door. As each of the believers entered the house they bowed graciously toward Qiang Hwang. Rusty waited for everyone to enter before he stepped inside. "If we're going to die today, at least we'll die warm with a full stomach," he said under his breath."

184

Chapter 21 - A Fatal Disclosure

Riding in the passenger's side of the truck, Major Hung watched as his vehicle approached the Mukden Prison. Mornings were appearing later, now that the end of fall was coming to the Liaoning Province. It was still dark over the Mukden Prison, and the smoke slowly rising from the chimneys gave it an eerie appearance. Without wind, the smoke hovered over the building, as if to protect the evil contained within its walls.

The promise of peace in China after the Nationalists had been defeated was proving to be false. It seemed there would be no end to the violence and mayhem that had swept over China. Major Hung found himself longing for the innocent time of his youth.

Hung exited the passenger's side of the truck and took one last drag from his cigarette before crushing it out under his boot. He stepped out toward the building and returned the salute from the guard at the entrance door. Once inside, he shed his coat and hat, and walked toward the main office. The orders to report to the prison had come early in the morning, and he was curious to find out why his presence was required.

As he entered the office, he found Colonel Li standing in the center of the room next to two young Chinese men seated with their hands tied behind them. Four guards stood at attention against the wall, awaiting the next command from their Colonel.

Major Hung placed his hat and coat on the table. "Good morning, Colonel."

Li had his arms folded in front of him as he continued to look at the two men. "Raise your heads!" he shouted.

As their heads lifted, Hung could see the cuts and bruises on their faces. They didn't appear to be fresh wounds, but were bad enough to indicate they weren't received too long ago. "These two thieves were caught stealing food from the warehouse. They told the men who arrested them that in exchange for their lives, they would provide valuable information about something that occurred three days ago. Out of curiosity, I thought I would see what these two pathetic pieces of filth could possibly have that would interest me."

Li slapped the man's face seated closest to him with the back of his hand. "Tell him what you told me."

The frightened man eked the words out as he looked at Major Hung. "Three days ago, me and my two friends were at the southern wall of the city and saw a man sneaking out through the part of the wall that had been knocked down. He was a big man, an American he tried to rob us-"

Li slapped the man in the head sharply. "Tell the truth if you want to live!" he ordered.

The young man lowered his head. "We thought he might have something of value, so we tried to rob him. The three of us surrounded him, and he fought us off. He killed my friend Chan and knocked me and Kun out."

"And these cuts and bruises on your face, did he do that?" Major Hung asked, waving his hand toward the man's face.

"Yes, Sir." The man raised his head high as he looked at Hung pleadingly. "He was skilled in the arts, Sir. He knew Kung Fu."

"Now tell the Major what he looked like," Li ordered.

"He was a big man, an American. He had light hair and blue eyes."

Li turned toward Hung. "It would appear as though Sergeant

Harrigan has slipped out of the Consulate, Major."

"But how could he, Sir? The Consulate has been under guard the entire time. He couldn't have gotten out without our knowledge. How could he have done that?"

"I intend to find out," Li responded. He turned toward the four guards as he spoke. "Now get this filth out of my sight," He said while pointing to the two men.

The guards picked the two men up from their seats and dragged them out of the room. Major Hung watched as they were led out, knowing they didn't have long to live. He turned his head back toward Colonel Li.

"We now have the American on a charge of murder, and I won't stop until he's in my prison. Get your men ready, Major. We're going to the Consulate. This time we won't be turned away!" Li ordered.

Major Hung responded as he turned to leave the office. "Yes, Sir, right away, Sir." As he closed the door behind him he remembered his encounter on the side of the road the day before. "You were there, Harrigan, I knew you were there."

Consular General Marsh sat on "The Rack," a name he used to refer to his bed in the prison cell. The accommodations were beyond horrible, and the smell of the prison made him nauseous. As a veteran of the First World War, he was familiar with the stench of death, and the Mukden prison reeked of it.

He'd been in the first sustained American offensive of the war, the Battle of Cantigny, fought on 28 May, 1918. Assigned to the American 1st Division along with 4,000 troops, under Major-General Robert Lee Bullard, they captured the village of Cantigny, held by the German 18th Army. The American success at Cantigny was followed by attacks at Chateau-Thierry and Belleau Wood, three of the most significant battles for the US forces in World War One.

The invading German Army had been particularly brutal to the French citizens in the early days of the occupation of France. The war-torn towns and the looks of despair on the faces of the civilians had haunted him. Marsh had seen his share of evil and man's inhumanity toward man, but nothing that could ever compare to the brutality of the Chinese Communists.

Returning home after the war, Marsh had watched Communism spread across the globe like locusts. It had even taken a foothold in the country he loved so much, the United States. He was now watching it consume the country of China at break-neck speed, and there was nothing he could do to stop it.

The jail guard came to his cell as he sat on the edge of his bunk and passed him a cup of water and a large piece of bread through the slot in the bars. He quickly gathered the bread and water in his hands before the guard could take them away, a lesson he'd learned at the hands of his keepers on the first day of his imprisonment.

He hadn't eaten for twelve hours, and the stale hard bread actually tasted good. The water on the other hand was horrible, and had the faint taste of petroleum in it. He told himself he didn't want to know what the bucket that brought the water was previously used for. Since being incarcerated, his daily sustenance was bread and water; or his 'three squares' as he called them, and they came at the discretion of the jailers.

After quickly devouring the bread, he gulped down the remainder of the foul water and looked around his cell. As he assessed his situation, he was interrupted by the voice of his captor.

"I see you're enjoying your accommodations, General," Colonel Li said with a smile.

Marsh stood and stepped to the cell door. "You know, Colonel, I'd give real money if you'd shut your mouth for just one damned day."

Li looked back at Marsh with contempt. He took a last drag from his cigarette and crushed it under his foot before responding. "General, your attempts at provoking me are futile. I would, however, suggest that you be a little more cordial toward me; it might help improve your stay here, since it's bound to be for a very long time."

Marsh smiled. "I survived the Germans Colonel; I can certainly survive the Communists."

"We shall see, General," Li responded as he turned to walk away. After taking a few steps, he stopped and turned around. "By the way, General, I'm on my way to the Consulate to arrest more of your colleagues. Thought you might be getting lonely." Li turned and walked away.

The General sat back down on the bed. "Well, Marsh, you're in the middle of it now," he said out loud. His head dropped as he thought about his wife.

The ten military trucks came to a halt outside the US Consulate. Major Hung stepped from the passenger side of the lead truck and began shouting orders to the soldiers exiting the back of the vehicles. Colonel Li exited from his staff car and stepped to the main gate with a look of determination.

Li barked his orders out at Private Bledsoe. "I need to see Mr. Parker and Captain Rivera immediately."

Bledsoe stood tall with his weapon at the ready. "They're on their way, Sir."

Gary Parker and Captain Rivera entered the courtyard, followed by the remaining Marines. Parker walked to the gate and addressed Colonel Li. "How can we help you, Colonel?"

Li nonchalantly pulled a cigarette from his coat pocket and slowly lit the smoke. After exhaling his first drag, he looked at Gary Parker. "We have evidence of a murder committed by one of your staff, Mr. Parker. We're here to question all of you and search the Consulate," Li said calmly.

"Murder. What in the hell are you talking about, Colonel? No one has left the compound! Who was murdered?"

"A Chinese citizen was murdered three days ago by Sergeant Harrigan on the edge of the city. That makes all of you here accomplices," Li replied.

Parker turned toward Captain Rivera. "Tell him, Captain; tell him what happened to Harrigan."

Rivera looked at Li and responded "We have no knowledge of Sergeant Harrigans whereabouts, Colonel. He went AWOL three days ago. We haven't seen him since."

Li took another drag from his cigarette and responded, "We'll find him, Captain, and he'll hang for his crimes. I believe the American phrase is 'You can count on it.'"

"Colonel, either way he's going to hang, whether it's by your hand or a military court martial for desertion. So you see, Colonel, it really doesn't matter."

Li was baffled by how cool Captain Rivera was regarding the charges. He expected to elicit a completely different response to his revelations. He looked back at Rivera to see him watching Li with a blank look. Angered, he decided to play his next card. "We're going to search the Consulate, Mr. Parker, and your radio will be confiscated this time."

Parker moved closer to the fence and spoke directly to Li. "Colonel, I'm not authorized to surrender the radio. I did, however, order Captain Rivera to surrender his weapons to you the next time you came here. We'll surrender the weapons and that completely eliminates any threat from this facility. Would that be satisfactory to you, Colonel?"

Li smiled as he responded, "Yes, Mr. Parker; that would be satisfactory."

Parker turned toward Rivera. "Captain, give the Colonel all of your weapons."

With no emotion on his face, Rivera turned toward Walter. "Brown, go to the duty hut and bring out the wooden box on my desk."

"Yes, Sir," Walter replied as he turned and ran to the building.

Rivera looked to the Marines in the courtyard. "Empty your weapons and pass them to the Colonel."

The men all stood still in disbelief. "That means now, gentlemen! Move it!"

The men all began emptying their weapons. As each Marine emptied their rifles, they passed them through the spaces in the gate. Brown arrived in the courtyard carrying the wooden box from Rivera's office. As he stopped next to Rivera, the Captain nodded toward Li.

Brown hesitated. "But, Sir, the-"

Rivera interrupted him. "Brown, just give him the pistols."

Walter stepped to the gate and passed the pistols through the bars until the box was empty, then stepped back behind Rivera.

Colonel Li looked toward Rivera. "And the ammunition, Captain?"

190

"Well now, it won't do us any good without the weapons, Colonel, now will it?"

"I suppose not, Captain." Li smiled. "I want all of you to know how much I appreciate this. And to show you my appreciation, I shall invite you all to Sergeant Harrigan's hanging," Li said with a huge smile.

An unemotional Rivera looked back at him. "I'll have to check my calendar, Colonel, but I'm almost certain I'll be busy that day."

Li frowned and turned away, ordering his men to leave. Rivera stood silent as Gary Parker turned and walked into the building. The men all gathered around Rivera with a questioning look.

Walter waited for the Chinese to leave before talking. "Sir, I don't believe it. Rusty wouldn't kill anyone unless they threatened him. He wouldn't do that."

Rivera looked at all the men standing around him. "I know, Brown. The charges are trumped up. Don't worry; if they'd have caught him, that dirt bag would have brought him here to show him off. I'm sure he's still alive."

Though still concerned, Walter was comforted by Rivera's words. What he said made sense, and he decided to accept Rivera's explanation for now. He looked toward the Captain. "Sir, all of those .45's were the old ones that are non-functional. They were from the bottom of the vault. I mean all the parts are there, but they'd probably blow up in someone's hand if they fired 'em. Those things are from the first world war."

Rivera looked at his men and spoke quietly. "You're not to speak of this to anyone here. All the serviceable .45's are in my office cabinet, along with the loaded clips. If the Chinese come over the walls, I want all of you to get to my office and grab a pistol and three magazines. I'm not gonna die in this shithole without a fight, understood?"

The men all smiled back at him and responded with a resounding, "Yes, Sir!"

As everyone filed back into the building, Walter's thoughts went to his friend. He knew that if Rusty had killed someone, it was either in defense or protecting someone else. He would have it no other way. He had a newfound respect for his Commanding Officer after what he'd done this morning. Now he finally understood the meaning of the old military phrase, "I'd follow him to the gates of hell."

Rusty stood outside, near the entrance to Qiang Hwang's house and looked out over the landscape. In spite of Qiang's hospitality, he'd posted people for watch around the property throughout the day. It had felt good to have a full stomach and a warm body after three days of trekking through the cold Chinese countryside. He was enjoying a hot cup of tea as he waited for the sun to go down. He wished it could have been coffee from Beth's Café in Philadelphia, but at this point, it tasted almost as good.

It was about a six hour hike to Haicheng, where they would cross the main road and hopefully avoid detection. The valley on the other side of the highway was far less populated, and they could move at a faster pace. His greatest fear, that An would go into labor, had taken a back seat to that of running into the Chinese Army. In spite of his best efforts, he couldn't get Major Hung's face out of his mind. His guts told him that they had been discovered; the only thing he didn't understand was why the Major hadn't reacted to what he saw last night.

Tao and Qiang came outside of the house and stood next to him. After being around Tao now for over two years, Rusty could tell when there was something on Tao's mind. He waited for his friend to speak.

"Rusty, have request," Tao said.

Rusty turned to face his friend. "Of course Tao, what do you need?"

Tao stood with his arms folded as he spoke. "Qiang want us to take grandson with us."

Rusty was taken completely by surprise at the request. He looked toward Qiang to see the old man with a huge smile and nodding his head. "Master I don't think we should do this. We still have so far to go, and it's still dangerous. I just think it's a bad idea." Rusty now knew why Qiang was so happy to open his home to these strangers. He'd seen an opportunity for his grandson to leave this conflict. "Doesn't he have parents?"

"Rusty, all Gan have is grandfather; all else-"

Rusty held up his hand to stop Tao. "No, don't tell me anymore. I

192

don't want to hear another story of loss in this country." Rusty was tired of the death, persecution, and sorrow that he'd been exposed to. It was taking a toll on him, and he wanted to be rid of the pain he'd been assaulted with since he arrived. He remained silent for a long time before he spoke. He nodded before he spoke. "Yes, yes, he can come with us."

Qiang stepped close to Rusty and grabbed his right hand with both of his. The old man's eyes filled with tears as he smiled up at the big man. When he took his hands away, Rusty looked down to see a roll of Chinese paper money in his palm. Rusty looked at Qiang and held the money back toward him. "No, I can't take this."

Qiang looked to Tao in a questioning manner. Tao spoke in Chinese to the man and waited for his response. After Qiang spoke, Tao turned to Rusty. "Rusty, he say this for boat to Japan, then for Gan when he in America."

Rusty held the money out toward Tao. "Master, I can't take this. You take it, please."

Tao kept his arms folded as he spoke. "Rusty, be great insult if you not accept. This is all money Qiang have. He trust you to take care of money and Gan. Qiang know he old man and not have long to live. Is great honor for you, Rusty, please take."

Rusty placed the money in his pocket and smiled at Qiang while bowing low toward him. He looked up to see Qiang smiling broadly. Qiang bowed low toward Rusty in return. He'd been humbled many times during his tour in China, but never so completely as now.

Tao reached out toward Rusty and held his hand tightly. "Thank you, Rusty."

Forcing himself to keep his emotions in check, he responded quickly. "No, thank you, Master." Wanting to avoid the emotional situation, he looked to the horizon and determined that it was time to leave. "Please get everyone ready, Master; we need to get going."

When Tao returned to the interior of the humble home, he found everyone packed up and ready to leave, sitting on the floor waiting for Tao or Rusty. Their efficiency and dedication remained a source of pride for Rusty. He never had to wait for them, nor did he doubt their dedication. As they all filed out at Tao's request, Rusty smiled at Qiang. "Thank you."

Tao translated the words to Qiang, who bowed toward them both. Qiang stood in front of his grandson, who had all his possessions in a bundle tied to his back. The two spoke softly to each other as the group waited for the young man to join them. Qiang pointed to Rusty as he spoke to Gan. The young man bowed to his grandfather and stepped toward Rusty.

As they turned to head toward the south, Rusty looked back to see the old man still standing outside his home, hand raised, smiling. Thirteen-year-old Gan stood next to Rusty with tears in his eyes, also looking back toward his home and the only family he had. Qiang raised his hand once more, turned, and disappeared inside. Rusty put his arm around Gan as they turned and continued forward in silence.

Chapter 22 - The Threat From Above

Rusty had led the believers around the remainder of the houses to the south of Anshan and was focusing on his next target, Haicheng. Since they had left Qiang's house, Gan hadn't been more than five feet from Rusty's side. The young man had a blank stare as he walked next to Rusty and hadn't looked anywhere other than directly ahead since leaving his home.

Strangely, Rusty felt a connection with the young man, as he too was raised by his grandparents. The loss of his father and mother at such an early age had been devastating. It's difficult to lose a parent when someone is an adult, but when you are as young as Rusty was, no one can explain it fully. His grandparents were always there for school and church functions, but it was nothing like having mom and dad present.

His thoughts wandered back to Philadelphia and his youth as he remembered his first high school baseball game. He smiled as he remembered his grandfather cheering from the grandstands when he hit his first homerun of the season. An avid baseball fan, his grandfather had hoped for a Harrigan to sign on with the Phillies in the hope of breaking the losing streak the team had been plagued with since its founding in 1883.

In spite of the financial hardships of the depression, his grandfather always found the means to take Rusty to at least one baseball game during the summer. One of Rusty's most prized possessions was a baseball autographed by his favorite player, number 17 from the St Louis Cardinals, Dizzy Dean. He had begged his grandfather to take him to the game when the Cards were in town for the 1935 season. The Cardinals had won the World Series the year before, and Dizzy Dean was one of their most prized players. After signing the baseball, Dean had patted Rusty on the shoulder and said, "There you go, young man" with a huge smile. Rusty didn't come down from cloud nine for a month. He'd even finagled the number 17 for his high school jersey. These were memories that would last his whole life.

Rusty reached his arm around Gan as they walked. The big man smiled down at the teenager as he held onto him. Gan smiled back as he looked up at him. A bond between the two had been forged.

Rusty could now see the lights of Haicheng in the distance, approximately five miles away. He raised his hand and stopped the group to check his map. Removing his coat, he once again pulled the flashlight, map, and compass from his pack and bent down to the ground.

After covering himself, he opened the map and turned on his light. His index finger moved to a spot just north of Haicheng, then he slowly moved his finger ten miles to the left, stopping at Ganwangzhen. The terrain surrounding Ganwangzhen looked to only have low rolling hills and appeared to offer plenty of cover for them during the day. He ran his finger farther south to the town of Gaokanzhen. The terrain was flat around the town, and he knew it would be more difficult to find cover to rest during the day.

He needed to get the group as far west from the road as he could and mentally calculated it would take them six hours to get there. The only thing he didn't know was what lay in the valley once they were on the other side of the road. He looked at his watch and found they had the six hours needed, but they still had to get farther south before they could cross. He turned off the light and rose to his knees. After returning the map, flashlight and compass to the pack, he stood and turned to Tao.

"We have about another hour of walking, then we'll turn west and cross the road."

196

"How long we have to go to Yingkou, Rusty?" Tao asked.

Rusty arched his back and stretched. "Two more days, maybe two and a half, if everything goes well. The real difficulty is getting through the valley on the other side of the road, and then, of course, getting through Yingkou to the docks."

Tao patted his friend on the back and walked away. "Then must go now."

Rusty smiled and started walking behind Tao. As he followed him, Gan remained glued to Rusty's right side, looking down at the ground ahead. Rusty placed his hand on Gan's shoulder, and when the young man looked up at him, Rusty smiled. Gan returned the smile, then looked back at the ground. Time heals all wounds, he thought.

The group was moving quickly through the countryside and never made a sound. They kept close to each other and although Rusty had expected some complaining, or even some talking between them, he never heard it, only saw only silent smiles when he looked back at them.

Rusty looked at the face of his watch and found they had walked for almost an hour in a southerly direction, so he stopped. The lights of Haicheng could be seen about four miles south of them. Without saying anything, he moved out toward the main road.

The road lay just over a low hill, three miles in front of them. Once over the hill, there would be no cover until they got past the fields on the other side of the road, something Rusty continued to worry about. He hoped that the conversation he'd been privy to overhearing with Major Hung was accurate, that the soldiers would be waiting in Yingkou, rather than posted along the highway. He certainly didn't have the manpower nor the weaponry to deal with a threat of that level. The main highway from Mukden was always busy with traffic during the day; he just didn't know how busy it would be during the night. He fought to keep from concentrating on the potential threats that flooded his mind. Deal with the now! he thought.

The group began the gradual ascent over the hill in front of them. The grade was certainly manageable, and it didn't appear to be slowing them. Rusty looked behind him to check on the group. None appeared to be having difficulty with the four percent grade.

Once at the top, Rusty stopped to rest. He bent over and rested his hands on his knees as he looked over the valley. He turned to Tao.

"Rest here for a while, then we'll cross the road."

The top of the hill was only three hundred feet above the valley, but it gave him an excellent view of the terrain. The road was only a mile from their position, but there was no cover for them either during their descent or while crossing the highway.

Traffic was minimal, with only the occasional truck driving through. He couldn't tell from his position if they were military trucks or commercial ones. He was hoping for the latter. The fields to the west of the highway posed a different threat. The valley was flat and unobstructed all the way to the mountains on the western edge. It looked flatter than Kansas, he thought. The moonlight glittered off the fields, but it was too far off to tell what the reflection was from.

Rusty sat down as he looked out over the valley, assessing the situation. Tao sat next to his friend and crossed his legs. "Rice paddies," Tao whispered.

Rusty's turned to Tao, his eyes open wide with disbelief. "What?"

"All rice paddy, Rusty," Tao repeated.

"I thought the growing season was over."

"*Is* over," Tao responded.

"But there's still water in them," Rusty protested.

"Water almost gone, can walk on edge."

"Oh, that's a comfort," Rusty said sarcastically. "We'll be out in the open."

"Still dark, Rusty, be okay."

He stared out over the uneven rice paddies. They would have to take a serpentine route through the maze, and that would take precious time from their already tight schedule. He took in a deep breath and let it out slowly. "Well, we better get going then, before some other surprise pops up." Rusty stood and started down the grade, with the group following.

Walter stood on the roof of the Consulate, staring down at the perimeter walls. There were Chinese soldiers everywhere he looked. After they surrendered their rifles, it seemed like there were ten times the soldiers around the complex. His gut told him that giving up their rifles would only embolden the Chinese. He expected Colonel Li to walk into the compound at any time and just take over. He found himself wishing that Rusty was still here; the pressure of leadership was weighing heavily on him. Walter walked around on the roof to keep the circulation going in his legs. The cold weather that set in was taking its toll on everyone at the Consulate, especially the Marines who were standing guard.

The door to the cupola opened behind him to reveal Corporal Manning. "Hey, Brown."

Walter reached into his coat pocket and pulled out the .45, handing it to Brian. "Here you go, Brian. I'm going in to get warm."

The Marines had reduced their posting to the position on the roof and kept one .45 there. "Better to have the high ground in case they come over the wall," was what Rivera had told them. By keeping a pistol on the roof, it would deprive Parker of the knowledge of its existence.

Walter walked into the kitchen for some alone time before he went on to the squad bay. Since the power had been turned off by the Chinese, the entire Consulate staff had huddled together in the squad bay for warmth and protection. Walter's claustrophobia had kicked in, and he avoided being around the others until the last possible minute. He always wanted to be dead tired and at the brink of exhaustion before he entered the room, so he could drop off to sleep immediately instead of looking around to see the others staring at him.

He sat quietly, staring at the wall with the pictures of the Consulate staff. Suspiciously absent was the picture of his friend, Sergeant Rusty Harrigan. As he looked at the wall, Captain Rivera came into the kitchen and sat across from him. "How's it going, Brown?"

"Good, Sir, just wanted some quiet time before going into the squad bay. Been feeling like a sardine lately with everyone in there."

Rivera smiled as he responded. "Yeah, I don't like crowds either, never have."

Walter raised his head and looked directly into Rivera's eyes. "Captain, do you think Rusty killed someone, or do you think Li's lying?"

Rivera leaned back and raised his eyebrows. "Wouldn't put it past

him to lie. Wouldn't be the first time that bastard has lied to us."
Rivera's head tilted to the side. "Still, I don't think he knew Rusty
was gone. Something happened for him to find out he's not here.
Maybe Harrigan did run into some locals as he was leaving."

"But to kill someone, I just don't see it. He had to be defending
himself."

"Whatever the case, Brown, there's good news in all of this."

With a curious look, Walter responded. "What do you mean, Sir?"

"It means he's still alive."

Walter smiled and nodded. "Yup, he is, just hope he stays that
way."

Rusty and Tao reached the bottom of the grade and lay down in
the prone position in the ditch next to the highway. They were on the
inside of a curve and couldn't see around the corner of the highway.

"Tao, go across the road and signal me when a vehicle is coming.
I'll send a few people across the road each time you tell me it's clear."
Tao didn't respond; he only nodded.

Rusty got up on his knees and looked for lights from approaching
vehicles. He motioned to Tao to cross the road. Tao sprang up, ran
across the road, and slipped into the ditch on the other side.

Once Tao gave him the go-ahead, he motioned for more of the
followers on the hill to move down next to him. Mee Ling, Ho, and
Gan ran the thirty yards down the side of the hill and lay in the ditch
with Rusty. Ho raised his right palm into the air, indicating for Rusty
to hold still. A commercial truck buzzed by them at a high rate of
speed as everyone lay still in the depression. After the truck was out
of sight, Rusty waved for more of the group to come down the hill.
They repeated the exercise until all of the followers were next to the
road.

Rusty looked across the highway to see Tao's open palm held in
the air. He turned to the group and motioned for them to lay low. The
lights from the trucks illuminated Tao's position as they approached.
The two military trucks buzzed past them with the wind from their
draft covering the group.

Rusty looked back up to see Tao giving him the go ahead. He ·

turned and motioned for three people to move out. Once they reached the other side, Rusty motioned for Ho, An, and Wu to get ready. Another vehicle sped past their position, and Rusty waved to the three to move.

As An was moving, she stumbled and fell to the ground, taking Wu down with her. Ho returned to help them up, and Rusty looked to see Tao's hand in the air. Ho got the two to their feet and hurried them off to the other side. Rusty could see the lights of the vehicle on the outside of the curve as An, Wu, and Ho slid over the other side.

Rusty looked up to see An's bundle lying in the middle of the road. As he rose to get it, Gan shot past him and darted out into the road. He snatched the bundle and ran back toward Rusty. As Gan dove into the ditch, the trucks lights shone on their location. Rusty could hear the truck's engines wind down as they approached. The brakes of the military trucks squealed as they came to a stop next to the followers in the ditch. Rusty slowly reached into his coat and retrieved the .45. He depressed the safety down with his right thumb and readied himself, his heart pounding.

The driver of the lead truck exited the cab and walked to the edge of the road. Rusty could hear the man in the passenger's side of the truck saying something, followed by a response from the driver, but he didn't understand what was being said. Rusty was looking ahead of him with the pistol ready in his hand.

Just three feet in front of him, he saw a stream of water coming down to the ditch as he looked on. Perfect, he thought. The stream stopped, and he heard the soldier get back into the truck. As the vehicles drove off, he could hear Gan and Mee Ling giggling behind him. As he sat up, he looked at the two of them and frowned. "Very funny," he said with a scowl.

Rusty and Tao resumed the process of getting the followers across the road until all of them were on the other side. Once they were all together, they slid the thirty feet down the embankment to the valley floor. Rusty looked at his watch, they had just two and a half hours to cross the ten mile wide valley before the sun rose.

They began the trek with the usual silence and determination they had exhibited throughout the journey. The rice paddies still had a few inches of water in them, so walking through them wasn't an option. The dikes, however, were eighteen inches wide, plenty of room for walking in the daytime, but difficult to maneuver in the dark. Of additional concern, the route wasn't straight. Rusty had to zigzag back and forth between the paddies, while trying to keep a westerly heading. The black silhouettes of the followers walking on the dikes at night offered an easy target for someone looking for them. That fact wasn't lost on Rusty; he kept his senses on high alert as they traversed the fields.

The temperature was slowly dropping, and the group knew that they had to get to Yingkou as quickly as possible. Tao and Ho's instincts, after years of wisdom, had warned of a chance of snow, something they surely didn't need at this point.

Rusty suddenly halted the group. The noise in the distance was faint, but familiar. His head turned to the left, then right as he tried to locate its origin. It was coming from their right, somewhere out of the north. His eyes scanned the horizon, looking for the noise as it grew louder. What could it be? Rusty thought. Was it a-

"Plane!" he shouted. "Get down!"

The group all fell to the ground, lying flat on the top of the dikes. Rusty looked to the right to see a light observation plane coming out of the north. The aircraft was at about three thousand feet and headed straight for them.

He shouted to the group, "Get behind the dike!"

The followers slid to their left and down into the paddy. As they got as low into the dike as they could, icy water covered their legs. Rusty peered over the top of the embankment to see the plane diving down into the valley. The aircraft dropped to a height of five-hundred-feet as it approached the followers. Rusty ducked back down and waited for the plane to pass overhead. The engine noise grew louder as the plane flew over the group. They watched as the pilot made a slow turn to the west, circling the fields.

"He see us, Rusty?" Tao asked.

Rusty kept his eyes on the plane as he responded, "I don't think so, but he's searching, that's for sure."

In the cockpit of the observation plane, the Russian pilot looked to the right of the aircraft as he circled. The Chinese observer sitting behind him in the tandem seat aircraft looked to the left. The moonlight glittered off the water in the paddies, producing a deceptive glare. Even at only five-hundred feet above the ground, they were finding it difficult to see anything. Back at the northern most part of the valley, the pilot set up a zigzag pattern, sweeping the fields as he moved south.

Rusty watched the plane as it moved back down the valley toward them. His jaw set as he saw the Russian red star on the side of the fuselage of the American Piper Grasshopper. "Great, we're being hunted by one of our old aircraft," he muttered.

The Piper made its way to the bottom of the valley, then turned out of sight. The believers climbed back onto the top of the dike and continued their trek to the tree line on the western edge of the valley.

"Rusty, you think he see us?" Tao asked again.

"No, he was in a search pattern and didn't alter it. We'll be fine, we just have to get out of these paddies." Rusty chose not to alarm the group, but knew the Chinese Army was closing in fast.

Chapter 23 - A Trial of Convenience

The sun was climbing over the horizon as Rusty and the believers entered the tree line on the western edge of the valley. They were just a few miles east of Ganwangzhen and a day's walk to Gaokanzhen, the last stop before Yingkou. The group walked deep into the trees and gathered around in a tight circle in an attempt to get warm. Their legs were wet from hiding in the rice paddy and each was shivering.

Tao placed his hand on Rusty's shoulder. "Rusty, must make fire, everyone need to get warm."

He knew Tao was right; he didn't like the idea of a fire, but knew it had to be done. Rusty nodded in agreement. "Yes, we need a fire. Keep it small and have everyone gather close around it. I don't want a big fire, especially since the Army is looking for us now."

Tao and Ho stepped away and began gathering wood for the campfire as Rusty dropped his packs and untied the tarp to cover the children. Everyone was shivering with the cold, huddling close to each other for warmth.

Rusty posted two guards at each end of the camp as wood was being piled in the center for the fire. The sun was fully over the horizon now, and Rusty's hope was that the smoke from their fire would look like the smoke from every other home around the valley. It shouldn't be an issue, so long as they kept the fire small, or at least he was hoping so.

Rusty broke open one of the remaining two K-rats and used the containers for kindling as Tao started the fire. Tao continued to add small pieces of wood to it until it was glowing with warmth. Everyone in the group took their shoes off and placed them close to the flames to dry them out, then began rubbing their feet to get them warm. Rusty pulled a fresh pair of socks from his pack and exchanged the wet ones on his feet for the dry. The followers were tired from the hard drive they had made during the night. The children ate voraciously from the fresh supplies given to them at Qiang's house as the elders sparingly nibbled at theirs.

As he ate from one of the cans of K-rats, Rusty surveyed the group of followers. Constantly assessing their condition and stamina had become a ritual for him. It was the only tool to gauge how far and how fast they could travel, since none of them ever complained. He smiled as he watched An weaving the strands of hair into her project. He could finally tell that the hair was being woven around the small pieces of wood to form a cross. It was only about four inches long, but ornate in its design. It was tightly woven, with a crosshatch pattern throughout. He smiled as he thought, for the baby.

Finished with his task of bringing stones to line the campfire, Tao sat to the right of Rusty and removed his shoes to get warm by the fire. As he rubbed his feet, he looked to Rusty's left to see Gan sitting next to him. "Have shadow now," Tao said with a smile.

Rusty looked to see Gan and then turned back toward Tao. "Yeah, I noticed."

"Grandfather tell Gan that you now family. Stay close to you."

"Oh great, not even married and I have a son," Rusty replied with a smirk.

"Is good arrangement, Rusty. You both lost parents."

"Good for whom, Master? Even if I get out of this, they'll send me to prison" he said while staring into the fire. "Won't be much help for him then."

"Have done good thing, Rusty. Have given hope to many people. If God is for you, no one can be against you."

"We'll see," he replied. A smile came across his lips as he thought back to his home in Philadelphia. "Gan and I both have grandparents who love us very much."

"What work grandfather do?" Tao asked.

He took in a deep breath and responded, trying to avoid becoming emotional. "He has a small grocery store in south Philly. He came from Ireland before the turn of the century and met another immigrant in New York. This man had a job promised to him in Philadelphia and said he could get work for my grandfather. My grandfather started working at a grocery store and learned all he could about the business. After ten years of working hard, he opened a small store himself."

"Grandfather good man, Rusty," Tao replied.

"Yes he is. He's worked hard during his life. They almost lost the store during the depression, but my grandmother kept the finances together, and they survived. After my parents died, they took me in and provided the best they could. I never went hungry, and I always had clothes on my back. There was always a lot of love in the house."

"Grandfather generous man."

Rusty mused over the comment and chuckled as he recalled a story. "My grandfather always helped others in the community. He was always there to help someone struggling, with some food or a few dollars. The people in the neighborhood loved him.

"One time, a young kid robbed the store and stole the money from the cash register. Some of the guys knew who had done it and brought him back to my grandfather's store. He got all the money back, but wanted to make a point.

"He made the kid work for a month in the store in exchange for not calling the police. After the month was over, he hired him to work there permanently, making deliveries. Shawn Murphy was his name. When he turned eighteen, he joined the Navy and has never once failed to send my grandparents birthday or Christmas cards. Granddad's a good man, and if I live to be a hundred I couldn't be half the man he is."

"You wrong, Rusty. You already good man." Tao waved his hand around the group. "Have helped all here. You give everything so others can live. Grandfather would be proud."

"Thank you, Tao, but I doubt this could compare," Rusty said

206

while staring into the fire.

"You good man; am proud have you as friend."

Rusty looked at his Master and smiled. "Thank you, Tao; you've been a good friend as well." He stood and stretched his back. "I need to relieve Chow so he can get warm." Rusty buttoned his coat and walked through the tree line. Always uncomfortable with praise or acknowledgement, Rusty found comfort in solitude; something else he inherited from his grandfather.

Consul General Marsh sat in a wooden chair in the center of the makeshift courtroom amidst a sea of Chinese Communists clad in their green military uniforms. The trial was being held by the People's Court in Mukden and was rapidly proving to be a show trial rather than a presentation of the facts.

With a working knowledge of both Chinese and Russian, Marsh was able to pick up on the gist of what was happening as he watched the court officials' one sided presentation of the case against him. He was being charged with beating two Chinese workers who had demanded back pay from the Consulate, an outright lie. The additional charges of inciting a riot and committing espionage had been thrown in for good measure after President Harry Truman had called upon American allies to withhold recognition of Mao's newly established government. Things weren't looking good for him.

The tall and powerful fifty-seven-year-old man was growing weaker by the day. His diet of bread and water was taking a toll on his health. His normally well groomed beard was now scraggly and long. His clothes smelled of the jail cell he was occupying, and he'd developed a nagging cough. In spite of his predicament, Marsh held his head high, refusing to give the Chinese any satisfaction.

He listened as the Chinese witnesses testified about Marsh's brutality and ill treatment under his employ. Marsh kept his eyes focused and his back erect as the lies continued. After the last witness spoke, the court was dismissed for the day. Marsh stood and waited for his escort back to his cell. As he was being led out of the courtroom, he looked to his left to see two Russian army officers standing on the side of the room smiling at him.

As a long-time member of the State Department and a WWI veteran, Marsh was intimately familiar with the politics of the new post World War II world. He knew of the incredible sacrifice and material support the United States and Britain had given the Chinese and Russian governments. Tens of thousands of his own countrymen had died to protect the two countries that now conspired to destroy the United States and Britain. No good deed goes unpunished, he thought. He glared back at the Russians with a look of contempt.

His guards led him to a truck parked out in front of the building and ushered him into the back. He was tired and hungry from the day's ordeal. He had sat in the makeshift courtroom for six hours without food or drink, and his back was on fire with pain. He was determined to deny the Chinese any satisfaction that he was uncomfortable, or in need of something, although he would have killed to have some eyeglass cleaner. The moisture from his breath was no longer doing the job on his glasses.

The truck stopped in front of the prison, and the guards motioned for him to get out. After climbing down to the ground, he straightened himself and walked to the main door. Once inside, he walked to his cell and waited for the "goons" as he called them, to open the door. Once inside, he turned and faced the door, waiting for what would surely be some insults from his keepers.

Marsh was surprised to see Colonel Li approaching his cell. He waited for Li to stop in front of him. "Good afternoon, Colonel. How may I help you?"

Li took off his coat and draped it over his left arm. "I just wanted to see if your accommodations suit you, Mr. Marsh."

Marsh crossed his arms and took in a deep breath looking around his cell. "I'd invite you in for tea and toast, but the guards seem to have missed my daily delivery of condiments." Marsh kept a blank stare as he looked back at Colonel Li.

"I wouldn't worry about it, Mr. Marsh. After tomorrow's proceedings, you'll be here for a long time. I'm sure we can work things out afterwards."

At that moment, the guard came with Marsh's ration of bread and water. Li stepped aside as Marsh took the rations. "Well, I see that dinner has arrived, so I'll leave you to dine. Have a nice evening, Mr. Marsh," Li said as he turned and walked away.

"And you as well, Colonel," he replied. Marsh waited for the guard and Colonel Li to get out of sight before he sat down. He took one last look to ensure he was alone before he voraciously devoured his ration. The bread and water were horrible, as usual, but he wolfed them down quickly in spite of the taste. His stomach groaned as the bread fell into his empty belly. He swore that if he ever got out of here, he'd never eat another piece of bread again. He began to mentally prepare himself for the next day's closing arguments and what was surely to be a harsh sentence. His head fell into his hands as he once again thought about his wife.

Rusty was lying on his back, sleeping soundly. The fire had provided the warmth he needed to nod off into a deep sleep. He felt a nudge in his ribs and stirred at the interruption. The nudge was replaced with a sharp shove to his rib cage. As his eyes opened he saw a rifle barrel pointed at him, just inches from his face. The Chinese man holding the rifle glared back at him.

Rusty turned his head to see Tao looking back at him as another Chinese man held a rifle toward him. "Well, so much for the fire being a good idea," he stated, while looking at the man.

He looked behind the men to see Chow Yun and Jie Meng bound and gagged. Rusty counted close to thirty Chinese men around the camp, all holding rifles on the group. Rusty slowly sat up as he addressed Tao. "Okay, Master, how do we get out of this one?"

Tao sat up and addressed their captors. After the conversation was over, he turned back toward Rusty. "He ask why we here."

"And what did you tell him?"

"Tell him we running from Army and going to America." Tao responded.

"I sure wish you'd quit telling people we're going to America!"

"Is okay, Rusty, they all rebels, fight against Communists."

"So why are the guns pointing at us?" Rusty asked.

"They see campfire and come to see who here," Tao responded.

"Now that they know we're not communists, could they put the guns down?"

Tao spoke to the man in front of him in Chinese and smiled. The rebel raised his rifle and shouted at the other men. All of them shouldered their rifles and stood back. Rusty stood, stepped toward Chow and Jie, and began untying them. "You're both fired," he said as he finished untying them.

"Sorry, Rusty," they said, in unison as they bowed toward him.

Rusty smiled halfheartedly. "It's okay; they probably would have gotten me as well. Don't worry about it," he said, slapping Jie on the shoulder.

Tao and the leader of the rebels were talking as he approached them. Tao turned toward him. "Rusty, they can help; he say we can go to camp. Not far from here, on way to Yingkou."

"Master, it's still light. We could be discovered." Rusty warned.

Tao spoke to the leader, then turned back toward Rusty. "He say be fine; no one see us, camp far off main road."

Rusty turned toward the leader to see him smiling and nodding. "Okay, it's probably better to get out of here anyway. If *they* found us, there's nothing to stop the Chinese Army from finding us. Let's go."

The followers all gathered their bundles as Rusty covered the campfire with dirt. He rolled his wrist over to find it was 1:30 in the afternoon. They still had five hours of daylight left. He gathered his bundles and placed them on his shoulder. He looked toward Tao and nodded. "Okay, let's get out of here."

Rusty fell in behind Tao and the leader of the rebels as they left the campsite. He looked to his left to see Gan walking close to him. "Just hope we can get out of here so I can comply with your grandfather's request."

Not understanding Rusty's words, Gan merely returned the smile.

Colonel Li was sitting in his office going over the day's reports when a knock on the door interrupted him.

"Enter!" he responded loudly.

Major Hung entered the room and closed the door behind him. "Good afternoon, Colonel."

Without looking up, Colonel Li barked out his question. "What news of the Christians and Sgt. Harrigan?"

Hung waited to respond until he had sat in the chair across from Colonel Li. "We have men posted in Yingkou and Dandong, and continue to patrol the roads between here and there."

Li looked up from his desk and set his pen down. "And what of the air patrol?"

Hung ran his right hand through his hair as he responded, "The Russian is in Dandong refueling and getting some rest; he was patrolling all night. When he resumes his search later this afternoon, he'll be moving back toward the area north of Yingkou."

Colonel Li lit a cigarette and leaned back in his chair. "Major, you're the best commander I have. You performed exceptionally during the siege of the city, and your tactics in finding the Nationalist have been brilliant. I find it difficult to understand; however, why you can't find a handful of Chinese Christians, led by an American." Li took another drag from his cigarette as he looked at Major Hung.

"Sir, we've covered every square inch of territory between Mukden, Dandong, and here. There's no sign of them. I believe they're in hiding somewhere."

"Major, they have to have supplies. They couldn't carry enough for more than four or five days, so either someone is resupplying them with food or they're stealing it. Someone has to have had contact with them." Li's voice rose as he continued. "It seems to me that you should be able to find them!" Li shouted, slamming the desk with his fist.

"Sir, I still believe the best approach is to wait for them to come to us, rather than wasting our time and assets trying to find them. Sergeant Harrigan isn't stupid. He knows how to travel through the countryside undetected. The best hope we have is to catch him in Dandong or Yingkou when he's attempting to leave China."

Colonel Li's jaw set, anger flushing his face. "Major, General Piao has told me that this has the highest priority. An American serviceman has killed a Chinese citizen. Finding him is the most important thing we have to accomplish, and I won't disappoint the General. Do you understand me?"

Hung sat up erect as he responded, "Yes, Sir!"

"Now get out there and find them, and don't come back into this office until you have him in custody."

Major Hung stood. "Yes, Sir!" He turned and exited the Colonel's office and closed the door behind him.

Chapter 24 - Joy in Troubled Times

Dark Gray clouds now covered the skies above the Liaoning Province, fulfilling Tao and Ho's prediction for snow. The cloud cover, combined with the rising temperatures, had made it warmer for the believers to travel, but the impending snow would most certainly slow their progress. The group was becoming weary from the continuous travel and concern for the older members had become Rusty's major focus. They needed rest, a decent meal, and he knew that wouldn't come until they reached Japan.

Rusty had another concern, however; their group of twenty-one people walking through the countryside had just ballooned to almost fifty, to include the rebels who now traveled with them. They had walked six miles in the open, and being discovered was now Rusty's primary concern. They had just crested a hill, and he looked down into a small valley ahead.

"How much farther do we have to go?" he asked.

Tao spoke with the leader, then turned back toward Rusty. "There," he said while pointing to a large barn at the bottom of the hill.

Rusty looked down into a small valley at what looked like a farm.

The narrow dirt path they were on continued through the farm and went up over a hill to the other side of the valley, which almost certainly led to Ganwangzhen. There were several buildings around the barn, but they appeared to be in a state of disrepair. It looked to be an excellent hiding place for the rebels to avoid bringing attention on themselves. Rusty was assessing the valley strategically when he heard An cry out behind him. He turned to find her lying on the road with Wu attending to her.

Rusty ran to An and dropped to his knees to assist her. Breathing heavily, An looked up at him and spoke between breaths, "Is time, Rusty!"

"Time for what?" he replied with a concerned but confused look on his face.

Kneeling next to Rusty, Wu excitedly shouted to him in Chinese. Still confused, Rusty stared blankly back at Wu as Lian Yi, one of the elderly women from the group, knelt next to him. "Baby coming, Rusty. Must get An inside."

Panicked, Rusty gathered An up his arms and started running for the farm house below them. Tao and the rebel leader were running ahead, shouting in Chinese to the farmhouse below them.

As they reached the bottom of the grade, Shan Wang, the rebel leader, was motioning for Rusty to enter one of the buildings, pointing to it frantically. Rusty stepped inside to see the interior of a bunkhouse with several beds lining the walls. Shan Wang pointed to one of the beds next to the entrance, and Rusty gently placed An on the bed. Two of the women from the rebel camp joined Hua Ling and Lian Yi from the followers and ushered all of the men from the bunk house.

Rusty stood outside, dazed, with a blank stare as Ho and Tao joined him. He looked at the two men in silence as he tried to collect himself. Suddenly, Rusty shouted in excitement, "We're gonna have a baby!" A huge smile came across his face as he grabbed Ho around the chest and lifted him off the ground. "We're gonna have a baby!"

After letting go, Ho and Tao stood back, laughing at Rusty. This was truly a joyous occasion, and the entire group was beaming, not only for An and Wu, but because they hadn't seen Rusty this happy in a long time.

★ ★ ★

Major Hung stepped out into the yard in front of the headquarters building. He put his coat on and walked to the column of six trucks parked at the end of the yard. One hundred men stood next to the vehicles awaiting Hung's orders to get into the trucks. He turned and walked to the last truck, watching the remainder of the ordinance and weapons being loaded into the rear. He wasn't going to be denied victory this time, no matter the cost.

Hung climbed into the lead vehicle and barked out "Let's go!" to the driver. As the caravan moved out of the yard, it turned toward the south. Hung lit a cigarette and puffed out a huge lung full of smoke. He'd grown weary of Colonel Li's focus on the Christians from the orphanage and even more tired of his obsession over the American soldier, Rusty Harrigan. He'd decided to put an end to this nonsense once and for all.

Hung had made the decision to start his search based on what he thought was his last contact with Harrigan and the group on the outskirts of Liaoyang. While he hadn't *seen* anything on that night, his guts told him that they had been there, watching him from the trees. He pulled his revolver from its holster and opened the cylinder. Once he determined all the chambers were loaded, he closed it and put it back into the holster. This time, he was determined to find the Christians.

The followers had all moved into the barn in the center of the rebel compound and were gathered around a large iron stove, getting warm. Rusty smiled as he watched Wu pacing around the barn, waiting for word about the delivery. He thought, It's the same all over the world. Every father nervously waits for word about their baby." He hoped one day to be waiting on word of his own child being born, but that was for some time in the future, after he found the right woman.

He stood, lifted the pot from the top of the stove and poured himself some tea. As the lone non-Chinese member of the group, he sat silent as the people around him talked among themselves in Chinese. While he was able to pick up a few of the words strewn throughout the conversations, he had to admit he was completely in the dark.

As he sat back down, Tao addressed him. "Rusty, Shan Wang say he can help with boat at Yingkou."

"Really? He knows a boat there we can hire?" he responded.

"Yes, he say man bring weapons to rebels from Philippines. Have big boat, can go Japan. He say use his name and can take to Japan."

Rusty smiled broadly. "Well, we just solved the biggest problem we had, Master." Rusty breathed a sigh of relief as he heard the news. "How far does he say it is to Yingkou?"

Tao spoke as he got up to fill his cup with tea. "One and half day walk, but now have Baby to take, maybe two day."

"Well, we can't leave until An is ready. She can't walk after having a baby."

Tao turned toward Shan Wang and spoke. Shan thought for a moment, then responded to him. Tao turned back toward Rusty. "They have cart, An can ride in cart, Rusty."

"That'll work; all we have to do is wait for her to get stronger, then we can leave. I'm starting to feel better about this, Tao. With a little bit of luck, this just might work. Things are starting to look up," he said with a big smile.

As they were basking in their good fortune, Lian Yi entered the barn and bowed toward Wu. "Have baby girl," a hysterical Wu shouted and ran from the barn. Lian smiled and bowed toward the group of people in the barn, then left.

Ecstatic about the news, Rusty stood and cheered. "Woo hoo! We need to celebrate."

The entire group of followers were cheering for An and Wu. As they were celebrating, Shan Wang came back into the barn with a bottle and some glasses, passing them around. He poured each member a small amount of the liquid, then raised his glass high for a toast.

Rusty leaned into Tao and whispered softly, "What is it, Master?"

Tao responded with a smile. "Is Bai Jio (bye joe), Rusty."

Shan Wang held his glass out toward everyone as Tao spoke softly toward Rusty. "Proper to touch glass, not let go during toast."

Rusty touched his glass and held it against the others as Shan spoke. "*Zhu ni tiantian kaixin!*" and then shouted "*Ganbei!*"

Rusty turned his head toward Tao. "What does that mean,

Master?"

"He say, 'Wishing happiness for you each day.' Then say 'Cheers.'"

Rusty watched as everyone downed the liquid in one swallow. He pulled the glass to his lips, threw the liquid back into his mouth, and swallowed. Tao watched the look on Rusty's face and smiled. Rusty choked the words out. "What's that made of, gasoline?"

"Is homemade, Rusty. You like?" Tao said with a huge smile.

Recovering from the burning in his throat, Rusty commented, "It tastes like it came from the engine bay of a Jeep."

As they were all celebrating, Wu came into the barn and spoke to Tao. Tao turned and looked at Rusty. "Wu say An want see you."

Rusty quickly walked from the barn and headed toward the bunkhouse. Once he reached the door, he slowly opened it and peeked inside to see An lying in the bed with her baby in her arms. As she looked up to see Rusty, she smiled and responded, "Rusty, come see baby."

He stepped to the bed and smiled broadly as he looked to see her beautiful baby girl. Hua and Lian were standing next to the bed and moved back as Rusty knelt down next to her. "She's beautiful, An." Rusty beamed with excitement as he looked at the newborn baby lying in An's arms. Her perfect face was outlined with jet black hair and she was bundled in the blanket.

Rusty gently touched her hair with his big right hand, then looked at An. "I'm so happy for you. She is beautiful An."

Wu kneeled next to Rusty and An as she reached out toward Rusty's hand. "This for you, Rusty," she said as she placed the handmade cross in his hand.

He looked at the cross, then back to An. "I can't take this, An. This is for your baby."

An smiled and patted his hand. "No, for you, please take."

He looked humbly at the cross made from her hair and nodded. "Thank you; thank you very much."

Wu spoke to Rusty in Chinese, then placed his hand on Rusty's shoulder. As Rusty turned toward An, she translated his words. "Wu say we want name baby after you. Baby girl name 'Rusty.'"

He leaned his head back and chuckled as he responded, "I think you could have picked a better name than that, An, especially for such a pretty baby."

"Please, Rusty; you honor us by giving name" she pleaded.

He nodded as he replied, "Of course I will; it would be my honor to have her named after me," he said as he shook Wu's hand.

An started to cry as she looked seriously toward her friend. "Rusty, you take others and leave for Yingkou. Now have baby, slow you down. Please, you leave."

Rusty's head jerked as he heard the words. "Absolutely not! All three of you are coming with us. We started this journey together and we're going to finish it together." He placed his big hand on her arm. "You're going to raise that little girl in America, so no more talk about leaving you here."

A tearful An smiled back at him and nodded. "Thank you Rusty. We all love you very much."

The emotional Marine quickly stood and patted Wu on the back. He smiled at the couple, then turned to walk away. His eyes welled up with tears as he looked down at the cross in his right hand.

Consular General Marsh sat erect in the center of the courtroom as he waited for his sentencing. He tried desperately to suppress his nagging cough, not wanting to let the Chinese know he was ill. He sat with a blank stare as the military members of the Peoples Republic of China entered the makeshift courtroom. A normally impeccably dressed man, he was disgusted to have to sit in dirty clothes, without a shower or shave. Personal hygiene had taken a back seat to his incarceration.

The guard standing next to Marsh poked him in the ribs, prodding him to stand. Once on his feet, he heard the judge pronounce sentence. His jaw set as he heard the sentence. "Ten years, hard labor." He fought to maintain his composure and avoid an angry outburst. He had hoped the Chinese would keep him in his cell for a few months, then release him and the other members of the Consulate. I may just have to tough this out, he thought. He stared down the soldiers as he was led from the courtroom and into the waiting truck for his ride back to the prison.

For forty years, Marsh had served his country, beginning with his military service in World War I. He'd never complained about an assignment nor turned down a posting because it was dangerous. He knew, as did all the other personnel in the Foreign Service, that at any time he could lose his life. But this time, he found himself in peril, because of the incompetence of the diplomats who had lost China to the Communists. He would never mention it openly nor speak out against his superiors, but he was disgusted at the diplomatic failure that had landed his staff in this predicament, and of greater concern, placed his wife in harm's way.

Marsh exited the truck and walked into the interior of the prison, in front of his captors. He entered his cell and turned around to stare down the guards as they closed the door behind him. He grabbed the bars of the cell in his hands and stared out at the hallway as he contemplated his situation.

Colonel Li stepped in front of his cell and calmly lit a cigarette. After exhaling, he looked at Marsh with a smile. "Well, Mr. Marsh, as I predicted, you'll be here with me for a *very* long time. Is there anything I can do for you to make your stay more pleasant?"

Marsh kept his eyes focused on Li as he responded. "Oh, I don't know, steak and potatoes would be nice," he said with a smile.

Li leaned in close toward Marsh as he spoke. "I wanted to be the first to tell you that soon you'll have a companion here at the prison."

"And who might that be, Colonel?" Marsh queried.

"It seems that Sergeant Harrigan killed a Chinese citizen during his escape. We don't have him yet, but rest assured we'll pick him up soon."

Marsh couldn't hide the surprise from his face. "I don't believe that, Colonel. Harrigan wouldn't hurt someone unless he'd been attacked."

"Oh, he did, and we have witnesses. Soon he'll be here at the prison with you, but not for too long, I'm afraid. Sadly, I'll be presiding over his execution." Colonel Li moved aside as the guard brought Marsh his ration of bread and water. "Well, what do you know, here's your steak and potatoes. I'll leave you alone to eat in peace." Li smiled as he turned and walked away from the cell.

Marsh stood in front of the cell door holding his bread and water as he digested the information he'd just received. His worst fears about Rusty had come true. The Chinese were after him, and there was nothing he could do about it.

Chapter 25 - Hung's Pursuit

Temperatures were dropping fast in the Liaoning Province, as attested to by the occupants of the US Consulate, who were covered in multiple layers of clothing. The stove in the barracks was stoked to its maximum and radiated heat for the 25 people gathered around it. They had burned every sensitive document in the complex and were enjoying additional heat from some of the wooden furniture that had been sacrificed for the cause.

Personal hygiene was also becoming a problem. Rivera had grumbled that the Consulate was beginning to smell like an old 'gym sock.' The always impeccably groomed Captain had gone way beyond a five-o-clock shadow and was extremely uncomfortable with his appearance. This certainly wasn't the first time he'd gone without a shower, but living in the Consulate was different than his time on Iwo Jima. The remainder of the Marines were enjoying the relaxed uniform standards, but were also disgruntled about the lack of hygiene. Everyone was looking forward to getting home.

The staff had taken to occupying their time with bridge tournaments. Even Walter had become a fan; the other Marines, however, preferred cribbage and acey-deucy. After consultation with Captain Rivera, Walter had the detachment of Marines studying military tactics from Rivera's vast library in the duty hut.

In spite of the full schedule the Consulate staff had carved out for themselves, there were still arguments and heated exchanges that broke out among them on a daily basis. Both Walter and Rivera were becoming more and more concerned, the longer the confinement dragged on. Walter was learning the lessons that Rivera already knew, "It's not the firefights of combat that tore men apart; it was the long periods of tedium in-between."

Walter was descending the stairs after his watch on the roof. Bundled in multiple layers of clothing, he had his arms crossed in front of him trying to get warm. He entered the kitchen to find Rivera seated at the table. He shivered as the words came out of his mouth. "Good morning, Captain."

Rivera was opening a tin of instant coffee, twisting the key around the top edge of the can. "Morning, Brown. How's the city looking?"

"Nothing going on, Sir. The goons are quiet, and it still stinks out there," Walter replied with a smile.

Rivera lifted the top off the can and set it on the table. He dug his spoon into the contents and poured it into the cup of hot water. His spoon rang against the sides of the cup as he stirred the brown liquid. His nose turned up as he spoke. "I'll never get used to the smell of this stuff. When I retire, I'm gonna open a cigar shop with a coffee bar in it. I want to spend the rest of my life smoking fine cigars and drinking Cuban coffee. Have you ever tasted Cuban coffee, Brown?"

"No, Sir," Walt responded.

Rivera took a sip of his coffee and wrinkled his face at the taste. He stared off into the distance and thought of his home town. "There was an old Cuban guy in downtown Riverside who opened up a cigar shop I used to go to." He smiled as he remembered the place. "He came there from Havana in the early twenties and opened a small store.

"He rolled his own cigars, damn those things were good. Me and my buddies used to go there and have a cigar on the weekends. The coffee was so strong it was served in small, dainty, little cups. If you drank more than two of those cups, your heart would race like a greyhound. It was sweet, but not too sweet, and went with the cigar perfectly.

"Sometimes his wife would even bring out food for us. That woman made the best chicken in the world." He turned his right hand in a circle over the table as he described it. "She would serve it with black beans and rice. I always tried to find out how she cooked it." Rivera smiled wide. "But she'd never tell me. It was cooked in a sauce made out of mangos and peppers, as best I could tell, and the flavor went all the way to your toes."

He looked up at the ceiling and chuckled as he reminisced about the store. "Damn, I miss that place." He looked back at Walter. "You have any place back home you miss like that, Brown?"

"No, Sir, my parents didn't have much money. I was born the year before the depression hit, so we didn't get to go to a restaurant until the war started. Dad got a job at a defense plant, and they were finally able to enjoy a few things. I do miss my mother's cooking, though." Walter smiled broadly.

Rivera looked at Walter, studying him. "You goin' back home after this is all over?"

Walter looked back at his Captain. "I like it back home, but it never really suited me, I was thinking about settling somewhere on the West Coast. I like the mountains and the ocean. Maybe Oregon or Washington."

"Whew, I don't think I could live with the rain. I like the sun too much."

Walter smiled back at Rivera. "Not me. Everything smells so fresh after the rain, and the smell of the ocean is like nothing I ever smelled before." Walter straightened his back. "Yup, somewhere in the Pacific Northwest, that's for me." Walter looked seriously at Rivera. "But first, we have to get out of here. Do you think they'll let us go, Sir?"

Rivera wrapped both his hands around the coffee cup, staring into the center of it. "I agree with General Marsh. He thinks they'll keep us here long enough to squeeze out as much political muscle from it as they can, then let us go. The only question is how long it will be."

"I hope it happens soon. The men are getting restless. We've had a lot of arguments breaking out; I think the guys are getting cabin fever. They really appreciated you helping out with standing guard, and reading from the library has helped, too, but they're falling apart, Sir."

Rivera rubbed the back of his neck with his right hand as he responded, "I know; tedium has become the new enemy. You can keep them occupied for only so long, Brown. I just hope the Chinese let us outta here before the lid comes off." Rivera could see that Walter was stressing over the situation and decided to set a lighter tone. "It'll work out, Brown. We'll be turned loose shortly; you can count on it. Now how about some of this *fine* coffee?" he said, with a disgusted look. They both laughed loudly.

The rebel camp had been in place at the old farm since 1945. The previous occupants had been chased off by the Nationalists and were never heard from again. Shan Wang had gathered the thirty-eight residents of the camp, mostly from young men who had lost family members to the brutality of both the Nationalists *and* the Communists. The forty-one-year-old man had been the leader of the rebels from the first day. The rape and murder of his wife by Communist troops had sparked the rebellious nature in him and stoked the fires of hatred he carried every day since.

Communist troops had been hunting the group for four years now, without success. The hidden valley they resided in had been the perfect choice. In spite of the efforts of the troops garrisoned in Yingkou, they had been unable to find them. To date, the rebels had been responsible for the death of over a thousand Chinese Communist soldiers and the destruction of countless vehicles. Every time troops came through the valley, the farmhouse and outbuildings were vacant and the farm looked abandoned. The rebels had an evacuation plan that would rival the finest armies of the world. The Communists had given up on the rebels being anywhere near the farm. They were all safe from the Communists, for now.

Twenty-five of the rebels, along with the group of followers, were seated around the stove in the barn, involved in conversation about the path for the believers. Rusty sat next to Tao and tried to gather as much from the conversation as he could. He'd been picking up words and phrases in Chinese over the past three years, but was still a long way from conversational. Shan was drawing lines and circles on the dirt floor of the barn with the end of a stick as Tao continuously nodded in acknowledgement.

Rusty's ever present shadow, Gan Hwang, was seated on the dirt floor next to him with his legs crossed, taking in the conversation. The young man had remained silent since he had left his grandfather and hadn't left Rusty's side the entire time.

Not unnoticed by Rusty, Mee Ling was seated on the ground next to Gan and would look at him with a twinkle in her eyes when she thought he wasn't looking. There was only three years difference between them, and they seemed to be comforted by each others presence. Gan was already a good looking young man, and Mee Ling was growing into a beautiful young woman. Rusty would smile whenever he watched the body language between them. No matter where anyone goes in the world, some things never changed.

After Shan was done with his explanation, Tao turned toward Rusty. "He say we can stay in old building near Gaokanzhen before go to Yingkou. Rebels use many times," Tao said, while pointing to the lines in the dirt.

Rusty leaned forward so Tao could show him. "Where is it?"

Tao pointed to an X drawn on the dirt. "This Gaokanzhen." He then moved the stick to an area below and to the right of that. "Here old building."

"Is it abandoned?" Rusty asked.

"Yes, Shan say all people gone, not used for many years," Tao responded.

"And how far is it?"

"Shan say ten miles from Yingkou, maybe fifteen miles from here."

Rusty rubbed his chin as he pondered the distances. "Can we get there without being seen?"

Tao bent down to the ground and rested on one knee as he pointed to the diagram. "Yes, he say old road here. Not be seen Rusty. Trail used by rebels for long time."

Rusty pulled the map from his rucksack and bent down to the ground, opening it out next to Shan's hand-drawn diagram. As he compared his map to the diagram, he was unable to find the area that Shan had spoken about. He turned toward Tao. "I can't see where it is and the trail isn't there, either."

Tao looked toward Shan and asked him a question. Shan knelt next to the two men and studied the map. He pointed to the area where the old building would be on Rusty's map. Rusty handed him his pencil and watched as Shan drew a line on the map, indicating where the trail would be. When he finished drawing the road, he placed an X at the spot where the building would be located. Rusty gathered the map as he sat down.

After folding the map back up, Rusty rubbed his right palm over his mouth as he studied their options. This last section of their journey was clearly the most dangerous, and he needed to weigh his decisions carefully. He sat back up in the chair and spoke to Tao. "Well, if An is up for the trip, we can leave tomorrow afternoon. Shan has given us the cart for her to ride in, so it shouldn't be a problem for her. We do need to leave as quickly as possible. I worry about them finding us here, and it only jeopardizes Shan and his group the longer we stay." Rusty looked toward Shan and asked, "Are you sure that your friend's boat will be there when we arrive?"

Tao translated the request, then relayed his response. "He say boat be there. Boat not leaving for another month."

Rusty smiled at Shan and replied, "Thank you."

Shan asked a question and Tao turned to Rusty. "Shan want to know why you help Chinese."

Rusty sat forward in the chair and placed his elbows on his knees with the fingers of his hands laced together. "Because God has led me to help them."

After Tao translated Rusty's words, Shan's brow furrowed as he replied to Tao. "He say, 'But we not your people. Why you help?'"

Rusty stared back at Shan. "Because these people are my brothers and sisters. They are my family, and I don't want to defy God." Tao lowered his head and grinned as he heard his friend's response.

Shan smiled as he heard Tao's translation. He spoke softly to Tao and nodded toward Rusty. "He say you given much for friends, given life for family. He say he like you very much. You good man."

Rusty smiled as he looked back at the man, nodding. "Tell him thank you, Tao, and thank him for his kindness toward all of us."

After Tao translated the words, he turned toward Rusty. "He say, 'It his honor to serve you.'"

Shan stood and bowed toward Rusty. The big man stood and returned the bow with a humble smile.

★ ★ ★

The sun was two hours from setting over the road to Yingkou, as the column of trucks slowed. Major Hung was looking closely at the landscape, attempting to determine the location of his suspected encounter with Sergeant Harrigan.

He'd been pushing his men hard and wasn't going back to Mukden without results this time. The column had stopped only once for rest and food since their departure. He'd decided begrudgingly when they needed rest. He'd already wasted enough time with the useless canvassing of the area north of Mukden and resented Colonel Li's involvement in the search efforts that caused the delays. Before departing Mukden, Hung had received the weather reports that said there was snow on the way, and he didn't want the Christians' tracks being covered in a blanket of snow. The hunt was on in earnest.

Major Hung shouted at the driver as he recognized the terrain. "Stop here!"

The driver slammed onto the brakes, pulling to the side of the road. As the remaining vehicles stopped behind him, Hung stepped quickly to the tree line where he thought the encounter had taken place. He stepped into the trees and looked around the area at the edge. He bent down to his knees and studied the ground around him. As he scoured the area, he saw what looked like two depressions in the dry grass. He studied the area around the depressions and saw a boot print at the bottom. The boot print looked to be where Rusty dug his toe in when he stood. Hung studied the toe print and smiled. "American military boots."

Hung stood and walked the area around the edge of the tree line until he found another print. The late fall had placed the grass in a dormant state and proved to be a better indicator for footprints, as the grass didn't spring back like it did in the summer. He called some of the men over to where he was and, after showing them the print, he spread them out to find the trail.

It didn't take long before one of the soldiers announced his find. As Hung stepped next to him, he responded, "Sir, it looks like the tracks move south, but there are many more footprints with it."

"Can you tell how many there were?" he asked.

"It's hard to say Sir; it looks like they walked single file. Maybe twenty or more."

After hearing the news, Hung turned toward his two trackers. "Follow the trail long enough to see if it turns west or not, then get back here and let me know."

The two trackers stepped out after acknowledging their orders. Hung walked back to the truck and retrieved his case from the seat. He stepped to the door of the truck and pulled the maps from inside, then opened them on the fender. With his Sergeant at his side, Hung ran his index finger over the twenty-five mile area from Liaoyang to Haicheng.

Sergeant Yeun stood next to him and listened for the Major's orders. "We can't afford to follow their tracks. That would take up too much time. We have to pick up their trail farther down the road. They have to stay close to the trees for cover during the daylight, so I think they would have probably crossed the highway into the valley somewhere before Haicheng. The majority of the valley west of the road is too open for them to move in, so they needed to be closer to the trees here," Hung said while pointing to the tree line south of the rice paddies.

"Could they have made it there by now, Major?" Yuen asked.

Hung looked up as he made the mental calculations. "Well, they couldn't make better than two miles-per-hour. There are old people and children in the group. Two, maybe three, thirty minute rests during the night, which would be about twenty-miles a day, with eleven hours of darkness." Hung looked back down at the map. "That would place them about here if they crossed the road at Haicheng," he said while pointing his finger in the middle of the valley to the south of the rice paddies.

"Shouldn't we proceed there now, Major?" Yuen asked.

"No, I want to coordinate the efforts with the Russian. I don't want to scare them off. If they get into the city, it'll take a month to find them. They would be able to hide anywhere. I want them in the open. Besides, they couldn't have gone farther than Haicheng. I want to be sure of where they are this time."

"The men are tired and hungry, Major; we need to give them rest," Yuen stated.

Hung leaned back, taking in a deep breath, then slowly letting it out. "Very well. That will work to our advantage. We'll go to Anshan and get food and rest. Tell the men to be ready for a hard march early tomorrow morning. We'll coordinate our search with the Russian and catch them by surprise."

As Hung finished his comments, the two trackers stopped in front of him. Breathing hard after their run back to the truck, one of the men spoke. "Major, we followed their tracks for two miles, and they moved southeast. It appears they're following the edge of the mountains."

Hung was nodding as he spoke. "Good, it appears then that their destination was, in fact, Haicheng. Get the men back into the trucks and we'll go to Anshan."

Major Hung had a smile as he folded the maps. "You're mine, Harrigan. I will have you in front of me tomorrow."

Chapter 26 - A Request Denied

As the morning sun fought to shine through the cloud covered skies, the six military transport trucks sped south toward Haicheng. Fully rested and fed, the soldiers were ready for the long push they were told the next two days would promise. In the lead truck, Major Hung was antsy for the hunt to begin. He'd been chain smoking since they left Anshan and looked forward to getting out of the truck.

He ordered the driver to slow as they came upon the area where he thought Harrigan might have crossed the road. "Okay, stop here."

Before the truck was fully stopped, Hung was stepping out of the cab and onto the ground. He dropped the cigarette onto the pavement and crushed it under the sole of his boot. Hung looked up to the sky to see dark, ominous clouds rolling in over the valley. He knew the snow would be on its way soon.

Major Hung addressed Sergeant Yuen as he stopped in front of him. "Okay, Sergeant, I want two groups of men, ten each, headed by the trackers. Send one north and the other south. We have about five or six miles to cover, and if my hunch is right, their trail will be close. You go north and I'll take the southern route. Contact me if you find something."

"Yes, Sir," Yuen said as he turned to assemble his men.

Hung buttoned his coat and put his gloves and hat on, readying himself for the trek. When his team was assembled, he ordered them to move out. The tracker led the column of men and diligently scoured the west side of the road. There was looser soil on the west side, which would make it easier to spot a footprint.

The six trucks had split up and were following each of the two groups from. Hung nervously looked at his watch every five minutes, cursing himself each time for habitually tracking the time. He continually looked to the west over the large expanse of the valley that was littered with rice paddies. He tried to get into the mind of his prey as he surveyed the terrain. Which route would I take? he wondered.

The Major was looking south toward Haicheng when he heard the tracker's voice bellow. "I have them, Sir!"

Hung sprinted to the front of the group to find the tracker fifteen feet below him on the valley floor. The tracker shouted back up to the Major, "This is where they crossed, Sir."

"Are you sure it's them?"

"Yes, Sir, it's the same American military boot print."

Hung spun around to one of the men. "Tell the drivers to take the trucks on to Yingkou, and have Sergeant Yuen, the rest of the men and the equipment catch up to us."

"Yes, Sir!" the man responded.

Hung was already sliding down the embankment before the soldier finished his response. Once he hit the bottom, he kneeled next to his tracker, who stated, "It's them, alright; no doubt about it. The tracks go off to the west, across the paddies."

"Very well." Hung stood to see the remainder of the men waiting. "Let's move out."

Major Hung knew he was close to finding his target. His men were rested and could set a faster pace. He also believed the Christians probably weren't moving during the daytime. Hung was now at the top of his game. This was what he knew, this was what he was trained for, the hunt.

It was late morning at the rebel camp, and the believers were slowly preparing their bundles to depart later in the afternoon. Everyone had enjoyed the rest, but was eager to move on. Tao and Ho were busy making sure everyone had enough food for the final leg of the journey, while Rusty combed over his map inside the barn, studying every detail for the trip.

He opened his last K-rat box and pulled the chocolate bar from the inside. He turned around and handed it to Gan and Mee Ling. They both smiled as they hurried off to share it with the others.

Rusty checked his pockets to ensure he had everything he needed for the final leg of the journey. As he emptied his right coat pocket, he pulled out the crucifix An had made for him. He grinned as he studied the cross. He'd received a lot of gifts over his short lifespan, but knew this one would be the most treasured. He sat back down in the chair as he looked at the gift in his right hand.

What started out as a rescue mission had turned into a life changing experience. Had anyone asked if he was a Christian prior to his time, he wouldn't have hesitated to reply "*Yes.*" What he had found out was that since his time with these people, he didn't have any idea what it was to be a Christian.

The sacrifice, determination, and trust in God that they had displayed had humbled him to his very core. Even in the face of humiliation and torture, they clung to God, holding tightly to Him while they endured all manners of persecution. His life had been forever changed, and his faith strengthened more than he could have ever imagined.

Ho approached Rusty. The big man looked up to his friend and smiled. "Yes, Ho?"

Ho stopped and bowed in front of his friend. "Rusty, An's cart done."

Rusty quickly stood and walked to the other end of the barn with Ho following. He stopped in front of the cart and looked at the dilapidated vehicle. It was a two-wheeled cart, with long arms out in front, connected together with a wooden rod at the end where two people could pull it. The cart looked like a large version of the rickshaws he'd seen in Mukden. The wooden wheels and spokes were beginning to rot, and the sides of the cart were in the early stages of falling apart. He could see where Ho had repaired portions of it with wire and rope, and lined the inside of the box with straw.

He turned to Ho and slapped him on the back. "Good job, Ho. It looks like it'll make it now. It's surely better than it was."

"Thank you, Rusty." Ho replied as he bowed.

"Are An and the baby okay to leave?" he asked.

"Yes, they fine."

"I think I'll check on her," he said as he walked from the barn.

Rusty was ready to leave the rebel camp. The down time to recuperate had been nice, but he was ready to get on with the final leg of the trip. The others had enjoyed not having to stand guard duty as well. Shan's men had posted themselves around the small valley, which freed the believers to get some well needed rest.

Rusty knocked on the side of the bunkhouse, then slowly opened the door. He looked to see An sitting in a chair holding her baby. She looked up to see him and smiled. "Please, you come in."

He looked down at the baby to see her fast asleep in her mother's arms, with Wu sitting next to them. Rusty knelt next to her and spoke softly. "We're going to leave in about three hours. I wanna get ahead of the storm. Will you be ready by then?"

"Yes, all ready," She said while looking at her husband and the baby.

"Ho has repaired the cart, so it'll be a nice ride for you. We have some blankets to cover you and the baby, so you'll be warm."

"Thank you, Rusty." An reached out and touched his hand. "Wu and I thank you for taking us," An said, with tears flowing down her cheeks.

An emotional Rusty couldn't respond. He stood with a smile and touched Wu's shoulder as he turned to leave.

The remainder of the soldiers had caught up with the advanced team, and Major Hung was pushing hard across the rice paddy dikes. He wasn't pleased about being in the open, but had to get across the valley as quickly as possible. Following the zigzag path that the believers had taken was slowing him more than he wanted, and his men were heavy laden with equipment.

Now at the midway point of the valley, Hung began sending

teams of ten men south at every mile. He wanted to close any escape route the believers may take. Each team was to turn west at predetermined points to choke off any escape route. If his supposition was correct that the believers were close, he wanted them surrounded. If not, the push toward Yingkou would cover a five mile area and he would have them trapped. He was setting his trap perfectly.

The tracker stopped on the dike in the middle of one of the paddies. Hung moved around the others to get up front. "What is it?"

Kneeling on the dike and looking down into the paddy, the tracker responded, "It's strange, Sir. The tracks go on-" he said while pointing west. "But it looks like they all slid down into the paddy."

Hung looked around the sky above the valley inquisitively. "They were hiding." His jaw set as he realized the reason. "That idiot Russian alerted them and they took cover behind the dike. He was flying too high."

Hung turned to his radioman. "Contact Yingkou and tell them we're heading toward them, then tell the Russian to get in the air. I want him sweeping the valley toward the north, starting in Gaokanzhen." Major Hung pointed toward the radioman with a glare. "And tell that Russian to fly low!" he ordered.

The Major turned to Sergeant Yuen. "Send another team south from here, and I want you leading the last one that breaks off. I need you on my left flank."

"Yes, Sir!" Yuen replied.

The Major motioned toward the tracker. "Let's move out."

The grass-covered airfield at Yingkou was a leftover from the Japanese occupation during the 1930's and 40's, although none of the Japanese aircraft that occupied the field remained. The lone exception was a Mitsubishi G4M "Betty" bomber that had crashed on takeoff in 1943. The rusting hulk rested at the west end of the grass field as a reminder to everyone who took off from the airfield. The forty-foot tall wooden tower and adjoining operations building, along with the three small hangars, were still intact, although in a state of disrepair. The only aircraft that currently occupied the field was a Soviet Yak 3 fighter, and the Piper Grasshopper that was awaiting Hung's orders.

The Russian pilot and his Chinese observer were sitting inside the operations building keeping warm next to the stove when the radio message came in. The Russian Lieutenant jumped to his feet and listened to the orders from the radio. He barked back into the microphone. "Copy."

The two men ran from the building toward their aircraft while they were putting their hats and coats on. Once at the aircraft, the pilot pulled the chalks from the wheels and performed a quick walk around of the plane, while the observer climbed into the rear seat. Entering the cockpit, the pilot cinched the safety harness around his waist and chest and depressed the start button. The A-65 continental engine coughed to life and was quickly brought to idle.

While the plane was warming up, the pilot pulled up the bottom half of the right side door and secured it tightly. With all the Piper's systems checking out, he pushed in the throttle partially and taxied to the end of the field. A quick check of the windsock alongside the airstrip revealed he would be taking off into the wind. The Russian threw his upper body forward sharply in the seat to check his harness to make sure he was securely strapped in, then pushed the throttle flush to the dash.

The little plane began moving, slowly picking up speed. The landing gear bounced on the field as the plane struggled to attain lift off speed. At forty miles-per-hour, the pilot eased back on the yoke and the little plane slowly lifted off the ground. Once in the air, he performed a banking right turn and put the aircraft into a northerly heading. The pilot looked at his watch and calculated a thirty minute flight to the southern end of the valley.

Rusty stood in front of the barn and looked to the sky. The dark clouds were down to three-thousand-feet, and the impending snowstorm wasn't far off. He knew they had to get going as quickly as possible. The cart had been pulled from the barn and was ready for its occupants. Tao, Ho, Shan, and ten other followers were milling around the area getting ready to leave.

Rusty looked toward Tao. "Master, please ask Shan if they would like to go with us. I know we can get them to America if they would just come join us."

Tao turned toward Shan and relayed Rusty's request. Shan smiled back at Rusty and took his hand as Tao translated the response. "Shan say he must stay. Too much work here to leave. He thank you very much, but must stay."

Rusty shook the man's hand firmly and bowed. "Thank him for us; he's been very kind."

Proud of the two words he'd learned in English, Shan responded, "Tank you."

"You're welcome," Rusty replied. He arched his back, stretching as he took in a deep breath. "Well, we better get An and the baby out here and get going."

As he turned to walk to the bunkhouse, he heard a faint noise off in the distance to the south. His eyes squinted as he looked to see where it was coming from. An explosion of engine noise erupted as the Piper Grasshopper screamed up over the hill to the south just above the road, surprising them all. The group didn't have time to react as the plane flew in just over their heads at an altitude of one-hundred-feet.

The pilot went into a banking right turn as he climbed to circle the valley. He pulled the microphone from its cradle and reported the contact to the soldiers on the ground, giving the position of the Christians.

Rusty turned toward Tao and Ho and shouted, "Get everyone out here now. We have to leave!"

Tao and Ho ran to the barn as Rusty made a beeline for the bunkhouse. Shan was yelling at the top of his voice at the other rebels to assemble.

The pilot made one complete circle of the valley, then turned north toward the soldiers on the rice paddies.

Rusty exited the bunkhouse with An and the baby cradled in his arms as Wu ran next to them. The rest of the believers were standing next to the cart, waiting for Rusty. Once he reached the cart, he laid An and the baby on top of the straw, then covered them with blankets.

He turned toward Shan and pleaded with him one more time to come with them. Shan declined after Tao translated his words and motioned with his hands for them to leave.

Rusty turned toward Chow Yun. "You and Jie pull the cart and I'll push."

"Okey-dokey, Rusty," Chow replied.

Rusty got behind the cart and leaned into it, starting it moving, while the rest of the group set off running to the south in front of them. As he pushed from behind, he turned to see Shan and the rebels gathering in front of the barn. He said a silent prayer for the rebels who had been so kind to them.

With the news of the discovery of the Christians, the soldiers were moving quickly through the paddies, just five short miles from the valley where the farm was located. Major Hung looked up as the Piper flew over the soldiers, wagging the wings of the aircraft. The soldiers waved back at the plane as he banked around them.

The radioman shouted to the Major as the plane turned southeast. "Sir, the pilot says the clouds are getting too low; he has to get to Dandong before the snow starts."

"Very well. Let's get moving; we have to get there quickly. The Christians have been alerted" he said as the men hurried through the last of the paddy dikes.

Every one of the believers was out of breath as they crested the hill. The cart carrying An was the last over the top. Rusty sighed and released his shoulder from the cart as they began the downhill run. The followers were still moving quickly to get out of harm's way when the snow started coming down in earnest.

Rusty knew the snow would both cover their tracks and slow the advance of the pursuers. He was breathing a sigh of relief when multiple rifle shots echoed off in the distance from the north. He looked at Tao and motioned for them to move. "Go, go, go!" He turned and ran back to the top of the hill, ducking down next to the trees.

Rusty looked down over the farm to see Shan's men running toward the barn for cover. All over the perimeter of the small valley, Chinese soldiers were emerging from the tree line. He laid on the ground as soldiers came out of the trees just fifty yards to the east of where he was lying.

As the soldiers got closer to the farmhouse, Shan's men opened up with their weapons, scattering the soldiers. From all around the valley, the Chinese returned fire on the farms buildings. The soldiers had effectively surrounded Shan's position. Rusty watched as soldiers out in the open were being picked off by Shan's men. He counted eleven soldiers down before they started pulling back to the tree line.

Just when he thought the advance had been repelled, he heard an ominous whistling sound over the valley. The ground in front of the barn exploded in a ball of fire. The next round hit the bunkhouse dead center, blowing the walls out with an enormous fireball. The entire building had been reduced to rubble. The mortar rounds were being "walked" toward the barn as each explosion tore through another structure. Rusty watched in horror as the last two rounds hit the barn, completely leveling the building.

When the mortar rounds stopped, the Chinese soldiers advanced on the burning debris. Rusty's jaw set in anger as he watched the soldiers shoot the rebels who were wounded and lying on the ground in front of them. He drove his fist into the ground hard as he stood and hurried back to the believers.

Chapter 27 - The Fatal Gift

Bobby was sitting on the couch with his elbows on his knees and his chin in his hands, deeply engrossed in Walter's story. By his reaction, Walter could tell he was clearly upset over the death of the rebels at the farm in China. His face had winced as he heard their fate.

Bobby interrupted Walter with an apologetic tone. "Mr. Brown, why didn't the rebels leave? I mean like, they could have come to America and lived. That's totally messed up."

Walter took a sip from his coffee cup before responding. "Bobby, would you leave the United States if someone took power who killed your friends and family? Would you leave if some politicians passed laws that took away your freedoms and arrested you for what you believed in or how you worshipped?"

Bobby pondered the question deeply before he responded, "But this is the best country in the world. Why wouldn't they want to come here? What happened to them in China could never happen here."

"You didn't answer my question, Bobby. If the government passed a law that said you couldn't worship the way you wanted to here in the US, would you pick up and move to Australia, Argentina, or maybe France?"

"I don't think I would."

"And neither did a lot of others around the world. Bobby, history is replete with examples of rebellions, Spain, France, Russia, Greece, and all throughout South America. There's hardly a country on the planet that hasn't had rebellions; people who fought back against oppressive governments. They all fought back against oppression, and you mean to tell me that you *think* you might?"

"No, this is my country. I'd fight back," Bobby replied sheepishly.

"And that's exactly the point. You *would* stay here and fight back. You'd stand up and be counted, because if *you* left the US, pretty soon others would leave because they saw people giving up. Those lawmakers would get their way, and sooner or later there wouldn't be anybody left to fight back."

"But the believers left; why didn't *they* stay?" Bobby countered.

"God had a different plan for them. He wanted them saved."

"Then why didn't he save the rebels?"

"Actually, although I don't speak for God, it appears to me that He did. He put Rusty and the other believers in front of them. It was their choice, and they chose to stay."

"But they died uselessly!" Bobby fired back.

Walter leaned forward before responding. "Not true. Rusty and the other believers were able to escape because the rebels stayed behind and halted the soldiers' advance. The believers wouldn't have been able to get away without their help. They sacrificed themselves, Bobby. They gave their lives so that others might live."

Bobby's head tilted to the side as he thought about what Walter had said. "Wow" he said softly.

Walter smiled inwardly as he watched the young man in front of him ponder what he'd been told. He continued the story after finishing his coffee.

Major Hung stood in the midst of the smoldering devastation with his jaw set as the snow fell around him. He'd lost men in the conflict, and he wasn't happy about it. He'd expected to find the Christians,

240

but instead had been surprised by a camp full of rebels. He cursed himself for stumbling into something he hadn't expected.

Sergeant Yuen approached him as he was surveying the damage. "Major, we've been through the whole area and there's no sign of the Christians. I don't think they came through here, Sir."

Major Hung started walking through the area with Yuen at his side as he pondered his options. "Sergeant, what happened up there on the hill?"

Sergeant Yuen was almost apologetic in his response. "We stumbled upon two of their perimeter guards, Major. We caught them by surprise, and the rebels turned their rifles on my men. I'm sorry it alerted the people in the camp, but they had to kill them, Sir."

Hung threw his cigarette onto the ground in frustration as he responded. "This whole thing is my fault. I was pushing too hard. I expected a bunch of unarmed Christians, not fully armed rebels. The only good that has come of this is that we finally found the rebels we've been looking for, after all these years." He looked into Yuen's eyes. "How many men did we lose?"

"Twelve men, Sir ; eleven in the valley and one up on the ridge."

The Major took in a deep breath. "Make sure they're taken care of before we leave."

"We will, Sir," Yuen replied. "Are we going to continue to look for the Christians, Sir?"

"Yes, as soon as we're done here, we'll go to Gaokanzhen." Hung waved his arm in a circle around the impact area. "Get this taken care of, Sergeant. We need to move on before the snow gets worse."

"Yes, Sir," Yuen responded as he turned and walked away.

Major Hung slowly walked through the debris as he analyzed his situation. He stopped when he saw one of the dead rebels lying on his back. His interest was piqued by something he saw protruding from the man's pocket. It appeared to be a linen-covered book with Chinese decorations on it.

Major Hung knelt on one knee, next to Shan Wang's body. He pulled the book from Shan's pocket and wiped the dirt from the cover. He slowly opened the book to find that it was a bible, translated into Chinese. "So you *were* here, Harrigan," he said softly.

241

He held his left thumb on the edge of the book and bent it backwards, riffling the pages. "What hold has this book on these people? How can one book change so many people's hearts and minds? What does this book contain that it can alter men's lives?" Major Hung looked at the book with a furrowed brow. He stood and put the book into his jacket pocket as he continued looking through the site.

The group of Christians turned onto the trail that Shan had marked on Rusty's map. The snow had covered the trail, and they were forced to look for a break in the trees to find it. The trail had veered off in a southwesterly direction and would put them at the far western end of Gaokanzhen, where the building Shan had told them about would be waiting for them. Rusty let the others go on ahead as the trail split off from the main road. He'd taken the position of Rear Guard, to ensure the Chinese soldiers wouldn't discover them or pick up their trail.

The snow was coming down hard now, and any evidence of their path should be obliterated within the hour. Rusty stood deep in the trees along the road, patiently waiting and observing. The light of late afternoon gave off little illumination and offered even less comfort in such a remote location. It was hauntingly quiet over the countryside, but in many ways, Rusty thought it could have been a scene from the Pennsylvania woods of his childhood.

The snow had come at the perfect time. Their escape was nothing short of a miracle, one that had also cost the rebels their lives. His fists clenched as the images of them dying flooded his thoughts. For the first time in his young life, he found himself not wanting to befriend anyone ever again. As soon as he got close to anybody, they wound up dead. He'd never been around such turmoil, such hate and corruption, and it was wearing on him. Like every young soldier who witnessed conflict, he was growing up faster than he wanted to.

Rusty checked his watch and realized that he'd been in place for just over forty-five minutes. The snow had accumulated enough to cover the believers' tracks. He took one last look to the north to ensure no one was coming, then moved out to catch up to the others.

Captain Rivera was sitting in the barracks with the other members of the Consulate staff, huddling around the stove. He had a blanket wrapped around his shoulders and was reading *For Whom the Bell Tolls*. The story of the Spanish Revolution, written by Ernest Hemmingway, was having particular relevance in his current situation.

The Assistant Consular General, Gary Parker, had been taken by Li early in the morning that day, and the staff was waiting for word of his fate. Parker had willingly agreed to go with the Communists, quieting the fears of the Consulate staff. They were waiting anxiously for any word of his condition.

Rivera's reading was interrupted by Sgt Walter Brown, who burst into the barracks. "Captain, Mr. Parker is back, Sir."

Rivera shot to his feet and quickly donned his coat as he rushed from the room. He was joined by Judy Francis, the administrative assistant, who ran behind him. They entered the courtyard in time to see Parker walking through the entrance gate and into the courtyard. Parker was walking slowly, with his shoulders humped over and his hands in the pockets of the coat.

Judy reached him first and hugged him tightly. "Are you okay, Sir?" she asked with concern.

Parker smiled at her as he responded, "I'm fine, Judy, just tired and hungry."

Rivera lifted Parker's left arm and wrapped it around his neck, then supported him with his right arm behind his waist. "Let's get you inside, Sir." Rivera looked to Walter. "Brown, get Mr. Parker something to eat and drink, will you." Walter ran toward building as Rivera helped Mr. Parker inside.

As Rivera helped Parker to a seat next to the stove in the barracks, Walter handed him a bowl of rice and a cup of instant coffee. Parker looked up toward Brown and smiled. "Thank you, Sergeant."

Parker ate voraciously as the group gathered around him. "Did they hurt you, Sir?" Judy asked.

After taking a sip from the cup of coffee, he responded while spooning more rice into his mouth. "No, I'm just tired; I've been standing for almost eight hours. That pompous ass General Piao and his crony Colonel Li kept firing questions at me."

"What did they ask you, Sir?" Rivera wanted to know.

Parker took in a deep breath between spoonfuls of food. "They were mostly curious about any contact we've had with Japan. I tried to tell them we can't use the radio, but they seem to be worried we're talking to headquarters."

"That's absurd. Why are they so focused on that?" Rivera queried.

"I think they've run out of ammo for keeping us here and want to dig up something they can use politically. It all points to them letting us go soon," Parker said while panning the faces of the people seated around him." He halfheartedly smiled as he looked at them. "I'd bet we're gonna get out of here soon."

"What makes you think that, Gary?" Judy asked.

Parker finished the last bite of food from the bowl and set it in his lap, lifting the coffee cup to his lips with both hands. He took a sip, swallowed the liquid, and sighed. "Because they looked frustrated. I think this has run its course, and there's not much else they can do."

General Marsh's wife looked pleadingly toward Gary Parker. "Did you get any word about Robert, Gary?"

Parker's brow furrowed as he looked at Vivian Marsh. "He was found guilty of treason and sentenced to ten years hard labor, Vivian," Parker responded as he clutched her left hand. Tears streamed down her face as she heard the words. Parker tried to console her. "Look, Vivian, they're not going to let us go without letting the General go with us. It's going to be fine. I'm confident they'll let us all go soon, including the General."

"Are you sure, Gary? Did you see him?" a tearful Vivian asked.

"No, I asked to talk with him, but they refused. The interesting thing, though, is that they went out of their way to tell me he was doing fine. That's another thing that leads me to believe we're getting out of here soon."

Parker looked around the group of people seated by him. "Look, the last thing the Chinese need is for any of us to be ill, injured or dead. The international community would erupt. Mao *does not* want anything to negatively impact his chances for international recognition. You can all rest assured that we'll be released soon." He looked toward Vivian Marsh. "And that includes the General, you have my promise."

★ ★ ★

Major Hung and his men were moving south, away from the farm, as the snow continued to come down. They had walked a significant distance from the farm and were only five-miles from Gaokanzhen. The bloody nose they had received at the farm was weighing heavily on them; a fact that hadn't gone unnoticed by their commanding officer.

The bodies of the soldiers killed at the farm had been carefully placed at the edge of the tree line, to be recovered after the push to Yingkou was over. The bodies of the rebels, however, had been left in the open. Hung had ordered that every rebel's body be searched to find anything of importance. Nothing had been discovered.

The team was led by his two trackers, who slowly perused the ground in front of them as they made their way to Gaokanzhen. So far, nothing had indicated to them that someone had travelled the road in front of them; the snow had effectively covered any signs.

Sergeant Yuen walked next to the Major in silence. The order for the men to remain silent had gone out at the farm. With the snow coming down, any noise made would be amplified and telegraph their position. The men had even taken steps to wrap the equipment on their backs, so as to not allow it to bang together and signal their position. At every mile they walked, the group was halted so Major Hung could listen to see if the Christians were making noise that he could pick up on. He was determined not to be caught by surprise again.

The Major had radioed the troops at Yingkou, ordering fifty men north to Gaokanzhen to meet up with them. The remaining troops had been ordered to stand guard at the city's northern edge, in case the Christians attempted to enter Yingkou. He had throttled back and was taking a more cautious approach to the hunt. Although he didn't expect to be surprised by rebels this time, he didn't want anything to interfere with him finding the Christians. He knew he probably only had one chance left to find them before they escaped.

The observation plane was in Dandong and grounded until further notice. The "Gutless Russian," as Hung referred to him, wouldn't go into the skies again unless it was clear. The task of finding the Christians would be on his shoulders alone, and he was determined not to fail in his mission.

Major Hung halted the men once more and listened closely for any noise. He looked around for anything that could be a sign that the Christians had come this way. He looked ahead to see the town of Gaokanzhen three miles in the distance. After five minutes of silence, he spoke softly to his Sergeant.

"We'll split up here. You take half the men and go to the western end of the city, and I'll go to the eastern end and meet up with the soldiers coming in from Yingkou."

"Very well, Sir," Yuen replied in a whisper.

The two groups split and began the final leg of the journey to Gaokanzhen.

It was midnight when the believers reached the building that Shan had told them about. From a distance, it looked like an old abandoned wooden warehouse. There were three outbuildings around the warehouse, one of which looked like an outhouse, to the delight of Rusty and the other followers. Walking off into the trees to perform their bodily functions had become an irritation to everyone in the group.

The building was small, with what looked like an office area at the east end. There were four doors on the north side that looked to be the entrance for individual storage areas. Rusty assumed they used to be for bags of rice, since they were so close to the rice fields. It was poorly constructed and appeared that it would fall down with a minimum amount of wind. It would, however, suit their purposes for the next eighteen or so hours.

Rusty directed the men to pull the cart into the storage area next to the office, to hide it from any onlookers. They stopped the cart just short of entering the storage unit and allowed An to exit. She gently handed her baby to Wu, then reached out to Rusty, who lifted her from the cart. Once on the ground, she took the baby from Wu and walked toward the office.

After the cart was safely put away, they all entered the office and welcomed what would be a semi-warm enclosure to rest in. The snow accumulating on the roof would help to hold the body heat inside the enclosure. The room was four-hundred-square-feet and was bare with the exception of two chairs and one old table. This looked to be a place that served Shan and the rebels well.

Rusty turned toward Chow and Ho. "Could you guys take the first watch? We're kind of out in the open here, and I need plenty of advance warning if someone is coming." Both men nodded in agreement. "And stick close to the tree-line; I don't want anyone seeing a lot of tracks in the snow."

Rusty dropped his packs on the floor and rubbed his shoulder. Pushing the cart with his shoulder for the last eight miles had taken its toll on his body. His legs were burning from the stress of plodding through the snow. He would certainly enjoy some much needed rest after this trip.

Chapter 28 - A Second Chance

Major Hung sat in the living area of a confiscated home at the east end of Gaokanzhen. The soldiers had bivouacked in a series of homes they had commandeered for the day until they could determine the location of the Christians. Hung sat at a small table and pored over the bible he'd taken from the body of Shan Wang.

In spite of his efforts to avoid opening the book, the draw had been too strong. He'd been reading portions of it for over six hours without a break and couldn't put it down. He would read for a while in one book of the Bible, then move to the next book. For the last three hours he'd been reading portions of the gospels, and was completely taken in by them.

Hung stood from the table and walked to the window to rest his eyes. He rubbed the back of his neck with both his hands as he stared through the glass. Why would this book cause two young men to sacrifice their lives? Why would these young men allow someone to shoot them in the head, or bury them alive, rather than deny what is written inside these pages? There was obviously much more information in the Bible that he needed to know, to understand such sacrifice. He needed to understand the mind of the enemy he was pursuing.

As he was deep in thought, he heard a knock on the door. He turned and walked to the front door, opening it to see Sergeant Yuen standing in front of him. "Come in, Sergeant." The Major pointed to the table at the side of the living area. "Have a seat."

Yuen sat at the table and looked at the book lying open before him. "Major, you do know it's illegal to have this book, don't you?"

Hung sat at the table across from his sergeant. "I know; I took it off the body of one of the rebels we killed."

"But, Sir, it needs to be destroyed. Chairman Mao insisted," Yuen protested.

The Major looked at his sergeant and responded curtly, "Sergeant Yuen, I, more than you, understand Chairman Mao's directives. The book will be destroyed, but not until I've studied it to better know the enemy. Do you understand?"

Sergeant Yuen was taken aback by his commanding officer's harsh response. "Yes, Sir!"

"Now, Sergeant, I need to know how we can proceed. I don't need your impudence, nor do I need a lecture about what Chairman Mao says. Am I understood?"

Yuen's back straightened. "Yes, Sir. I'm sorry, Sir," he quickly responded. "Sir, the men have arrived from Yingkou, and together with our team, the city has been swept. We found no signs of the Christians."

"How many men were left in Yingkou?"

"There are fifty men remaining on guard at the northern edge of the city, in case the Christians try to enter," Yuen replied.

"And Yingkou has been swept?"

"Yes, Sir, the men have been looking for the Christians constantly since their arrival."

"And what of Gaokanzhen?" Hung queried.

"The same, Sir. Our combined forces have searched the entire city."

Hung stood and walked back to the window, staring out into the sky as he evaluated his options. He spun around and walked to the table, opening the maps. He ran his finger over the areas to the east and west of Gaokanzhen, speaking as he studied the map. "We know they were here at the farm," he said, while pointing to where the farm was located. He drew his finger down toward the south. "If they went south from there, they would have travelled through the same area we came through." He moved his finger to the east. "If they turned and went east, they would have been out in the open and easier to spot."

Yuen interrupted, "But if they went east, Sir, they would be in a better position to get closer to the industrial area of Yingkou, where they could better avoid being seen as they went through the city."

Hung rubbed his forehead with his hand. "Sergeant Harrigan is smarter than that. He would stay hidden for as long as possible." His finger moved across the map to the western side of Gaokanzhen. "But if he turned toward the west after they left the farm, he could stay close to the tree line by the mountains all the way down to Yingkou."

Yuen put his finger on the map next to the hills along the western side. "But, Sir, that's extremely rough terrain, and he has a lot of old people to move through there. Besides, that would put them five miles west of the city when they got to the coast."

Hung ran his hand through his hair as he studied the map. "Harrigan would know we would concentrate our forces on the main roads and paths to Yingkou." He drove his finger down hard on the map east of Yingkou. "That's where he would go." He looked up at Yuen. "Form the men into ten-man teams. We'll send one team west and look for them against the mountains. Send one team east to the main road, then have them move south into Yingkou. Send two teams south into Yingkou and have them split up when they get to the dock areas; the Christians have to leave by boat.

"The docks are spread all over the coast line, so we'll need as many men there as possible. I'll take one team north and see if I can pick up a trail, and link up with you after I've reached this area." Major Hung pointed on the map to a spot five miles east of where they had turned southeast to enter Gaokanzhen. "Keep in radio contact and inform me of any discoveries."

Hung stood straight as he finished. "They couldn't have left the country yet. There hasn't been enough time. They have to be close." He gathered the papers from the table and placed them into his pack. He placed the bible into the right pocket of his jacket, and then put it on. "Let's get going, Sergeant. Time is running out."

Yuen looked at the pocket of Major Hung's jacket where he had placed the bible. "Yes, Sir."

The snow had all but ceased in the area surrounding the old warehouse. The clouds above were still dark and ominous, but were now at three thousand feet and moving west rapidly. Now in the light of day, the believers could see that the building they rested in was concealed on three sides by tree cover. The eastern end was exposed and offered little cover for someone approaching from that direction.

As far as the eye could see, the ground had been covered in two feet of fresh snow, presenting an almost tranquil setting. Rusty and Tao were seated at the table in the office area reviewing their strategy for the nightfall. It was now noon and Rusty knew they wouldn't be able to move for another five or six hours. He was avoiding the urge to press on, but the need to get to the docks was weighing on him. He had to remain focused and stick to his plan.

The trip to the dock in Yingkou would only take about six hours and should put them at the boat dock somewhere around midnight. Rusty was relying heavily on Tao's skills and knowledge to find the place where they were to meet with the owner of the vessel. With his elbows on the table, he rubbed his forehead up and down fiercely with the fingers of his left hand. Time was running out, and he had to get the believers to the boat before the Chinese soldiers found them. He let out a long breath as he focused on the map.

Tao placed his hand on Rusty's arm. "Be okay, Rusty. Think too much. Be at boat tonight, all be fine."

He lifted his head from his fingers and rubbed his chin. "I know, Master," he replied quietly. "Just worried about the soldiers finding us. They got way too close yesterday."

Tao was worried as well, but saw no benefit in adding to Rusty's stress. He stood and touched his friend on the shoulder. "Must eat, Rusty. Have food before leave. Need to be strong for tonight." Tao stepped away from the table to check on the others and allow his friend to think about the events that would unfold later in the afternoon.

★ ★ ★

Sergeant Yuen and his men moved through the trees at the base of the mountain five miles south of the farmhouse they had attacked. The tracker was out in front and was carefully scouring the surroundings for any signs. He stopped as they reached the trailhead that broke off from the main road the believers had taken. The tracker stepped into the trees and bent down next to the ground. As he scraped the snow away down to the dirt, he looked to see the cart track depressions filled with snow. Without saying anything, he waved to the men behind him to follow.

As the tracker made his way through the narrow pathway, Sergeant Yuen looked around for any potential threat in the trees around them. The order for silence by Yuen was being adhered to by the men. They all moved through the trees with both stealth and purpose.

The tracker stopped next to one of the trees and looked closely at the branches. He pulled a small piece of cloth from the end of one of the branches. He turned toward Yuen and spoke softly. "They came through here, Sergeant."

"Do you know how long ago it was?"

"Based on the amount of snowfall, I would guess about twelve hours ago. The tracks were covered well."

Sergeant Yuen spoke at a normal volume. "Let's get moving; we have a lot of ground to make up."

The men moved out quickly as the tracker continued forward.

Rusty was sitting on the floor finishing his last packet of crackers from his K-rats. The crackers hadn't gone down well, and he found himself dreaming about a T-bone steak. He took a long drink from his canteen in the hope that the taste could be washed out of his mouth by the aluminum flavor of the container. He was wrong.

Everything had been completed in preparation for the believers' final journey. The only thing that remained was for the sun to go down and mask their departure. He looked across the room to see An and Wu staring at their baby, cradled in An's arms. He started daydreaming about the day he would have his own child, a son he could take hunting; a daughter he could watch going to the prom. He smiled wide as the thoughts flooded his brain. If he could only-

The front door to the building burst open and Chow Yun charged inside. "Rusty, soldiers coming! Coming from north," he said while pointing behind him breathing heavily.

Rusty shot to his feet as the others in the room stood in panic. Chow Yun was breathing heavy from running in the snow. Rusty tried to calm him. "Slow down, slow down. Take a breath and tell me how many soldiers are coming."

With his chest heaving he choked the words out between gasps. "Coming from north Rusty, ten men!"

Rusty looked back at him with his brow furrowed. "How far away are they?"

"Two, maybe three miles. Must hurry, coming fast, Rusty!"

Rusty turned and immediately sprung into action. "Tao, get everyone out of here!" He turned toward Lian Yi. "Lian, carry the baby for An and Wu. We won't have time to get the cart ready. Ho, you and the other men are gonna have to carry An." He turned toward Tao and Ho. "I'll stay here and keep them busy while all of you get away!"

"Rusty, we stay, help you!" Tao stated emphatically.

"No! I want you all to get everyone to the boat!" He looked at his friend and barked at him. "You need to go now!" Rusty bent down, grabbed his rucksack, and handed it to Tao. "Take this with you. All the papers you need are in there in case I don't get to the boat in time."

"Rusty, must-"

Rusty cut him off before he could finish. "We don't have time to argue about this, Tao. All of you leave now! I'll follow as soon as you've gotten far enough away!"

The believers rushed from the building, led by Ho. Tao turned back toward Rusty as he was exiting the door and looked at his friend with concern. Rusty didn't speak; he only nodded and smiled in return.

Rusty pulled the .45 from his pocket and set it on the chair. He then grabbed three of the clips from his other pocket and set them next to the pistol. Looking around the room for something to give him cover, he tipped the table up on its edge and rested it against the door.

He picked up the .45 in his right hand, and pulled the slide back with his left, just enough to see the round in the chamber. Cocking the hammer all the way to the rear, he lifted the safety with his thumb and held the pistol down at his side. Standing to the side of the window, he peered out waiting for the approaching soldiers.

His plan was to keep the soldiers busy for as long as he could, then make an exit out the rear window and hopefully catch up to the others. In spite of his reassurances to Tao, he knew instinctively it didn't have a chance of success. He held up his left hand and looked at it closely as it trembled. He opened and closed it several times in an attempt to stop the shaking, but he couldn't. He took in a deep breath and quickly let it out as he stared out the window.

As he surveyed the woods, he saw what appeared to be movement thirty yards in front of him. Squinting to get a better look, he confirmed his suspicions. There were ten men moving toward him, spread out over a fifty-yard distance parallel to his location. He lifted the .45 and pointed it toward the window. He spoke out loud as he stared through the window. "Wait, Harrigan, wait for it, not yet." As the men stepped into the clearing he tightened his grip on the pistol and took aim.

With loud explosions, the three rounds exited the barrel, shattering the glass panes and buzzing past the soldiers' heads. Rusty dove down to the floor and behind the table. Bullets rattled against the wooden sides of the building as the soldiers returned fire.

Jumping back to his feet, he fired three more rounds through the glassless window, striking one of the soldiers. The men ducked back into the trees and took cover. Rusty could hear someone shouting orders outside as he gripped the pistol tighter in his hand.

The return fire coming from the trees was fierce as the rounds entered the structure, splintering the wooden sides. Rusty covered his head with his arms as the pieces of wood fell all around him. He waited for a pause in the fire, then jumped up again, firing two rounds, emptying the pistol. As he turned to dive back down, a bullet grazed his left shoulder, driving him to the floor hard.

Breathing hard, he rolled over onto his side and pulled himself against the table. His shoulder throbbed as he pressed his right hand against it to apply pressure. He picked the pistol back up and depressed the magazine release, dropping the empty magazine from the weapon. With one hand, he slid another magazine into the weapon. Striking the .45 on the bottom against his thigh, he locked the magazine into the well, then depressed the slide release, chambering a round.

254

"Okay Harrigan, time to get outta here!" he said out loud. He looked up to the three-by-three window and took in a deep breath. "This is gonna hurt, a lot!" After waiting for another lull in the fire, Rusty jumped up and fired three rounds out of the front of the building, then ran toward the rear window, jumping head first through it with his arms in front of him. He groaned in pain as his body fell onto the snow-covered ground.

Rusty quickly got to his feet and started running south through the trees. With the pistol still in his right hand, he pressed the side of the weapon against his left shoulder, trying to stop the throbbing. His heart was pounding as he weaved in and around the trees, trying to keep forward momentum. He turned his head around to look for anyone following him, but couldn't see anyone. As he turned his head back around, the rifle butt hit him hard in the face, driving him backwards onto the ground in a heap. The big man was out cold.

Light gradually entered Rusty's eyes as he struggled to regain consciousness. He could see figures walking around in front of him, but they were blurry. He blinked several times, trying to focus, as he heard men in front of him speaking in Chinese. He struggled to raise his hands, but found them to be tied behind him.

Rusty was pretty sure his nose was broken, based on the throbbing pain and the taste of blood in his mouth. His situation was less than desirable, and from what his senses were telling him, it wasn't about to get any better. He raised and lowered his head, blinking as the figures in front of him slowly came into focus.

Directly in front of him, was what he believed to be the largest Chinese man he'd ever seen. The Communist soldier was well over six-feet tall and built like a wrestler. The man was standing with his arms behind him, legs spread, as he stared at Rusty.

He turned his head to see the man who was clearly in charge, barking orders at everyone. The man looked at him and spoke in Chinese, none of which he understood. Rusty responded to him, "I don't understand what you're saying."

The big man in front of him threw a roundhouse punch to Rusty's face, throwing his head to the side. Rusty slowly raised his head back up and spit blood from his mouth onto the floor in front of him. He took a deep breath and waited for the next blow as Sergeant Yuen continued to bark orders toward him in Chinese.

Rusty looked at the man and repeated his plea, "I still don't understand Chinese, and saying it louder isn't going to help!" he fired back.

Sergeant Yuen nodded toward the big man. The next blow came to Rusty's gut, tipping the chair over backwards. As the two soldiers picked him back up, he saw the man who had hit him smiling down at him. Rusty rolled his head around and moved his jaw, trying to alleviate the pain.

Sergeant Yuen shouted at Rusty for a third time as he looked into his eyes. Rusty chuckled as he responded, "I guess you're just too stupid to figure it out." Rusty leered at Yuen and spit a mouth full of blood at the Sergeant's feet. The rifle butt struck him in the head from behind, and for the second time within the hour, he was knocked out cold.

Chapter 29 - Wisdom Revealed

For the second time, Rusty was waking up after being knocked out by the Chinese soldiers. His nose was broken, and his lower lip had a large gash on it from the beating he'd taken. There were cuts and bruises on his face, and he was relatively certain that he had broken ribs as well. He'd personally learned that the Chinese were extremely effective at torture. Rusty fought to regain consciousness.

He could hear the sound of a truck engine approaching from outside the building. Based on the elevated activity of the goons standing in front of him, he assumed it was someone of importance. The door of the building opened to reveal Major Hung.

Hung entered the room and closed the door behind him. He stepped toward Rusty with a smile. "Sergeant Harrigan, good see you again."

Rusty rotated his head around his neck in an attempt to relieve the pain. "Nice to see you, too, Major. I see that Communism has made the Chinese a kinder and gentler nation," he said, while straightening his back.

Major Hung pulled the remaining chair around and placed it in front of Rusty, with the back facing forward. He sat down as he spoke. "You must tell us where other Christians are. You take Chinese citizens against will."

"I'm afraid they're gone, Major. By now, they're on their way to the United States. You missed them by one whole day. You should have gotten here earlier and you might have seen them," Rusty said with a smile.

Hung turned toward Sergeant Yuen and nodded. The Sergeant hit Rusty's face with a hard blow from the back of his hand. "Not stupid Chinese, Harrigan!" Yuen shouted.

Rusty turned his head back to the front and smiled. "Well, what do you know, it speaks English."

Yuen raised his hand to strike Rusty again, but Major Hung held up his left hand to stop him. "Must forgive Sergeant Yuen; he in bad mood. You kill one of his men."

Rusty leered at Yuen. "My aim was off; I was hoping to kill two of them." Yuen hit Rusty in the face, hard.

"Can do this for whole day, Sergeant Harrigan," Hung stated with a smile. "Must ask again, where Christians?"

"I told you, they're gone, I stayed behind to keep you busy until they could get away. Is that too difficult to understand?"

Hung raised his hand and motioned for the big Chinese soldier to move forward. He looked into Rusty's eyes as he spoke. "Sergeant Harrigan, can make you talk, choice yours."

Rusty raised his voice as he responded, "I stayed behind so they could leave, okay?"

The chair tipped over backwards as the big Chinese soldier hit Rusty hard in the face. As the two men lifted him back upright, Rusty was spitting blood from his mouth and breathing hard. "Where Christians?" Hung repeated his demand.

With his head down and breathing heavily, Rusty spoke between gasping breaths. "They're gone."

Major Hung turned toward Sergeant Yuen and barked out his orders in Chinese. All of the men left the building, leaving Major Hung and Rusty alone. He moved closer to Rusty as he spoke. "See you in trees outside Liaoning."

Rusty tried to contain his surprise at Hung's statement. If he knew they were there, why hadn't he taken action to capture them? What was he up to? Rusty chose his words carefully before responding. "I know, I suspected you knew we were there." He couldn't understand why the Major was telling him this.

Hung pulled the bible from his jacket pocket and held it out in front of Rusty. "You die for this?" he asked.

Weak from the beatings, Rusty forced himself to focus his eyes to see one of the translated bibles from the orphanage. His mind raced as he wondered where Hung had gotten the book. Had the believers been captured? Had the Chinese killed them? He had to know.

"What's that, Major?" he asked coyly.

"Was found on rebel at farm. You give to him?"

Rusty shook his head as he responded, "No, I didn't."

"Ask again, Sergeant Harrigan, you die for this book?"

The Major's response told him the believers were safe. But why wouldn't he try to bluff Rusty into believing they had been captured? Major Hung was up to something, and Rusty was confused as to what it could be. Major Hung stood and retrieved the .45 from the top of the table. He cocked the hammer of the Colt automatic and pointed it toward Rusty. "You deny Jesus, or I shoot," Hung said while pointing the pistol at Rusty's head.

Rusty was confused as Hung repeated the demand. "Deny Jesus!"

Every muscle in his body tightened as he prepared himself for the explosion from the .45. He was about to die, and there was nothing that could stop it, except for complying with Hung's demand. He took in a deep breath and responded slowly, "I can't do that, Major," he replied.

"Why you not deny Jesus? I shoot you."

"Because I'm more afraid of Him than I could ever be of you."

"Why afraid of Him? I can kill you."

"You can't kill a Christian Major, but He can send me to hell if I deny Him. Go ahead and shoot; there are worse things in this world to worry about than dying," Rusty responded.

"You be dead, not understand. Why you not deny Him?"

Weak and hurting, Rusty forced his eyes wide open. "He died for me, Major. I can do no less for Him. Now get on with it. I'm ready to die, and quite frankly tired of seeing all the evil you and the Communists have brought into this country. Just do it and quit threatening me."

Hung lowered the pistol to his side as he looked at the big man. He'd watched the same response at the prison when Colonel Li had killed the two young Christian men. He'd never seen such loyalty to a cause, not even to the Communist ideology that had swept over his nation. He slowly lowered the hammer of the .45 and placed it back on the table.

As he sat back down in front of Rusty, he spoke in a low voice while holding the bible out in front of him. "Have read some of book, what mean 'I am truth, way, life, no one come to Father but through me?'"

Rusty's brow furrowed as he looked at the Major. "You've been *reading it*?"

Major Hung nodded as he looked at him. "Yes, have been reading. What this mean?"

Not fully understanding what had just happened, Rusty stammered for a response. He tried to keep it as simple as he could, still not completely grasping what had just transpired. He lowered his head as he responded, "John 14:6, Major, it means that we have to place our trust in Him. We have to deny ourselves, pick up our cross, and follow Him no matter what. We have to turn our lives over to Him, *completely*. It means that if you don't *know Him*, He won't represent you on the day of your judgment, and you won't get into the kingdom." Rusty raised his head and stared at Major Hung. "It means nothing you do by yourself can bring about your salvation. He's the only one you can trust to save you."

Hung looked back at Rusty with a confused look, "Not understand."

Rusty's head fell back down as he responded, "Don't worry, Major. Keep reading and you will."

With a blank look, Major Hung stood and placed the bible back into his coat pocket as he looked at Rusty. He picked up the sheathed K-bar knife from the table and walked behind him. He slid the knife inside the belt of Rusty's pants, then draped his shirt over the weapon.

260

He stepped around in front of him and spoke quietly. "Sergeant Harrigan, not all Chinese like what happens here. They not all evil." Hung took a deep breath. "Am going to Gaokanzhen to get Colonel Li. He come from Mukden. We be back soon, Harrigan. Sorry, can do no more to help," Hung said before exiting the building.

Rusty sat silently as he contemplated what had just happened. "It *is* true; for every Christian you kill, ten more take their place." He smiled through his swollen lips as he thought about what he'd just experienced.

Hung stood outside and addressed the other soldiers. "I'm going to Gaokanzhen to meet Colonel Li and bring him here. I don't want Sergeant Harrigan beaten any further. He needs to be alert for the Colonel." He looked to Sergeant Yuen. "Do you understand, Sergeant?"

"Yes, Sir!" Yuen responded.

"Very well; we'll be back soon," he said as he stepped into the truck.

Rusty heard the engine of the truck come to life outside the building as he struggled to get to the K-bar inside his belt. His fingers groped for the weapon as he heard the truck drive off. He quickly lowered his hands and let his head fall forward as the door to the room opened. Once the eight soldiers had entered the room, Sergeant Yuen stepped over to Rusty and slapped his left shoulder with the back of his hand. Rusty moaned in pain as Yuen struck his wound.

Sergeant Yuen smiled as he looked down at the big man. "Not stupid Chinese, stupid American. Soon Colonel Li be here, then you see who stupid." Rusty closed his eyes tightly as he fought off the pain from the blow.

The soldiers relaxed around the room, sitting on the floor or leaning against the wall, waiting for the arrival of their Colonel and the additional troops from Gaokanzhen. Rusty looked around the room, evaluating his situation. Even if he could cut the ropes and get free, the best hope he had was to take out one or two of the soldiers before he was killed. He focused on the .45 on the table and thought if he could just get to the pistol, his odds would be greatly increased. Either way, he knew he was going to die today, in spite of the assistance Major Hung had given him.

His fingers slowly moved upward toward the knife, as he tried not to let the soldiers see his movements. He could feel the bottom of the scabbard as his fingers inched closer to the handle. Sergeant Yuen stood from the chair as he saw Rusty struggling. He hesitated as he heard a low thud coming from outside the door.

The soldier on sentry duty outside looked down in horror as he saw the arrow shaft protruding from the center of his chest. He breathed out his last breath, then fell over on his back.

"What was that?" Yuen shouted as he looked to the men standing closest to the door.

The big Chinese soldier was leaning against the wall next to the door and started to respond. Before he could get a word out, he was struck in the neck from behind. The clenched fist had driven through the wall and broken his neck. The man's lifeless body fell forward onto the floor.

Before the soldiers could react, Tao Chung and Ho Shen burst through the door and into the room. Sergeant Yuen pulled his pistol and raised it toward the intruders. Tao spun the staff in his hands fiercely, striking Yuen's arm and breaking it. With one fluid motion, Tao pulled the staff back and drove the end of it into Yuen's forehead, knocking him out.

Ho jumped forward, lowering himself to the ground and spinning his right leg, cleaned the legs out from under two of the soldiers. He drew his right fist back close to his body and punched the men in their chests, killing them both with the powerful blows.

With the staff in his right hand, and one of the ends tucked behind his right shoulder, Tao spun low to the ground, striking one of the soldier's legs with the free end of the staff. Once he was down, Tao spun the staff over his head with both his hands, then brought the end of it crashing down on the man's throat, killing him.

As another soldier raised his rifle toward Tao, Ho leapt into the air and kicked out with his right foot, raising the barrel of the rifle into the air. The weapon discharged and the bullet went harmlessly into the roof. Ho let loose a flurry of blows to the man's head, knocking him unconscious. His body crumpled to the floor as Ho turned to face another soldier.

Tao started spinning the staff over his head and brought the end of it down on top of the soldier's head standing closest to him. The man fell forward and onto the ground in a heap. Tao and Ho turned toward the last soldier as the man raised his rifle. The eerie whistling noise followed by a thump from behind caught them all by surprise. The soldier fell forward, exposing the arrow in his back. Chow Yun stepped into the room with the bow in his right hand and bowed toward his friends. The entire conflict had lasted less than a minute.

Ho stepped behind Rusty and pulled the knife from behind his back. He quickly sawed through the ropes, setting his friend free. Tao and Ho looked with concern at Rusty's blood-covered face and at the blood oozing from his shoulder. Tao picked Rusty's coat up off the floor and carefully put it around him. Chow Yun put the bow over his shoulder and helped Ho get Rusty to his feet. Rusty picked up his .45 from the table and placed it into his pocket as they walked from the building.

"How did you know I was in trouble?" Rusty asked them through blood stained lips.

"Friend tell us," Tao responded as he pointed outside.

Rusty looked up to see Gan Hwang standing outside looking at him. Rusty forced a smile through his swollen lips. Gan ran to Rusty and hugged him tightly as he was being held up by Chow and Ho.

"Gan watch soldiers catch you. He come back, tell us," Tao said as he patted Gan on the shoulder. He placed a serious look on his face. "Must hurry, Rusty. Must get to boat," Tao pleaded as they helped Rusty walk from the building.

"Where *is* everyone, Master?" Rusty asked.

"Others at boat, Rusty, must hurry. Soldiers come soon," Tao responded.

The four men helped Rusty through the deep snow as they set off toward western Yingkou. He fought back against the fatigue that had covered his entire body as he forced his legs to move through the snow. He clung tightly to the two men holding him up as they moved out as quickly as possible.

The diesel engine of the troop truck wound down as it came to a halt in front of the old warehouse. Colonel Li looked through the windshield to see one of the soldiers lying on his back by the front door with an arrow in his chest. He leapt from the truck and immediately began shouting to the ten men in the rear of the truck.

Major Hung exited the rear of the vehicle to see the dead soldier on the ground and shouted to his men, "Surround the building!" he ordered.

As Colonel Li pulled his pistol from its holster, Sergeant Yuen stepped from the building. Unsteady on his feet, and trying to regain full consciousness, he addressed his Colonel. "They got away, Sir!"

Li was furious and lashed out at the sergeant. "What do you mean, *they* got away?" he demanded.

Yuen was supporting his broken arm with his left hand as he reported to Li. "The Christians came back, Sir, and rescued Sergeant Harrigan."

Colonel Li shot past Yuen and entered the room. He looked around to see the five dead soldiers lying inside the room. The two men who had been knocked out were sitting in the chairs holding their heads in their hands.

"How many Christians were there, Sergeant?" Li demanded.

Yuen replied sheepishly, "Two, maybe three, Sir."

"You expect me to believe that two men did all of this? What kind of a fool do you take me for?" Li barked back.

One of the soldiers entered the building and looked at Colonel Li. "Sir, we found their tracks. There are four sets of tracks coming into the building, then five going back out, Sir."

"Very well, take five men and set out after them. We'll take the remainder with us and meet up with you in Yingkou," Li ordered.

"Yes, Sir!" the soldier replied.

Li looked around the room and lit a cigarette. When he stepped behind the chair that had held Rusty, he saw the K-bar knife lying on the ground next to the rope. He picked up the rope and looked at the end, finding it to be cut off evenly. He lifted the knife into the air and looked at Yuen. "And how did Harrigan get this knife, Sergeant?" he asked, while Major Hung looked on in silence.

"I don't know, Sir; he didn't have it when we questioned him." Yuen's voice quavered as he looked toward Major Hung. "You need to ask the Major, Sir. He was in here alone with Sergeant Harrigan."

"And exactly what do you mean by that, Sergeant?" Hung

264

responded toward Yuen in a raised voice.

Yuen remained silent and leered toward Hung as Colonel Li slowly turned toward the Major. "I'll only ask you once, Major. What happened to Sergeant Harrigan?"

Major Hung remained silent as he stared back at his Colonel. "What happened here?" Li repeated.

While staring at the Major, Sergeant Yuen addressed Colonel Li. "Sir, look in the Major's jacket pocket."

Li stepped toward Hung and reached into his coat pocket. He pulled out the bible and slowly opened it. After fanning quickly through the book, he looked up at his subordinate. "This is a bible, Major. You know this is illegal. Why do you have it?"

Major Hung's jaw set as he looked toward the Colonel. "I took it from one of the rebels we killed yesterday."

"And why didn't you destroy it, Major?" Li demanded.

"I kept it Colonel, to better understand the enemy."

Colonel Li's lips snarled as he looked at his subordinate. "You're lying, Major; I see weakness in your face, the same way I saw it in your face the day we killed those Christians at the prison."

Major Hung responded to Li with a blank stare. "No, Colonel, *you* killed those men at the prison. The blood is on your hands, not mine."

Colonel Li took a drag from his cigarette as he responded in a calmer manner. "I now see what has happened. You've been caught by the trap of these Christians." He took a last drag from his cigarette and dropped it to the floor, crushing it with his boot. "You'd like to follow this Jesus, wouldn't you, Major?"

Hung swallowed hard as the realization of his fate hit him. "I would, but I don't think He would have me after all of the horrible things I've done."

Colonel Li removed the revolver from his holster. "Well, Major, it appears you'll have the opportunity to ask him." With an emotionless face, Li lifted the revolver and fired twice into Major Hung's chest. With wide eyes and mouth agape in shock, Major Hung fell backwards onto the ground. Sergeant Yuen and the other two men looked on in horror as they watched their Major die.

Colonel Li turned toward Sergeant Yuen and calmly addressed him. "Sergeant, you'd better have more loyalty toward me than you did toward the Major. Now get these two men into the truck. We need to get to Yingkou and stop the Christians."

"Yes, Sir," Yuen replied with a quavering voice as he looked at the body of Major Hung.

Supporting his broken arm with his left hand, he turned toward the two soldiers, nodding. The two men stood and walked from the building as Yuen turned one last time to look at the body of the Major. Slowly, he walked from the building.

Chapter 30 - The Final Leg

The five men fought their way through the countryside as a second wave of snowstorms was fast approaching the southern Liaoning Province. The frigid air had brought Rusty back into focus, but was doing nothing to alleviate the pain in his face, much less the pain in his chest and shoulder. Chow Yun and Ho Shen helped him keep his balance as they struggled through the snow. They had been walking at an accelerated pace for over an hour now, and Rusty was exhausted.

"Stop; please stop. Just let me rest for a minute," Rusty pleaded.

As the five men came to a halt, Rusty bent over with his hands on his knees, breathing hard. He coughed several times as he tried to catch his breath. Bending over farther, he cleared his throat and spat into the snow. The snow in front of him was bright red from the blood. He scooped a small amount of clean snow with his right hand and placed it into his mouth, in the hope of soothing the pain. He rolled the snow around in his mouth, trying to get some relief. He slowly stood upright, clutching his ribcage with his open right hand. The intense pain seared through his left side.

Tao placed his hand on Rusty's right shoulder. "Must go now. Please, must hurry."

Rusty spoke between ragged breaths. "Please, Master, just another, minute." As much as he wanted to, Rusty knew if he sat down to rest, he'd never get back up, but he needed to stop walking for just a moment. With his hands on his knees, he spoke to Tao. "Master, Major Hung said he retrieved a bible from one of the rebels at the farm. He showed it to me, and it was one of the bibles that Ho had translated. Did someone give him a bible?"

"Yes. I give to Shan Wang."

"Why would you give away your bible, Master?" Rusty asked.

Tao looked at Rusty after checking to the north. "Shan ask why we Christian, so I give bible to him. Very sorry, Rusty."

"Don't apologize; it probably saved my life. He'd been reading it, Master, Major Hung had been reading it!"

Tao smiled at his friend. "All things good from bible, Rusty. Then probably good thing he read it."

"I hope he continues to read it," Rusty responded.

"Yes, be good thing," Tao said as he continued to look behind them to ensure the soldiers weren't coming. He knew they would be following, but didn't know how much of a head start they had. He looked at his friend and wished he had time to treat his wounds. He was additionally grieved that he didn't have time to clean up Rusty's face. Tao could barely recognize Rusty through the blood covering his face.

Tao nervously pleaded with Rusty for a second time. "Must go, now!"

Rusty raised his head and nodded. "Okay," he said after taking in several deep breaths.

Tao and Ho lifted his arms and placed them on their shoulders. The men stepped out into the darkness, following the tracks they had made during their previous journey to Yingkou. Only three miles separated them from their final destination.

Lights from the lone military truck pierced the darkness ahead as Colonel Li watched through the windshield. The driver remained silent as he focused on the snow-covered road ahead. They had just passed through Gaokanzhen and were heading due south toward

Yingkou. Li looked at his watch and calculated that twenty minutes would put them in the southern end of the city.

Li had a blank stare as he looked into the darkness ahead of the truck. The only thing that could be heard in the cab of the truck was the blower motor from the heater. It was even drowning out the noise from the diesel engine. Li puffed on his cigarette as the day's events flooded his mind.

The radio message he'd received telling him the Christians had been located was the good news he'd been waiting for. Bringing Sergeant Harrigan in front of the People's Court in Mukden would give him and General Piao the political victory they needed, not to mention how satisfying it would be to see the look on General Marsh's face. He was looking forward to that for sure.

The "New Order" in China was finally becoming a reality, and he was proud to be a part of it. The dream of expelling the western powers from their homeland had been a part of China's history for hundreds of years. Many people had died, and even more would have to die before stability could be achieved, but the dream had been fulfilled; the western powers no longer had a choke hold on his country. He took a last, long drag from his cigarette and crushed it out in the dashboard ashtray.

As he looked out the side window, a vision of Major Hung's face fell over him. His eyes closed, trying to blot the image from his mind. The Major had been with Colonel Li for six years, and he'd never once questioned his loyalty, until this day. His teeth gritted as he thought of the Christians and how they had taken the Major from him. This country will never be safe until we've eliminated all of the Christians, he screamed inwardly.

As he closed his eyes tightly, trying to rid himself of the Major's image, the driver spoke out, "We're here, Sir."

Colonel Li looked up to see the lights from Yingkou just ahead. The truck slowed as they came into the northern edge of the city. Only a handful of people were walking on the streets, and none would look toward the military truck. The people of China had lived in fear of the military, first from the foreign military powers, and now from their own soldiers. The streets were emptying fast.

In the distance, Li could see the shimmer of the ocean beyond the lights of the dock area. They had arrived in the center of the city, and if Colonel Li was correct, they had arrived before Harrigan and the four other Christians.

He barked at the driver as he saw the soldiers come into view. "Stop here!"

"Yes, Sir," the man responded as the truck came to an abrupt halt.

Colonel Li exited the truck and stepped toward the men. Expecting to see Major Hung, the soldiers snapped to attention and saluted nervously as Colonel Li approached.

He returned the salute and addressed the ranking enlisted man. "Sergeant, how many men are covering the dock area?"

"We have fifty men covering the docks, Sir, from the east to the west."

"And none of the Christians we're looking for have made it here yet?" Li asked.

"None that we've seen, Sir. No one has passed us, from any direction."

"And you're covering the entire dock area, Sergeant?"

"There are some small fishing docks at the western end, but we checked them earlier this afternoon and no one was there. The entire dock has been checked, Sir."

"Are there any boats at the western end?"

"Just a few fishing boats at the far end, Sir, but no one is on board."

"How far away, Sergeant?" Li pressed.

"A mile, maybe a mile and a half, Sir."

Li turned and looked to the driver and gave him the signal to turn the engine off. The men in the rear of the truck immediately exited and formed up in front of the Colonel. He looked at Sgt. Yuen and saw his right arm swollen from the injury he'd sustained earlier in the afternoon. "Sergeant, stay here with the truck. The rest of you come with me." Colonel Li followed his instincts and led the ten men toward the western end of the waterfront. His gut told him that the remote status of the western end of the docks would be ideal for Harrigan and the Christians to sneak past the soldiers. The men stepped out quickly toward the west.

★ ★ ★

The snow began to lightly fall as Rusty and the four men entered the western end of Yingkou. Lighting for the city was limited, which offered them good cover as they made their way down the streets toward the dock. The green metal lampshades attached to the poles along the dock only allowed light to focus downward in a cone shaped fashion, creating dark spots between the lamps. It was eerily quiet as the five men cautiously made their way toward the water. They couldn't see a single person walking in the city anywhere they looked.

Tao stopped and held his hand up, halting the group, as he heard men running behind them. Rusty leaned against the wall of one of the warehouses and tried to breathe as quietly as possible. They were tucked between two buildings and strained to hear exactly where the men were coming from.

Tao eased out into the open from behind the building and saw five men coming from the north. The falling snow amplified the sounds of the men as they moved toward them, telegraphing their location. He fell back in behind the building and turned to Ho and Rusty.

"Five soldiers coming from behind," he whispered to the others.

Chow Yun knocked an arrow in his bow as Tao peeked back out around the building. He quickly moved back in. "Not there," he whispered, pointing to their rear.

Ho moved silently to the other end of the building, and stepped back to check the other side of the alley. He moved back in as he saw one of the soldiers working his way toward them. He held up the index finger of his right hand, indicating there was one man coming. He moved to the opposite side of the alleyway and waited. When the soldier came into view at the entrance to the alley, Ho grabbed his right wrist and pulled him into the alley. He reversed the movement and bent the soldier's wrist back toward him, flinging the man up into the air and down to the ground in front of him. The quick hard blow to the man's chest silently killed him.

Ho dragged the man farther into the alley and laid him on the ground against the building. He picked up the soldier's rifle, and handed it to Gan. The young man grasped the rifle and pulled it in close to his chest with a panicked look.

Tao leaned out of the other side of the alley slowly, to see one of

271

the soldiers coming toward them. The man was alone and on the opposite side of the street. The soldiers were working their way through the area, checking each of the alleys between the buildings. Tao pointed to Gan and motioned for him to stay with Rusty and Ho. Tao whispered in Chow's ear, and Chow Yun raised the weight off his left foot as he prepared to move.

Tao nodded to Chow and lowered himself to the ground. Chow moved to the opposite side of the alley and took aim, letting the arrow fly. The arrow entered the soldier's neck and passed through his throat, half of it protruding out the other side. His hands went limp at his side as he fell forward. Tao and Chow ran the fifteen yards to the other side of the street and took cover.

Rusty and Ho looked out from the alley just as Chow was pulling the soldier behind one of the buildings. Rusty placed his right thumb on the .45's safety, with his finger resting on the trigger as he breathed hard against the pain in his chest.

Ho looked across the street and saw Tao motioning for them to move south. With Ho and Gan supporting Rusty from both sides, the three men moved out into the street, staying close to the buildings as they worked their way closer to the dock.

They had moved a hundred yards when Ho yanked Rusty into an alley behind him. Unsteady on his feet, Rusty fell to the ground behind Ho with a loud thud. Alerted by the noise, the soldier walking on the other side of the street stopped and raised his rifle toward the noise. He slowly started moving across the street.

From out of the shadows, Tao moved quickly toward the man, and with one continuous move, tore the rifle from his hands and spun him around. As the soldier threw a punch with his right hand, Tao stepped to the inside of the blow and deflected it with the back of his left hand. He moved his right foot forward and brought his open right palm up and alongside his right temple, driving his right elbow up and into the soldier's face. Before the man could fall, Tao twisted his right arm, bringing him down to the ground. He dragged the soldier back into the shadows as Chow retrieved the rifle.

Rusty had seen a different side to the men whom he'd known all this time. He'd watched these gentle and decent men whom he had grown to respect turn into silent and deadly killers. The efficiency of their movements and the speed with which they dispatched the enemy had surprised him. Although he understood the theory behind the

Martial arts, he'd never seen it brought to the forefront in its practice at this level. Despite having been trained in the art, he was feeling wholly inadequate as he watched its deadly purpose being utilized to its maximum efficiency. He had a newfound respect for the men who were with him.

As they moved closer to the water, Rusty strained his eyes to locate the boat where the followers waited. Over the buildings to the south and west of where they were, he saw what appeared to be two masts. He calculated the distance to be about two hundred yards. He pointed with the .45 in his hand. "Is that the boat, Ho?" he whispered.

"Yes, boat there," Ho replied quietly.

Ho waited for the signal from Tao before he moved out. His eyes scanned the area, looking for the remaining soldiers. He knew there were still two of them somewhere, but he couldn't see them. He turned his head slowly, allowing his ears to scan the area for any sound of the soldiers.

Ho looked across the street and saw Tao pointing toward the south, indicating that they could move out. He lifted Rusty's arm up over his shoulder and slowly moved around the building in front of them. He scanned the area as he checked to the right for signals from Tao.

As they moved south, Rusty could now see the starboard side of the sixty foot fishing trawler tied up to the pier. The bow was pointing west, and the boat gently rocked back and forth as the waves moved into the harbor. The vessel was dark and showed no signs of life as they drew closer. When they were thirty yards from the ship, Tao held his hand up, telling them to stop. Rusty, Ho, and Gan ducked into the darkness of the alley behind the last building on the dock. They would have to move the last twenty-yards out in the open to get to the trawler.

The three men watched as Tao and Chow moved through the darkness to the boat. They quickly stepped over the side rails and onto the ship, kneeling on the stern behind the rail, keeping watch for the soldiers. Rusty saw Jie Meng exit the cabin with his bow in front of him. Jie knelt next to Chow and Tao. Both of the men had arrows knocked in their bows.

Ho saw Tao waving at him, giving the "all clear" signal. As the three men stepped out from the building, Ho heard a noise behind him. He turned back north to see two soldiers pointing rifles at them.

273

Ho immediately stepped in front of Rusty as the two rifles fired. He was lifted from his feet as the rounds impacted his chest. Ho groaned as he fell to the ground behind Rusty.

"Nooo!" Rusty screamed as he looked at his friend lying on the ground in front of him. He raised the pistol toward the men and in an uncontrolled rage continued to fire the .45 until the two soldiers fell to the ground.

His chest heaving, Rusty dropped the empty pistol onto the ground next to him and looked into Ho's eyes. The two bullets had struck Ho in the center of his chest, and he was bleeding profusely. Rusty cradled his friend's head in his hands as he looked into Ho's eyes. "We need to get you to the boat, Ho," he said as tears filled his eyes.

Ho coughed between words. "No, must go, Rusty."

"We won't leave you Ho; you have to come with us!" Rusty pleaded.

Through blood-stained lips, Ho responded to his friend, "All be fine, Rusty, must go now." Ho smiled at the big man as a calming peace fell over his face. "Rusty, am blameless before God."

Rusty smiled back at his friend, tears streaming down his face. "Yes you are, Ho. You *are* blameless before God."

Ho's eyes closed slowly as the last breath exited his body. Rusty lifted his friend to his chest, rocking him back and forth, sobbing.

Behind them, the diesel engine of the trawler roared to life. Rusty could hear Tao yelling at them to get on the boat. Gan helped him get up from the ground, placing Rusty's left arm over his shoulder. As they moved away, Rusty continued to look behind him at the body of his friend lying in the snow.

The running lights on the trawler came on as Tao cast off the bow line. When Rusty and Gan came into the open from behind the building, they heard soldiers coming from the east. Rusty turned and saw Colonel Li running toward them, along with the ten soldiers flanking them.

He shouted to Tao, "Cast off!"

Tao removed the stern line and jumped onto the boat as Rusty and Gan ran toward them. Nearly spent, Rusty forced his legs to run faster against the pain enveloping his body. Gan dropped the rifle from his left hand and clutched Rusty's left arm tightly as they ran toward the boat. Rusty pushed at the air with his open right palm as they got closer. "Go, go, get moving!" he shouted.

The diesel engine thumped louder as the throttle was opened. The trawler began moving alongside the pier, slowly gaining speed. Rusty and Gan were just feet from the stern of the boat as it moved alongside the dock.

Colonel Li stopped in his tracks and raised the rifle to his shoulder, carefully taking aim at the two men running toward the trawler.

Rusty and Gan leapt into the air for the last five feet of distance as the rifle in Colonel Li's hands discharged. The round struck Rusty in the lower back as his hands stretched out for the rope fender on the stern of the boat.

A shocked Colonel Li dropped the rifle on the dock in front of him as he looked down to see two arrows protruding from his chest. His mouth opened wide as he fell over onto the wooden dock.

Rusty clung tightly to the fishing nets hanging over the fender as the lower half of his body drug through the frigid water, blood streaming behind him as the trawler pulled away. Tao and Gan held onto his arms pleading with him to hold on. Rusty looked at them and smiled, as his eyes slowly closed.

Chapter 31 - Bobby's Hope

Walter Brown took the last sip from his coffee cup and sat back in the recliner. "The End," he announced.

Bobby sat up erect on the sofa. "What do you mean, 'The End?' Rusty just dies? That really sucks, Mr. Brown."

Walter reached out and placed the empty coffee cup on the end table. "He had completed his mission, Bobby. He got the Christians out of China. God sent him to get them to safety, and he did. By anyone's standards, that's a successful mission."

"Oh, and then God just lets him die. That's sooo not cool," Bobby protested. "Weren't you mad about it when you heard he'd died?"

"Yes, I was. But, Bobby, without Rusty getting the believers out of China, so many good things would've never happened," Walter explained.

"What good happened by him dying, Mr. Brown?" Bobby asked, sarcastically.

Walter leaned forward with his hands clasped together. "All of the believers made it to America."

"Yeah, but he still died! What good is it if they all made it here without him? He was the reason they were able to get here, then he gets killed," Bobby said angrily.

Walter smiled broadly as he responded, "Well, let's just look at what happened to them, Bobby. Tao finally got to go to Texas. He worked at a church in Houston helping Chinese immigrants transition to life in America. He had a long life of joy and fulfillment, and passed away in 1972 at the age of ninety-three. He literally helped thousands of immigrants, Bobby. He touched a lot of people's lives." Walter picked the coffee cup up from the table and held it out toward Bobby. "Could I talk you into getting me another cup of coffee, please?"

Bobby took the cup and hurried into the kitchen. He spoke loudly from the other room as he poured another cup. "What happened to the others, Mr. Brown?"

Walter turned his head toward the kitchen as he spoke loudly. "Mee Ling and Gan Hwang settled here in Washington. They were adopted by a Christian couple in Renton. Both of them went to the University of Washington and graduated with honors." Walter lowered his voice back down to a normal level as Bobby entered the living room. He took the cup of coffee from Bobby and sipped from it. "Thanks, Bobby. They eventually got married and had two children."

"No kidding? How cool is that? Are they still here in Seattle?"

Walter set the cup down and looked at Bobby sadly. "No. They went back to China in 1986 for missionary work and were never heard from again."

Bobby lowered his head as he responded, "Were they killed?"

"Don't know, Bobby. We got a few letters from them at first, then the letters just stopped. Their children still live here in the area, though." Walter hesitated before responding again. He smiled as he thought about the others. "Wu and An Zhao went to Indianapolis and opened a Chinese restaurant. They're still there, although they're in their eighties now."

"What about their daughter, Rusty?" Bobby asked.

Walter beamed as he spoke of her. "She eventually went to MIT and wound up working at NASA. She's sixty-two now and getting ready to retire. She fell in love and married someone she worked with at NASA and had six children.

"An and Wu had three other kids after Rusty, two boys and one more girl. They're all doing well." Walter took another sip of his coffee. "Chow Yun and Jie Meng settled in Denver, where they opened a Kung Fu studio. They both married wonderful women and had a passel of children. They're still there. I get letters from them from time to time."

"And the other believers, where are they?" Bobby asked.

"Hua Ling, Lian Yi, and the remainder of them went to San Francisco. They found Ho Shen's family, who helped them all settle into the community. A lot of them have passed away, but they all had good lives, Bobby, good lives because one man got them out of China."

Bobby leaned forward in his seat. "What about the people from the Consulate? What happened to you guys?"

"The Chinese let us all go, including General Marsh. We left in December and were home in time for Christmas. We were taken out of China by boat, where we met up with a US ship in the Gulf. After a two week trip, we landed in San Francisco."

Bobby leaned forward in his chair as he queried Walter further. "What happened to the Marines at the consulate Mr. Brown?"

"Four of us were recalled for Korea, myself, Manning, Sheridan, and Captain Rivera. All of us made it back except Rivera."

With a sad look, Bobby asked with a reverent voice, "What happened to him?"

"He was with the 1st Marine Division and was killed at the battle of the Chosin Reservoir on the twenty-seventh of November, 1950."

Bobby sat silent as he heard the news of the man whom he had grown to respect during the story. After several minutes of silence he spoke. "But the others made it out okay, right?"

"Yes, they did, Bobby. Everyone got out of the Marine Corps after Korea, though. I guess we'd all had enough of the killing."

"Did you ever see the other Marines again?" Bobby asked.

"Yeah, I did. We used to get together every few years for

reunions. They finally stopped in two-thousand and three, though."

"How come you stopped going?"

"Manning died. He was the last of them, except for me." Walter took a sip from his coffee and sat back in the chair.

"Did the other Marines ever find out what happened to Rusty? I mean, like, did you tell them all of the good things he did?"

Walter took in a deep breath before responding. "I told them years later at one of the reunions. The only regret I have is that I never got a chance to tell Captain Rivera. I think he would have appreciated what Rusty had done. The guys all eventually came around as to why he had done what he did. It took a while for them to see it, but they eventually realized he did the right thing."

Bobby was reaching for something to salvage how he was feeling about Rusty's death. "Are you guys sure he died that day?" Bobby mused. "I mean, isn't it possible he could have survived?"

"We all held out hope that he could have survived, but eventually we accepted his death. They used to say that he could have made it to Japan and survived. Some said he could have made it to the Philippines. There was even a wild story that said he survived and lives in Australia."

"What do *you* think happened to him, Mr. Brown?"

"Oh, Bobby, his wounds were too severe. Even if he could have survived the beatings, he had lost way too much blood. And then being shot by Colonel Li. No Bobby, Rusty Harrigan died that day."

"You don't think he could have made it back to Philadelphia?"

"No, son; even if he'd survived, the military would have hunted him down. There's no place in this country that he could have survived in. He would have been a hunted man. Besides, Philadelphia is the first placed they would have looked for him."

Bobby lowered his head as he spoke. "It sounds like you miss him very much, Mr. Brown."

"Bobby, there's not a day goes by but what I don't think about him. He touched a lot of lives, including mine. His sacrifice gave others life. He had that Heart of Service I spoke about, more than anyone I've ever met. So you see, Bobby, if Rusty hadn't left the Consulate and gotten all of those people out of China, none of them would have lived, and all of the incredible accomplishments they achieved once they got here wouldn't have happened. Just look at what he did by sacrificing his own life."

"Wow, he really was a great man, wasn't he?" Bobby said with a humble grin.

"Yes, he was, the greatest man I've ever known."

The two of them stood as they saw headlights flash in the window of the living room. Walter rolled his wrist over and looked at his watch. "Ten-thirty; didn't realize we'd been talking so long. Looks like your parents are home."

"Mr. Brown, it was a great story, thank you," Bobby responded as he shook Walter's hand.

"Bobby, I think it would be okay if you called me Walter from now on. I believe you earned it for sitting through the ramblings of an old man," he said with a chuckle.

"Thank you, Sir," Bobby said as the front door opened.

Kirk and Maria stepped into the foyer to find Walter and Bobby waiting for them. Maria had a smile of relief as she looked at the two. "Did everything go okay, Walter?" she asked.

Walter patted Bobby on the shoulder as he responded, "We had a good time, Maria. I'm afraid we ate you out of house and home, though. You're gonna have to buy more ice cream," he said with a smile.

Kirk looked at the old man. "That's okay; I'm sorry we didn't have anything ready for you guys," Kirk said with a confused look as he stared at his smiling son.

Walter rubbed the back of his neck as he addressed the two. "Jerry and Inger never showed up. I guess they decided to go home."

Maria held out an open palm as she spoke. "No, they called us on the cell phone as we were going through Gig Harbor. They're right behind us. They got delayed for a while at the hospital."

"It's just like Jerry; he'll be late for his own funeral," Walter said with a chuckle.

The 1986 Ford pickup truck entered the driveway as they all turned and looked through the front window. "Here they are now,"

Maria announced.

They all watched as Jerry and Inger exited the truck and walked to the front of the house. Kirk opened the door to let the two people into the home. Inger entered first. The eighty-three-year-old grandmother was dressed in slacks and a sweater, with her white hair done up at the back in a bun. The attractive older woman had small cuts on the left side of her face from the vehicle accident they'd been in. The five foot four inch elderly woman smiled as she saw her son and daughter-in-law waiting for them.

Jerry Hanson followed his wife through the door, closing it behind him. The eighty-five-year-old man had his left arm in a cast and sported the same cuts on his face that his wife had. His body bore the scars of a lifetime of hard work in the construction trade. Almost bald, the old man had a large belly that hung over the belt of his pants. His huge hands still had the calluses he'd earned after a life of hard work. He smiled as he saw his family and his friend.

Maria screeched when she saw the condition her father and mother-in-law were in. "Oh no! I didn't know you guys were hurt so badly!" she said as her brow furrowed.

Jerry tried to comfort his daughter-in-law as he stopped in front of them. "It's okay, honey, it looks worse than it really is."

"What in the world happened?" Kirk demanded as he looked at his parents.

"It's not a big deal, son. We were going north on I-5 and some guy changed lanes behind us. He clipped the left rear of the car, and it slid us sideways into the next lane. There was another car coming up fast from behind and T-boned us in the left side. The cuts are from the glass in the window when it shattered from the impact."

"And your arm? What happened to that?" Maria asked nervously as she pointed to the cast on his left arm.

Jerry smiled as he responded. "Broke it when the guy T-boned us. It's nothing, Maria; we're both fine, honest." Jerry's eyes opened wide as he looked at the plaque in Maria's right hand. "Wow, let's get a look at this," he said as he reached out to take the award. Jerry held it out in front of him with his right hand, allowing Inger, Walter and Bobby to see it. "The Governor's Humanitarian Award, wow!" he said with a huge smile.

281

Jerry slowly handed the award back to Maria as he spoke. "We're all *very* proud of you, Maria. I wish we could have been there, honey."

"That's okay, dad. You guys are okay; that's really all that matters."

Bobby's head lowered as he realized that his grandparents could have seen his mother receive the award had it not been for him. Sadness fell over him as he looked at his family enjoying his mother's acknowledgement.

Kirk tilted his head to the side, looking at his parents' injuries. "If you guys look like this, the car must really be in bad shape," Kirk stated.

"I'm afraid it's a total loss," Jerry replied, sadly.

"Don't you think we can have it fixed Dad?" Kirk asked.

"No, too bad, too. I'm *really* gonna miss that car." Jerry reached into his pants pocket, retrieving the key ring and holding it out toward his son. "This is all that's left of it." Just before he dropped the keys into Kirk's hand, Bobby looked at it closely. Attached to the key ring was a cross made from hair, with small pieces of wood woven into it.

Bobby's mouth fell open as he looked at his grandfather. Tears immediately filled his eyes as the realization hit him. He quickly stepped in front of Jerry, hugging him tightly. The old man was caught off guard as he stood silently, staring at his grandson. A stunned Maria and Kirk looked on with wide eyes at their son hugging his grandfather.

No one knew what to say as they watched Bobby embracing Jerry. This was no longer the hostile and withdrawn son they had known for these past months; something had changed him. After several minutes, Bobby let go of Jerry and looked into his eyes. "Granddad, if you still want to, maybe we could go to a Mariners game sometime," he said with a huge grin.

Still in shock, Jerry looked at the others in the room. He slowly responded to his grandson, "Well, yes, I'd like that very much, Bobby. We can go to the first game of the season that they're in town if you'd like."

Bobby let go of Jerry and stood back looking at him with a huge smile. "I'd like that, Granddad." He turned toward his parents, holding up the notebook in his right hand. "I've got to go upstairs. Mr. Brown gave me a lot of homework to do, and I have a letter to write."

Walter interrupted, "Don't forget, Bobby, we have to train once you finish your homework."

Bobby smiled as he responded, "Thank you, Mr. Brown."

"No, Bobby, thank *you*," Walter replied with a smile.

Bobby started up the stairs and stopped. Turning around, he smiled at his grandfather. "I'm sorry I haven't gone to a game with you, Granddad. I really am sorry."

With a blank look, Jerry responded, "That's okay, Bobby; we'll make up for it."

Bobby smiled widely at his grandfather, then turned around and continued up the stairs.

The five people stood silently as they looked at each other in amazement. "I just don't get it," Jerry stated.

Maria turned toward Walter. "What happened here?"

"Nothing. We just had dinner and talked," Walter said with a smile.

Jerry raised his hands and looked around at the others. "What in the world just happened?" he repeated his demand.

Walter turned toward Jerry. "Nothing happened; Bobby and I just had a nice evening together." He looked at his friend with a huge smile. "You wouldn't happen to have a piece of Beeman's, would you?"

Jerry reached into his pocket and retrieved the pack of gum, then held it out toward Walter. He took a stick from the pack and handed it back to Jerry. "Thanks, bud."

Still confused, Jerry looked over the faces of the people in the room. "I don't understand!"

Walter put the piece of gum into his mouth and slapped his friend on the right shoulder. "Don't worry, Jerry, you will."

Walter turned and walked to the door. He stopped just before opening it and turned back to look at his friend. "We still on for pinochle Friday?"

With a still confused look on his face, Jerry replied, "Yeah, I'm still okay for that."

Walter smiled at his friend before stepping through the door. "Okay, see you then." He winked at Jerry as he spoke. "Oorah!"

THE END

Author's Note

This book was written to pay tribute to two groups of people in Mukden, China, during the horrors they endured in the late 1940's and early 1950's at the hands of the Chinese Communists.

First, to the loyalty, honor, dedication, and professionalism displayed by the staff of the United States Consulate. Their bravery and sacrifice from 1945 to 1949 is unparalleled. In the face of incredible brutality, these brave men and women stood fast, holding tightly to their convictions and their duty. They were true heroes.

And last, to the tens of millions of Chinese Christians who suffered persecution and even death for their beliefs, beliefs that are still outlawed in China to this day.

Acknowledgements

From the bottom of my heart I would like to thank the many people who helped me get this book to print.

To Michael Garrett, editor extraordinaire. Brian Schwartz, for his consulting skills. To Christian Bakken for the incredible cover art. Xalan Czace, Jill Hess, Sherrie Yellico, Jan Craddock, and Irma Schell for your patience and support. To Charlie, our Bernese mountain dog, who laid on the floor next to me as I punched away at the computer keyboard. And lastly to Claire, my love, and my best friend.

Made in the USA
Charleston, SC
03 June 2016